ACKNOWLEDG

*****

The author wishes to acknowledge the
invaluable assistance of the following people:

Miguel Baldenegro, U.S. Border Patrol, Intel Asst.
Lawrence J. Koep, M.D.
Russell Ahr, Sp.Asst. to the District Dir.for INS in Phoenix, AZ
Laura C. Fulginiti, Forensic Anthropologist
Sharon Loggia, CRC, Donor Network of Arizona
Harold Perlman, Pharmacist
Dr. Bob Koch, DVM
John and Mary Hays, Arizona Ranchers
Tom, Margaret & Cynthia Rigden , Arizona Ranchers
Elizabeth B. Lewis, Ph.D, Historian, Journalist, Author

Also,
Christopher R. McAllister, U.S. Border Patrol Intel Agent
Roy Z. Pierce, Jr., U.S. Border Patrol, Sr. Patrol Agent
Donna Jandro and Tina Williams, Editorial Services
Brandon Williams, Computer Consulting
Chris Lovelace, Systems Engineer
Courtney Lovelace, PR
Kelly Scott-Olson and Christy A. Moeller,
ATG Productions, Phoenix, AZ

Extra special thanks to:
**My ever-patient husband, Jerry, for accompanying me on
exhaustive research trips and putting up with me
and
Retired Police Captain and U.S. Border Patrol Intelligence
Assistant, Mike Baldenegro, for his advice and immeasurable
assistance during the researching and writing of this book.**

To

my loving family
and wonderful friends

Thanks for your encouragement

1

A scant fifteen minutes had elapsed since my vacation had officially started and my purse was ringing already. I stifled a sigh of irritation and dug the phone out, glancing at the number on the display screen. "Too late!" I muttered, dropping it onto the passenger seat. "I'm not answering." I cranked up the volume on the radio, tightened my grip on the steering wheel and headed across the desert towards the imposing monolith of Castle Rock. The ragged peaks, now glowing a peachy-coral in the late afternoon sunlight, cut a serrated pattern across a sky of clear sapphire blue.

Considering I'd had no more than a handful of days off since I'd taken the job at the *Castle Valley Sun* seven months ago, I was psyched, I was jazzed, and I was in no mood to tackle even one more problem, no matter how small. For two whole wonderful weeks there would be no copy to write, no deadlines and no employee issues. Whatever it was would just have to wait until Tugg could handle it on Monday.

The phone chirped a few more times and then quit. Good. My dad always said to be careful what you wish for and he was dead-on right, as usual. Along with the newly acquired notebook computer, the handy little cell phone had been on my 'must have' list for months and, in theory, was supposed to make my life easier. It had in many ways, but it was also a royal pain in the butt. Being accessible 'twenty-four seven' wasn't exactly what I'd had in mind.

I hummed along with the upbeat melody, swung onto Lost Canyon Road and headed home, my mind busy with the details of my upcoming trip to California with Tally. A chill of delight shot down my spine at the thought of just the two of us spending some much-needed R & R in a new setting away from the pressures of work. He'd promised that we'd take time out from the horse show to spend at least one day at the beach. I could hardly wait to bask in the cool sea breeze. I'd survived my first sizzling summer and so far, was less than impressed with what was loosely described as autumn in Arizona. Back home in Pennsylvania, there would be a frosty nip in the air and the forested hills would be a breathtaking tapestry of crimson and gold. But as I drove through the cactus and rock-strewn desert, there was nothing to hint that it was the second week of October, except it was a little less hot.

At that moment the jaunty voice of the radio announcer cut into my thoughts with the optimistic declaration that a weather change was definitely on the way—for sure, this time, he insisted. Right. Predictions of rain by effusive TV meteorologists had been bandied about for weeks, but I hadn't seen anything even remotely resembling a cloud since the last summer storm had swept through town six weeks ago dumping an inch of rain in less than an hour.

The phone jingled again. Damn! I should have powered it off. The office number showed on the screen again. I debated a few seconds, then pushed the button and said in a mechanical monotone, "You have reached the cell number for Kendall O'Dell. She is currently in holiday mode and cannot comprehend anything you may say in reference to work. Please refer all problems to Morton Tuggs. Thank you."

There was an extended silence and then I heard Ginger mutter, "Well, I'll be a dimpled duck's butt. Now I've heard everything."

I couldn't help bursting into laughter.

"Sugar, is that you?"

"Yeah, it's me. But whatever it is, I don't want to hear it."

"Well, good gravy, girl, don't get yourself all in a snit," she said, giggling. "I just called to remind you to bring that big ol' ice bucket and pretty red-flowered tablecloth to the party tonight."

"I won't forget. You still need me there before six?"

"I've got a million and two things left to do, so I could use a little extra help getting things ready and...could you hang on a second while I grab the other line?"

She clicked off and I smiled to myself. Ginger could always find an excuse to throw a party. Get a new car? She'd have a party. Relatives visiting from out of state? Why not celebrate? This evening's shindig was the official welcome for our new reporter, Walter Zipp, who'd thankfully come aboard less than three weeks ago after a fruitless four-month search. His reasons for moving to Castle Valley were rather vague, something about caring for his wife's elderly aunt. In light of his impressive credentials, it was surprising when he didn't blink at the sizeable salary cut. But, considering the circumstances, I sure wasn't about to argue with him.

"Okee dokee," she sighed, coming back on the line again. "Could you do me one more favor and pick up a couple of bags of ice?"

"I thought that was Lupe's responsibility."

"I don't even know if she's coming for sure," Ginger grumbled. "And here I was really counting on her homemade enchiladas for the main dish."

"What's the problem? Is she sick?"

"She says no, but something's bothering her. She's been real quiet and keeping to herself. But, most important, she ain't been laughing at my jokes the past couple of days."

I smiled to myself. "This does sound serious."

Completely missing my quip, she continued, "I know it. Her eyes were all puffy and red when she came in this morning and when I asked her about it, she clammed up tighter than a Mason jar lid. Right after you left, some woman called asking for her and two seconds later, she skedaddled out of here, looking real worried and mumbling something about maybe not being able to make it tonight."

That had to be bugging Ginger big time. She made it her mission in life to keep close tabs on everyone's business. Secrets drove her to distraction. But, her news was unsettling. Lupe Alvarez was one of our most dependable employees, and one of only two people capable of handling both classified and display advertising. She was always on time for work, eager for overtime hours and, since I'd been at the *Sun*, had never once left early. On weekends, she maintained housekeeping and babysitting jobs as well. Oh boy. The last thing I needed was a personnel crisis just before leaving town.

"I'll give her a call when I get to the house," I said, watching a roadrunner skim across the road in front of me and disappear into a cluster of creosote bushes. "Maybe I can find out what's wrong."

"Thanks, sugar. See you in a few."

Within ten minutes, I was standing barefoot on the cool terra cotta tile in my living room checking for phone messages. My parents had called and Tally was going to be late getting to the party because of some problem at the ranch. The rest were hang-ups.

I looked up Lupe's home number and dialed. Busy signal. Good grief. She must be among the handful of people left on earth without call waiting. I shed my clothes all the way into the bedroom and stuffed them into the hamper. I couldn't put it off any longer. The mountain of laundry had to be done before I could even begin packing the suitcases that stood beside my bed. A quick shower refreshed me and after I'd zipped myself into a sleeveless cotton jumpsuit, I lugged the hamper to the kitchen, started a load of wash and then set out the ice bucket and tablecloth before trying Lupe's number again. This time it rang.

"*Hola?*"

"Lupe, this is Kendall. Ginger told me you left work early. Is everything okay?"

A long hesitation. "I...I had to take care of some...personal business."

"So, you're not sick?"

"No."

"Good." Did I detect a hint of wariness in her voice? "Ginger says you may not be coming to the party tonight?"

There was another drawn out silence. "Oh...well, no, I mean, I suppose I can come for a little while."

"That's great. So, you're still bringing enchiladas and picking up ice?"

"Yes."

"You're sure everything is okay? Is there anything you want to talk about?"

"No! I mean...it is nothing important. See you there." Click.

My reporter's antenna vibrated as I cradled the phone. Hmmm. Normally, she was outgoing and talkative. Today, however, not only did her voice sound lackluster, I detected an undertone of distress. Disturbing. And then I stopped myself, remembering the promise I'd made myself earlier to put all concerns of the job and my co-workers on the back burner for the next two weeks. Maybe it would be better to find out what was bugging her before I left town though, so my mind would be at ease.

By the time I arrived at Ginger's faded pink adobe house an hour later, Walter Zipp's dented green Bronco was already parked next to our co-worker Jim's sassy little Toyota truck. I smiled to myself. They'd been assigned to bring the ingredients to make margaritas and I had a feeling they'd gotten the party off to an early start. Walter would be enjoying a bachelor's night out, having explained earlier that his wife would be unable to join him since she opted to stay with her ailing aunt.

A foot-stomping country tune was wafting out the screen door as I paused to pet Ginger's fluffy gray and white cat. "Hey there, Churchill," I murmured, when he threw himself down and rolled over to invite me to scratch his tummy. "I've been thinking a lot about adopting one of you furry felines. Maybe when I get back from the coast, huh?"

"How about you take him with you right after the party?"

I looked up to see Ginger's younger brother, Brian, standing at the door with a devilish grin plastered on his face. I took the bait. "Really? You think Ginger would be okay with that?"

"No, but it would sure be fine with me..." Several sharp barks interrupted his sentence as his grandmother, Nona, rolled up beside him in her wheelchair. Her little brown dog, standing stiff-legged on her lap, glared daggers at the cat. "...and I'm positive Suzie would be more than happy to see him gone too," Brian concluded, shouting over the shrill yipping. Churchill rose, leveled a look of disdain at the watery-eyed pooch, and with a regal air, sashayed away, tail aloft. I smiled. The cat had attitude.

"Well, if it isn't Miss Kinsey O'Dale." The old woman's eyes sparkled with mischief as Brian swung the screen door open for me. True to the many years she'd spent as a Broadway actress, and well known for her outlandish theatrics, she was predictably overdressed for the occasion in a red sequined dress and matching hat adorned with two enormous white ostrich feathers.

Grinning, I leaned down and planted a kiss on her brightly rouged cheek. "Hi, Nona, great to see you too." Hard of hearing, she'd called me 'candle' the first time we'd met and since then, seemed to delight in finding some new way to mispronounce my name. The little game amused both of us.

"Sis is out on the patio having a major coronary," Brian said, pointing towards the kitchen. "Jim and that new guy are no help at all. They've been chugging margaritas for the last half hour."

I gave him a wry smile. "Hey, that's okay. It's taken us forever to get somebody to sign on at the paper, so we sure don't want to scare him off. Let 'em have a good time, I'll help out."

He wheeled Nona away from the door and back in front of the TV as I entered Ginger's cluttered kitchen. I shook my head in amazement at the tower of unwashed dishes in the sink. Plastic grocery bags were scattered everywhere and a jumble of paper plates, cups, napkins, pop and liquor bottles covered every available square inch of counter space. Ginger was way ahead of me in the worst housekeeper category. At least I washed the dishes every couple of days.

"Oh, there you are," she said, rushing through the patio door, looking totally frazzled. "I guess I'm running a tad behind."

"You should have orange traffic cones posted at the doorway to warn people. It looks downright dangerous in here," I said with a laugh, pushing aside tortilla chip bags to set the ice bucket down. "Here's the tablecloth. I'll wash these dishes and then you can tell me what else needs to be done."

"Bless your little heart," she crooned, pushing a damp strand of strawberry blonde hair away from her freckled face. 'I don't know what I'm gonna to do about getting some more food. How fast could you whip up a passel of enchiladas?"

I made a face at her. "Right. Betty Crocker, I'm not. Just chill, okay? I called Lupe. She says she'll be here."

Ginger clasped her hands and rolled her eyes heavenward. "Thank you dear Lord."

It took every second of the next hour, but between Ginger, myself and Brian we managed to get the chairs and buffet table set up outside, light the candles, and start a cheery fire in the clay chimenea before we attacked the mess in the kitchen. Jim and Walter lounged outside the open door in lawn chairs cracking jokes and supervising our activities. They were well into the second pitcher of margaritas as twilight set in and the rest of the newspaper staff and their families began to arrive.

"Bet you can hardly wait to get away on your trip with Tally," Ginger said, edging me a coy smile as we spooned salsa and guacamole into hand-painted bowls. "You gonna wear that sexy new bathing suit you bought in Phoenix last week?"

I winked. "That was my plan."

"Ah, romance," she sighed, delicately fanning her face. "I'm tickled pink to know you two ain't scrappin' no more about you doing that Morgan's Folly story."

I shot her a meaningful look. "He hasn't mentioned it this week...so far anyway."

Ginger tossed the empty salsa bottle in the trash. "Well, sugar, you can't blame him for being a mite peeved. You should've told him what happened right away."

A mite peeved was putting it mildly. "I know, I know. I've done my utmost to make it up to him these past couple of months and I think things are finally getting back to normal. We both need a break from the office routine and...other things. I think this is just what the doctor ordered."

"Where is our handsome cowboy, anyway?" Ginger asked, scooping up the bowls.

"He said he'd be late. Some kind of trouble at the ranch."

"Not problems with his Ma again?"

I grimaced. "No, thank goodness, it's not Ruth this time. I don't know. It has something to do with a couple of his ranch hands. What about Doug?" I inquired, referring to her current companion. "Why isn't he here?"

"He's bartending at a private party over at the tennis ranch."

"Too bad, we could have used an extra hand," I remarked, tossing empty tortilla chip bags into the trash.

She rolled her eyes. "Tell me about it."

We set the last of the munchies on the table, greeted all the guests and then helped ourselves to margaritas before collapsing into the lawn chairs. Brian had made up a WELCOME, WALTER sign on his computer and it flapped in the balmy breeze as a dazzling array of stars sparkled overhead. Everyone had told me the Hunter's moonrise this time of year would be spectacular and they weren't kidding. Little by little the horizon began to glow like a second sunrise, snuffing out the stars, and suddenly there it was, climbing majestically above the crest of Castle Rock like a giant cantaloupe-colored disk. The effect was spellbinding and murmurs of awe rose from the small gathering. I knew it was just an optical illusion but the sheer enormity of it seemed unreal, dwarfing the peaks below.

More people streamed through the door, filling the small back yard. "Ready for the hot-seat again?" I remarked to Morton Tuggs as he and his wife, Mary, settled into lawn chairs next to me. "You sure you're going to be up to it?"

"Oh, yeah. I'm feeling fit as a fiddle," he said, patting his paunch. He really did seem vastly improved since his ulcer surgery. "Anyway, it's going to be a whole lot easier with Walter here taking up the slack while you and Tally are gone."

"I'll second that." I raised my glass. "Attention, everybody! My esteemed co-editor and I would like to propose a toast to officially welcome our new man on the street, Mr. Walter Zipp."

There was applause and a rousing chorus of agreement from the staff while another round of margaritas was poured. Brian re-filled my glass and Ginger leaned in to whisper, "You sure Lupe's coming? It's a quarter past seven." Her worried gaze roamed over the crowd gathering around the buffet table, picking at the chips and dip. We had a cauldron of refried beans simmering inside, but that hardly constituted dinner.

"We'll just ply them with more appetizers till she gets here," I assured her, trying to quell my escalating uncertainty. It was long past the time she should have arrived.

To keep everyone's mind off the fact that the main course had not yet materialized, I suggested we all share the funniest or most bizarre story we'd ever covered. Tugg entertained us with several gems from his early days as a cub reporter and Jim had us all in stitches as he repeated his golden toilets along the freeway story. I, of course, shared my last two big assignments and then we urged Walter to tell us all a little about himself and his last job in Sierra Vista. He hoisted his bulky frame from the chair and gave us a lopsided grin. "I'm happy as a pig in shit to be here," he slurred, running a hand through his short-cropped brown hair, "cuz there's big trouble brewing down south."

Oh. Good opening. The mothers of some of the younger kids exchanged startled glances, so I quickly interjected, "Well, we're all equally happy to have you here but trouble sounds like a *good* story opportunity to me.'

"Not if you live and work there now, it isn't. I'll tell you what," he said, hitching up his pants with one hand. "The ranchers and just plain everyday God-loving Americans living near those border towns have about had it with those damned illegals. They're pouring across like cockroaches and are just about as easy to catch. And, I'll tell you what, if you add the growing number of White separatist groups springing up to that equation...well, you mark my words, people, there's going to be bloodshed before this is all over. I'm glad to be out of it. Real glad."

Bleary-eyed, Jim piped up. "Hey, man, there's nothing funny or weird about that story."

Walter edged him a look of mild annoyance. "Oh, yeah? Well, try this on for size. The last piece I was working on before I left, and this is just one among several other strange stories, concerned a particular jumper they caught in Morita."

"What's Morita?" Ginger asked, casting a pensive eye at her watch.

"A ghost town about half a mile or so from the Mexican border. Not much left but the mine and a half a dozen buildings. Anyhow, the caretaker cornered this wetback hiding in a shack and turned him over to the Border Patrol."

"Why does a ghost town need a caretaker?" I asked.

"Cause it's on private property and there was an accident there last year, but that's another story," he said with an impatient swipe of his hand. "So anyway, this Mexican claimed...."

"Hate to tell you, Walter," Jim cut in, "but this still ain't funny and it sure ain't weird." He turned to all of us and said, "Let me tell you guys the one about the lady who kept a cow in her bedroom."

Walter put up a hand. "Keep your pants on, Jimbo. I intend to win this contest under the most *bizarre* heading if you'll just let me finish."

Jim continued to look skeptical while everyone else leaned forward a few inches.

"The guy claimed—and I don't know what the hell he'd been drinking or smoking before they nabbed him, but get this, he said he'd been hunkered down in some bushes the night before and witnessed a whole van load of people getting waylaid by aliens."

Jim's face twisted in disbelief. "What the hell does that mean? He *is* an alien."

"No, dummy. He didn't mean illegal aliens. He was talking about space aliens. Little green men from Mars."

The amazed silence that followed his remark seemed to emphasize the strangled gasp. We all turned around in time to see the glass casserole dish fall from Lupe's hands and shatter on the concrete patio. Her dark eyes glassy with horror, she muffled a cry with her hand and fled.

Seconds later, Tally appeared in the doorway and, like the rest of us, stared in shocked dismay at the remains of our enchilada dinner. He looked up and shrugged. "Was it something I said?"

2

I hadn't realized just how hungry I was until dinner evaporated before my eyes. My stomach rumbling in protest, I pulled my eyes away from the tomato and cheese covered lumps to meet Tally's quizzical stare. "No," I said quietly, "we can thank Walter here for frightening Lupe with his UFO story."

"Shame on you, Walter!" Ginger wailed, jumping to her feet. "You've gone and ruined supper for everyone. Now what am I gonna do?"

He drew back, looking defensive. "Well, gee whiz. How could I know that was gonna scare her? Geez, I'm glad I didn't mention anything about the other weird part of the story concerning the cattle..."

Nona's terrified scream aborted his words and everyone froze. "Stop her!" she shrieked, pointing to Suzie, who was eagerly wolfing down large bites of enchilada casserole. "She might swallow a piece of glass!"

"Suzie, come!" Brian shouted, making a grab for her. The dog artfully sidestepped him, snatched another mouthful and then executed a forward roll through the sauce. Brian lunged for her again, but slipped in the gooey mess and would have fallen if Tally hadn't grabbed the back of his shirt. When Churchill suddenly appeared from out of nowhere, Suzie took off after him, barking madly.

Suddenly, everything looked like a scene from an old Marx Brothers comedy. Some of the kids, shrieking with laughter, joined in the chase while the adults cursed and tried to hang onto their drinks and food as chairs flew in all directions. I tried, but couldn't suppress a shout of laughter as the dog wove in and out among the startled guests, anointing everyone she touched with enchilada sauce. Above the mayhem, I heard the sound of a car engine starting and glanced over the fence in time to see headlights flash on. The laughter died in my throat. Oh man. It must be Lupe. She was going to get away before I discovered why Walter's seemingly innocuous remark had caused such a violent reaction. I sprinted for the side gate and ran out to the dimly-lit street, yelling, "Lupe, wait a minute!"

In response to my shouts, she turned her head in my direction for a second, then shoved the car into gear and floored it. Disappointment mingled with anger as I watched her taillights vanish around the corner. Why had she run away from me? I made one of my instant decisions and swiveled around only to collide with someone in the shadows. My heart contracted and I let out a squeak of fright as arms closed around me. "Whoa!" came Tally's soothing voice, "what's with all the drama tonight?"

When I recovered my breath, I said, "Jesus, Tally, you scared the crap out of me."

"Sorry. Where are you going in such a hurry?"

"To get my car keys and go after Lupe."

"Why?"

"Why?" I stared up at his finely-chiseled features outlined in the moonlight. "Ginger's party is in complete shambles and you're not the least bit curious to find out what caused it?"

He shrugged. "Well, I gather something Walter said spooked her, but is it really necessary for you to go chasing after her right this minute?"

"She lives ten minutes away. I can be back in a flash." I started to draw away, but his hands tightened on my shoulders.

"Kendall, for the life of me, I don't know if I'll ever understand why you feel the need to dash off half-cocked at the slightest provocation. You might want to think about working on your overly-impulsive behavior."

I smiled sweetly. "Tell me something I don't know."

His weary sigh spoke volumes. "Okay, then, how do you think Ginger's going to feel about you skating out in the middle of her party?"

"She'll be pissed."

"Then why do it?

"But, what about Lupe?"

"What about her?"

I swallowed my agitation and pulled away from his grasp. "All right, I won't go right now. But, you saw her. She was in a total panic. Something set her off and I'd wager it's more than just a story about UFOs."

He folded his arms and regarded me with skepticism. "I don't suppose you'd buy into the notion that the dish just slipped out of her hands and she left out of plain old embarrassment?"

He had a point, but it was more of an adrenaline boost to believe otherwise. "I suppose it's possible, but Ginger said she's been acting kind of weird all week, and today she got a phone call that sent her tearing out of the office right after I left. I really had to lean on her to come here tonight. Nope. Something's definitely wrong."

He looked away from me and for a few seconds there were no sounds except for the echoes of conversation from Ginger's back yard and an owl hooting from a nearby saguaro. I could tell by his rigid posture that something else was on his mind. Unlike me, he was very capable of keeping his emotions in check and his mouth shut.

I tilted my head to one side. "What's wrong at the ranch?"

He didn't answer.

"Come on, Tally, I can tell something's bothering you."

He lifted his hat and raked his fingers through his thick hair. "Damned INS is on my back again. They're claiming some of my hands are undocumented, but as far as I could tell they checked out okay. I got a Notice of Intent this afternoon that I'm going to have to deal with."

"What's that?"

"I've got 72 hours to show evidence that they're here legally."

"I see. Are you sure that's all?"

He cleared his throat uncomfortably. "Um...you *are* coming to California with me next week, aren't you?"

"Of course I'm going with you, silly. I've been looking forward to this trip for weeks. Don't worry, I'll be ready to leave Tuesday at the crack of dawn just like we planned."

"Uh-huh."

"What does uh-huh mean?"

He blew out a protracted sigh. "I know you well enough to recognize all the signs."

I bristled. "What signs?"

"It's been about two months since your last adrenaline fix."

I laughed. "Oh, come on. Who's being dramatic now?"

"I mean it, Kendall. You're like a bloodhound and it's going to bug you to no end if you don't find out what's going on with Lupe. Am I right?"

I linked my elbow through his and pulled him towards the house. "Well, Mr. Know-it-all, I'm afraid you're wrong this time. Nothing is going to stop me from going with you and that's a promise."

He edged a dubious look at me. "I'm going to hold you to that."

There was no mistaking his solemn tone. He was right, of course. I was burning with curiosity about her strange behavior, and if he hadn't intervened, I would already be at her place. But I certainly had no intention of altering my vacation plans. And anyway, we weren't leaving for three whole days. That should be plenty of time to ferret out the answer.

We'd just set foot on Ginger's front porch when the screen door flew open to reveal our pressman, Harry, and his family tromping out one by one followed by Al Robertson and his wife.

"Hey! Where's everybody going?" I asked, stepping aside to allow Harry's three small children to scoot past. "The party's not over already, is it?"

"It is for us," Harry replied gruffly. "The kids are starving and if we hurry we can make it to Angelina's before they close. I don't know about you guys, but I don't feel like lapping my dinner up off the patio."

"Oh, dear," I said under my breath. Ginger must be having a major cow. How could I have even entertained the thought of chasing down Lupe? What kind of a friend was I anyway?

I left Tally standing there talking to Al and headed for the back yard, dodging the tide of people streaming towards the front door. On my way through the kitchen, I spotted the two bags of ice Lupe had brought, melting in the sink. I stuffed them into Ginger's freezer and went outside once again. Brian stood among the jumble of overturned chairs grasping the wayward Suzie against his sauce-streaked shirt while Ginger knelt on the patio sopping up the mess with a wad of paper towels. "Well, I beg your pardon," she griped to Walter, who was still seated in his chair, looking befuddled, "if you hadn't scared the bejesus out of her we'd all be eatin' supper right now instead of wearing it."

He exchanged a look of pure frustration with Jim and then turned to face her. "Okay, okay. I'm sorry as hell. What do you want me to do about it?"

As more and more people jostled past me, grumbling their goodnights, my heart went out to my generous, fun-loving friend. Without thinking, I blurted out, "I have an idea. Why don't we *all* go over to Angelina's for Mexican food and...and...well, dinner's on me!"

Ginger sat back on her heels and stared at me, her eyes shiny with tears. "I can't let you do that, sugar."

I waved away her protest. "Of course you can."

"Nope," Walter exclaimed, rising from his chair. "Ginger's right, Kendall. This fiasco was my fault. *I'm* buying dinner for everyone."

Jim hiccupped loudly. "Walter, my man, you are one cool dude."

Ginger pushed to her feet with a grunt and threw the soggy towels into a trash bag. "Well, gee, that's real nice of you."

Walter nodded. "It's settled then."

Jim staggered when he rose from the chair and Walter grabbed his arm. "Steady there, Jimbo, I'll do the driving."

I was really curious to hear the second part of Walter's story that had been aborted by Suzie's shenanigans, but now didn't seem the time. Later, definitely later.

The news of the free dinner spread like wildfire and within minutes, cars roared out of the driveway and a curtain of dust hung in the air as the caravan disappeared down the dirt road towards the south end of town. It suddenly occurred to me that Angelina's was only a mile or so from Lupe's house and a plan began to percolate in my mind. I pulled Ginger aside, whispering, "I need you to do me a favor."

She listened intently as I explained my strategy. "So, if all of you ride with him, then we'll have to take separate cars. I'll scoot over there, check things out and then join you at the restaurant."

Her honey-colored eyes sparkled with mirth. "Ain't you the sneaky one?"

"I prefer to think of it as surreptitious."

"Tally ain't dumb."

"Look, you told me yourself that your car keeps dying. Just explain to him that it would be better for everyone to ride with him. He can put Nona's wheelchair in the back of the pickup."

"Bet you a dollar to a donut, he ain't gonna buy it."

"Tally's too much of a gentleman to refuse, trust me."

She shook her head in disapproval. "You're bad. Can't this wait 'til tomorrow?"

I set my jaw. "Ginger, I don't know if this will even develop into a story, but I haven't taken an interesting assignment for over two months! I mean, Tally's really happy with things just sailing along at an even keel, but I need...I need, I don't know...something. Just to satisfy my own curiosity, I want to follow up on this. Please."

An unreadable light glowing in her eyes, she stared at me long and hard before heaving a conciliatory sigh. "Give me a minute to clue in Brian and Nona."

"Thank you." I gave her a quick hug, but she looked unusually agitated as we parted. I busied myself at the kitchen sink and within minutes I heard her corner Tally in the living room. I glanced up at his reflection in the window as she explained her transportation dilemma and noticed his expression of polite interest turn decidedly dubious. Doubt assailed me. Was this thing with Lupe a big enough deal to risk antagonizing him? I was the first to admit that Tally was the best thing that ever happened to me, even though Ginger described our relationship as fire and ice. His steady, easy-going disposition had a definite grounding effect on my volatile one. So, why was I doing this? Was it my way of rebelling against his overprotective behavior, or was I shying away from his recent overture that we take our relationship to a new level of commitment? Even though he hadn't voiced it aloud, I knew his vision for our future together didn't include my career. Was I ready to settle into ranch life?

"Not yet," I muttered to myself when I heard Tally graciously agree to drive Ginger's family to Angelina's. My heart fluttered when I heard the click of his boots on the tile floor behind me and I could barely make eye contact when I looked around.

"Guess you heard I'll be chauffeuring Ginger's family with me." It was a statement, not a question.

"Yeah, yeah. That's really nice of you. I'll...be along just as soon as I finish up here," I said, plunging my hands into the soapy water. The glint of speculation in his dark eyes made me cringe inside, but he didn't say another word, just turned and walked out.

I closed my eyes and sighed. He *had* to know and I felt like a naughty schoolgirl caught smoking in the bathroom. The instant his truck left, I was out the door and in my car heading towards the Hispanic community located south of the railroad tracks. I kicked around the idea of phoning Lupe but dismissed it. The element of surprise might yield better results. As I entered the narrow labyrinth of streets crowded with bars, rundown shacks and boarded up buildings, bright moonbeams filtering through the tall tamarisk trees illuminated the occasional shadowy figure ambling by. My shoulders tensed. On second thought, this might not be the safest place in town for a single Anglo woman. Oh well.

I'd been to Lupe's place only once before, but that had been during the day. Now all of the ramshackle trailer parks looked alike and I couldn't remember the name of hers. Rats! Without the benefit of streetlights, I had to rely solely on the full moon as I drove along the unpaved roads looking for something familiar. I was close to kicking myself in defeat when I spotted the water tower. Of course! It stood near the entrance to her park. I turned into the entrance marked Shady Grove, cruising slowly, until I saw her car adjacent to the dimpled silver Airstream trailer at the end of the second row.

I parked a few spaces away and got out. The warm night air was filled with the sounds of music, kids crying and dogs barking. A dim light glowed in one tightly curtained window when I rapped on the metal door. I thought I heard movement inside, but then nothing. I knocked again and called softly, "Lupe? It's Kendall. I want to talk to you."

The light went out and I sighed with annoyance. What kind of a game was she playing? "Come on, Lupe, open the door. I know you're in there."

Silence prevailed for another few seconds and then the door edged open a crack. I could barely make out her face in the light from nearby trailers. "I can't talk to you." Her words sounded muffled, like she'd been crying.

"Why not?"

"I just...can't."

"Is this about Walter's silly story?"

Silence.

"Okay then, if this has something to do with your job..."

"I...I might not be coming back to work. I have to go away for awhile."

My stomach dropped to my shoes. "Oh no. Please don't tell me that. You know Al's scheduled to be gone for a wedding three days next week. I can't leave Tugg with no one to handle advertising."

She choked, "I'm sorry."

I stood there watching my vacation vaporize before my eyes along with my promise to Tally. But the tragic pitch of Lupe's voice superceded both problems.

"Look, whatever it is, maybe I can help..."

"No one can help me."

"Why not?"

"Because...I've done something very, very bad."

"Let me in, Lupe. Right now."

She hesitated at my tone of authority, then the lamp flashed on and without further protest she turned away, leaving the door open. I stepped inside and shut it behind me.

She collapsed in a heap on the frayed loveseat in the tiny living room and wept uncontrollably into a dishtowel. I sat down on an adjacent wicker chair and patted her shoulder, waiting for her to regain control, wondering what kind of trouble she was in. It struck me that I really knew almost nothing about her other than what was in her personnel file. She'd begun her career at the newspaper as a carrier, advanced to the pressroom and finally worked her way into classified ads where she'd been for the past two years. About her personal life though, I knew nothing.

"Would you like something to drink?" I asked when her sobs subsided and she raised her tear-stained face. She nodded wordlessly and I walked the three steps to a kitchen so small it looked like it belonged in a dollhouse. Pity for her meager living conditions blended with feelings of profound dread. What shocking information was she hiding? Did I really want to know? I opened several cupboard doors, snagged a glass and filled it from the tap. "Here." I handed her the glass and sat down again. "I'm listening whenever you're ready to talk."

She took a few tentative sips, but seemed to be having trouble swallowing. Finally she quavered, "You're my boss. I shouldn't be telling you this."

"I'm also your friend, okay? And I can't help if you won't tell me what's wrong."

She shook her head. "You won't believe me anyway."

"Try me." My tone conveyed more bravado than I felt.

She stared straight ahead, hollow-eyed, before returning her gaze to me. "You can't tell a soul. Not even Tally." She picked up a well-worn Bible from the side table and placed my hand on it. "Promise."

"Lupe, I don't know if..."

"Promise, or I won't tell you one word."

3

I hesitated several seconds, but it was long enough for two conflicting thoughts to flash through my mind. The adventurous side of me wanted desperately to know her secret, but at the same instant, the logical part of my brain screamed for me to hit the door running before I involved myself further. I contemplated the steadfast intensity of her gaze a split second longer before answering, to my own surprise, "All right. I promise."

She sat unmoving and I could tell by her anguished expression that she was still waging an inner battle. Then suddenly, she blinked as if coming out of a trance. She set the Bible down and rose her to feet, pacing the small room several times before stopping to face me. "The story Walter told about the man at Morita...the one about the alien abductions...I think it has to be true."

My mouth sagged open. "You're kidding, right?"

"I know it sounds loco, but I've been down there the past two weekends searching for some clue...anything." She drew in a shallow breath, whispering, "But there is not a single trace of them."

An uneasy feeling nudged me. "Trace of who?"

A look of pure misery clouded her features. "My brother, Gilberto, and my Uncle Raymond both disappeared ten days ago."

I gawked in disbelief. "Oh, come on, Lupe, get real. There's no way..."

Angry tears jumped to her eyes. "See? I knew you wouldn't believe me." She marched to the door and yanked it open. "You can go now." The rock-hard gleam in her steady gaze punctuated the finality of her words.

At that moment I really didn't know what to think of her outburst but I put up an obliging hand. "Calm down. It's just that...well, that's a pretty amazing statement." I patted the chair next to me. "Why don't you sit down here and start at the beginning. I'm sure there's a reasonable...."

"There is a witness."

"To the...ah...abduction?" It was an effort to conceal my skepticism.

"Yes. He claims he is the only one who got away from...from the sky people."

Her preposterous statement sent a shock wave through me. "Okay. I'm ready to hear more."

She closed the door, returned to the sofa and sat with clenched fists to her lips for another long minute before saying in a barely audible voice, "I feel like I am dying inside. I honestly don't know what to do or where to turn for help."

I shifted uneasily. "So...I gather you haven't reported this situation to the authorities—sheriff, Border Patrol, INS?"

"No."

"Why not?"

Her quick glance reflected a mixture of exasperation and chagrin. "Don't you understand? I can't. If *la migra*, you know, the INS finds out what I've done...they'll deport me."

The thought that there was still time to cut and run did occur to me, but she looked so distraught, I was unable to move an inch. "Lupe, why don't you start at the *real* beginning of the story?"

She hung her head, avoiding my eyes. "You have probably figured out that I'm not here legally. My green card is counterfeit and so is my driver's license."

My heart sank like a stone, but I maintained a stoic expression. "Go on."

"I came across with my stepfather, but he...he got into some trouble...." Her voice trailed off.

"What kind of trouble?"

"Smuggling drugs. He shot a Border Patrol agent...and now he's in prison."

"Christ."

"I had everything planned so carefully," she said, nervously kneading her hands. "I have worked like a slave to send money home all these years to help the rest of my family have a better life, but much of it went for my mother's sickness." Her thick dark hair fell across her face when she bowed her head again and fingered the silver crucifix at her neck. "It was never enough, Kendall. Never enough. No matter how much I sent. God finally took her last month."

I put my hand over hers. "I'm so sorry." Words seemed totally inadequate.

She swiped away fresh tears. "You know, it's bad enough that I was not there with her when she died, but now I have to live with what I have done." Renewed panic lit her eyes so I kept my voice low, soothing. "What exactly did you do, Lupe?" Her hangdog expression had me holding my breath.

"I paid a *coyote* to bring them across the border."

I cocked my head. "Your brother and uncle?"

She nodded.

My insides went hollow. "How much?"

"Three thousand dollars."

"Oh, man." I'd read stories like this where the smugglers accepted the money and then abandoned the people in the desert. "Why would you even consider becoming involved in something like this? Why couldn't your relatives wait and apply to enter the country legally?"

She flicked me a look of disbelief. *"¡Dios Mio!* That could take years! Do you know how hard it is to find any kind of decent paying work in my homeland or to put food on the table? Do you have any idea of what it's like just to even survive there?" Her Hispanic accent grew more pronounced as her agitation increased.

I stared at her a few seconds before answering quietly, "I guess I don't."

In a halting voice she recounted an existence burdened with poverty, crime, illness and living conditions so wretched I could hardly believe she was talking about life in this century, let alone a country within a few hour's drive of where we now sat.

When she finished, I glanced around again at her sparse living conditions and thought about all the overtime hours she worked, her weekend jobs, the crappy old car she drove, her meager wardrobe. Where was my brain? I should have guessed long ago. It struck me also that the newspaper could be in trouble by having an undocumented worker in our employ. It seemed no matter what direction we took someone was going to suffer. A rush of sympathy engulfed me when I thought of Tally's dilemma with his ranch hands. What a strange coincidence that we should both experience the identical problem the same night. "Lupe, tell me more about this witness. Is he still around? Have you talked with him?"

"Not directly." She looked away from me again and my sense of unease heightened. Why the furtive behavior? "Is this the same guy Walter was talking about?"

"No. The information comes from a small boy."

I was dumbfounded. "A boy? How old?"

"Four, maybe five."

I sat back hard, staring at her. "Let me get this straight. You're ready to quit your job, go traipsing around the desert hunting for who knows what, and risk getting yourself deported, all on the basis of some fairy tale told by a kid you haven't even talked to?"

Her jaw tightened. "Sister Goldenrod thinks he's telling the truth."

"Sister *Goldenrod*? And who on earth is she?" I hadn't realized my voice was rising until Lupe chided, "You don't need to shout. I thought you were going listen to the whole story?"

I held out my hand in a placating gesture. "You're right. I did promise."

"She is the one who put me in touch with the *coyote* in the first place."

"And?"

"She called this afternoon to tell me about this little boy."

I couldn't decide whether the story was getting better or worse as she relayed the tale of the Guiding Light Mission, which served as a sort of unofficial halfway house for illegal immigrants. The woman calling herself Sister Goldenrod was the minister at the small church located less than a mile from the border town of Sasabe.

"Sasabe? Is that southwest of Tucson?"

"Yes. Why?"

Hadn't Tally mentioned helping out a rancher friend of his in that area several times in the past few months? I wished now I'd paid more attention to him. "Oh, nothing. Go on."

According to Lupe, Sister Goldenrod administered shelter, food and comfort to the local homeless population and to the hardy souls who were lucky enough to make it across the miles of desolate landscape and evade the Border Patrol. She didn't believe that she was doing anything wrong and stubbornly maintained that she was merely doing the Lord's work.

A young family who had recently crossed over happened upon little Javier wandering in the desert. He was severely dehydrated and hallucinating about space aliens having supposedly waylaid the van where he and others had been hiding. Unwilling, or unable to take the boy with them, the couple had left him at the mission where he was now in the Sister's care. The problem, Lupe explained, was that the child appeared so traumatized by the event he couldn't remember many details. And even Sister Goldenrod, with her kind ministrations, had been unable to coax the boy out from under his bed because he maintained that the aliens might find him.

"I think hallucination is the operative word here," I said, watching her crestfallen expression. "Look, obviously something happened, but it's pretty farfetched to believe that we're dealing with a UFO abduction."

"Then where is my family?"

I shrugged. "I don't know. But I'm afraid that without the assistance of the authorities in that area you don't stand a chance in hell of ever finding them."

She glared at me. "Are you saying I should forget about them?"

"Of course not. We just need to think of a way to approach this that won't get you deported." My gaze strayed to my watch and I flinched in surprise. Good heavens! Tally and the gang were expecting me at Angelina's. How was I going to explain being over an hour late? At that second, my cell phone bleated a 'low battery' warning and handed me the excuse I needed to explain why I hadn't called.

Lupe must have noticed my discomfort because she rose from her chair and said apologetically, "Thanks for listening. I know there's nothing you can do, but just talking about it has helped."

It may have helped Lupe, but I doubted I'd be sleeping tonight. "Look, I don't want you running around down there asking questions and drawing attention to yourself. Maybe an immigration lawyer could tell us what your status is. Let me give it some thought," I said, picking up my purse. "Maybe I could make a few calls...."

Lupe's sharp intake of breath arrested my words. "What?"

Realization gleamed in her smoky eyes. "You're right," she said softly. "I can't ask the authorities for help...but you can."

Speechless, I stared at her for a few seconds. "Me? How?"

"Don't you see? You're a reporter! No one is going to think it's strange if *you* are asking the questions."

She was absolutely right. No one would think it the least bit odd. But, as her proposal sunk in, equal parts of consternation and excitement churned inside me. My reporter's intuition whispered, 'Go for it! This might be a great story,' while my rational side warned, 'Reality check, what about you and Tally?' I shook my head sadly. "Lupe, I can't. As tempting as it sounds...."

"Please," she choked, collapsing to her knees in front of me. "Come with me, even if it's just for a few days. I don't have anyone else to turn to." She buried her head in her hands, sobbing hysterically. "Please help me find out what happened to them!"

Pity squeezed my heart. What should I do? How could I just ignore her anguished plea? I patted her shoulder while thinking that there must be a way to assist her without jeopardizing my trip with Tally. I did some quick calculations. We weren't planning to leave until Tuesday anyway, so...what if I took the next few days to do a little detective work and got back in time to leave on schedule? What would be the harm in that? "When were you planning to leave?"

"Tomorrow morning."

"Okay, how does this sound? I'll go with you and see what I can find out, but only if you promise to do me a favor in return."

Her bloodshot eyes mirrored uncertainty. "What?"

"We'll take separate cars and you'll come back to work on Monday morning, then Tugg won't be left hanging. I'll have three full days to snoop around and still get back in time to leave with Tally on Tuesday. That way, everybody should be happy. And if I don't come up with anything substantial, I give you my word I'll take the last few days of my vacation when I get back from California and we'll make an additional trip. It's that or nothing."

The seconds ticked by as she considered my proposition and finally nodded her acquiescence. "Okay."

I breathed a sigh of relief. Sort of. The plan sounded plausible, but getting it past Tally presented the next major obstacle, considering that my obvious subterfuge tonight put me at a distinct disadvantage when it came to presenting my side of the argument that was sure to arise. Lupe and I talked for several more minutes and then she accompanied me outside. "I'll never be able to thank you enough," she said with a tremulous smile. "I'm sorry to cause all this trouble."

"No need to apologize."

"I feel so bad about spoiling Ginger's party." She gestured towards her car. "The other pan of enchiladas is on the back seat. Do you want to take it back to her house?"

At the mention of food, sudden hunger gnawed at my belly. I'd probably missed a great dinner at Angelina's. "I'm sure the party is over now. Don't worry about it. Get packed and get some sleep. What time were you planning to leave?"

"Around seven. It's close to a four hour drive."

"I'll be here." I started towards my car, but stopped and turned when a thought struck me. "By the way, where will we be staying overnight? Should we reserve a motel room?"

An indulgent grin creased her lips as she slowly shook her head. "I can see you have never been to Sasabe. It is a very small place. Sister Goldenrod let me stay in one of the rooms she keeps ready for her um...unexpected guests, or maybe you would want to drive back and find a motel in Green Valley."

"That bad, huh?"

"Not fancy at all," she said with a little shrug.

34

"Well, I'll bring my sleeping bag in case I have to rough it for a couple of nights."

She thanked me again and I headed to the restaurant nursing my own pangs of guilt. Crap! Just as I feared. There were only a few cars remaining in the parking lot when I arrived and Tally's truck was not among them. I groaned aloud and goosed the car down the road towards Ginger's place, dread pooling inside me as I imagined the impending confrontation—one provoked by my own impulsive actions.

When I approached her driveway and saw Tally's truck parked beneath the streetlight, my heart did a nervous little dance. He was leaning against the door twirling his hat in his hands. Not a good sign. Gravel crunched under the wheels as I braked, jumped from the car and started walking towards him. Might as well get it over with.

I was filled with regret. It should have been a night for romance. The soft breeze caressing my face carried the dusky-sweet scent of desert plants and felt surprisingly cool. Was this the weather change I'd been waiting for, the one that would herald an end to the sweltering summer heat?

Silvery moonlight, more brilliant than any I had seen before in my life, beamed down on me like a spotlight, exposing all my weaknesses. I flashed Tally a sheepish grin designed to diffuse the situation, but his response sent my spirits plummeting. The mosaic of light and shadow playing across his rugged features revealed the tight set of his jaw and the agitation smoldering in his hooded gaze. Why did he have to look so tall, so imposing and so damned sexy? Before I could utter one word in my defense, he said coolly, "It's really comforting to realize that on your list of important things, I rank somewhere below Ginger's dirty dishes and Lupe's personal problems."

"You know that's not true."

"Really? You could have fooled me." He made an exaggerated point of staring at his watch then lifted his gaze to me. "All I know is that it's past ten o'clock and I've spent exactly five minutes with you all evening."

"I'm sorry. I had every intention of coming to Angelina's after…"

Tersely, he interjected, "After cooking up your little scheme with Ginger. Shame on both of you. We waited at the restaurant until poor old Nona finally fell asleep in her chair."

I sighed heavily, pressing one hand against my forehead. "I'm sorry. I don't know what else to say. But, I was right. Lupe does have a serious problem and I, unfortunately, am going to have to deal with it."

He seemed unimpressed by my explanation and his lips flattened into a hard line. "Sorry is not going to cut it. I know you're accustomed to using deception to wheedle information from other people, but I don't appreciate you using it on me and I sure as hell don't like being put on the spot."

Although I probably deserved his wrath, I stuck my chin out and shot back, "Before you get your shorts all in a knot, I did try to call you, but the battery on my cell phone died so…" I winced inwardly as the words left my mouth. Even I knew how lame it sounded and my face flamed with embarrassment.

He arched one dark brow. "I see. And apparently Lupe's phone wires were also cut?"

I squirmed under his accusing glare for a moment before saying, "That's a little bit overly-dramatic, don't you think?"

"You're the one who gets off on drama and duplicity."

"That's not fair. Besides, you forced me to do it that way."

"*I* forced you?"

"Yes! You made it very clear you didn't want me going over there tonight and I'm not accustomed to asking anyone's permission to do my job. I didn't want to have an argument with you in front of everyone, so…"

His gaze softened marginally. "What kind of trouble is she in?"

"Well…I can't say."

Grimacing, he squeezed his eyes shut. "Why does this sound familiar?"

I knew he was referring to my first assignment when I'd arrived in Arizona last spring. On Tugg's request, I'd had to work undercover and been unable to tell him why. "This is nothing for you to have a freckled cow over. I agreed to go with Lupe down to the southern part of the state for just a couple of days to check some things out."

He quit twirling his hat and jammed it on his head. "I see."

"No, you don't see. Lupe's gotten herself involved in…well, something pretty awful and she begged me to help her. She also swore me to secrecy."

"This is exactly why I didn't want you to get yourself involved. Can't this wait until after our trip?"

"I don't think so."

His sigh of exasperation filled the space between us. "I know you're not that excited about the horse show…."

I cut in, "Don't assume things. Lupe said that if she can't resolve this problem, she's not coming back to work."

He cocked his head to one side. "At all?"

"At all. And since Tugg and I agreed that we wouldn't leave each other in a bind, if Lupe takes off I won't be able to go with you anyway because we'll be short-staffed." I explained the bargain I'd made with Lupe, concluding with, "You're going to have to trust my judgement on this one."

He shot me an incredulous look. "You mean like your last two assignments? In case you've forgotten, I had to save your beautiful butt the first time, and the second time I was the last one to know that you'd almost gotten yourself killed."

"So that's it. I thought we weren't going to have this discussion again. Admit it, you're not really upset about tonight. You're still pissed at me over that Morgan's Folly story. How many times do you want me to apologize? I was wrong. I should have told you sooner. This time I'm telling you right up front. Lupe's in big trouble and I'm going to do my best to help her if I can."

He shook his head slowly. "Do you have any idea how aggravating you can be?"

"Me?" I hoped my beguiling grin would thaw his anger. "I don't mean to worry you but this is…this is what I do."

His eyes were luminous with disappointment. "I guess I was hoping that things would settle down, and that maybe you'd develop a little appreciation for what *I* like to do, but I guess ranching doesn't hit your hot button."

"Tally, I love you, but please don't try to corral me like one of your wild horses. I'm not ready to be put out to pasture just yet." Oops! His face closed up and I regretted the words the moment they left my lips. Why, oh, why couldn't I stop and think things out before saying them? I rushed to slide my arms around him. "I'm sorry. I didn't mean that the way it sounded." I laid my cheek against his neck. "You know you're the most important thing in my life." I cherished the feel of his strong arms around me and I thought again how we seemed a testimony to the opposites attract theory. The fact that he appeared to have a clear vision of who he was and where he intended to go in life had a steadying influence on me. And compared to my impetuous ways, his dependable disposition was like a buoy in the rough uncharted waters of our still evolving relationship.

He stiffened and held me away from him, his eyes searching mine. "Kendall, I know I can't change you any more than you can change me, but I hope you'll think this through before you go running off chasing UFOs or some nonsensical thing."

I blinked my innocence. "Who said anything about UFOs?"

He dropped his hands from my shoulders and jerked the truck door open. "I'm not stupid."

"I never said you were."

"You think I haven't figured out that this must have something to do with Walter's crazy story? I have eyes. I saw how Lupe reacted. Why in the hell you have to insinuate yourself into this I don't know but if you insist, I hope you'll watch that pretty ass of yours this time."

"I'm glad you like it." Much to my dismay, he did not respond to my coquettish grin. "Please don't worry. I'll be careful." I held up two fingers. "Scout's honor."

He looked unconvinced. "Where did you say you were going?"

"Sasabe. Isn't that near the...what ranch was it you were telling me about?"

"The Sundog. Champ Beaumont's spread." A thoughtful expression softened his features. "Actually, I have some unfinished business there. Maybe I'd better come along to protect you from yourself."

"Tally, you can't. I promised Lupe I wouldn't tell anyone about this."

He clamped his mouth shut, wheeled around and climbed into the driver's seat. Simultaneously, he slammed the door shut and started the engine.

"Wait a minute," I shouted, running towards the open window. "Aren't you coming over to the house?"

Staring straight ahead, his jaw line resembled granite. "Not tonight. But while we're on the subject of promises, I hope you'll remember yours." He shoved the truck into gear, then turned and leveled me a look of warning. "I'm leaving for California at five o'clock Tuesday morning with or without you."

4

Tally's abrupt departure left me standing in the moonlit road choking on a pearly cloud of dust. Indignation tightened my chest. I hadn't suffered from an asthma attack for weeks, since that last time we'd had words. "Damn it, Tally!" As the taillights on his truck winked out and the roar of the engine faded, hot tears stung my eyes. No matter how I tried I couldn't seem to stay in his good graces. Leave it to me to damage his masculine sensibilities again by mouthing off without thinking. Ruefully, I decided that perhaps I should think about registering my tongue as a lethal weapon. But at the same instant a shadow of remorse wrapped around my heart, another part of me rebelled. Was this my future with him? Was I going to have to sacrifice my dreams to make this relationship work?

A slight thumping sound from behind startled me and I whirled around to find Ginger standing near the trash dumpster shaking her head sadly. "I told you he was gonna be madder than a cornered badger."

I fisted my hands on my hips and glared at her. "Ginger King! You were eavesdropping."

She wrinkled her pug nose and waved away my protest. "Oh, Flapdoodle. I just happened to be taking out the garbage. How could I help but overhear y'all yapping at each other like a couple of angry coyotes?"

She was right, we'd hardly been whispering. I kicked up a puff of dust and blew out a weary sigh. "Just once, I wish he'd stay put and finish a conversation like a mature adult. But no, he always quits right in the middle and drives off in that damn truck!"

"Men don't like confrontation."

"I don't know what to do with him. We just can't seem to see eye to eye on some things. You know he hasn't come right out and said it yet, but I'm getting the sense that he'd be happier if I never took another assignment. Out of town, anyway."

Ginger leaned back against the fence post and studied me for a second before saying, "Well, my stars and garters! How'd you expect him to react? It ain't like you been taking a walk in the park. You've gone and gotten yourself into some pretty tough scrapes these past few months."

I hitched my shoulders defensively. "Maybe, but I didn't plan it that way. Things...just happened." I stared up at the moon as if the answer to my dilemma lay hidden somewhere in the dark craters. "I can't win. I adore Tally, but I don't want to sit around the Starfire knitting potholders all day like Ruth. It's hard to explain, but it really gets my blood running to chase down an interesting story." In my mind, I was already projecting ahead to the possible intrigue awaiting me. Strong intuition convinced me that this feeling of cold. excitement in my gut could not be wrong.

Ginger's unusual silence drew my attention back to her. Our eyes locked and I was surprised by the expression of suppressed anticipation in her honey-colored eyes. "What? Why are you staring at me like that?"

"I'm not staring. I was just thinking that...well, I know you two've got some big-time differences to overcome, and I'm sure you ain't in the mood for another lecture, but dang it, girl, wake up and smell the coffee! Guys like Tally don't come down the pike everyday."

"You think I don't know that?"

She flicked me a doubt-laden look. "Sometimes you don't act like it. Look, Doug and me don't always see eye to eye, but nine times out of ten I can get him to come around to my way of thinking."

"I don't think compromise is part of Tally's nature."

She mulled that over a few seconds and then tipped her head sideways. "You suppose it might be the fact that he's so much older than you?"

I gawked at her. "He's only thirty-four! You make him sound ancient."

"You know what I mean. He just seems so much more...settled, more set in his ways."

"Is that a euphemism for saying that I'm immature and flaky?"

"Of course not."

She looked hurt, so I reached out and touched her shoulder. "I know you mean well, but cut me some slack, would you? I think he's still got some serious issues to work out about his first wife, and I went through this same drill with my ex-husband ragging on me to quit my job and raise a bunch of kids."

Ginger stared at me as if I'd lost my mind. "So? If Doug popped the question tonight, I'd be ready to get hitched in the morning."

"Well, that's you."

"I think you're missing the big picture here, sugar."

I glanced sharply at her. Not only was she unusually serious, her inexplicable expression of feigned innocence indicated something was up. "Okay, Ginger, out with it. What are you not telling me?"

She bit her lower lip and jammed her hands into the food-splattered apron. "Nothin'."

"Are you sure?"

"It's just that...well, you should've been with us at dinner tonight instead of gallivanting around town after Lupe. I was watching Tally's face real careful when he was playing around with Harry's kids. He looked happier than a frog on a lily pad, if you get my drift."

"Subtle you're not. Why don't you just come right out and say it? I know what the score is."

"I don't think you do," she muttered.

"Hey, why should I rush things? One divorce and a broken engagement in the span of three years is not a track record I'm proud of. I intend to proceed at my own pace, thank you very much."

She looked positively pained. "I still don't think you ought to go running off like a spring filly when the stallion's in the barn. Excuse me for living, but I thought he really rang your bell."

Ginger was priceless. "He rings my bell just fine," I said with a wide grin. "But I think you're both overreacting. I'm not going to jump the Grand Canyon on a motorcycle for Christ's sake! I'm just going to help out a friend and maybe get a good story while I'm at it. And we weren't going to get to see much of each other until Tuesday anyway. He's driving up to Prescott to get that new horse and I'd planned to run a thousand errands and clean my filthy house. But, as it turns out, I'm going to have to deal with something rather important that's come up."

Her eyes turned crafty. "I heard. So, what's all this about Lupe being abducted by space aliens? Come on, I promise I won't tell anybody."

"Of course you won't, because I'm not going to tell you."

"Girl, you're making a big mistake if you ask me," she said, her voice rising shrilly. "You're going to fool around and spoil things with Tally if you ain't careful."

Her urgent tone made my heart skid to a stop, then restart with erratic thumps. "What makes you say that?"

She reflected on her fingertips a few maddening seconds before blurting out, "If you weren't so danged pigheaded you'd see things real clear like me. Instead, you're so all fired busy thinking up ways to provoke the poor guy you ain't seein' what's right in front of you."

"Ginger, what the *hell* are you talking about?"

She said nothing, just stared at me wide-eyed with her lips pinched shut. Her chest heaved as if she were about to burst. "Are you going to tell me what's going on with Lupe?"

"Nope."

Pouting, she looked away, folding her arms. "Then I ain't tellin' either."

Waves of exasperation pounded at my temples. Mindful of my short temper, I bit back the host of barbed retorts that leaped to my tongue, saying instead, "Well then, I guess it's a draw. I won't know your secret and you won't know mine." Even though I was burning to know what she was concealing, I stomped to my car and flung the door open. "I have to pack and get up early. I don't have time for games." I broke a fingernail jamming the key into the ignition and the engine purred to life as she rushed up to the open window wailing, "Sugar, please don't be mad at me."

Keeping my own bruised feelings at bay, I surveyed her anxious expression. "I don't get it. I've known you for six months and I love you dearly, but never once during that time have you ever been able to keep a secret. Why are you starting now?"

She shrank under my incriminating glare. "I've already said more'n I'm supposed to. You know I'd tell you if I could, but this time I just can't. I promised her...."

"You promised who?"

In pure Ginger fashion, she dramatically clapped both hands over her mouth and backed away shaking her head. Then she turned and ran into the house, slamming the door behind her. For a minute, I just sat there in a trance-like state with the engine idling, trying to make some sense of this whole disastrous evening. I toyed with the idea of pounding on her front door and demanding that she explain her cryptic statement, but one glance at the clock on the dashboard made my decision. I was leaving town in eight short hours.

I don't even remember driving through the downtown area and I was, as my grandma used to say, 'riding the pity train', as I turned onto Lost Canyon Road for the second time that day. The giddy elation I'd felt this afternoon was a distant memory in the wake of the unsettling confrontations with my two favorite people. Under normal circumstances, I would have savored the vinegary creosote-scented breeze blowing in the open window and been transfixed by the splendor of the moon-splashed landscape. But not tonight. What a difference a few hours can make. I eased into the carport and trudged up the brick walkway. Inside, I listlessly flipped on lights and then made a beeline for the answering machine, energized with anticipation. Would there be a message from Tally assuring me that he wasn't angry and that everything would be all right? Nope. My already low spirits nose-dived. How on earth had I managed to complicate my life in such a short period of time? Strange. We were all prisoners of our promises.

I wouldn't have thought I'd be able to eat, considering my morose disposition. However, since I'd never had dinner, I raided the refrigerator. Three pieces of cold pizza and an entire pint of chunky chocolate chip ice cream later, I was if not satisfied, at least replete.

In my bedroom, as I stuffed clothing into my bag, the phrase 'shit list' came to mind and it drew a wry smile. How ironic. I was most certainly on Tally's, Ginger was on mine, temporarily anyway, and if I backed out on Lupe I'd be on hers. But if I did nothing at all I'd be on my own.

It was a long mostly sleepless night spent listening to the far-off hoot of owls and the mournful wail of coyotes as my thoughts meandered from one puzzling issue to the next. Why was Ginger, of all people, being so obtuse? How was it that she and some other unnamed woman were privy to information affecting me and Tally? Why wouldn't she tell me?

That thought dovetailed into my impending journey and his reaction to it. Okay, I'd be the first to admit that I'd gotten myself into a few jams in the past. Remembering my smug assurance that this time would be different sent a little ripple of doubt through me. How could I know that? Would the day ever come when I would react to a situation with cool detachment using my head instead of leaping blindly into the unknown? The outcome of my two previous assignments had been nothing less than astounding, but the premise of this one was downright spooky. UFO abductions? It seemed preposterous, but logic dictated that there might be some connection between the bizarre story relayed by the Mexican national in Walter's story and this young boy. Wasn't it too much of a coincidence to think otherwise?

I thumped my pillow and turned over, my mind swimming with last minute details. I must not forget to take my notebook computer and the charger for my cellular phone. Should I bother packing a jacket? And what if Sister Goldenrod had no room for us? What then? I really *was* flying by the seat of my pants and I might have to suffer the consequences of my rash decision. I sat up and clasped my knees, watching the scarlet numbers on the digital clock turn over 5 a.m.—ridiculous. I threw off the covers, showered, and then dressed in jeans and a T-shirt, brewed coffee in the kitchen. After the second cup, it occurred to me that the person I really should talk to before embarking on this trip was Walter Zipp. He had personal knowledge of the area and could clue me in on the data he'd gathered for his UFO story. The hour hand on the clock nudged six. It was too early to call him now, so I'd contact him later from the road.

I finished the laundry, washed the dishes, swept the floor and then lugged the bags to the front door. The moment I stepped outside, a rash of goose bumps chased up my arms. Wow. For the first time since I'd been in Arizona, I felt a definite chill in the air. The jacket was a good decision. After I'd loaded the trunk, I paused for a moment, savoring the supreme serenity of dawn, my favorite time of day. Not that I didn't relish the drama of the brilliant sunsets too, who wouldn't? Perhaps it was because all the day's events were behind me whereas there was something exhilarating about starting fresh each morning, waiting for new adventures to unfold.

The autumn sun had taken on a different character from the fiery beginnings of a summer day when it rose harsh and bold to claim skies of flawless blue. Now it was more subtle, softer, the opaque light slowly transforming the horizon to pale turquoise. Above the towering spires of Castle Rock, feathery jet contrails shocked a brilliant white by the eminent sunrise, fanned out like silvery bicycle spokes.

Reluctantly, I pulled my gaze away and returned to lock the front door, mindful that the sounds of the desert had also changed—the subdued, repetitious cooing of the mourning doves having been replaced by the cheerful racket of the incoming winter birds.

As I backed the car out and headed down the road, mentally primed for a new challenge, there was only one thing wrong. The familiar burn of excited anticipation in my stomach was tempered by the heaviness in my heart. As much as I wanted to ignore it, I really hated to allow the cavernous rift between Tally and me to stand unresolved for three days. I reached for the cell phone and then pulled my hand away, setting my jaw. Why should I be the one to give in? For once, I'd wait until he called first. I battled with myself for another five miles or so before I felt my resistance crumbling. I grabbed the phone. "O'Dell, you're a wuss!"

I knew from experience that the whole Talverson clan rose before dawn, so I had no qualms about dialing his number. It rang five or six times before I heard a woman's voice say dully, "Hullo."

Crap. Double crap. Why did it have to be his mother? I swallowed my resentment, saying sweetly, "Good morning, Ruth. Sorry to call so early, but I really need to speak to Tally."

There was a momentary silence before she said, "Who is this?"

I did a slow burn. She knew damned well who it was. This was another one of her silly games. Anything to put a rift between me and Tally. Not for one second did I buy into the supposition that she was still suffering from the severe depression following the death of Tally's father—a depression supposedly spawned by the reprehensible actions of Tally's former wife. Was it my fault that I bore such an uncanny resemblance to the late Stephanie Talverson? Why couldn't Tally acknowledge that his mother's ceaseless hatred for the woman spilled over onto me?

To myself, I fumed, 'Get over it, lady', but I managed to keep my voice even, controlled. "It's Kendall."

"Hmmph. Hold on, let me see if I can find him." I heard her put the phone down and then nothing for a long time. Had I lost the signal? I pulled the phone away from my ear and watched the little 'in service' message pulsating. No problem on my end. I pressed it against my ear again, and then I heard noises. It sounded like pots and pans clanging. Cupboards being opened and shut. Silverware clattering. The innocent sounds of breakfast preparations.

My face flamed. The old witch! She must have set the phone down and gone on about her business, never even telling him I'd called. I fought the urge to turn the car around, drive to the ranch and confront her. I couldn't. It was almost seven o'clock.

I punched the END button and tossed the phone onto the passenger seat. By the time I pulled in front of Lupe's trailer, my heart rate had slowed to a dull roar, but the beginnings of a headache tapped at my temples. Okay, one thing at a time, I would have to deal with Tally's mother later.

I took a few slow breaths and got out just as the trailer door swung open. "Hi," Lupe called out, as she shouldered a stained nylon overnight bag and kicked the metal door shut behind her. I could tell by the dusky smudges beneath her eyes that she'd probably slept as poorly as I had. We took a few minutes to work out the logistics of the trip. Since she didn't have a cell phone, we settled on a series of hand signals to communicate and then, with the map spread out on the hood of her car, we studied the various routes and decided to stay on the Interstate for the majority of the trip. I agreed to follow her and we made plans to stop somewhere in Tucson for an early lunch.

The hour's drive to Phoenix flew by and as we merged into the heavy traffic on I-10, I congratulated myself again on my decision to stay in Castle Valley and not take the job I'd been offered at the Phoenix newspaper. I had to admit it. I was spoiled now. Spoiled by the exquisite isolation, the friendly down-home people, unobstructed views of the mountains, fresh unpolluted air. After years of living in what seemed like little more than a furnished closet in Philadelphia, my little desert town seemed like a haven from the rush and crush of people and traffic always associated with large cities. And Phoenix was no exception. As we headed south, on the now familiar route to Tucson, I breathed a sigh of relief when we finally got beyond the miles of lookalike shopping centers, industrial parks and the endless sea of tan and pink stucco townhouses capped with red-tile roofs. Cookie cutter housing developments, which seemed to have sprung up overnight, were gobbling up the vacant desert land at an astounding rate.

Lupe's car seemed to be straining to maintain freeway speeds. Clouds of blue-black smoke poured from her rear exhaust pipe and it appeared that any moment it might burst into flames. I was beginning to have serious doubts as to whether she would even make it as far as Tucson, so I pulled up even with her in the middle lane and gestured a questioning thumbs up while mouthing, 'Is everything okay?'

She returned my signal with a self-assured smile so I dropped back behind her. Apparently she had more confidence in her old car than I did. It was approaching nine o'clock, so I dialed Walter's number, hoping I'd given him enough time to sleep off what was probably a doozy of a hangover.

The line rang and I couldn't help grinning. Was this great or what? I was flying down the Interstate at 65 miles per hour, in the middle of nowhere and was able to conduct business. How had I ever managed without this little marvel of technology?

"Yellow?" came a sleepy voice.

"Walter?"

"Last time I looked."

"Hey, it's Kendall. Hope I didn't wake you."

Big yawn. "Well, sorta, but that's okay. Guess it's time to haul my butt out of bed. What's up?"

"I'm on the road heading down to your old neck of the woods for a couple of days to help out a friend, and I was thinking that if I have some time left over I might follow up on that story you were working on."

A lot of throat clearing and then, "Which one?"

"The one about the UFO sighting." He'd find out soon enough from Ginger that the friend was Lupe, but I'd honor my promise as long as I could.

Extended silence, then a gruff, "Why?"

"Oh, I don't know. The premise intrigues me."

A short hesitation. "Where'd you say you're going again?"

"Arivaca and Sasabe."

"I hope you realize that you're driving right into a powder keg that could explode at any minute." His tone sounded ominous.

"What do you mean?"

"The Knights of Right are planning a series of protest rallies in that area this weekend."

"I gather they are one of the White power groups you mentioned?" I asked, tightening my hold on the steering wheel as a strong gust of wind buffeted the car.

"Yep."

"What are they protesting?"

"A couple of things. For starters, two years ago, the Feds nabbed their leader in a sting operation. I think the guy's name is Arthur Lane, or Andrew, I forget, anyway last week he was sentenced to eight years in prison."

"For what?"

"Other members of the group swear it was a trumped up charge of setting fire to a Hispanic church.

Because it was labeled a hate crime, the Feds got involved. They videotaped a bunch of these guys practicing field maneuvers out in the desert, innocent stuff in my book, but they swooped in and arrested all of them on weapons charges, acting on a tip that the group was training to carry out some terrorist plot someplace."

"And?"

"They couldn't make that one stick."

"And the second thing?"

"The ranching community is up in arms because one of their own is in trouble for flashing a phony badge and then allegedly drawing a gun on a couple of immigrants he caught cutting up some of his irrigation line. Now one of those bleeding heart liberal humanitarian groups has hired an attorney to represent the illegals in a lawsuit. Can you believe that? Man, I'm telling you, everything is upside down."

"Sounds like a great human interest story to me."

"Yeah, well, trust me, that whole situation's going to get a lot dicier before it gets better."

"So I'm gathering, but back to my original question. Got any suggestions on who I should talk to regarding our supposed extraterrestrial visitors?"

Rather than trying to give me all the particulars at that moment, he suggested that I read some of the articles he'd written that were posted on his former newspaper's website. Awkwardly, I shouldered the phone and jotted down the web address on the pad beside me while keeping a wary eye on the road. Both lanes were choked with aggressive truck drivers that passed us like jets and bore down on the proliferation of hapless out-of-state visitors like a fleet of destroyers. It made for ticklish driving conditions and it wasn't lost on me how dangerous it was to

54

try and simulate an office situation while hurtling down the highway.

"If you're going to talk to anyone though," Walter droned on, "you'll want to get hold of a gal in Arivaca by the name of Mazzie La Casse."

"Mmmmm. Who's she?" His response was drowned out by the roar of a diesel truck charging past. "What was that again, Walter?"

"I said she presents herself as a psychotherapist as well as a UFOlogist. She facilitates one of those encounter groups for people who claim they've been space-napped. I think they meet every now and then at the New Life Community Church in Arivaca."

"Super. Anyone else?"

"Oh, man, I can't remember the names of all the wackos I talked to, but some of them are mentioned in the articles. You also might want to read about the corresponding piece I was working on right before that one."

He sounded so wistful I decided to follow a hunch. "Walter, level with me. You're too good of a reporter to have just abandoned stories this compelling in midstream. Are you sure Lavelle's ailing aunt is the only reason you left Sierra Vista?"

His hesitation answered my query. "It wasn't my idea to leave things hanging, but...well, things were getting too hairy and way too close to home, so we packed it in."

"So, what's the scoop?" I asked, downshifting as Lupe slowed behind an old panel truck hauling a load of poorly tied together hay bales.

"Hold on a minute, I've got another call," Walter said, clicking off.

While I waited impatiently for him to return to the line, I took the opportunity to take in the ever-changing vista of the Sonoran desert. On either side of the highway, irrigated farms burgeoning with lettuce and other crops I couldn't identify, temporarily checkerboarded the parched landscape in varying shades of green. In fallow fields, tractors churned up clouds of dust that whirled away towards rock formations so devoid of vegetation that they looked like piles of crumpled-up paper bags. But even though the terrain differed greatly from the lush greenery of Pennsylvania, it seemed everywhere I traveled in Arizona was like driving into a calendar picture. I loved every inch of this sun-scorched state and the expectation of exploring new territory had my stomach tingling with anticipation. Or was it hunger? Probably both.

"Okay, I'm back. Listen, I'd rather you didn't spread this around or Lavelle will have my hide."

Oh great. Another secret. Another promise to keep. "I'm all ears."

"Back in July, the 14th to be exact, do you remember hearing the story of a Border Patrol agent by the name of Bob Shirley?"

I searched my memory but came up empty. "No, what about him?"

"He was found shot in the temple inside his truck on the reservation not too far away from that old mining town I was telling you about last night."

"You mean Morita?"

"Yeah," he said with a despondent sigh. "It was a real shocker. He was a helluva nice guy and a dedicated agent."

"Sorry to hear that, Walter, but why is telling me this going to upset Lavelle?"

"Because he was her cousin, her favorite cousin since she was a kid."

"I see. I gather there's a lot more to this story."

"Yep. For Lavelle, his death piled onto all the other problems we'd been struggling with. The last year down there we were besieged by the humongous increase of illegals tramping through our property at all hours of the day and night. They wore a goddamn path through the yard! Our place was broken into twice, once when she was home alone, and it scared the ever-living crap out of her. And then, after what happened with Bob...well, she just couldn't handle the strain of living there anymore."

The phone hummed loudly, obliterating some of his answer. Damn, was I going to lose the signal? I pulled the antenna up. "Sorry, Walter, can you repeat that?"

"...authorities are calling it suicide, but a lot of folks in that area aren't buying the official explanation."

"What about you?"

"I wish I knew for sure."

The note of glum skepticism in his voice kicked my pulse up a notch. "What makes you say that?"

"I don't know. There's just something fishy about the whole thing." He sounded grumpy.

"Like what?"

"Like, what in the name of glory was he doing out there on the Indian reservation so many hours after his shift change?"

"So, he was officially off-duty. Who found him?"

"One of the tribal police. He was parked on a really rough, isolated stretch of dirt road that runs past Morita and comes out near Newfield not far from the San Miguel Gate. It had been dragged just a few hours earlier and...."

I interjected, "What do you mean dragged?"

"Border Patrol vernacular. The agents drag tires behind the vehicles to blot out footprints and such. That way when they're looking for signs of jumpers, they can tell approximately when the last group crossed and how many. Although, according to the stories Bob told us, these people are wising up."

"How so?"

"He filled me in on some of their tricks. Smugglers especially, employ some pretty crafty maneuvers like gluing scraps of carpet to the bottoms of their boots. The tribal police call 'em carpet walkers," he added as an aside, "but now these people are getting really inventive and using the same type of boots as the Border Patrol to throw agents off the track. One resourceful guy even carved cow prints on the soles of his boots."

"Wily coyotes," I murmured, "but getting back to the situation with your wife's cousin, were any footprints found near his truck?"

"Oh yeah, a bunch. It could be that a group of crossers mistook him for their ride, rushed the truck and who knows what happened from there. But the locals think he was most likely ambushed by drug traffickers."

"That's scary."

"No kidding, but here's the rub. The forensics team found only his fingerprints on the weapon and they couldn't find anything to prove that he *didn't* take his own life."

"Well, it *is* a pretty sophisticated science now, you know that." I wondered if he was reading too much into the situation considering his personal involvement. "They're not often wrong." Silence met my ears. "Tell me, Walter, did your wife's cousin leave a note of explanation?"

"Sort of."

"What does 'sort of' mean?"

"It was unfinished. The FBI found a notepad on the seat beside him. It said, *I can't do this anymore,* but get this, he never signed his name."

"Any idea what he meant by that statement?"

"Considering all the circumstances? Yeah, I might."

5

And the circumstances proved to be interesting indeed. Walter confided that Bob Shirley, along with three other agents and a Customs Inspector, were about to be indicted for alleged involvement in a major cocaine trafficking ring based in Tijuana, Mexico. Theoretically, that was the reason he'd chosen to take his own life.

"I thought I knew the guy pretty well and I'm having a hard time grasping that he'd be involved in anything so...so unsavory," Walter grumbled.

"He wouldn't be the first agent to fall from grace. Just a few months ago, I read about four or five others who were arrested for simply looking the other way when the loads were brought across. And these were people with long and distinguished careers. Supposedly they'd pocketed in a few months what they'd normally make in a year's time. That has to be pretty tempting for some people."

"I never voiced it to Lavelle, but don't think the thought didn't cross my mind."

"Walter, tell me something. Do you know if he was having financial problems? What does a Border Patrol agent make a year anyway?"

"I gathered things were tight, but I think they were doing okay. He'd just gotten a promotion a few months prior to his death and I think Lavelle said he was up to forty-seven, maybe forty-eight grand a year. Nowadays, that's probably not a whole hell of a lot considering he was supporting three kids, a wife and his mother-in-law. But still...."

"Did he strike you as the kind of a person who'd be involved in something like that?" I asked.

His short silence was telling. "Boy, you think you know someone and then find out you really didn't." He went on to divulge that following the agent's death had come the revelation that he had apparently been linked to one of the many White power groups operating in the area the past few years. It was alleged that he'd even been spotted at a rally. This additional fact had added to Lavelle's burgeoning humiliation and spurred their hasty departure. But my interest level really shot through the roof when Walter added as an aside that Bob Shirley had also been the apprehending agent in the case of the Mexican migrant found in Morita, the one claiming to have witnessed the UFO abduction.

"Hmmmm. Now, *that* grabs my interest. What's your take on that?"

His deep sigh hissed in my ear. "Probably just a coincidence, but I never got to pursue that angle because Lavelle wanted to get the 'hell out of Dodge' when this all came down."

"Did you talk to his widow about it?"

He snorted, "Loydeen? That netted me a big fat zero."

"Why do you say that?"

"Every time I tried to talk with her about Bob's death, including just a few weeks ago when we drove over there to tell everybody goodbye, she flat refused. The strange part is she wouldn't discuss it with Lavelle either and she seemed...."

A crackling buzz obliterated his answer and I only caught bits and pieces of his conversation for the next few seconds before the line went dead this time. Rats. I tried several times to dial him back, but the 'no service' message continued to blink back at me. Oh, well, I'd call him later. I had enough information for starters.

Food was uppermost on my mind when we arrived on the outskirts of Tucson. I pulled up beside Lupe again and pointed to my mouth. She got the message and took the next exit. Within minutes we were seated at a booth inside a noisy coffee shop crowded with truckers, uniformed Hispanic workers and boisterous groups of tourists all decked out in shorts and brightly-printed shirts. A harried-looking waitress wearing a stained blue apron slapped menus on our table, asked if we wanted coffee, and then sprinted away.

"Are you hungry?" I asked Lupe, perusing the menu with interest. Everything looked yummy, especially the Grubstake Special that included juice, a short stack, eggs, grits and homemade biscuits.

"A little. I guess."

I looked up at the expression of utter misery reflected in her jet black eyes, and my heart went out to her. In addition to suffering the loss of her mother, how would I feel if my brother and uncle had disappeared under such bizarre circumstances? I probably wouldn't have any appetite either. When I broached the subject, she shot me a warning look and inclined her head towards two middle-aged men at the adjacent table. I edged them an unobtrusive glance. Who did she think they were? Undercover Border Patrol agents? It was possible. Okay. I'd fill her in on Walter's conversation later.

Hoping to take her mind off her troubles, I filled the void with chatter about work and then lightened the conversation with a few details about my upcoming vacation with Tally. Apparently I failed miserably, as she had shredded her paper napkin into a pile of confetti. We ordered our food and went over the roadmap again. Besides a few sparsely situated towns which included the ghost towns of Oro Blanco and Ruby, vast empty stretches of land, including the Tohono O'odham Indian Reservation west of Sasabe, was all that awaited us. Only then did it hit me what a monumental task I had undertaken. What had I been thinking? What were the chances of me finding anything concrete in such a huge area in three short days?

"Just in case we get separated," I said, sliding her a sheet of paper, "how about giving me specific directions to the mission."

She sketched out a simple grid and handed it to me just as the waitress slid a plate of *huevos rancheros* in front of her. My breakfast was piled high on a platter big enough to hold an entire turkey. Wow! If my younger brother Shane had been there with me, he'd have hooted with laughter and accused me as he always did of having an appetite like sumo wrestler. As always, thoughts of my family sent a pang of homesickness shooting through me. But at least I had Christmas to look forward to. During the last conversation with my parents, we'd agreed that I would host the family for the holidays.

Lupe's depression appeared to deepen with each passing moment and she seemed jumpy and distracted, picking listlessly at her eggs while I managed to polish off every bite. When I asked, she whispered, "It makes me nervous to be so close to the...uh, you know, so close to Mexico. Until this thing happened, I did not want to risk coming down here at all."

"I see." It was after eleven by the time we left the restaurant, gassed up and dumped a quart of oil in her car. Mellow music from a favorite tape provided a relaxing environment for me as I followed Lupe south on I-19 towards the border town of Nogales—all virgin territory to me. The Santa Rita Mountains, a massive cathedral of rock cloistering a host of shadowy canyons, was a commanding presence to the east while the peaks to the west were partially obscured by drab gray mesas of slag deposited by the local copper mining company.

"Same to you," I muttered under my breath as yet another irate motorist, who apparently didn't think 65 miles per hour was fast enough, honked and roared past while issuing me the famous one-fingered salute. Enough. Weary of Lupe's dawdling pace, I pulled in front of her and checked my rearview mirror periodically to keep her in sight.

To my delight, a fleecy film of white clouds appeared on the horizon, bringing to a close seven straight weeks of pristine blue skies. But the rising wind was presenting a problem. Tawny dust devils, having siphoned up sand, leaves and other debris from the bone-dry desert floor, performed a dizzying ballet in traffic, splattering their gritty contents in all directions. If it kept up, we might be in for a full-blown dust storm, which would make driving even more hazardous, I thought as three eighteen-wheelers, apparently in a race to see who could reach the border first, rumbled past. I was relieved to see the sign announcing that only twenty miles remained until our exit. Good. Armed with the additional information provided by Walter, I was anxious to get started on my sleuthing. For Lupe's sake, I prayed that the little boy at the mission would be able to shed some light on the puzzling disappearance of her relatives. Knowing just the little I did about this intriguing case galvanized my senses. Was Tally right? Was I an adrenaline junkie? If so, how was I going to change that? Did I even want to?

Thinking of him spawned a twinge of disappointment. Obviously Ruth had never told him I'd phoned, but why hadn't he taken the initiative to call me? No doubt he was still annoyed about my decision to help Lupe. Couldn't he see past his own pigheadedness? Couldn't he grasp that I'd had no option but to pursue this situation as best I could? My thoughts roamed back to Ginger's evasive behavior last night. It galled me to no end to know she was sitting on inside information concerning Tally and some other woman. What was behind her roundabout references that I took him for granted? The tiniest ember of doubt flickered inside me. Now that I really thought about it, there had been times these past few weeks when he'd been distant and rather withdrawn. I had attributed it to ongoing problems at the ranch, but I'd been so immersed in putting out fires at the office that I hadn't really pressed him for details. I vowed right then that I would give him one hundred percent of my attention next week and amply demonstrate the depths of my feelings for him. I grinned to myself. The new skimpy two-piece bathing suit should set the stage nicely.

At Arivaca Junction, I pulled over and signaled for Lupe to take the lead again. Other than the Cow Palace Saloon and the Long Horn Grill that sported a gigantic steer's head complete with long white horns, there wasn't much to the place, just a few scattered businesses and some ramshackle houses. The streets seemed mostly deserted.

We waved goodbye to a smiling young Mexican girl sitting in the bed of a pickup truck selling bunches of dried red chili peppers, and drove onto a well-maintained road flanked by palo verde trees, prickly-pear cactus and thick clusters of mesquite and ironwood. Secured inside miles of range fence, herds of cattle grazed peacefully on the soft contours of golden grasslands sweeping westward towards the eye-catching Baboquivari Mountains. I thought the jagged peak piercing the now mostly cloudy skyline looked a little like an enormous brown shark's tooth.

The road gradually deteriorated into a series of sharp turns and sudden dips that had my stomach doing cartwheels. As the car rattled over yet another cattle guard, I decided that this particular route would be inadvisable for anyone prone to carsickness. There was very little traffic other than an occasional pickup or SUV. After a few miles of breathing the blue curtain of oil-laden smoke from Lupe's car, I dropped back behind her. Why risk an asthma attack?

I have to admit that what happened next was totally my fault. Yes, I was gawking out the window at the breathtaking scenery. Yes, I was thinking about a hundred different things and I was most certainly driving too fast. As I rounded a sharp curve and descended into a wash, it took a second for the dark image ahead to penetrate my foggy brain. "Sheeeeit!" I floored the brakes and skidded to a stop mere inches from a gigantic black bull. Shaking and gasping for breath, three things occurred to me in quick succession. I had not hit him, I was not hurt, and the bull hadn't budged one single inch. Instead of fleeing in terror, he just stood there, chewing, flicking his tail, and staring straight at me with a wicked gleam in his dark eyes. This imposing beast bore no resemblance to the gentle doe-eyed cows that my brothers and I had petted on visits to dairy farms when we were kids. I shuddered to think of what would have happened had I plowed into him. I would have been dead meat.

My sudden stop had killed the engine, so I turned the key, hoping the noise would scare him. It didn't. Should I risk getting out to try and shoo him away? I surveyed the sharpness of his horns and decided that would be a dumb move. No way was I a match for what looked to be three thousand pounds of beef on the hoof. When I laid on the horn, he lowered his head and pawed the ground as if in challenge. Now what? There was not quite enough room to drive around him without hitting the road sign, so I shouted out the window, "Okay, big guy, move it. Now!"

His response to my demand was to shake his head and snort a gross-looking gob of bull snot onto my windshield. "Jesus!" Apparently pleased by his performance, the bothersome bovine turned his rump towards me and decided to treat me to more of his bodily functions by depositing an enormous pile of dung in the road. Some of it dropped onto my hood and front bumper. He turned back to me, nostrils flaring, and I swear he wore a look of smug triumph on his broad face. I moaned in disgust, rammed the car in reverse and backed to the top of the rise, hoping that I would seem less of a threat.

I looked in all directions. The range fence on either side of the road appeared to be intact, so where had he come from? In the distance I could see a ranch house and a few outbuildings, but no other signs of life. No people, no cars—nothing but a few red-tailed hawks gliding in the steady wind. Surely by now, Lupe had noticed that I was no longer behind her, so why hadn't she doubled back?

Wait, I had my cell phone! I grabbed it, then paused. Who was I going to call? Tally? And tell him what—that I was being held hostage in the middle of nowhere by a cantankerous bull? He would laugh himself sick. But, the more I thought about it, the less humorous the situation became. What if another driver happened upon him at night? Perhaps the sheriff's office could notify the rancher or animal control? I dialed information but got dead air. The 'no service' notice blinked at me again. "Stupid, useless phone," I muttered, stuffing it back into my purse.

There was nothing to do but wait, so I rolled the window down all the way and stared out at the mountain-rimmed valley. I really had nothing to complain about. Who could ask for a more beautiful setting? It was blissfully quiet, and as the cooling wind fluffed my hair and whispered through the tall desert grasses, I filled my lungs with the fragrant scent. I sat there for at least ten minutes until the bull grew bored with me and leisurely wandered into the brush. All right! I shoved the car into gear and stepped on it, hoping to catch up with Lupe. I'd only gone a mile or so when I saw two vehicles ahead pulled over to the side of the road. One of them was hers. When I got closer, shock zapped my heart. Lupe was leaning against the side of her car, arms folded tightly, talking to a tall, burly man clad in a khaki shirt and slacks. Uh-oh. The large letters on the side of the white and green vehicle parked behind hers proclaimed U.S. Border Patrol. All four of her car doors were open, as well as the trunk. Her bag was on the ground beside her, the contents strewn about.

I mouthed a silent, 'Oh, my God!' as I drew alongside them and Lupe shifted her gaze to me. Her usual burnished copper skin tone had faded to ashen gray and I prayed that I was the only one who noticed that behind her expression of subservient impassivity lay a hint of panic. Filled with an awesome dread I waved and parked my car in front of hers. Stay cool, I cautioned myself as I got out and strolled towards them. And be prepared to lie your head off. "Is there some kind of a problem?" I asked, keeping my voice light, my face impassive. He couldn't hear my heart thundering, could he?

"Afternoon. Do you know this woman?" the man asked, inclining his blonde crewcut towards Lupe, while absently flicking what looked to be her driver's license between his fingers.

"Sure do. She's a friend of mine."

"And how do you know each other?"

"We work together at the *Castle Valley Sun* newspaper."

"Is that so?" His close-set green eyes reflected profound doubt. "And what's *her* position?"

It irked me that he continued to talk about Lupe as if she weren't standing right next to him or was a person of so little consequence that he could not address her directly. I swallowed my annoyance. "She works in our advertising department."

One sandy brow crept higher. "Full time?"

"Yes, sir." My gaze strayed to his nametag that read Hank Breslow, and then back up to meet the unwavering suspicion in his eyes.

"And you are?"

I issued him a bright smile even though my mouth was as dry as cornstarch. "Kendall O'Dell. I'm the editor of the paper. So ah...what's going on?"

"You tell me."

I edged a glance at Lupe who stood silent as a stone. I wasn't sure what kind of a game he was playing and I didn't really care for his impudent attitude, but I knew we were treading on quicksand. "We came down to do a story on the...um, rally in Arivaca this weekend." I silently thanked Walter and maintained an expression of stoic calm.

Some emotion I could not fathom flickered behind his steady gaze. Wordlessly, he lowered his eyes to study the driver's license again. The wind sounded awfully lonesome whistling through the tall straw-colored grass and I was very conscious of our isolation. Suddenly, I felt resentful towards Lupe for putting me in the position of having to lie for her, but then a twinge of guilt chilled me. Hadn't I voluntarily injected myself into this situation?

"Where did you say you were born again?" the agent asked, finally shifting his attention to Lupe.

"Florence, Arizona." The falsehood slipped out with practiced ease.

"And your mother?"

"Hermosillo."

His eyes bored into hers. "Have you got a copy of your birth certificate with you?"

At that, I had to bite my tongue to keep from jeering, 'Oh, come on. Who carries their birth certificate with them in the car?'

Never flinching, she fished something from her wallet and extended it to him. "I have my Social Security card. Will that help?" The slightest inkling of indolence surfaced in her smoky almond-shaped eyes. She knew she'd won. So did Agent Breslow.

He made a show of studying her card, just to keep her on edge, I think, and then handed it back to her along with her driver's license. "You ladies have yourselves a nice day," he said, squeezing out a synthetic smile. A glimmer of skepticism still persisted in his eyes as he climbed into his Chevy Tahoe, slipped on a pair of mirrored sunglasses, revved the engine, and then ever so slowly cruised away.

When he was out of sight, I turned back to find Lupe's show of bravado dissolving as she slowly slid to her haunches and took in great gulps of air before pinning me with a look of terrified rage. "Where were you?" she screeched.

I felt foolish and impotent. "Well, you see, there was this big bull in the road, and there wasn't anything...."

"That guy just came at me out of nowhere," she cut in through clenched teeth. "If you'd been here with me this wouldn't have happened." She clapped her hands alongside her head and collapsed to the ground as if her legs would no longer support her. "Holy Mother of God," she murmured in a quaking voice, "I was afraid of this. Do you know how close that was?"

Stung by her accusation, my face warmed with guilty embarrassment. "Lupe, I'm really sorry. I got here as soon as I could but you see this bull wouldn't let me get past..." The excuse sounded so silly, I halted my explanation and fired a question at her. "What reason did he give for stopping you?"

She looked up at me ever so slowly. "Reason? What reason would he need other than the fact that I'm Mexican?"

I knelt beside her. "Okay, Lupe, calm down. Fortunately, nothing happened. You're gonna be okay. I'm going to be with you the rest of the trip."

"What about when I go home tomorrow night? If we had come in the same car, he probably would not have stopped me."

I put out a hand to help her up. "You don't know that for sure. Be realistic. With the situation down here as volatile as it is, you might get pulled over again whether I'm here or not. Anyway, you seemed to have your ducks all in a row or he wouldn't have dropped it."

She took my hand and clambered to her feet. "I did do pretty good, didn't I?" she said, a faint grin brightening her grim features.

"Your acting skills are to be commended," I agreed dryly, but the heavy weight in my gut reminded me of how tenuous her situation was and could be again any time in the future.

I helped her get her things back into the car and I led the way this time. On the outskirts of town, I noticed a Border Patrol vehicle parked behind a clump of mesquite on a dirt side road. As we drove past, I glanced at the occupant and a feeling of apprehension pooled in my belly. Agent Breslow was sitting inside with his field glasses trained on us. Was he spying on us, making sure our alibi was accurate? I suppressed an impish desire to wave at him, instead refocusing my attention on the road. It would not be wise to piss this guy off.

It was almost one o'clock by the time we pulled into what I'm sure was normally the sleepy little town of Arivaca. But, not today. Among the rows of cars, pickups and motorcycles parked along the main street, vehicles from the Pima County sheriff's department stood out prominently. Uniformed deputies were out in full force, and only blocks ahead I could hear angry shouts from a sizeable crowd gathered in front of the La Gitana Saloon to my left. They waved placards that read TACO BENDERS GO HOME! THE KNIGHTS OF RIGHT ARE PREPARED TO FIGHT! BEANERS STEAL AMERICAN JOBS! THE ONLY SOLUTION IS WHITE REVOLUTION! On the opposite side, a smaller contingency of counter demonstrators screamed back while brandishing their own signs—AMNESTY FOR ALL! DOWN WITH WHITE RANCHER BIGOTS! DISCRIMINATION IS THE REAL CRIMINAL! A news crew with microphones in hand stood beside a white van sporting call letters from a Tucson television station. Nobody looked very happy.

I glanced in the rearview mirror at the look of fear plastered on Lupe's face. While the situation presented an enticing story angle for me, I could only imagine what she must be thinking in light of her close call with the Border Patrol. Now she would have to endure the hateful slurs and degradation of her heritage just to get through town. Even with the umbrella of protection afforded by sheriff's deputies, it did not seem like a great idea. Why hadn't I thought this out ahead of time? Even though our trip would have taken longer, we could have traveled state route 286 directly to Sasabe and avoided this messy situation. No wonder she'd been so apprehensive. She knew what the score was far better than I did. "What an idiot you are," I muttered under my breath.

I waved her down a side street, got out and walked back to her. "Due to the ah...circumstances, I think it's best if you leave your car here and we'll go on to the mission in mine. We can pick yours up later or tomorrow after this thing breaks up. Okay?"

Lupe angrily swiped at the ribbon of tears trickling down her cheeks. "Why? Why do they hate us so much?" she asked in a voice shaking with emotion. "Why should it be a crime to want to work hard so we can send money home to feed our families? That's not a lot to ask for! Can't they understand that people..." she paused, swallowing hard, "that some people are willing to die for such a small dream? I think this problem cannot ever be solved."

Being a White, legal, well-fed Irish-American citizen whose ancestors traced back to the seventeen hundreds, made it difficult for me to place myself in her shoes. "Hey, never say never," I said, trying to bolster her spirits, even though I silently agreed that there did not appear to be an equitable solution at hand anytime soon. "You stay here. I'm going to scope out the situation and ask one of the deputies if there's another way to get to Sasabe other than driving right though the middle of that mob."

"Okay." Her voice was faint, devoid of hope.

I left her sitting there with the doors locked and hiked back to the main street. Oh, man. What was I getting myself into? The cries of the assembly grew louder with each step. Dozens of curious onlookers stood about listening to speeches and there was sporadic applause and cheers mingled with harsh rhetoric shouted from both sides. I shouldered my way to the front for a better look and a little ripple of recognition snaked through me when I read the name on one of the inflammatory signs. ARIZONA COALITION OF RANCHERS SUPPORTS CHAMP BEAUMONT! HELP PROTECT PRIVATE PROPERTY

RIGHTS FOR AMERICAN CITIZENS! OPEN SEASON ON WETBACKS!

Beaumont? Wasn't he the rancher Tally had visited several times these past few months? Could he be the same person Walter had mentioned, the one who was now in legal trouble regarding an episode with some illegals, as well as the target of a lawsuit filed by an advocacy group?

I studied the divergent group with interest. This was not an all male crowd. There were women of all ages present and I was frankly startled to see a sprinkling of dark Hispanic faces among the opposing groups. But then, why should I be surprised? I'd learned during my previous trip to southern Arizona that many of the Mexican-American families also resented the influx of illegals, especially the criminal element. But it was particularly unnerving to note that the most vocal protesters among the throng of Stetson-hatted ranchers were a menacing band of tattooed skinheads. Fists to the sky, they used bullhorns to shout out harsh threats of death and destruction directed towards the smaller group of Hispanics who were flanked by well-dressed whites comprised of men and women that Tally would have dismissed as 'a bunch of lily-livered liberals.'

The very character of the air had changed. It fairly crackled with palpable levels of hostility and indignation, obliterating the sense of peace I'd experienced such a short time ago. Walter was right. This was a volatile situation that could easily get out of hand. As the noisy throng pressed closer, my claustrophobia began to bother me big time. I looked around for a way out and my heart gave a little jerk of surprise when I recognized Hank Breslow among the sea of faces. My lips tightened in irritation. Had he followed us into town? And, if so, why?

Jostled and shoved as the crowd lurched forward, I had a hard time keeping him in sight. He was in a heated discussion with someone, but I could not see who he was addressing. Just then, a young woman with bright raspberry hair and enormous multicolored tattoos on both biceps shoved a clipboard into my hands. "Sign this, and we'll throw this wetback-loving bastard out of office," she snarled, her silver-ringed nostrils flaring. Her T-shirt read AVENGE BOB SHIRLEY'S COLD-BLOODED MURDER!!

Confused, I stared at the form and read the explanation above the signature lines. It was a recall petition for Congressman Lyle Stanley. I remembered vaguely that he'd been pressing to ease border restrictions and that he was also married to a Hispanic woman who was the daughter of the Mexican consul in Douglas. I declined to sign and she hastily swiped it from my grasp.

My apprehension level rose as the expressions of the crowd grew more intense and the shouting escalated. Part of me longed to stay and report on the unfolding drama, but I reminded myself why I was here in the first place. When an egg splattered on the forehead of a guy standing not two feet from me, I decided it was time to go. I turned around and pushed my way to the fringe as law enforcement officers waded into the fray.

With a gasp of relief, I dislodged myself from the shrieking clutch of humanity and started back to where Lupe waited. As I passed one sheriff's deputy climbing from his patrol car, I said, "Excuse me, sir, is there another road to get to the Guiding...er..." I coughed away the remainder of the sentence, regretting that I'd almost given away our covert destination of the mission. "I mean, is there another way to get to Sasabe other than this route?" I asked, nodding in the direction of the main highway.

He appraised the situation with the crowd before fixing me with a distracted frown. "You could take Ruby Road. It connects with another dirt road that winds through some mighty rough country real close to the border." He hooked his thumbs in his belt and looked me up and down. "Personally, I wouldn't recommend that you travel it alone."

I blew out a sigh of pure frustration. From the first moment I'd decided to undertake this project, it had been fraught with an unbelievable series of problems and roadblocks. Was there a message here?

"See that little church over there?" he advised, pointing to our right. "Turn left behind it and take 3rd Street all the way out to the clinic. Make another left and then a right onto the main road. You'll intersect with route 286 in about eleven miles. Got it?"

"Yes, thanks." I turned away and suddenly remembered the wandering bull. I retraced my steps and reported the incident. He didn't look the least bit surprised and, in fact, I gathered from his apathetic reaction that it wasn't an unusual occurrence. Oh, well. I'd done my duty.

I trotted back to Lupe, who quickly transferred her bag to my trunk and then locked her car before jumping into the passenger seat next to me. I didn't say anything, but thought locking it was a futile effort considering that the window behind the driver's seat had a piece of cardboard taped onto it in place of the window glass.

When we rounded the corner, her features fused into a motionless mask of alarm. She glared at the protesters and mumbled something in Spanish.

"What?" I asked her.

She slid me an uneasy glance and scrunched low in the seat. "I was praying to God that we get to the mission without any more trouble."

"We'll be okay now," I assured her as we left the teeming mob behind us, crossed the main street and drove behind an unpretentious white block building that housed the New Life Community Church. Ah, yes. This was the place where the alien abduction encounter group met. Contacting and hopefully arranging a meeting with UFOlogist Mazzie La Casse would be on my list of things to do this evening.

The little cemetery to our left was well kept in comparison to the series of crumbling brick and adobe houses we passed along the way, many of which appeared abandoned. There were piles of old cars, overflowing trash dumpsters, a mashed-in horse trailer, and the constant din of barking dogs standing stiff-legged in weed and junk-infested back yards. Grimly, I thought that this was certainly not the initial view of town the local chamber of commerce would have approved of.

When the sign reading Arivaca Medical Clinic loomed before us, relief poured through me. Since we hadn't seen a single person after leaving the main road, I allowed my tight shoulders to relax. As we passed the one-story brick structure, I turned to Lupe with a triumphant grin. "See? Home free. Where there's a will, there's a way, my dad always says."

Instead of returning my smile, she stared straight ahead, eyes bulging with horror. Following her gaze, I thought my heart was going to vault out of my chest. Dead ahead of us, blocking our entrance to the main road was a bright red Dodge 4x4 pickup with monster tires. Lounging alongside were two young guys dressed like cowboys, but the three other men sprawled lazily on the tailgate had their heads shaved smooth as cue balls. Muscle shirts emphasized the blood-red swastikas tattooed on their chests and arms. All had cigarettes and beers in hand. Uh-oh.

I stood on the brake while my fevered brain sized up the scenario in nanoseconds. Five strapping young guys, three of them skinheads, and lots of empty bottles scattered on the ground. Add two women alone in a car, one of them Hispanic, and the situation looked pretty dicey. I swallowed hard, tasting the remains of the Grubstake Special in the back of my throat.

The daring part of me wanted to climb from the car, confront them, and demand, 'Okay, dudes, how about moving this puppy out of my way,' but my uneasiness skyrocketed as they stared back at us, their expressions of good-humored camaraderie slowly turning to menace. When one of them reached behind and pulled a baseball bat from the truck bed, Lupe screeched, "Kendall, let's get out of here!"

I hit the door lock, shoved the car into reverse, but almost jumped out of my skin when a figure loomed behind us in the rear-view mirror. I pulled my foot off the gas so fast, the car hopped like a rabbit and the engine died. Before I knew what was happening, the stranger began pounding the trunk of my car with his fists. "How many goddamn beaners have you got stuffed in here, huh?" he shouted, following his question with a string of racial slurs and expletives targeted at Hispanics.

What should I do? Just back over him? My hesitation cost me. Before I could decide my next move, the others had surrounded the car like a pack of coyotes encircling their prey.

6

"Do something!" Lupe screamed, clawing at my shoulder. "Get us out of here!"

I wanted to, but surprise and fear held me immobile while two of the guys gleefully poured the remainder of their beers onto my windshield. With wicked smiles plastered on their youthful faces, they then proceeded to lick the foam off while the other four pounded on and rocked my car from side to side. One of the muscle-bound skinheads, with a wild and dangerous gleam in his eyes, brandished the bat at Lupe and shouted his intentions to slay all wetback invaders. As her terrified screams grew louder, in a strange sort of way I felt removed, like I was in a scene from a gang movie. Above the babble of voices I kept waiting for someone to call, 'Cut!' Looking back, I can convince myself that their bluster was mostly for show and that they never intended any real harm other than to scare the crap out of us. But, at that moment, I was unsure.

Somehow, I willed my inert limbs into action and rolled the window down a crack. "You morons better back off! I'm calling the sheriff right now!" With trembling hands, I fumbled in my purse for my cell phone and made certain the guy in the black Stetson with his face squashed grotesquely against my window, saw me dial 911. They couldn't know that the 'no service' message was still blinking. Goddamn worthless device.

One of them shouted a warning to the others and they tossed the beer bottles into the air and sprinted for the truck. Hooting and hollering like cowboys at a rodeo, they piled into it and shook their clenched fists at us before disappearing around the corner in a cloud of dust.

In the breathless silence following their dramatic exit, Lupe and I exchanged a look of stunned horror. It took several minutes for me to regain my composure and, as my erratic breathing and thundering heartbeat began to subside, it was not lost on me that my association with Lupe had now made me a target of the animosity that prevailed in this highly-charged atmosphere. Word spread swiftly in small close-knit communities. There was no question that inquiries on my part regarding the disappearance of her relatives would place me on the wrong side of prevailing sentiment. This latest demonstration of hostility was unlike anything I'd ever experienced before in my life and it shook me to the core.

I turned to her. "You okay?"

Pasty-faced and visibly shaking, she nodded and spat, *"Hijos de puta!"*

I'd picked up a couple of Spanish phrases in the past six months and recognized this one as highly uncomplimentary. For Lupe, who rarely swore, it revealed her extreme distress. And who could blame her? "Still want to stay?" I asked, thinking that we'd already wasted almost two precious hours of our short trip. "Or should we get the hell out of here now?"

She pressed fingertips to her eyelids for a few seconds then said with a catch in her voice, "I can't. I can't leave until I find out what happened to Gilberto." She paused and turned to face me, her eyes glistening with unshed tears. "But…I also don't want you to have any more trouble with these…stupid bigots. I was wrong to bring you down here into this awful situation."

It was indeed awful, and I had a feeling things could get even worse, but I had no intention of breaking my promise to her. There was no point in dwelling any longer on the incident, so I started the engine and turned onto the main road. We traveled in glum silence for a few miles and then in a move designed to lighten the mood, I flashed her a playful grin. "Why do you suppose these guys all want to look like Humpty-Dumpty?"

Her mouth sagged open. "Who?"

"Humpty-Dumpty. You know. The shaved head thing? It's supposed to be intimidating, but I think they look kind of silly, don't you agree?"

She seemed to be thinking it over and finally edged me a sly look. "The big guy, the one that looked like a moose? I especially liked the earrings he was wearing, didn't you?"

"Loved 'em." It was heartening to see the tense lines around her mouth relax. The rest of the trip to Sasabe was uneventful. Pushed by the steady wind, the milky glaze of clouds that had coated the sky all day was breaking up into lacy puffs of white. As we skimmed along the recently patched two-lane road, a bright golden nugget of late afternoon sunlight peeked through and I felt my spirits lifting. When we swung onto Route 286, I wondered if the craggy collection of tilted buttes to the south of us lay in Mexico. We couldn't be too far from the border at this point. Several large yellow signs announced that we were entering the Buena Vista Wildlife Refuge and a smaller one advertised that the Rancho de la Osa Guest Ranch was only a few miles ahead.

"What does *osa* mean?" I asked Lupe.

"Bear," she answered in a distracted tone. We'd only traveled another mile when she shouted, "There!" Pointing towards a strange-looking fence constructed of stones and old truck tires, she directed, "Turn right on that dirt road. The mission is maybe half a mile from here."

As we buzzed over a cattle guard and headed towards the foothills to the west, my stomach growled. How could I be hungry again so soon? Was it the pristine air and wide-open spaces, or perhaps being removed from all the daily pressures of work? Whatever the reason, I found myself wondering where we were going to find dinner out here in the middle of nowhere. I had a few sodas and apples in the cooler, but that wasn't going to cut it.

"Is there a place in Sasabe to eat?" I asked Lupe, carefully avoiding the carcass of a dead skunk lying in the middle of the road. The lingering stench of its perfume had us pinching our nostrils for a few seconds as we crept past.

She turned to me, looking uncertain. "I don't know. The last two times I was here the Sister was kind enough to let me eat in the kitchen with some of her…guests."

I caught her meaningful glance. "Sounds good to me." I was looking forward to meeting this woman. And although I had mixed feelings about her questionable motives in regards to her assistance of undocumented immigrants, I could not deny that she must possess a heart of gold to risk the possibility of arrest in order to carry out her convictions.

"There it is," Lupe announced, pointing towards a white cross perched on a red-clay roof. It was just barely visible above the thick fields of ironwood and mesquite. Her pinched expression and tightly clasped hands conveyed her growing agitation. I could hardly blame her. What news awaited her? Would this lost child confirm her worst suspicions?

I turned right into a rutted driveway lined with unevenly spaced boulders and got my first look at the whitewashed walls of the Guiding Light Mission. Enclosed behind a fence fashioned from the long spiny branches of the Ocotillo cactus, the simple Spanish-style building, adorned with a gracefully curved bell tower, stood alone and rather forlorn-looking in the middle of a weed-choked dirt lot flanked by a few thirsty-looking palo verde trees. But my eyes were drawn to the rambling house to the right of it. It was painted the brightest, most garish pink color I'd ever seen. And the paint looked fresh. To our left, the hulking remains of several abandoned cars of early 70's vintage lay in a jumble of trash beside a dilapidated garage that housed a dented brown Bronco. The only other dwellings were three tiny sun-bleached shacks on the north side of the church.

I parked the car in front of the wide arched doorway of the mission and got out. What a godforsaken place to build a church, no pun intended. There were no other houses in sight and the place looked abandoned. "Are you sure she's here?" I asked Lupe, as we trudged through the gate.

"She's probably in here," she replied, pulling on the brass handle. The ancient hinges emitted a grinding squeal as the carved wooden door opened and a draft of cool air welcomed us inside the sanctuary. It took a few seconds for my eyes to adjust to the dim light filtering through smudged stained-glass windows and falling in multi-colored slats over the dark rows of low wooden pews.

"Sister Goldenrod?" Lupe's called out, her voice tentative.

There was no echo and the sound of her words vanished as they left her lips, almost as if the thick adobe walls had absorbed them. She called again, but there was no response. Lupe's brows dipped in concern. "How strange. She's knows I'm coming today."

We backed out the door and I pointed to the garage. "Is that her Bronco?"

"Yes."

"Well, she's obviously around here someplace." I grinned at her. "Why don't you check out the Pepto-Bismol house and I'll look over by the garage."

"Okay."

The strong gusts of wind rushing around the side of the little church whipped my hair into a tangled mass and stirred up little puffs of dust behind Lupe as she walked across the sandy parking lot. I took off towards the garage and spotted another structure behind it that I hadn't noticed on the way in. The long one-story building looked as if it might once have been a stable. There were piles of rubble everywhere, including the remains of several other dwellings with only the stone chimneys standing. Had there been a whole community here at one time?

As I wandered among the glass and trash-strewn foundations, the significance of the piles of blackened timber and charred remnants of furniture penetrated fully. I ran my finger along what looked like the remains of a mangled steel window frame and it came away blackened with the sooty evidence that there'd been a fire here and it appeared to have been fairly recent.

The deep silence surrounding the whole place was disturbed only by the moan of the incessant wind. I doubled back towards the garage and followed a pair of rolling tumbleweeds into the three-sided structure. There had been a fourth wall at one time, but it lay to one side, collapsed into a heap like giant dry matchsticks. Inside, against one wall, cardboard boxes of all sizes and shapes were piled high. I stepped closer to investigate but froze in my tracks when a terse voice behind me ordered, "Stop right there and turn around real slow!" Cha-chunk! The unmistakable sound of a shell being chambered turned my insides to mush.

Hardly daring to breathe, I did as the voice bid and found myself staring down the barrel of a shotgun. To my amazement, the bearer of the weapon was a pint-sized woman wearing a grimy ball-cap turned backwards over a haystack of graying blonde hair. Well, who was this? My voice seemed to have deserted me as I gawked down at her, dumbstruck by her odd appearance. I had a height advantage of a least a foot, and the situation might have been comical except the deadly expression in her hazel eyes told me that she meant business.

"I've warned you people about trespassing on church property," she growled, aiming the gun right at my nose, "and I damn well meant it."

My muscles tensed when she waved the barrel within inches of my face. Jesus, she had her finger on the trigger. Better say something, I urged my frozen vocal chords. "Ma'am, if you'll let me explain...."

"Shut up!" Her sardonic grin revealed a row of uneven yellowed teeth. "Back to finish the job, huh? Very clever sending a woman in plain clothes instead of the usual assortment of thugs. But you're not fooling me. I know who you really are."

I swallowed the lump of fear clogging my throat. "Who do you think I am?"

"Sister Goldenrod! What are you doing?" Lupe's sharp inquiry and the thud of running footsteps sent a wave of relief pouring through me. Sister Goldenrod? Not exactly the way I'd pictured her. My brother Pat would have pronounced her facially challenged, but for me, the combination of her irregular horse-like features and pudgy body rekindled memories of my childhood toy Mrs. Potato Head.

The woman's gaze flickered to Lupe as she sprinted into the garage, and then swung back to me. "I caught another one of these damn undercover Border Patrol agents snooping around here again." She shoved the barrel against my right shoulder. "I ought to wing her just to make my point."

Wide-eyed with fright, Lupe gasped out, "No, wait! This is Kendall O'Dell. She is my boss. She's here to help me find my brother and my uncle."

The woman's bushy charcoal brows, badly in need of plucking, dipped lower. "What do you mean she's your boss?"

"She's the editor. You know, from the newspaper where I work."

The woman fired her a look of outrage. "Are you nuts? You brought a goddamned reporter with you?" She grabbed Lupe by the arm and shoved her out the door, snarling back at me, "You! Don't move an inch!" Walking with an odd crab-like gait that rolled her body from side to side, she squired Lupe towards the rusted-out remains of an old Pontiac where someone had spray-painted the side of it with the warning: THIS IS PRIVATE PROPERTY! IF I CATCH YOU HERE I WILL SHOOT YOU. Wished I'd noticed that sooner.

The sheer relief of not having a loaded shotgun pointed at me left my knees softer than overcooked noodles. I'd certainly had more than my share of adrenaline for one day, I decided ruefully, leaning my body weight against a pile of empty crates while I assessed this very un-ministerlike woman whose girth almost exceeded her height. Trying to picture her in the pulpit preaching to a congregation strained my imagination.

Now out of earshot, she proceeded to give Lupe a thorough dressing down. I could tell by the pointed finger jabs in my direction that she was discussing my fate.

A full five minutes passed before they turned and began walking back towards me. I pushed to my feet. The look of cautious expectancy on Lupe's face indicated that she had prevailed, but Sister Goldenrod was still evil-eyeing me as they re-entered the garage.

Sister Goldenrod said, "I'm going to take Lupe's word that you're going to keep your yap shut about my little visitor, is that right?"

I mustered a placating smile. "That's correct. I am a reporter, but rest assured that I'm here unofficially. I don't plan to do or say anything that would jeopardize her situation or yours, or his for that matter."

She looked uncertain, but inclined her head toward the pink house. "I hope I don't regret this. If the Border Patrol or INS gets wind that I'm hiding this child, my ass is grass and *he* will be deported to God knows where. You got that?"

"Got it." For a supposed woman of the cloth, she sure had a foul mouth.

The three of us fell into step. "Has the boy been able to tell you where he's from or how he got here? Was he traveling with relatives?"

Sister Goldenrod's breath came in wheezy gasps as we crunched along the gravel driveway. "I don't think the little guy even knows what country he's from," she replied with a sad shake of her head. "Probably Mexico, but he might have come from someplace in Central America, El Savador, Costa Rica, who knows? All I've been able to gather so far is that he and his family lived high in the mountains and that he and his mother came here to find his father. He also keeps babbling about bright colored lights and horses chasing him. At least I think that's what he's saying." She turned to Lupe. "You'll probably have better luck than me understanding him. That is, if he'll even talk to you."

"Lupe told me about his weird abduction story," I put in. "Has he been able to furnish any more details about that night?"

She pursed her lips as if debating whether to answer me or not, and finally said, "Not many. You know how it is with kids and their imagination. It's hard to tell fact from fiction, dreams from reality. But something strange must have happened out there in the desert to make him so traumatized. I mean, it's taken me days to get him to come out from under the bed. Now he insists on staying in the closet because he's afraid these sky people will find him, whoever they are," she said hitching her broad shoulders. "He sneaks out to use the bathroom, but that's it. He won't even come to the kitchen to eat, but that's fine by me, because I haven't even shared this with my staff. Loose lips sink ships and all that."

Lupe and I exchanged a contemplative glance as the woman heaved her bulky body up the three steps leading to a rickety screen porch. With time and gravity working against her, the cut-off overalls she wore emphasized the blue-veined rolls of thigh fat jiggling above her knees. Swinging like pendulums, her enormous boobs drooped almost to her waist. Not a flattering getup to say the least.

Once inside, we walked through a small living room furnished with a jumble of frayed castoff furniture that looked like it had come from a thrift store, past a spacious kitchen and then followed her down a long narrow hallway surfaced with brownish-red Saltillo tile. The sound of our footsteps was drowned out by the continuous squeal from the evaporative cooler on the roof as it puffed gusts of moist air through rusty overhead vents. The place was much larger than it appeared from outside, the rambling hallway opening into a series of small rooms that gave me the impression of a rabbit warren.

When we reached the last door, she put a finger to her lips and edged it open to reveal a tiny cubicle hardly bigger than a walk-in closet. The bed, a cot actually, filled most of the room and the sloping concrete floor suggested that it might have been an outside storage area at one time. A blanket hanging from a narrow window blocked out all but a hint of the late afternoon sunlight and it took a minute or so for my eyes to adjust to the murky twilight.

"You stay here," she whispered hoarsely, pointing to the spot where I now stood. "Too many visitors at once might scare him."

She switched on a dim floor lamp and motioned for Lupe to accompany her. To keep the peace, I did as she asked, but I was more than a little irked by her brusque behavior. This woman could definitely use a personality transplant.

"Let me talk to him first," Sister Goldenrod said, pulling a door to my right open. She bent down and said softly, "It's just me, Javier. I've brought a pretty lady for you to talk to."

One pretty lady, not two. She cast a backward glance to make sure I'd caught her little dig and then switched to Spanish. I heard the sound of a muffled voice, high and tense. She continued to converse with him in soothing tones before turning to face us. "He says he's hungry, so I'm going to get his dinner. I'll be back in a few minutes." She waddled past and then turned to glare at me. "Make sure you don't do or say anything to upset him."

A hot flash of anger warmed my face. I had half a mind to tell this infuriating woman exactly what I thought of her, but I squeezed out a strained smile instead. After she left, I whispered to Lupe, "What's her problem anyway? Are you *sure* she's really a minister? She's got a mouth like a cowhand and has a gigantic cob up her butt!"

Her wan smile was apologetic. "She just needs some time to learn to trust you. She's really very sweet when you get to know her better."

I grimaced. "Are we talking about the same person?"

She waved away my remark and edged the closet door open further. I moved the floor lamp closer and peeked in. Illuminated by the soft halo of light sat little Javier, huddled in the closet beside a stack of boxes. A thatch of shiny black hair framed his perfect oval face and I thought he had the biggest, most beautiful cocoa-brown eyes I'd ever seen. But they were frightened eyes.

Haunted eyes. What on earth had happened to create such an expression of abject terror? The stuffy closet smelled like a combination of food, sweat and old shoes. I bent down, smiling. "Hi, Javier, my name is Kendall," I said, pointing to my own chest, "and this is my friend, my *amiga*, Lupe." I knew he didn't understand me, but was hopeful that he'd respond to a friendly face.

He pulled what looked like a ragged stuffed bunny closer and stared at me with suspicion. Sensing his unease, I pulled back, motioning for Lupe to take my place. She was cracking her knuckles and appeared anxious as she sank to her knees without pretense and began to question him. I could tell by the taut set of her shoulders and jaw that she was fearful of the little boy's answers. I heard her mention her brother, Gilberto, and, obviously frightened by the subject matter, Javier began to shrink further and further behind the clothing. I wished then that I'd taken the time to learn more Spanish. I knew some of the usual phrases and enough to order Mexican food, but not much beyond that.

When the boy refused to answer question after question, Lupe's soft voice grew louder and more desperate. "¡Si me puedes contestar mi hijo! Quiero saber que le paso a mi hermano?"

Javier let out a frightened wail and Lupe sat back on her knees, eyes misty with frustrated anger. "¡Ay Caramba! He will not answer my questions."

I laid a hand on her shoulder. "Calm down, you're scaring him."

Just then, Sister Goldenrod re-entered the room with a tray of food in her hands. When she realized that I'd disobeyed her direct order to stay put, she banged the tray on a scarred chest of drawers. "I told you to stay away from him! Now you've got the poor baby all in a dither."

Before I could defend myself, Lupe leaped up to confront her. "You lied to me! You said he would tell me about my brother, but he refuses. You have to make him talk to me!"

She jerked her thumb towards the doorway. "Okay, that's it. Take your nosy friend and get out of here. Now."

Lupe stomped one foot. "No. We're not leaving until he tells us what he knows." From there, the two of them lit into each other. Faces contorted with anger, their heated exchange fluctuated between English and Spanish and behind me, cowering in his dark hideaway, Javier's cries of distress grew louder.

How dumb was this? The idea of having driven almost 300 miles for nothing snapped my patience. I pushed the closet door shut. "Lupe, be quiet! And you," I said, locking eyes with Sister Goldenrod, "put a sock in it!" My dad's favorite expression produced the desired result. Gawking at me, her mouth opened and closed silently like a dying bass. "This is getting us nowhere, and obviously neither of you can handle this situation with anything remotely approaching objectivity," I continued, keeping my tone cool and rational, "so I'm going to give it a shot now."

I turned to Lupe. "You are going to act as my interpreter, and you," I said to my goggle-eyed tormentor, "are going to get off my back and leave us alone for a few minutes. Please."

An avalanche of emotions tumbled across her broad face and for several seconds, I thought she was going to object. But, she surprised me by leaving the room without another word. Good. Maybe we could make some progress. I turned around, not really sure what I was going to do. When I eased the door open, my heart constricted with pity at the sight of the little boy jammed into the furthest corner sucking his thumb.

Acting on instinct, I sat down cross-legged so as to appear less imposing. "Tell him you're sorry you yelled at him," I instructed Lupe, inviting her to join me on the floor, "and that we are here to try and help him."

Appearing chastened, Lupe began to speak to him softly and his gaze darted back and forth as he studied our faces. I maintained a friendly grin and felt elated when he finally pulled his thumb out and smiled, murmuring, *"Que bonito pelo rojo tienes."*

"What did he say?" I whispered.

"He thinks your red hair is pretty."

I beamed him a huge smile. *"Gracias.* Okay, now ask him if he can remember what happened to the other people who came here with him."

I could see the spark of fear reappear in his eyes the moment Lupe introduced the topic and I cautioned her to maintain a calm tone. When he finally answered, he kept repeating the word *pesadilla* again and again. "What is he saying?" I asked. "What is *pesadilla?*"

A look of confused frustration dominated Lupe's face. "It means nightmare. He says he is afraid to sleep because he dreams of the monster bugs with the big scary eyes. He's frightened that they will find him and cut him with their sharp claws. He says he was hiding inside the toolbox in the van so they did not know he was there."

"Anything else?"

She spoke to him again and then turned to me. "He's saying something about his mother not being afraid to come to the crossing place, but that he was because he was very scared to see the horse."

"He's afraid of horses?"

She questioned him again and sat back shaking her head. "He says he's not afraid of all horses, just the black one." We shrugged puzzlement at each other and she added, "I know. It makes no sense to me either."

I frowned at her. "So, is he dreaming this stuff, or did it really happen?"

She spoke to him again and his eyes misted as he whispered his response with trembling lips. Lupe's hand flew to her mouth and she choked out, "Oh, no. This cannot be true."

A sharp pang of apprehension stabbed my heart. "Why? What did he say?"

"That if my brother and uncle were in that van, they were also stolen away by the sky people and that they are most surely dead by now."

7

Lupe's face turned the color of wet cement as we traded a look of horrified disbelief. Monster bugs with sharp claws? Even as I tried to keep my mind open to all reasonable possibilities, the logical part totally rejected the idea of extraterrestrial visitors. It was easier to believe that his interpretation of events was a product of his delusional state of mind, resulting from exposure and dehydration, rather than embrace such a creepy fantasy. There were well-documented cases of people found wandering in the desert suffering from hallucinations. Could something else he'd seen before induce such a fable? Did people have TV in these isolated areas of Mexico and Central America? Video games? Probably. In travel magazines I'd seen photos of satellite dishes in the most remote corners of the earth.

"Ask him about these colored lights," I urged Lupe. "Isn't it possible that he's talking about the moon? You saw how bright it was last night. Could he have seen a reflection of something?"

She spoke to him again and his response deepened her frown. "He does not think so. He remembers his mother telling him that if they crossed during the dark of the moon there was less chance of being caught by *la migra.*"

He was right. Two weeks ago there wouldn't have been any moonlight. Then what *had* he seen? "Can he describe these lights?"

She questioned him again, then sat back on her heels with a sigh. "He says he looked up in the sky and saw a flying disc with lights that sparkled like a rainbow. There was also a blue beam that shined down on him so bright it blinded him like the sun."

Little shivers traced the back of my neck. This was just too, too weird. How could he possibly be making this up? "Okay, ask him if he can describe these bug-eyed creatures."

Javier sobbed out his answer and pressed his eyes shut. "He doesn't want to talk anymore about the bad night," Lupe said in a disconsolate tone. "He wants to eat his dinner now."

"Let's leave him alone for awhile," I said, rising to my feet, feeling more perturbed than ever. "Maybe we can get more information from him later." I picked up the tray from the dresser and set it on the floor next to him. He didn't waste any time diving into the food and my own stomach was growling with nervous hunger when I eased the closet door shut behind us.

Out in the hallway again, I could tell by Lupe's silence that she was deeply disturbed. Javier's story was totally unbelievable, but if even a fragment of it had some merit, it was obvious he'd experienced something frightening. But I could not even begin to fathom what it might have been.

I glanced over at Lupe. Her hangdog expression prompted me to stop and place a hand on her arm. "Listen to me," I said, forcing her to meet my eyes. "Before you get yourself worked into a lather, remember there is no proof whatsoever that *your* relatives were in that particular van."

A tiny ray of hope flickered in her eyes. "I guess that's possible."

"Of course it's possible. We don't know how many people crossed the border that night, or where they went after they got here. When you contracted with this…person you paid, where was he planning to take them?"

"To Tucson. They were supposed to call me when they arrived and I was going to drive down to get them. Gilberto has friends working in Phoenix who said they would get him a job right away."

I nibbled my lip for a second. "Could they have been apprehended and returned to Mexico?"

"Maybe, but why would I have not heard from them for so long?"

I shrugged. "What if they're stuck in the system? Maybe they're being detained somewhere like a stash house, or drop house, whatever they call them, or perhaps they're just hiding out someplace. What about the *coyote*? Can you contact him again?" The look of anticipation brightening her features had me praying I wasn't planting false hope.

"I'll ask Sister Goldenrod if she can help us find him."

"Good. Now, I wonder if she's got a telephone I can use."

The heavenly aroma of baking cornbread had my mouth watering as we entered a kitchen so huge it boasted three refrigerators, two stoves and six tables with benches. The layout of the room reminded me of a private Amish home I'd visited with my family years ago on a trip to Illinois. The stern-faced woman and her three white-capped daughters had served up a scrumptious six-course meal that I'd never forgotten—especially the peanut butter pie. I rested my hands on my hips, taking it all in. So, this was Sister Goldenrod's soup kitchen for the needy and hungry. At that moment, I definitely qualified as one of the hungry.

A young Mexican girl with coal black hair braided to her waist stood at one of the stoves stirring two steaming cauldrons of something that smelled delectable. At the adjacent stove, Sister Goldenrod, wearing elbow-length oven mitts, bent down to pull pans of golden-brown bread from the oven.

"Can we do something to help?" Lupe asked her.

She glanced around, her expression sour. Apparently she was still ticked off at me for ordering her from Javier's room. Well, too bad, she'd just have to get over it. After a hesitation, she jerked her head towards the refrigerators. "You can wash and chop vegetables." She removed her apron and hung it on a nearby hook. "Celia will show you what needs to be done, I have other things to do right now."

"Sister Goldenrod, would you mind if I use your telephone?" I asked, searching the room for one. "My cell phone isn't working in this area."

She dispensed a look of indifference. "As long as they're local calls, I don't care."

Somehow, I needed to get into the good graces of this woman or I'd never gain her cooperation. "I have a phone card, so you won't be charged for any long distance calls and," I added, bestowing her a high-wattage smile, "I'll be more than happy to make a donation to the mission in exchange for dinner."

She considered my proposal and nodded. "The Guiding Light Mission gladly accepts all donations."

A door to our right suddenly banged open and everyone's attention focused on a stocky, balding man staggering into the room, straining under the weight of two large wooden crates. He deposited his cargo on the floor with a loud grunt and then straightened slowly, grimacing and massaging the small of his back. "Son-of-a-bitch!" he groused. "A guy could get a hernia lifting shit this heavy."

Sister G edged him a look devoid of sympathy. "You sure took your sweet time getting back here. Make a few stops along the way, did we?"

His expression darkened and he opened his mouth to answer when his gaze fell on Lupe and me. Surprised admiration replaced his look of annoyance. "Well, howdy doody do," he said, rubbing the stubble on his chin. "The clientele around here is definitely improving." His mouth stretched into what I'm sure he thought was a beguiling yellow-toothed grin as he attempted to tug the soiled white tank top down over several inches of exposed and very hairy skin on his protruding belly. "Froggy McQueen at your service. And who might you two lovely ladies be?" Froggy puffed out his chest and smoothed his remaining hair, apparently perceiving himself to be a real attractive guy.

"They're here on a private matter that does not concern you," Sister Goldenrod said, moving towards him.

"I'm hoping your trip to Tucson and Green Valley netted you more than two paltry crates of melons. Or did you drink up the remainder of the food money on your way back?"

His brown eyes smoldered. "Oh, ye of little faith. Yeah, there's more stuff. So, I stopped for a few beers along the way, so what? And if we're going to talk money, I think I'm the one...."

"Bring in the perishables and store the rest in the garage. Now!" she snapped, brushing past him out the door. He shrugged and allowed his appreciative gaze to linger on us a few seconds more before he followed her out, singing, *"Froggy went a courtin' and he did ride, uh-huh..."*

I turned to Lupe and made a pretense of fanning myself. "What a total stud muffin. Hold me back."

Maintaining a solemn expression, she replied, "Yeah, he's really hot. Please don't make me fight you for him." Giggling like schoolgirls, we turned towards Celia, who frowned at us in confusion. The brief encounter appeared to have buoyed Lupe's spirits temporarily anyway, and for that I was glad. I listened as Lupe translated the girl's instructions, which were in Spanish, of course, and for the next hour and a half we earned our keep by chopping a ton of onions, celery, lettuce and tomatoes. Dinner consisted of albondigas soup, cornbread, salad, and refried bean burros. Simple fare, but it smelled delicious and would most likely be quite filling.

As if an unheard dinner bell had sounded, two scraggly-looking White guys probably in their fifties, along with several young Mexican men, filed in the kitchen door just as Lupe and I set our plates down at one of the tables. Maintaining deferential expressions, they accepted the handout in silence and nodded at us politely as they moved to the far end of the room. They ate with gusto and left quickly. But, as I took my last mouthful of buttery cornbread, it was obvious that the majority of the "guests" expected to eat this mountain of food had not yet arrived. Most likely, that would occur when darkness fell.

When we finished, Lupe said she was going back to see if she could coax more information from little Javier, so I decided it was a good time to make my phone calls. As I passed a small window outside the kitchen door, my eyes strayed to the horizon. In sharp contrast to the fiery brilliance of summer sunsets, this evening's grayish-yellow twilight smudged with thin black clouds seemed rather insipid. At least the wind had died down.

A movement near the garage caught my attention. Ah, yes, the beguiling Froggy. He was busy unloading cardboard boxes from a camper shell mounted crookedly on a dilapidated orange pickup. I smiled to myself remembering my exchange with Lupe, but I was more than a little curious about his role here at the mission, not to mention the origin of his unique nickname. What did he do other than fetch food for the soup kitchen? More intriguing yet was the dubious relationship between him and Sister Goldenrod. She didn't act like any minister I'd ever met and he didn't treat her like one. There was no sign of her outside, but dim light streamed through the stained glass windows in the chapel. Was she preparing for Sunday morning services? Perhaps I'd attend.

I turned away and went hunting for a telephone. I was anxious to make contact with Tally. It seemed as if we'd been out of touch for days instead of hours. Had Ruth ever given him my message? Had he tried to reach me on my cell phone? I also needed to find a jack so I could hook up my notebook computer and go online to find the articles Walter had recommended that I read.

No sign of one in the kitchen or dining room, but I finally located a smudged white phone beside a pile of old magazines on the floor beside one moth-eaten chair in the living room. I punched in the myriad of numbers required and as I listened to the rings, my heart surged with hope that Tally would answer. But what if it was Ruth again? My body tensed at the thought. I'd love to tell the bitchy old lady off just once, but I counseled myself to stay cool.

"Hello?"

Faint relief softened the pangs of disappointment. It wasn't Tally, but it wasn't Ruth either. "Hi, Ronda, it's Kendall, " I said, settling myself on the hard tile floor, "is that good-looking brother of yours around?"

"Nope, you just missed him. He and Jake took the big horse trailer downtown to see if they could get the axle fixed. He said they had a couple of other errands to run before they head out for Prescott in the morning."

I swallowed my frustration, hating the phone tag game. "Wish I could convince him to invest in a cell phone."

Her laugh sounded brittle. "That'll be the day."

"Well, what time do you expect him back?"

"I dunno. Ten, ten-thirty. You want him to call you?"

I hesitated. What if Sister G retired early? She might not take kindly to being awakened, especially if the call was for me. In addition, I wasn't even sure where I'd be spending the night yet. "I guess not. Just tell him I called and my plans are still on track to be back there Monday evening."

"Okay."

Ronda, like Tally, did not waste words. But, at least I felt confident he'd get this message. I would like to have added 'Tell him I love him and miss him like crazy' but she and I weren't that close, so I concluded with, "Thanks."

Click.

With a sigh, I cradled the phone. Picturing the four of us living under the same roof was a hard pill to swallow. In my heart of hearts, how could I fault Tally's love and loyalty for his own family? That was part of what made him so special. Was I a selfish bitch to want him for myself?

I shook off my darkening mood and went to retrieve my computer from the car. It was as quiet as a tomb outside minus the usual insect chorus of summer nights that I was accustomed to. The fresh country air had a brisk wintry feel to it that made me glad I'd brought along the jacket. I was actually looking forward to being cold after sweating my brains out these past months.

Froggy's truck was still parked beside the garage, but there was no sign of either him or Sister G. The lights in the mission were dark. Perhaps they'd returned to the kitchen.

Back in the living room once more, I hooked into the phone line and accessed the Internet address Walter had given me earlier. I scrolled through the options, finally finding his byline. As I read each article, waves of uneasiness chilled me. The description of the alleged 'abduction' related by the Mexican national sounded eerily like Javier's improbable story, including the description of bright, pulsating lights and extraterrestrial creatures with bulging eyes. The man also provided the startling information that they appeared to have a tiny slit for a mouth or no mouth at all. According to Walter's account, the terrified man had actually wept with relief when Agent Bob Shirley had arrived in Morita to arrest him for illegal entry. Prior to being transported back to Mexico, he'd been held for three hours in the detention center at Border Patrol Headquarters, where he'd been photographed, fingerprinted and given something to eat and drink. During that time, he had repeated the bizarre story of his encounter, telling authorities that he'd actually witnessed people being led into the dark entrance of an alien spacecraft. He claimed that two of the creatures had pursued him on foot until he'd eluded them by accidentally falling into a ravine, where he'd cowered beneath a rocky overhang frozen with fear for hours until dawn broke. Even in daylight, he'd not felt safe and had wandered aimlessly for hours before he'd found a hiding place in Morita. I looked up from the screen, frowning. Why would aliens give chase on foot? Why not beam him up to their space ship?

"Oh, come on," I whispered under my breath. Real or not, this was spooky stuff. But that wasn't all. Walter had written several other pieces that involved the disturbing discovery of butchered cattle and horses found on some nearby ranches, which imitated exactly a rash of mutilations on Texas and New Mexico ranches several years earlier. My pulse picked up a beat or two when the article identified one of the ranches as the Beaumont spread. Did Tally know about this? If so, he'd never mentioned a word of it to me.

A group of Arivaca teenagers, allegedly involved in the practice of witchcraft, had been arrested earlier on charges of animal cruelty involving dogs and cats and were considered prime suspects. They, however, claimed innocence and pointed fingers of blame at a local recluse by the name of Russell Greene, who lived within several miles of the mutilations. But, psychotherapist and UFOlogist Mazzie La Casse was quoted as saying, "I don't believe for a second that these kids or any other resident of this planet is responsible. The recent sightings of UFOs in this area and northern Mexico, combined with the advanced level of surgical precision required for such expert removal of body parts from these animals, is ample evidence to me that the authorities should not jump to conclusions, but try to keep their minds open to the idea that there may be a connection. The majority of abductees report that specific medical experiments were performed on them by highly skilled beings. I believe this to be the work of extraterrestrials."

Was this woman serious? She was someone I definitely needed to speak with. And soon. But before I contacted her, I decided to see what other information I could find on the Internet regarding the UFO phenomenon. To my surprise, the subject of UFO sightings, landings, abductions and alien contact was more widespread than I imagined. Site after site directed me to yet another site. There was a ton of information on the 1948 Roswell, New Mexico crash landing of a 'manned' alien spacecraft and the subsequent cover-up by the U.S. Government. Many people believed the closely-guarded Area 51 in Nevada was part of a secret government experiment involving some type of collusion between the military and the extraterrestrials. Apparently the intergalactic visitors were providing advanced technology to produce new types of aircraft. What, conspiracy theorists wanted to know, were the space aliens receiving from our government in exchange for their expertise? It all made for fascinating reading, but it was getting late. Reluctantly, I returned to the Sierra Vista site and continued to scroll through the remaining articles Walter had written concerning Bob

Shirley's death. There wasn't too much more than what he'd told me earlier except for the fact that, because he'd died on the Tohono O'odham Indian Reservation (which I learned meant 'people of the desert'), there was some finger pointing among the various agencies regarding the initial investigation. The FBI claimed that the tribal police had contaminated the crime scene, making it difficult for them to gather evidence, the lack of which forced their conclusion of suicide. The tribal police claimed it was the fault of Border Patrol agents, who had arrived first, along with county sheriff's deputies. Bob Shirley's distraught wife blamed all of them for bungling the investigation.

Scrolling back several pages, I found links to other articles featuring border problems and several of them centered on the thankless job confronting many of the agents. It seemed the greatest irony that, on the one hand, these well-trained men and women were charged with protecting the borders of the United States from illegal immigrants, and on the other were increasingly called upon to rescue these same people. Scores of human rights organizations bemoaned the number of deaths that had occurred during the hottest part of last summer, eighty-five fatalities in all, and placed the blame squarely on the Border Patrol. In response to criticism, and at taxpayer expense, specially trained agents of the Border Patrol Search, Trauma and Rescue team, or BORSTAR, were routinely dispatched to patrol the deserts and waterways, such as the Rio Grande, in search of injured or dying border crossers. On the flip side, the government employed the latest sophisticated tracking and surveillance equipment and even arranged for sting operations to intercept groups of aliens entering with cunning smugglers. There were several telling quotes from one agent who agreed to be interviewed only if he remained anonymous. He revealed only that he was thirty-two, married with children and that he'd been with the agency five years. "I think I'm getting jaded and frankly, I don't know how much longer I'm going to want to do this. This whole thing has become a public relations nightmare. Think about it. After 20 weeks of intense training at the academy and for twenty-eight thousand lousy bucks a year to start, most of the time we sit on our butts for eight hours staring at jackrabbits. But then if things do get hot, *we're* the bad guys for doing our job when we do capture these jumpers crossing our borders. Countless hours are spent filling out forms before driving them back to the border, and then we're processing the same SOBs later the same day! We're constantly tested for firearms proficiency, but you better not draw your weapon on José or your own government will come down on your head with a vengeance. The whole mess is completely nuts."

I shook my head. It didn't sound like a vocation I'd be interested in. Yawning, I stretched and hit the exit key before beginning my search for a phone book. After a couple of minutes, I located a frayed copy wedged beneath a scarred end table. I looked up numbers for both Mazzie La Casse and Loydeen Shirley. Both resided in Arivaca.

I dialed the UFOlogist first and a woman picked up on the second ring. I identified myself and asked if we could meet the following morning for an interview. Also, could she arrange for me to sit in on one of the support groups she led for those suffering from the alien abduction phenomenon? I hoped I was maintaining a professional tone, but it wasn't easy to discuss such an outlandish topic without a trace of skepticism creeping into my voice.

"I can inquire," she replied, sounding dubious, "but I wouldn't count on it. For the uninformed, I know this is an implausible subject, but I take their stories very seriously. Frankly, I can't imagine any of them being amenable to discussing their very personal, very disturbing experiences in front of a reporter. For the record, Ms. O'Dell, these are not uneducated people. Many of my clients are highly educated professionals like doctors, lawyers, teachers and even law enforcement officials, not a bunch of crazies as you might think."

"I never said they were. If it will help though, I can assure them of anonymity."

"We'll have to see," she replied, her tone still wary.

I decided not to push further on the phone. "I'd be glad to buy you breakfast. Any suggestions on where?"

Her high-pitched laugh had a nasally quality. "There aren't a lot of choices. How about I meet you at La Gitana. There's a small café there, besides the saloon. Do you know where it is?"

"I do. What time?"

"Nine-thirty would be most convenient for me."

"See you then." Next, I dialed the number for Loydeen Shirley. There was no answer, no answering machine message, no voice mail. Okay. Perhaps a personal visit tomorrow after breakfast was in order.

I cradled the phone, glancing at my watch. Lordy, I'd tied up the phone line for almost three hours. I closed the lid and with computer in hand, retraced my steps towards Javier's room to find Lupe. The soft clink of flatware and the murmur of voices from the kitchen stopped me. I stuck my head around the corner, and even though I'd been expecting it, a shock of surprise zigzagged through me. The room was overflowing with people of all ages, and not just Mexicans. Among the tables of copper-skinned people sat a family of Orientals as well as swarthy Mediterranean types and one White family with young children. Considering that there must have been forty people in the room, it was relatively quiet. I wondered how they had all arrived without me being aware of it. A few looked up and stared at me with apprehension, but most kept their eyes averted or concentrated on their meal. The odor of sweaty, unwashed bodies almost usurped the aroma of food.

"Hi," said a sweet-faced blonde girl of perhaps four seated alongside a younger boy at the table closest to me. A weary-eyed woman with an acne-splotched complexion, who couldn't have been much older than me, cradled a baby in her arms. On second thought, she may have been younger than twenty-nine, and that gave me pause.

"Hi, yourself," I said, returning the child's friendly grin. "Getting enough to eat?"

"I yike cownbwead," she said, stuffing a much too large piece in her mouth, leaving a trail of yellow crumbs down her arm and onto the floor.

"Darla," her mother scolded, slapping specks from the child's lap. "Mind your manners."

Across from them, a bearded guy with long stringy hair, wearing torn jeans and a soiled T-shirt, looked up at me, his inquisitive eyes reflecting my own curious appraisal. I probably didn't look like I belonged here. He did. 'Do you come here often?' sounded like a really lame question, so I substituted, "Sister Goldenrod sure knows how to whip up a fine meal."

The woman crossed herself and hugged the sleeping baby to her breast. "Amen," she agreed, nodding. "I don't know how we'd have managed these past few months without her help. There just ain't been a lot of good-paying jobs to be got around here lately."

I wondered why they would choose to live in such a remote place that offered few employment opportunities in the first place. My gaze traveled around the room. I knew why the others were here. They probably hadn't eaten a square meal in days, maybe weeks, maybe never. But the woman's husband, if he was that, looked able-bodied. His thin lips stretched into a sardonic gap-toothed grin making me think of Sister Goldenrod and Froggy. People around here were in serious need of dental work.

He crooked his finger at me, so I leaned down. "You wanna know why there ain't much work around these parts anymore?"

I already knew, but asked, "And why is that?"

"Because these goddamn border-jumping assholes will work for fly shit and that leaves nothin' for the rest of us," he whispered, his face reddening with anger.

I drew back. Interesting vocabulary and really bad breath. Boozy breath, which would help explain his belligerent attitude. I looked around to see if anyone else had overheard his remark, but it didn't matter. It was doubtful that anyone in the room spoke English.

But in a sudden about-face, his expression altered. "Evening, Sister Goldenrod," he crooned, staring over my shoulder, looking downright angelic. "Mavis an' me and the kids sure do thank you for sharing what little you have with us and may the Lord reward you for your kindness."

"Thank you, Tom," she replied, reaching out to ruffle the little boy's hair. "I certainly hope so." She waddled over to the stove to converse with Celia in Spanish while another heavy-set Hispanic woman, whom I had not seen before, began clearing the tables. I was anxious to ask

Sister G some pointed questions about how she justified harboring illegals on American soil, but this was not the time or place.

I returned the young girl's goodbye wave and started down the hall again to resume my search for Lupe. She'd been in with Javier an awfully long time and I wondered why. When I entered the room, my question was answered. Sprawled fully clothed on the cot, she lay sound asleep. When I eased the closet door open, I saw Javier's small form huddled under a thin blanket, his thumb firmly tucked in his mouth. At least now, he looked to be at peace. Would he sleep the innocent sleep that a child should, or would nightmares of his recent ordeal bring him screaming to consciousness? I hoped not.

I pulled a threadbare quilt over Lupe and tiptoed out. Hitting the sack sounded pretty good to me too. I'd slept very little the previous night and it had been a tiring, stress-filled day.

I stopped by the kitchen again to ask where I'd be sleeping and noticed that the family with the children was gone and only one other table was still occupied. Sister G was nowhere in sight. I did my best to communicate my question to Celia and she pointed towards the side door. I needed to get my things from the car anyway.

The dim yellow glow from one bug-encrusted light fixture did little to penetrate the thick gloom. I closed my eyes, allowing them to adjust to the dark. Shouldn't the moon be up by now? Groping my way to where I'd left my car, I realized that a dense blanket of clouds had rolled in, obscuring the ever-brilliant starlight that usually dominated the Arizona night sky. The wind had picked up again.

The dark outline of my Volvo was only a few yards ahead of me when I stumbled over something. Gasping with surprise, my car keys clutched in one hand, the computer in the other, I had only a fraction of a second to react. Rather than drop the precious laptop, I raised my right hand to catch myself. I slammed into the car window and the keys went flying. "Damn." Fighting off the sense of disorientation, I set the computer case on the ground. Where was the moonlight when I needed it? And, of course, my flashlight was inside the locked car.

"What else could possibly happen today?" I fumed, wondering what I'd tripped over. With a groan of frustration, I dropped to my hands and knees and began patting the ground. This latest mishap might have been comical except it hadn't exactly been a red-letter day so far. And it was no one's fault but mine. In my search, I encountered something round, about the size of a baseball. It took me a couple of seconds to realize it was an orange, no doubt dropped during Froggy's produce delivery earlier. Cripes, I could have broken my neck.

Flat on my belly, my head and shoulders underneath the car, my fingers finally closed around the elusive bunch of keys. "Thank God," I muttered with relief, pushing to my knees. But before I could get to my feet, the crunch of footsteps in the gravel froze my movements. The clamor of angry voices coming at me out of the darkness reversed the heavy silence. Instinctively, I stayed down out of sight.

"Why can't you leave me alone? I'm running this place on a wing and a prayer, trying my best to redeem myself and do something useful with the rest of my life. Why can't you do the same?"

"Give me a frickin' break. Try and remember who you're talking to. You mess with the Frogman and you're gonna be real sorry, Sister Madam Reverend Goldenrod. Christ Almighty, where'd you come up with such a corny name anyway?" The raspy voice ripe with sarcasm belonged to Froggy McQueen and I wasn't surprised when I heard Sister G seethe, "Goldenrods just happen to be my favorite flower, as if it's any of your business, and what gives you the right to speak to me like that, you cretin?"

"Oh, please. Get down off your pious sanctimonious horse. You might be able to fool other people, but that high and mighty shit won't work on me."

She let out a squeak of anguish. "Look, I can't pay you the full amount right now, you're gonna have to give me more time."

"Yeah, right. Like you ain't got additional sources of income."

"What are you getting at? You mean the pittance I get from those lousy donation letters? Not hardly."

"Froggy's running out of patience."

"Listen to me. I'm expecting Sister Agatha and some of the other big shot church elders from Tucson to be here sometime next week. If everything goes as planned, if somebody doesn't open his big yap and mess things up, there should be a sizable contribution to the mission."

"That would be mighty fine indeed. You just remember our agreement."

"I'm sure you won't let me forget."

"Hey, I don't expect any more than what's due me."

"What's *due* you? This is nothing more than goddamned blackmail."

"Now you're hurting my feelings," he whined. "I been doing my best to help you out around here and my silence on this particular matter simply means a small supplement to my living expenses. Just consider it a deposit to the National Bank of Froggy."

"It's blackmail, you...you miserable drunken...."

"Ah, ah, ah," he interrupted, his tone hardening. "Let's not say anything we'll be sorry for."

Sister G could only splutter as he strolled into the dim circle of light wearing a smug look of triumph. He banged through the side door, so I edged my head high enough to make out Sister G's lumpy silhouette shuffling off in the direction of the little wooden shacks behind the church.

Slowly, I rose to my feet. Well, well, well. How very intriguing. Froggy was in possession of information concerning Sister G's past that I would very much like to have. Would it confirm my suspicions about her legitimacy as a real minister? What *was* the criteria for becoming a minister anyway? Could *anyone* just start a church? Did one have to file papers or graduate from a seminary with a degree in theology? I'd have to check that out.

I unlocked the car door, laid my computer on the passenger seat, retrieved my overnight bag and walked towards the first small dwelling. A rectangle of light appeared suddenly as Sister G opened the door and I caught a glimpse inside the tiny room packed wall to wall with mattresses and cots, all occupied by the grim-faced Mexican families who'd been in the kitchen earlier. No doubt the other two shacks were also filled to capacity.

She sucked in a startled breath when the light fell on me. "What do you want?"

"Just wondering what the sleeping arrangements were."

She shut the door quickly and moved past me. "Where's Lupe?"

"Conked out in Javier's room."

"Well, I don't really have any extra rooms. I have a lot of guests tonight."

"I can see that. Say, um, aren't you worried about getting caught?"

Her steps faltered. "Caught doing what?"

Okay, I'd play the game. "Harboring undocumented immigrants."

"Look here, O'Dell," she said coldly, "I have no knowledge of that and neither do you. I'm simply here doing the Lord's work. I don't need to see people's papers to know whether or not they are human beings in need of help."

She had a point. If cornered, she could always claim ignorance. Well, no sense getting into another pissing match with her right now, it was getting late and I needed a place to crash. I fell into step beside her as she ambled towards the pink house. "Listen, I'm sorry we got off on the wrong foot today, but I am curious about something you said earlier."

"What's that?"

"When you thought I was an undercover agent with the Border Patrol, you said something about me coming back here to finish the job. What did you mean by that?"

She exhaled a wheezy sigh. "We had a big fire here a while back and I think someone in their ranks is responsible. I'm just lucky the wind shifted when it did, or it would have burned everything to the ground. As it is, five buildings were a total loss."

"What makes you so sure it was someone with the Border Patrol?"

"Because they've been on my case since we opened our doors. They're pissed off at me, the ranchers are pissed off at me, the goddamn INS is pissed off at me just because we've been doing the humanitarian deed of putting up water stations to help save some lives."

"And how long have you been doing this type of humanitarian work?"

She paused and turned around, looking annoyed. "Why do you want to know?"

I shrugged. "Just curious, I guess. It's my nature to ask questions."

An upward eye roll. "No kidding." She reached for the kitchen door handle. "Look, this old place was falling to ruins when I took over, let's see, almost two years ago. Besides a barrel of elbow grease, I put in a lot of my own savings to help restore some of the buildings. The sanctuary and this house are both over a hundred years old and need constant repair."

I followed her along the winding hallway until she stopped at a door and swung it open. "I have an extra bed in my room. You're welcome to bunk there if you like," she said pointing to a narrow cot crammed into the corner of the tiny, angular room.

I wasn't keen on the idea of sharing a room with her, but hey, what choice did I have other than sleeping on the floor in the airless little room with Lupe and Javier? I set my overnight bag on the floor, switched on the lamp and then caught a movement out of the corner of my eye. I glanced up at the low eaves and it was all I could do to keep from screaming my lungs out at the sight of a huge, shiny black spider dangling in a web not two feet above my head. A mass of shivers engulfed me as I executed a backward leap that almost knocked Sister Goldenrod to the floor. "Jesus H. Christ!" I gasped, whirling around to make a mad dash for the doorway.

"What's the matter with you?" she screeched from behind.

From a safe distance of ten feet, I raised a trembling finger. "The...there's a humongous spider hanging over the bed. A black widow, I think."

She blinked slowly. "So?"

Her look of bemused irritation said it all. People who do not have a spider phobia can never in a million years understand the raw terror these eight-legged creatures can generate. "I can't sleep with that thing hanging there. You're going to have to kill it."

She glared daggers at me. "I will do no such thing. Beulah has been living here almost as long as me."

"You *named* the spider?"

"Listen up, O'Dell," she said with a tired sigh, dropping onto her large four-poster bed. "Beulah stays. That's the only spare bed I've got. Take it or leave it."

Well, it was her decision, her place and her spider, so I was out of there. Suddenly camping out in my car didn't seem like such a terrible idea. "If you'll hand me my bag, I'll be going now."

8

Now what? I was contemplating the idea of spreading out my bedroll on the living room floor when halfway down the hall a door opened and Froggy McQueen stepped into my path. "I...ah, couldn't help but overhear your dilemma, Miss O'Dell, and I think maybe I can be of service." His smile appeared genuine, but he couldn't disguise the crafty gleam in his eyes.

I stared down at him, noticing for the first time the bushy tangle of gray hairs protruding from his nostrils. In fact, Froggy seemed to have an abundance of hair everywhere but on his head. Even his ears were fuzzy. I suppressed a shudder of repugnance and forced a polite smile. "And just exactly what did you have in mind?" He made a great show of reaching over to push the door open wide enough to reveal two twin beds. "*Are you lonesome tonight?*" he crooned in a terrible imitation of Elvis Presley, "*are you lonesome tonight? Are you sorry we drifted apart?*"

I'm sure my mouth was hanging open a mile. "Excuse me?"

"In other words," he said, grinning wickedly while executing a grand sweep of his hand. "I'd be more than happy to share my quarters with you."

I'll bet you would, you disgusting little...horny toad. With extreme difficulty, I swallowed back a hundred caustic retorts and weighed my position carefully. If I alienated this guy it would make it much harder to extract information from him. "That's very kind of you, but you see I'm having a really bad asthma attack," I said, patting my chest and forcing a tiny cough, "so I'm going to have to sleep..." Where? Think fast! "...out on the porch."

"It's gonna be freezing outside," he said, apparently hoping to dissuade me.

I smiled sweetly. "I need the fresh air. You do understand, don't you?"

His smile sank out of sight, replaced by a look of complete bafflement. Before he could utter another word, I added, "But, thanks for your generous offer. Good night now."

Pervert. With shivers of revulsion skating down my spine, I pushed past him before I said something I'd regret. And that wouldn't have taken much.

"Okay, sweet thing," he called after me in an oily tone I'm sure he meant to sound enticing. "But if you change your mind and want to get toasty warm, you know where to find Froggy."

I hated it when people referred to themselves in the third person. The image of spending the night under the same roof with this odious little man derailed my plans of sleeping in the living room, so I headed outdoors once more. Would this aggravating day never end?

I got about ten steps from the door when it dawned on me that I'd best use the facilities now because there sure weren't any outside that I knew of. I did a quick turnabout, let myself quietly in the kitchen door, and started towards the bathroom I'd seen adjacent to Javier's room when a slight sound from the direction of the living room halted my steps. Moving with stealth, I peeked around the doorway. Froggy stood in the dim lamplight dialing the phone. I pulled back out of sight, breathing shallowly. Who would he be calling at this late hour?

"Hey, diddle diddle, it's the cat with the fiddle," he intoned, keeping his gravelly voice low. "Little boy blue *do not* blow your horn, but the sheep's in the meadow, the cow's in the corn."

What the hell? Struggling to make sense of what I'd just overheard, I nearly missed his abrupt cradling of the phone. Oh, crap! On tiptoe, I hotfooted it around the corner and ducked into the kitchen. Seconds later, I heard his door close. The after-effect of yet another adrenaline jolt left my whole body tingling. I sat down on one of the benches until the sensation subsided, thinking I'd had more than enough shocks for one day.

So what had that been all about? Froggy certainly had a thing for songs and now nursery rhymes. Innocent sounding as it may have been, the call was obviously some sort of a signal. But for whom? There was no way to check because the phone he'd used was so ancient it didn't have a redial button.

To conceal the fact that I'd been eavesdropping again, I returned to the kitchen and banged the door as if I'd just come in. Making no attempt to muffle my steps, I made my way along the hallway once again. When I passed Froggy's door, I heard the hinges squeak softly. The icy chill on the back of my neck told me he was watching, but I entered the bathroom without turning to verify it. I washed up quickly and was back outside in less than fifteen minutes.

Walking towards my car looking skyward, I almost gasped aloud at the sheer magnificence unfolding. The driving wind had ruptured the thick cloud cover, allowing intermittent beams of moonlight to shine through the ragged openings like a flashing neon sign. Long shadows chasing across the rugged landscape created a rather hypnotic effect. I could have stood there in the exhilarating breeze watching the moon play Peek-a-boo with the silver-edged clouds all night, but fatigue won out.

Now that it was my only choice, I must admit I didn't relish the idea of spending the night in my car. I would have preferred to camp out in the open, but thoughts of Froggy roaming about, not to mention the legion of other strangers present, squelched that idea.

It was no easy task to accordion my long frame into the sleeping bag on the back seat. After locking the doors, I rolled the windows open a few inches to stave off my claustrophobia, but in spite of the soothing wind whispering through the palo verde branches, sleep proved to be elusive. I shifted to my left side and adjusted the rolled up jacket pillowing my neck. Just think, if I hadn't agreed to take part in this peculiar undertaking I'd be cuddling with Tally right now.

Time passes at a sluggish pace when it seems as if you're the only person awake on earth. But it does give one time to be introspective. Lying there staring up at the distant carpet of stars winking back at me like a million rhinestones, I began to look at them differently. I began to question my own beliefs. Sure, I'd read science fiction novels dealing with the possibility of life on other planets, I'd seen all the long-running TV shows and movies addressing the subject, but was I really ready to accept the fact that there might be alien forces kidnapping people here on earth? No. But then, was it logical to believe that we human beings were the only intelligent life in the entire universe? Was there really something to these alleged UFO sightings? How else could one explain the similarities between Javier's tale and that of the Mexican immigrant found months ago in Morita? And, what about all those animal mutilations? No doubt UFO enthusiasts would solemnly intone that it was the work of the extraterrestrials, just as Mazzie La Casse had, but it made more sense to assume that this was the work of someone very human in origin. And if so, what would be the purpose of such a heinous act? A feeling of helplessness crept over me. What had possessed me to think that I could tackle something this ambiguous in two short days? I tried to clear my head, but my mind flitted from one disturbing theory to another like hungry hummingbirds around a feeder.

"Stop it," I said out loud. If I were to get any sleep at all, this was definitely the wrong subject to explore alone in the dead of night. I turned my thoughts instead to Tally and the promise of fun that lay ahead for us in California. But gradually, the memory of our quarrel and his parting words to me eclipsed my happy fantasy. I was reluctant to admit that perhaps he was right, but I couldn't help wondering if I'd made a huge mistake agreeing to take this on.

Somewhere between reflections of self-recrimination and the immensity of the task that lay before me, I fell into a tortured sleep filled with disquieting dreams. The final one had me running for my life across the desert, pursued by monstrous winged creatures astride wild-eyed black horses. Consumed with panic, my heart slamming against my ribs, I could only move in slow motion. A vacant house appeared, but each shadowy room I tried to hide in was inhabited with spiders of all sizes, shapes and colors. I tried to escape, but the space creatures closed in, trapping me. When one enormous yellow spider began crawling up my arm, I awoke with a strangled shriek of terror and sat up, banging my head on the headliner of the car. "Owww!" I rubbed the injured spot and massaged the dull pain in my neck. The sensation of pure horror evoked by the dream lingered on for long minutes, clinging in my memory like some viscous fog.

"Get real," I warned myself, holding my wrist aloft, squinting to see the time. Four-thirty-five. I groaned softly. Too early to get up, too late to get a decent night's sleep. Which was just as well, as I had no intention of chancing a return of the nightmares.

It was then I realized the swiftly-moving shadows outside my window were not caused by clouds, but by people. Dozens of them were running through the clearing, many more than had been in Sister G's kitchen the night before. "Holy cow." I hunched lower and watched with amazement as the dark stream of humanity drifted past me. Even the smallest child made not one sound. Shifting my weight so I could see out the back window, I saw a glint of moonlight reflecting off glass, illuminating the outline of four vans parked at the mouth of the driveway. Official transportation, I presumed. How was it I'd not heard them?

Witnessing the clandestine event, one that was probably occurring a hundred-fold all along the U.S./ Mexican border at this very instant, gave me an odd thrill. How many gringos, outside of authorized government officials and the smugglers themselves, ever got a chance to observe something like this? Not many, I wagered, observing one tall figure in a low-slung western hat motioning people into one of the vehicles.

I glanced back towards the shacks and saw the silhouette of another lone figure disappearing into the darkness. Sister G watching her flock being herded to safety? Was it really her sole mission in life to assist these unfortunate souls, or was she entangled in the actual trafficking process? Is that what Froggy meant when he'd accused her of having additional sources of income? I thought about the cryptic nursery rhyme—*Little boy blue don't blow your horn,* and decided it made more sense to concentrate on his activities. Since he believed that I was outside on the porch, had he warned the van drivers to cut their engines and coast silently into the driveway? And, the sheep's in the meadow and cow reference was obviously code announcing that the illegals were now on church property waiting for transportation.

The faint growl of an engine seemed to validate my theory. One of the vans rolled away. Two minutes elapsed before the second one left and several more before the third headed east towards the Sasabe road. The entire operation had been carried out with military precision in less than twenty minutes.

Trying to focus in the poor light made my eyes blurry, so I held them closed for a few seconds and then looked out again at the fourth van. Something was different. The driver had not started the engine and it sat there for another five minutes before the headlights blinked three times. Away in the distance to the southwest, I saw three answering flashes. How odd.

The minutes dragged by until the muffled purr of the engine alerted me. The van eased out to the road and headed south towards the border. Huh? Was the driver directionally challenged? Less than thirty seconds later the headlights of an oncoming vehicle appeared from the direction the other three had gone. My God, it was the Border Patrol! Had agents already apprehended the other three vans? Would this one chase down number four? But the SUV did not appear to be in pursuit. It cruised by the driveway slowly and I watched until it disappeared from sight. No siren blared, no emergency lights blazed. I continued my vigil for another ten minutes, but nothing else happened. I could make no sense of what I'd just seen.

Edgy, crabby, and suffering from pangs of guilt, I stuffed the jacket under my neck and curled up on the seat again, trying to get comfortable. I, Kendall Shannon O'Dell, a law-abiding United States citizen, had witnessed the entire illegal operation go down and had done nothing to stop it. But what if the smugglers were armed? What could I have actually done? And when the Border Patrol arrived, shouldn't I have alerted them to the situation? Why hadn't I?

As I pondered the plight of little Javier, of Lupe, of the despondent faces of the people in Sister G's kitchen last night, an odd sensation of remorse engulfed me. These desperate souls, including this most recent group of young men and families, were, at great risk to themselves, breaking our immigration laws in order to flee lives of poverty, despair and corruption. They were willing to sacrifice everything familiar in order to seek a better life for themselves and their children. For the first time I actually thought about the dark-haired men and women who toiled in our fields, bussed our tables, bagged our groceries, washed our cars, mowed our lawns, cleaned our toilets—and were happy to do so. Somehow, thinking of these things lessened the guilt enough so that I drifted in and out of broken sleep until the first signs of daybreak appeared.

With profound relief, I extricated myself from the car, stretching my stiff limbs and stomping the circulation back into my feet. No way was I doing that again tonight. But then, I shouldn't have to. Lupe would be going back home this afternoon, which would make the cot in Javier's room available. But did I really want to stay at the mission with her gone? It just might be worth driving the distance back to Green Valley to find a nice comfortable motel tonight.

It was downright chilly, so I pulled on my jacket and watched the shadows slowly surrender to the ruby glow on the horizon that gradually ripened to a radiant shade of scarlet-orange. The fiery tide of light chased away the goblins of the night as it spread across the rolling grasslands to the foothills, finally igniting the granite face of Baboquivari Peak to a breathtaking shade of crimson. "Wow," was all I could muster in the way of adulation as my grandma's old proverb, *Red at night, sailor's delight, red in the morning, sailors take warning,* came to mind.

Behind me, the kitchen door squeaked open and all I could think about was hot coffee and an even hotter shower. I exchanged a wave of greeting with Celia, grabbed my overnight bag from the car and hurried inside. After helping myself to a mug of aromatic coffee, I made a beeline for the bathtub, passing Sister G in the hallway, all decked out for Sunday services. The vision of her simply styled salt and pepper gray hair, the long flowing white robe, along with the Bible clutched in her right hand, imparted an aura of dignity she'd lacked yesterday. For the first time since my arrival, she favored me with a smile that was almost amicable.

"Will I be seeing you in the chapel this morning, Miss O'Dell? My sermon begins promptly at eight."

I hesitated. I planned to leave early with Lupe so she could retrieve her car before we met the UFOlogist for breakfast, but I was also curious to hear what this woman had to say. "I have an appointment in Arivaca at nine-thirty, but I'll certainly stay as long as I can."

She sniffed in approval, squaring her shoulders. "Good. I'll expect to see you there." She continued down the hall and I watched her until she was out of sight. It was true. People often assume a different persona when they don costumes and uniforms.

Forty-five minutes later, freshened up and feeling much improved, I opened the door to Javier's room, expecting to find Lupe in the closet grilling him for more answers. Instead, she was still sprawled on the cot. Apparently ten hours of sleep wasn't enough for her. And since I'd slept maybe two at best, I couldn't work up a lot of sympathy. "Hey, come on, we've got things to do," I said, whipping the blanket off her. "Time's a wastin'."

She cracked her eyes open and met mine. "I'm sorry, I don't feel very good this morning." Her voice sounded faint and her skin had a grayish tinge.

"What's wrong?"

"I don't know. I think I'm running a fever."

I laid my palm across her forehead. It was burning hot. I winced inwardly. Oh, great. This was all we needed.

She struggled to a sitting position, sniffling. "I'm sure it's just a cold. The kids I was babysitting last weekend were all sick. Don't worry, I'll take some aspirin and be fine soon." As if to contradict her statement she sneezed twice.

I perched on the far edge of the cot to think. This trip had been one huge headache since its inception. Perhaps it was time to cut bait. "I don't think we have any choice but to head back," I said as Lupe's eyes drifted shut again. "One of us has to cover the office tomorrow, and I can't expect you to do it if you're sick."

Her lids popped open and accusation flared in her bloodshot eyes. "But...but you promised!"

"I know I did, but this thing is turning out to be way, and I mean *way*, more complicated than you can imagine. If I stayed another week, it's doubtful I'd be able to find out what's really going on."

She grabbed my hand. "I will not break my promise to you. I'll go back home early, stay in bed today and get better. Tomorrow morning I will be at my desk. Please, Kendall! What if it was your little brother, your uncle that was missing? Could you just go away and do nothing?"

I studied her grief-stricken face while trying to imagine my own family embroiled in such a tragic situation. "No, I couldn't," I said, stifling a weary yawn, "but there are quite a few things you don't know yet."

Squaring her jaw, she leaned back against the wall and pressed the blanket to her chest. "Then tell me."

I watched her frown deepen as I relayed my telephone conversation with Walter, recapped the contents of his articles, shared my suspicions about Sister Goldenrod and Froggy and then described my early morning experience.

"So...what do you think?" she asked, her eyes searching mine.

"To be honest, I don't have a clue."

She was silent for a few seconds. "What were you planning to do today and tomorrow?"

Just thinking about it made me tired. "Talk to Bob Shirley's widow, see if I can extract more information from Froggy and Sister G, and then make a trip over to Morita to question the caretaker. If I have time, I'd like to visit some of the ranches where these animal mutilations took place, find out if anyone saw anything unusual. Even then, I may not have any answers for you."

"But at least you can try," she said in a small voice. "Please."

The guilt was full-blown now. If she kept her end of the bargain, sick or not, I had no alternative but to keep mine. "Okay, I'll stay and do what I can."

The gratitude shining in her dark eyes heightened my sense of responsibility towards her, but also feelings of dread. Something terribly weird was going on here and my instincts told me the outcome would probably not be something she'd want to hear. "We still have to get your car. Do you feel up to having breakfast with me and this lady UFOlogist?"

She threw off the blanket. "Give me twenty minutes and I'll be ready."

We looked in on Javier before leaving, noting his empty breakfast tray on the floor beside him. Sister G must have fed him early. But then, she may have already been up at the crack of dawn for other reasons. He and Lupe exchanged a few sentences and when he edged me a shy smile, my heart warmed and broke at the same instant. What was to become of this little guy? "Were you able to find out anything new from him before you went to sleep last night?" I asked Lupe after she closed the closet door and shouldered her overnight bag.

"Not much. He did say that when he was running from the creatures, he fell into an arroyo and slept for a long time. When he woke up, he had trouble remembering exactly what happened."

"Fell into an arroyo," I repeated. Why did that sound familiar to me? "He slept a long time? Sounds more like he knocked himself out. Perhaps he's suffering from temporary amnesia."

Lupe nodded in agreement. "I just asked him to talk about anything that came into his head."

"And?"

"Well, he talked more about his momma. She is very pretty, very young. He said his father stopped sending money home to them and that's why they were coming to look for him. He also said before they were picked up by the *coyote* at the border, his mother told him they were taking the same path through the desert to the special crossing place that his great-grandfather and other relatives had used for many generations to come to this country."

"Word of mouth," I mused. "Now, if we could only find out where that particular spot is. And if your brother and uncle crossed at the same place, then maybe we can make a connection. Did you ask Sister G to see if she could contact the *coyote*?"

"She says she does not know the name of the man since all of her information comes second and third hand, but she will try to find out. "

"Good."

I glanced at my watch as we stepped into the hallway. "While you're getting your shower, I'm going to listen in on Sister G's sermon. Will half an hour be enough time?"

She pressed a tissue to her nose and nodded. "I'll be ready."

I turned to go when something occurred to me. "One more thing. Did Javier say anything else about seeing this horse he's so afraid of?"

"No, why?"

"Just curious. I can't seem to make a correlation between that and the UFO memory."

"Maybe they rode from his home to the border on a black horse."

I shrugged. "Beats me. Well, see you shortly."

Quilted gray clouds hung overhead when I stepped outside and strolled across the clearing. An impressive number of cars and pickups were parked near the old mission. I watched with interest as a well-dressed Mexican family with four children piled out of a late-model mini-van and trooped inside the wide double doors which now stood open in welcome. Inside the tiny sanctuary, the parishioners were packed shoulder to shoulder in the wooden pews. Curious heads turned in my direction so I smiled in return, seating myself in the back pew in hopes that I could make my escape later without disturbing anyone.

At eight sharp, Sister G limped to the podium and asked us to bow our heads in prayer. In the wake of yesterday's inauspicious introduction, together with all the other things I knew and didn't know about her, I was surprised by the passionate tone of her sermon. It contained thought-provoking messages of love and truth, good versus evil, and the need to practice kindness and tolerance to those different from us. The dialogue was generic in nature, included quotes from the Bible and preached all-encompassing, familiar and nonsectarian themes. None of the rough edges of this coarse woman were apparent today. Okay, so maybe she really was a minister. That made the entire situation even more puzzling.

It was time to go, so I quietly got up, dropped the donation check I'd promised her into the collection basket near the door, and slipped outside. A few raindrops spattered on my head as I made my way across the parking lot. "Way to go Grandma," I murmured, thinking about her weather proverb. Perhaps a good drenching would wash the accumulation of crud off of my car. I fetched Lupe from the kitchen and we retraced the previous day's route to Arivaca, again passing very little traffic along the two-lane road. She was silent most of the way, but suddenly said, "Tell me again why we are meeting with this woman? How is she supposed to help us?"

"I don't know that she can, but according to the stuff I read last night on the Internet, these people research UFO sightings and related stories. What's really important for us is the fact that she hosts this abduction encounter group. I want to hear if there are similarities between their accounts and Javier's."

"But what about our promise to Sister Goldenrod not to tell anyone about him? And what about me? How much do I tell her? What if she repeats the story to INS or someone else?"

As if to emphasize her fears, Lupe stiffened as a Border Patrol van sped past in the opposite lane. "Until we can determine how trustworthy she is, we'll have to be careful how we word our questions," I answered after a brief glance at her pained expression, "so, if it makes you feel better, I can handle most of the interview."

She sneezed into her hands and mumbled, "sorry" as she fished in her purse for tissues. "I hope you don't catch this."

"Me too." I opened the window a little further to let in fresh air. She blew her nose again before saying, "I'd feel better if you ask the questions. You know as much as I do about this mess, probably more."

I agreed and slowed speed as we entered the town limits of Arivaca. A sizeable number of cars and trucks were lined up in front of the café and parked at odd angles on the opposite side of the wide street. As we rolled past La Gitana, my pulse accelerated when a big red pickup truck backed out a few car lengths ahead of us.

"Oh, no," Lupe whispered, her watery eyes widening with anxiety. "Not those bastards again!"

The same young dude with the black Stetson who'd tongue-washed my window yesterday, narrowed his eyes at us in a menacing fashion as he and a companion drew even with my car. His hostile scowl, designed to be intimidating, didn't invoke the fear in me it had yesterday because there were plenty of witnesses milling about town this morning. Boldly, I returned a glare of my own.

"Not such a big shot today, " I muttered to Lupe, watching him disappear around the corner in my rear view mirror. "I'm going to make it my business to find out who that guy is."

"Be careful. I can tell by his eyes that he has an evil heart," Lupe remarked, dabbing the end of her nose.

I had a suspicion that the young man's hatred was directed more towards Lupe than myself but, because we were together, that also put me squarely in his sights.

After retrieving her car without incident, we returned to the main street, Lupe following close behind me. Preoccupied with the appetizing prospect of what to order for breakfast, it took a few seconds for the ominous sound of squealing tires to penetrate my thoughts. My insides clenched at the sight of the familiar pickup rounding the corner a block ahead of me and barreling in my direction. "Shit!" What was this moron doing now?

Apparently playing a dangerous game of cat and mouse, or who would flinch first, he aimed the grill of his truck at me and floored it. Thinking about it afterwards, I couldn't remember the exact sequence of events. While frantically motioning for Lupe to pull over to the side of the road behind me, I noticed a little orange cat dart from underneath a parked car and run directly into the path of the truck. The young cowboy saw it too, but did not slow down. "Stop it, you idiot!" I shouted, absorbing the wrath of his demonic smile as he cut the wheel away from me at the last second. The next thing I knew I was staring at the terror-glazed eyes of the little cat as it slammed into my windshield. "Oh, my God!" It clawed desperately for a foothold, but when I instinctively hit the brakes, the ginger-colored bundle of fur tumbled off the hood and disappeared beneath the car with a sickening thud.

9

Choking back ragged sobs, I scrambled from the car and knelt down beside the motionless cat, positive that I'd snuffed out an innocent life. Blood oozed from its little pink nose and there was a jagged cut behind one ear where it had probably hit the edge of my bumper. "Oh, kitty, I'm so sorry." I placed a finger on its neck feeling for a pulse. Was that a faint heartbeat or my own trembling hand?

Lupe arrived at my side, crying, "What happened? Oh, my God! Did you kill it?"

"I don't know," I said, stroking the dust-covered fur while trying to swallow around the knot of remorse clogging my throat. "I...I tried to stop, but it was too late."

"It wasn't your fault, lady," said a raspy voice from behind. Turning, I stared up into the concerned brown eyes of a gray-bearded stranger. Two younger men wearing Levis and soiled T-shirts walked up and stood beside him as he doffed a ragged hat in my direction before placing it over his heart. "Say a prayer, gentlemen. It looks like the last of the little feller's nine lives has run out." He cocked his shaggy head at me. "I can get some newspaper to wrap him up in, if you like."

Guilt and anger burning a hole in my chest, I turned my attention back to the cat. It twitched a couple of times, blinked, and then was still again. It took a mighty effort not to burst into tears. I pressed fingers to my temples and pulled in a few deep breaths. "Just...let's just wait a minute. I don't think it's dead, but I need someone to help me." I looked up at the men. "Is there an animal hospital around here?"

"Nope," answered one of the younger men. "The closest one is in Green Valley, but hey, Matt," he said, knuckling his companion on the shoulder, "Payton's in there having breakfast. Go get him. He'll probably know what to do."

A tiny spark of hope flared inside me as I watched the third man lope across the street and disappear inside La Gitana. "Who's Payton?" I asked, rising to my feet and trading a hopeful glance with Lupe, who looked every bit as distraught as I felt.

"Payton Kleinwort. I think he used to be a veterinary assistant or some such thing," the bearded man replied, finger-combing his shoulder-length hair behind his ears before replacing his hat. "Nice fella."

A moment later, the front door of the café flew open and a slender man wearing khaki shorts, a long-sleeved shirt and hiking boots trotted towards us with Matt following close behind. Without saying a word to any of us, he knelt to examine the cat. Breathless, I waited in agony for his verdict. What ironic timing. Two days ago I'd voiced the desire to adopt a cat of my own and instead, I'd probably ended up killing one.

"Is it alive?" Lupe asked, placing a comforting hand on my arm.

"Yes, but this little critter needs professional medical attention right away. What exactly happened?" His expression grave, he pushed his steel-rimmed glasses up the bridge of his narrow nose. The trace of condemnation in his sage-green eyes nudged my guilt thermometer several degrees higher. I repeated the incident with Lupe chiming in her version from the sidelines. "Whoever this guy is, he ought to be locked up," I said through gritted teeth. "He's a complete psychopath." The knowing look circling among the four men prompted me to dryly observe, "So, I gather you all know who he is."

Payton Kleinwort rose to his feet, brushing the dirt from his knees. "Everybody knows Jason Beaumont."

I gawked. "Beaumont? Of the Sundog Ranch?"

A look of appraisal flickered in his eyes as he nodded. "One and the same. But, he's really not a bad kid, just mischievous sometimes." His sheepish expression suggested there was a lot more to tell, but I wasn't in the mood to listen to anyone defend him. "Mischievous, my foot. He's a sadistic bully. We've had two run-ins with him and his buddies in less than twenty-four hours. I think he should be reported to the authorities for harassment and reckless driving at the very least, which I think I'll do when I get to Green Valley."

The older man shook his head slowly. "It wouldn't do you any good, my dear. Champ'll get the kid off the hook just the same as every other time."

I really did want to hear more about the people Tally had been visiting these past few months, but the injured cat took precedence. "Lupe, help me get this poor little thing into my car."

"Now? What about our meeting with the...the UFO lady?"

Darn. My warning look was rewarded by her blank stare. My intention had been to not publicize our get-together, but I'd neglected to inform her of that fact. Oh, well, too late. "This can't wait. I'm going to take it to Green Valley. You go on ...."

"Whoa, whoa, whoa," Payton cut in. "It won't be necessary for you to inconvenience yourself. I was on my way over to the Sundog this morning anyway to visit my son, so I'll take the cat with me and you can come check on it later."

I'm sure I looked utterly baffled. "That's really kind of you, but what...I mean why...?"

"At one time, Payton here used to be a member of the high and mighty Beaumont clan," the bearded guy informed us, underscoring his statement with a conspiratorial wink I didn't understand.

"Until he got his ass good and kicked," added the second young man, smirking just a bit as he jabbed his friend Matt in the ribs. For the first time I took note of their appearance. Both had shaved heads and sported tattoos on each arm. I wondered if they'd been at yesterday's rally.

"I don't know if I'd have had the patience to put up with the raft of crap you did for as long as you did," the older fellow tacked on with a sad shake of his head.

"Well, Joe, given enough time, things have a way of evening themselves out." Payton's indulgent smile belied the sheen of irritation in his eyes, but when he turned back to me his tone was almost apologetic. "Once upon a time, I was married to Champ Beaumont's daughter, so...."

Oh, my. My frazzled brain finally re-engaged. "I see. Jason Beaumont is your brother-in-law."

"No," he said, kneeling to cradle the cat to his chest. "Former brother-in-law."

For the first time I noticed the cluster of freckles on his bare arms and that his receding carrot-red hair was almost the same shade as my own. He rose and headed across the street towards a bronze pickup with a camper shell, so I hurried to keep step with him amid the flurry of scornful remarks peppering the air behind us.

"Hey, miss!" shouted Matt. "Maybe that space lady can contact one of her flyin' saucer buddies to send one of them aliens down to doctor up the cat. You know, perform one of them miracle cures."

"Yeah," his friend chimed in, "maybe she could talk one of 'em into doing that mind meld thing and save you a trip to the vet!" A bawdy chorus of laughter followed.

Payton edged me a look of chagrin. "Don't pay any attention to them. They're just having a little fun with you."

My concern for the cat kept me from appreciating the situation. "Sorry, I'm still a little fuzzy from all that's happened. I still don't understand why you're taking the cat to the Beaumont ranch?"

"Open, please," he said, indicating the passenger door. I did and he gently laid the limp cat on the seat, adding, "My mother...I mean my ex-mother-in-law's brother, Dean Pierce, lives at the ranch now. He retired from veterinary medicine about six months ago, and just so you'll know," he said lifting the cat's tail and peering closely, "this is a little female. By her size I'd guess she's five or six months old."

"She's just a baby. Well, I can't begin to thank you enough for your help, interrupting your breakfast and everything."

"No problem. You're obviously an animal lover like me."

I followed him around to the driver's side. "Do you think she'll be okay?" I asked as he pulled on the handle. "The last thing I need is to have this kitten's death on my conscience."

He glanced over at the limp feline before turning back to me with an encouraging smile that changed the whole complexion of his rather bland face. "I can't guarantee anything, but trust me when I say this kitty will be well cared for."

"By the way, I'm Kendall O'Dell from Castle Valley." I stuck out my hand and he enfolded it in his own. "Glad to meet you, Kendall O'Dell from Castle Valley. What brings you to this area?"

"I'm a reporter."

He tilted his head to one side, looking faintly amused. "If you're looking for excitement, you're going to be sorely disappointed."

"Oh, I don't know. Yesterday was pretty exciting."

He climbed into his truck and started the engine. "You mean the rally? Well, thank goodness it's over and we can get back to our normal peace and quiet. But, I expect that's not what you want to hear."

"I was thinking maybe I'd stick around a few days to see if anything else interesting develops."

A meager smile twitched at the corners of his mouth. "Considering your choice of breakfast companions, I gather you'll be focusing on the search for possible alien life forms."

I ignored his mild disdain. "Who knows, maybe I'll get lucky."

"Don't hold your breath," he said with a wry grin. "The most stimulating thing that's happened in this town in the last two years was the big bash hosted by my beloved ex-wife last summer to celebrate our divorce." He backed into the street.

Not sure how to respond to that, I shouted, "Hey, wait a minute. How do I find the Sundog?"

"It's impossible to miss. Anyone in town can tell you," he yelled, gunning the truck down the road to Sasabe.

As I watched him speed away towards rocky foothills crowned with misty-blue clouds, I sent up a silent prayer. Just knowing the injured kitten would soon be in good hands soothed my shattered nerves. Considering the number of weirdos we'd come in contact with since our arrival, we were lucky the benevolent stranger had offered to help.

"Angels come in all shapes and sizes, don't they?" Lupe remarked, walking up beside me.

I grinned at her. "I don't know as I'd go that far, but he certainly qualifies as a Good Samaritan."

"Some things aren't easy to explain away," said a husky female voice from behind.

We swung around to face a statuesque woman clad in a garnet-colored ankle-length dress accessorized with an impressive silver concha belt. Straight blue-black hair framing her hollow cheeks partially obscured a mysterious smile that urged me to challenge her statement. "Mazzie La Casse?"

A nod. "And which one of you is Miss O'Riley?"

I raised a hand in greeting. "It's O'Dell." I was struck by the candid intensity emanating from her dark eyes, and it chased away my preconceived notion of a wild-eyed eccentric.

After I introduced Lupe, we walked the few remaining yards to the restaurant's weather-beaten front door past a sign announcing: **Welcome to the oldest bar in the oldest continuously inhabited townsite in Arizona.** A tiny notice in the window brought a smile to my lips. OPEN WHEN WE'RE HERE, CLOSED WHEN WE'RE NOT. The screen door whined loudly as we followed her inside. The place was small, warm and crowded, but the appetizing aroma of frying bacon helped revive my stress-dulled appetite. The noisy buzz of conversation dropped to a low murmur as we drew the curious stares of the locals, most of them seniors. Ah yes. The only eating spot in town would be gossip central—a good thing normally. However, it was disappointing to realize that the small dining area had no quiet alcove or out of the way booth. "Is there another room where we can talk privately?" I whispered to Mazzie.

She hooked a thumb beneath the strap of her large shoulder bag and shrugged. "They could serve us in the bar, but I'm not sure it would be any better."

"Okay, this will have to do," I said, noting the apprehension in Lupe's momentary glance. We chose the only remaining clean table, near the kitchen entrance. While a young, gum-chewing waitress in overly tight jeans sloshed coffee into our cups, we reviewed the sticky one-sided menu. Apparently the novelty of our arrival had diminished somewhat because only a handful of inquisitive stares from the surrounding tables continued to come our way. Normally, I would have used my little tape recorder for the interview, but I knew the noise level of the room would make it difficult to decipher later.

"I'd like to take some notes," I said, watching Mazzie stir cream and sugar into her coffee before taking a tentative sip.

"That's fine," she said, folding her hands around the cup. "But before we begin, I'd like to be frank about a few things. If you're seeking information for a feature article concerning the subject of UFO sightings, alien abduction or the witness experience, I can help you. If you're looking for tabloid sensationalism, or if your questions are designed to try to discredit my work here, I'll conclude our interview."

Clearly she was in no mood for ridicule and I wondered if she'd overheard the remarks made earlier by the group of men in the street. "Actually, my questions to you pertain to a personal matter, so...." I paused to make eye contact with three seniors at the adjoining table practically falling off their chairs eavesdropping. When they averted their eyes, I said softly, "Perhaps we can just start with some general background information until we can find someplace more private to talk."

I noted, as her probing gaze darted back and forth between us, that her eyes were such a deep shade of mahogany it was difficult to see her pupils. "There's a little picnic table out back. Perhaps when we're through eating and," she paused and glanced outside at the soggy-looking clouds, "if it's not raining, we could talk there."

"Super."

"All right. What do you want to know?"

I flipped to a fresh page in my notepad. "For starters, your credentials as a UFOologist?"

"I studied at the Roswell, New Mexico site with other researchers for two years and then I worked with Dr. Hadlyn Stouffer at the Harkins Institute for UFO studies in

California for almost twelve. I've written numerous magazine articles, I can get you copies if you wish, and I've also co-authored two books on sightings in Europe and South America before beginning my own studies here."

"What made you choose this particular area?"

"The proliferation of sightings that started about two years ago and their possible connection to the animal mutilations on some of the ranches in this area."

I hunched forward, keeping my voice low. "Then I'm sure you know about the abduction story told by the immigrant apprehended in Morita awhile back."

"Yes, indeed. I'm sorry I didn't have an opportunity to talk with him before he was deported. From the accounts I read in the newspaper, he was obviously suffering from the severe mental aftershock that is commonly associated with these occurrences." Her expression grew wistful. "He might have found it helpful to have the support of our encounter group."

"As a psychotherapist, what exactly is your role in that setting?"

She took another sip of coffee before saying in a matter-of-fact tone, "It's my job to help clients deal with the fear, depression and anxiety associated with the abduction experience."

"What's your take on this guy's story that an entire van load of his countrymen was…well, *space-napped*? Are you aware of any other situations where abductees have simply vanished from the face of the earth?"

"There's no one way to answer that. In addition to eyewitness accounts right here, there are documented cases from all over the world relayed by people who have never communicated with one another, yet share similar experiences of seeing bright pulsating lights in the sky.

Many report being surrounded by a strange cloud and then ending up miles away from the abduction site, hysterical, disoriented, and sometimes suffering from temporary blindness and sleep paralysis. One recognizable factor in all of these cases is the unexplained blocks of missing time."

Her expression grew more animated as she warmed to her subject. I cautioned myself to maintain a professional demeanor, as what she was saying sounded totally inconceivable to me.

"But to answer the second part of your question," she continued, motioning to the waitress for more coffee, "no Missing Person reports are filed on illegal immigrants, so how can one know if these people actually disappeared? Perhaps they just returned to Mexico. And how can one say for a fact that extraterrestrials are responsible for the hundreds of people that disappear each year without a trace, and not just those who've braved El Camino del Diablo?"

"El Camino del Diablo?"

"The Devil's Highway. It's located west of here, towards Yuma. No one knows how many poor souls have perished trying to make it across that godforsaken stretch of desert." She arched a commiserating brow at Lupe before continuing. "Ninety-five percent of UFO sighting can be explained logically, but that leaves five percent that cannot. Think about it. That translates to several million people, including small children, who suffer the aftereffects of these unexplained encounters."

"Like what?" Lupe asked, unable to hide the gleam of anxiety in her eyes.

"In addition to the mental shock I mentioned, abduction victims share other common themes such as trauma, often times recurring nightmares, depression and psychosomatic illnesses. There are numerous accounts of bizarre medical experiments performed on them such as surgical implantation of tracking devices, sexual examinations, and encounters with the aliens themselves. Female abductees give frightening accounts of having fluid extracted from their abdomens and tell disturbing tales of stolen human embryos. In the cases I've handled personally, the majority of my clients have responded well to treatment. And in all but the most severe ones, these people are able to cope with what has happened to them and rebuild their lives."

The fact that this obviously intelligent and educated woman showed no trace of skepticism concerning this far-fetched subject left me more disturbed than ever. "I'm sorry to sound dubious, but short of someone producing biological evidence, living or dead, what makes you so sure these people aren't just making this stuff up?"

Her face registered annoyance. "To what end? To be scorned by colleagues, friends and family? Let me tell you, just being a therapist places me on the fringe of this ridicule. UFOlogists are constantly on the alert for deliberate disinformation, false leads or people just out there to make money or a run for their so-called fifteen minutes of fame. After years of research, and having listened to hundreds of these witnesses, believe me, I've learned how to separate the actual abduction cases from the hoaxes."

The arrival of our breakfast brought the conversation to a temporary halt. While Mazzie munched on fruit and dry wheat toast and Lupe picked at her oatmeal, I dug into ham, eggs and hash browns. I was glad of the respite, because as knowledgeable as she appeared, I was having a big problem buying into this whole theory without bursting out with, 'Give me a break!' Okay, maybe I could admit that somewhere out there in that ocean of stars there might be other worlds populated with life forms, but I was still having a devil of a time accepting at face value the reality of extraterrestrials tinkering around with human beings.

By the time we finished eating it was ten-thirty and only a few old-timers remained, shooting the breeze, smoking and edging glances rife with curiosity our way. As strangers in a small town, I acknowledged that we were providing a welcome diversion, but I didn't care to provide them with their day's entertainment by allowing them to overhear the actual reason for our visit. I glanced out the window at the threatening clouds and suggested we finish our conversation outdoors while we had time. I dropped some money on the table to cover our tab.

When we stepped out the back door, the cool wind gusts carried the damp smell of imminent rain. I inhaled deeply, savoring the weather change.

The backyards of the restaurant and the neighboring properties were all piled with an amazing assortment of junk ranging from rusting appliances and old furniture to broken-down cars. As we settled around the splintery picnic table set beneath the gaunt limbs of an emaciated tree, Lupe sneezed several times.

"You sure you want to sit out here?" I asked, watching her slip into the sweater she'd had tied around her waist during breakfast.

"I'd rather be someplace where we can talk in private."

Mazzie appraised us in silence before saying, "So, do you want to tell me the real reason you wanted to see me?"

Her thick brows dipped lower in concentration as I conveyed the information we had, leaving out only Lupe's relationship to the missing people and Javier's hiding place. When we finished, she wore a look of eager concern. "Can you arrange for me to speak with this child?"

Lupe and I exchanged a questioning glance before I turned back to her. "I'm afraid not. We've given our word that his location remain a secret for now, but in your opinion, how much credence should we give this boy's story?"

She pursed her lips together for a few seconds before answering. "I don't really know what to make of the black horse he refers to, but the rest of his story is very consistent with other abduction accounts, including his memory loss, which we refer to as 'doorway' amnesia, and also his depiction of the monster bugs."

Cold tremors danced along the base of my neck and I could tell by Lupe's fearful expression that she felt the same. I think I'd have been happier if Mazzie had announced that it was all the product of a child's active imagination.

"Let me show you something," she said, reaching for her bag. She thumbed through some folders and pulled one out, opening it in front of us. "There are three categories of extraterrestrials that have been described in vivid detail and even drawn by the abductees themselves after being regressed under hypnosis. The most common type has been nicknamed the 'grays.'" She pointed to a sketch of a fragile-looking creature dressed in a coverall. "The description is almost always the same— approximately four feet high, grayish-white hairless skin, an elongated, bald head and black almond-shaped eyes." She moved her finger to the opposite page. "This one is a blend between a human and an alien. We call it the humanoid. As you can see, it looks very similar to us, except that abductees describe them as being over seven feet tall. Finally, there are these." With dramatic flair, she flipped the page and pushed it in front of us. Lupe's gasp of horror sent a shockwave tearing down my spine. "This one," she said, tapping the page for emphasis, "known as the mantis, sounds very much like what this child is describing."

"As in praying mantis?" I asked, staring at a pair of bulbous eyes set in a long insect-like face minus a nose and mouth. The claw-like webbed fingers appeared almost reptilian and I knew that if I'd come face to face with this ugly thing in the middle of the night, I'd be having nightmares too.

"Exactly. The other thing that leads me to believe he is telling the truth is his description of the classic Oz Factor." The excited catch in her voice had Lupe and me trading another quizzical glance as she swiftly paged through the folder again. I had to remind myself that we weren't admiring pictures of purebred dogs and cats, we were looking at renderings of space aliens, for heaven's sake! Oh, man, I could only imagine Tally's reaction. But, no matter how outlandish it sounded I had to ask myself one question. If Javier was fabricating the story, how could a child so young describe the mantis creatures with such dead-on accuracy?

"Eyewitnesses," Mazzie exclaimed, "have reported being struck by a bright beam of blue light that leaves them paralyzed. Then they're taken to a 'house' where time flows at a different rate, all sounds of the environment cease and they find themselves in a domed room subjected to terrifying examinations by creatures with glowing phosphorescent eyes."

"*Dios Mio,*" Lupe whispered, breaking into sobs. "To think that any of these things have happened to my... to my friends is too awful to think about," she sobbed, stumbling from the table. She fled to the door marked *Damas* and slammed it behind her.

"Do you want to go after her?" Mazzie asked, eyeing me with sympathy.

"No, let's leave her alone for a few minutes."

The wind sang a dismal little tune as it whined around the bare branches of the scraggly tree. A few drops of rain struck my face and she began gathering her papers together. "It isn't just a friend of hers missing, is it?"

I hesitated for a fraction of a second. "I can't say."

She pinned me with a knowing look and said softly, "You don't have to."

"Thank you very much for your time and insight on this subject. You've given me a lot to think about," I said rising with her. "I'd still be interested in sitting in on one of your encounter groups. Here's my card."

"I'll think about it." She nodded goodbye. As I watched her slip through the restaurant door, I decided that being in possession of the additional knowledge on this bizarre topic had not really simplified my job one bit and I could not shake the disturbing sense of foreboding growing deep inside me.

10

For a long moment, I stood staring at the neighboring tin-roofed adobe cottages beyond the wire fence separating them from the restaurant's back yard. Judging by their condition and the architecture, I deduced that these sturdy, time-weathered structures had been rooted there in the same spot for fifty or sixty years. My gaze roamed from the picnic bench to a rusted wheelbarrow full of faded flowers, and on to a colorful ceramic chicken perched on the windowsill. Trying to marshal my disjointed thoughts, I drew comfort from the homey sights. Eventually, I walked over to the outside restroom and tapped on the door. "Lupe, are you all right?"

"Yes," came her muffled reply. The latch snapped and she stepped out, dabbing at the corners of her eyes. "I'm sorry. Maybe it's because I'm not feeling so good, but I couldn't listen to her anymore. I can't bear to think of what has happened to Gilberto and dear, sweet Uncle Raymond. These creatures...they must have stolen them away for one of these terrible experiments." She gulped and swallowed hard. "Kendall, what am I going to do? Tell me! What can you do? What can anyone do?"

Sharp hysteria edged her voice, so I laid my hands on her trembling shoulders and forced her to meet my eyes. "Lupe, there may not be anything either of us can do at this point but pray. But let's have a reality check before we talk about this any further, okay?"

She nodded in silence.

"I don't know how much of this space alien stuff I'm willing to buy into. Granted, Mazzie La Casse does not strike me as a nut case, just the opposite in fact, and there appears to be an extraordinary number of people who, for whatever reason, believe that they've had some sort of encounter with... some kind of beings, and it sounds suspiciously like Javier may be one of them. Even so, I think we should keep our feet planted securely on terra firma if we're going to progress with this investigation. Do you get what I'm saying?"

A half shrug accompanied her "No."

I ushered her towards the door. "Logic dictates that we're dealing with a human factor here, not space creatures, so that's how I'm going to have to proceed."

If anything, she looked even more disconcerted and just a little bit angry. "You think someone is... pretending to be a spaceman to scare people? Why? Why would anyone do that?"

"I don't know. But that's the assumption I'm going with for now."

She stared at me with alarm. "I don't know if that makes me feel better or worse."

I agreed with her wholeheartedly as we stepped inside once again. All eight of the tables were empty and the waitress waved cheerfully as we headed towards the front door. It was then I noticed the large, somewhat crudely drawn mural of a woman covering one entire wall. "Who do you suppose that's supposed to be?" I muttered to Lupe as we pushed open the screen door and stepped outside in time to see Mazzie La Casse preparing to climb into a silver Honda.

"Maybe it's the gypsy," she replied, yawning her disinterest.

"What?"

She waved an impatient hand back at the restaurant sign. "La Gitana. It means gypsy."

"Oh. Gotcha," I said, distracted by the sudden commotion in the street. Four young boys, shouting something at the tops of their lungs, pedaled their bikes in mad pursuit of a dented pickup truck painted solely with gray metal primer. I couldn't make out much about the driver through the dark armor of window tint except that he wore a broad-brimmed hat pulled low over his face. As the truck turned left onto Ruby Road, two other boys standing on the sidewalk lobbed rocks and yelled in unison, "Russell Greene will cook your spleen and eat it on rye bread. Run before he breaks your neck or you could wind up dead, dead, dead!"

The man rewarded the boys' lame limerick by lowering the window just enough to flash his middle finger at them. Russell Greene? Why did that name sound familiar? The boys gave chase, pelting the tailgate of the departing vehicle with rocks before it vanished in a curtain of yellow dust.

"Now what do you suppose that was all about?" I said to no one in particular.

Mazzie peered over the top of her car and shook her head in disgust at the gang of pre-teen boys now hooting with laughter. "Poor tragic soul. He was one of the people implicated by the authorities in connection with those animal mutilations I mentioned."

My attention gauge shot up. Of course. He'd been mentioned in one of Walter's articles I'd read last night. "Why is he a suspect?"

She glanced at her watch. "About twenty years ago he was piloting a private plane with his brother and girlfriend onboard when it crashed during a terrible snowstorm in Montana or Colorado, I forget which. Anyway, the two passengers died instantly. Because he was lost in such a remote area and wasn't found for weeks," she paused, her expectant gaze sliding between Lupe and me before concluding with, "he…and this is just one of the versions I've heard…he ate the flesh of his own brother and his girlfriend to survive."

Lupe stifled a gasp and looked like she was going to lose her breakfast. "Not an appealing visual," I admitted, suppressing a little shudder of horror, "but I don't understand the correlation to the animals."

She looked askance at the six raucous boys racing past her car before she returned her attention to us. "The rumor going around is that he still harbors a taste for raw flesh."

I'm sure my face reflected the same look of horrified disbelief as Lupe's.

"As I told you, I don't think the animal mutilations are human in origin," she said with a careless wave. "But, I did try to talk to him one day a few months ago about several eye-witness sightings in the proximity of Morita…."

I cut in, "Whoa. What does he have to do with Morita?"

She eased herself behind the wheel, pulled the door shut and rested her arm on the window rim. "He's the caretaker over there."

How interesting. "And what did he say?"

"Not much. He was getting into his truck outside the feed store so I ran over and knocked on the glass. I asked if I could talk to him about reports from several campers in the area, who said they'd seen bright, pulsating lights hovering over the mountains. There had also been sightings further west on the reservation and east towards Ruby that same weekend."

"And?"

"He wouldn't even talk to me, just shook his head and drove off." Her face glowed with excitement as she motioned for me to come closer. "Listen, I hope you'll reconsider allowing me to visit with the boy. By employing hypnosis, it may be possible for me to tap into repressed memories that might reveal important clues about what he saw."

Still feeling unsure about the whole weird subject, I sidestepped her request. "I'll check into it." I thanked her again for her time, and when her Honda disappeared around the corner, Lupe blew her nose for the umteenth time, asking in a clogged voice, "So, what should we do now?"

Taking note of her ashen complexion, I said, "I plan to pay a visit to Loydeen Shirley before I go find the Sundog. You, I think, should go straight home to bed."

"But what about Sister Goldenrod?"

"What about her?"

"If I leave now, I won't get the information from her about the *coyote*...and my bag is still there."

I thought about that for a moment. "Is there anything in it that you can't live without until tomorrow night?"

"No, I guess not."

"Then there's no problem. I'll pick it up later and tell her why you had to leave early. If she balks at sharing the information with me, I'll suggest she call you at home."

She nodded, her expression one of profound relief. No doubt she was suffering as much from emotional overload as she was from her cold.

As we started across the street towards our cars, a strong gust of wind rushed in sending paper scraps and leaves whirling in all directions. "So much for the rain," I muttered, watching the storm clouds sail away towards the Santa Rita Mountains. A single shaft of sunlight punched through the gray mist as Lupe settled into her car. I looked up at the bright patch of blue and smiled. "Looks like you'll have nice weather for your drive home," I told her as she fastened her seat belt. "I'll call you if I find a phone," I added, glaring at my useless cell phone and its non-existent signal.

"All right." When she revved the engine, black smoke poured from her exhaust pipe.

I fanned away the fumes. "Oh, and if I were you, I'd stop and put another quart of oil in this puppy when you get to Tucson."

She nodded, but her watery eyes reflected concern as she put the car in reverse. "If you do go to Morita, please be careful. I don't think I would want to meet a person who would eat another human being."

"Don't worry, I'll be fine. And you take care going home." As I watched her car sputter away down the road, part of me wished I was going with her, but I steeled my resolve. A promise is a promise is a promise.

The fourteen raindrops bequeathed by the much-anticipated non-storm had done little to dampen the parched ground. A steadily rising wind stirred up a hazy sheen of dust, and I could taste the grit in my mouth as I trudged back to La Gitana and stuck my head in the door. Matt, his buddy and a third man who looked vaguely familiar were camped out at a table, flirting with the buxom waitress, who giggled as she slapped Matt's hand away from her rear-end. Her face reddened when she spotted me. "Hi, you forget something?"

"No, I was wondering if you could give me directions to the Sundog Ranch."

"Sure thing."

I scribbled the directions in my notepad. "And could you tell me how to get to 44 West 1st Street?"

"Who you trying to find, honey?" the waitress asked, popping lavender bubble gum.

"Loydeen Shirley."

She pointed out the window. "Go past the ceramic shop over there and turn left. Her house is set back a ways from the road on the right hand side. You can't miss it."

"For being a stranger in town, you sure seem to know a lot of people," Matt observed, rocking his chair back on two legs. "But I guess it's a reporter's job to nose around, huh?"

How could he know that? I caught the extra emphasis he'd placed on the word 'nose' and while I found his cocky attitude annoying, the cold predatory gleam in the third man's mustard-colored eyes had me recoiling instinctively. In a matter of seconds, I took in his KNIGHTS OF RIGHT-STOP THE INVASION! T-shirt stretched across a well-muscled chest, and bare arms that bore tattoos of skull and crossbones and prominent swastikas. He was one scary-looking dude.

I dragged my gaze back to Matt and kept my face expressionless while trying to remember who else knew I was a reporter besides Sister Goldenrod, Payton Kleinwort and of course, the Border Patrol agent who'd waylaid Lupe yesterday. But, considering how small the town was, I shouldn't be surprised that news of a stranger would spread like wildfire in a strong wind. "It's a tough job, but someone's got to do it." I waved at the waitress. "Thanks for your help."

"No problem."

I couldn't get out fast enough and the strong sense that curious eyes were boring into my back as I crossed the street to my car set my nerves on edge. The thick-necked guy with menacing eyes bore a slight resemblance to the moose with the earrings yesterday who'd roughed up my car, but then there were so many men here with the shaved head look, it was difficult for me to be sure.

It took me all of five minutes to locate the white slump-block house sitting along a rutted unpaved road only a few blocks from the small downtown area. A FOR SALE sign at the mouth of the driveway leaned at a forty-five degree angle and the weed-choked lawn looked as if it hadn't been mowed for months. A pale green car bearing a University of Arizona sticker in the back window sat adjacent to an older model Chevrolet. I parked and took note of the empty birdbath and dead flowers in the small rock garden adjacent to the front porch. Apparently Loydeen Shirley wasn't too concerned about curb appeal because the place projected an aura of decay and sad neglect.

An aged Bassett Hound lying on a ragged mat thumped its tail and looked up at me with forlorn brown eyes. "Hi there, doggie," I said, knocking on the screen door and then kneeling to scratch him behind the ears. The tail thumped harder. After a minute dragged by and no one answered, I knocked again, louder this time. Finally, I heard a bubbly cough and shuffling steps. The door squeaked open far enough to reveal a cranky-faced woman wearing a ratty housecoat and crown of curlers. A cigarette smoldered in one hand. "Loydeen Shirley?"

"No. Who are you?"

I flashed a cheerful smile. "My name is Kendall O'Dell and...."

"If you're here to look at the house you need to call for an appointment."

"I'm not here to see the house."

Her bloodshot eyes narrowed to slits of suspicion. "Then what do you want?"

"Walter Zipp and I work for the same newspaper."

Her indifferent shrug annoyed me, so I tried another approach. "Walter's wife, Lavelle, was Bob Shirley's cousin. Perhaps you knew him?"

"Of course I knew him, he was my son-in-law." I had the distinct sense she would like to have added 'you idiot' but she snapped, "Why do you want to see Loydeen?"

I remembered what Walter said about the woman's reluctance to discuss her deceased husband, so I rustled up my most beguiling smile. "I was just in the area and thought I'd stop by to visit. Maybe I could chat with her for a couple of minutes."

"About what?" She sucked so hard on the cigarette I thought she was going to inhale the whole thing and then before I could say another word, she burst into a fit of coughing. Holding onto the doorframe for support, she hacked and gagged and wheezed so violently I thought she was either going to barf or check out altogether. Not sure what to do, I called out, "Is there anything I can do?"

"Jesus, Grandma!" A young woman with spiky brown hair appeared out of nowhere and rushed to the woman's side. "You're not supposed to be up." She shot me a startled look and shouted, "Wait there, I'll be right back," as she led the still-coughing woman away.

Oh, my. I eased my weight onto an old wooden Adirondack chair beside the door and leaned my head back, suddenly feeling bone weary. Two nights of lost sleep were catching up with me. I wished I could close my eyes and lie down on the mat beside the dog. "Want some company, fellah?" As if he understood, the hound raised his freckley brows and wagged his tail.

As I sat there listening to the lonesome whisper of the wind dancing through the high grass, I sensed more than just an air of disregard surrounding the place, an actual pall hung over the house. But then, it had only been three months since Bob Shirley's untimely death.

I think I may have actually dozed off for a few minutes when I heard the hinges on the screen door squeak. I blinked and looked up as the lanky girl stepped onto the porch and pulled the front door shut behind her. She wore heavy eye makeup, hip-hugger jeans and a midriff T-shirt that showed off her belly button ring. "Hi, I'm Jennifer Shirley." Her open, friendly smile was a welcome contrast to her grandmother's brittle reception. "Grandma says you know Walter and Lavelle."

"That's right." I introduced myself and handed her my business card.

Reading it, she plopped down next to the dog and ruffled his floppy ears. "How's my old Buster doing?" Expectantly, she turned back to me. "So, you work with Walter? How are they liking Castle Valley?"

"Just fine, I think."

"I felt bad that I didn't get to say goodbye when they came by a few weeks ago, but I was away at school. Say, your hair is really cool. Are you a natural redhead? I'm thinking about dyeing mine red," she said, fluffing her short bangs.

She seemed anxious to talk and that was great, as I was anxious for information. I thanked her for the compliment and motioned towards the green car. "So, you attend the U of A in Tucson?"

At the mention of school her face lit up. For several minutes, she chattered on about her hopes to major in microbiology, work for a big pharmaceutical firm and find the cure for cancer. Lofty goals.

"Do you come home often?"

Her enthusiasm diminished. "Twice a month. Sometimes my two brothers drive down, and once in a while my big sister comes to help out," she said, stuffing my card into the front pocket of her jeans, "but it's not much fun being here anymore. In fact, it's like a morgue. There's nobody to talk to most of the time."

"Why is that?"

She drew her knees up to her chin and sighed. "As you could probably tell, Grandma's got emphysema, so she can only talk for two minutes before having a coughing fit. She's not supposed to smoke, but she gets on my ass if I say anything."

"And your mother?"

Her swift shrug and upward eye roll told me a lot. "She pops Prozac all day or else she's zonked out on sleeping pills...." Her voice trailed off and she stared straight ahead blank-faced momentarily before meeting my eyes again. "Why do you want to talk to her?"

"I wanted to ask her some questions about your dad."

Little distress lines fanned out across her forehead. She lowered her eyes and absently petted the dog again. "Good luck."

"Why do you say that?"

"Because, she gets totally paranoid if we try to talk to her about him." She paused to clear her throat. "Maybe things will be better when we sell this place and she moves up to Tucson. Bad vibes here now."

"Your brothers, are they at the university too?"

"Yeah. Carl's got one more year, I've got two, but Todd just started."

I did a quick calculation. Tuition, room and board for three college students would add up to a substantial amount of cash. Would the financial burden have pushed Bob Shirley to abandon his principles and become involved in drug smuggling to augment his income?

"We'll be there for the rest of this semester anyway," she said, sounding despondent. "If the house doesn't sell and we don't get the grants we applied for...well, we may all have to drop out."

"Losing your dad has obviously been pretty hard on the whole family emotionally and financially."

"Nothing will ever be the same."

I flipped open my notepad and leaned forward. "Jennifer, I'm hoping you can answer some questions for me. I'm trying to help out a friend who's in some serious

163

trouble. I can't give you specifics except to say there are bizarre similarities between her current predicament and something that happened involving your dad. I'm trying to figure out if there might be a connection between these two situations."

The color seeped from her face. "What are you talking about?"

"Did your father ever discuss his work?"

"Sometimes." A cautious note had entered her voice.

"Did he ever talk to you about one particular immigrant he arrested in a place called Morita?" I consulted my notes and tacked on, "It happened the last week of June."

Her eyes fogged for several seconds then cleared. "Oh, you mean the guy who thought he saw a space alien or something?"

"Exactly. What was your dad's reaction to his story?"

"At first we all laughed about it, but then later on...." She hesitated for a few seconds before fixing me with an odd look. "You know, so much was happening around that time, I hadn't really thought about this until now."

I leaned closer. "What?"

"A couple of days afterwards, when Todd was joking about it at dinner, my dad just suddenly lost it. I mean he got really mad and said he didn't want us to discuss it ever again."

"Really? Did you think that was strange?"

She hitched one thin shoulder. "Kind of."

"How would you rate your dad's state of mind during that time period? Did he seem depressed?"

"Well...I wouldn't exactly call it depressed, but I did overhear him talking to Mom that he was bummed about his job and he was thinking about quitting."

"Why?"

"He was totally...well, disillusioned is the word he used. Half the time he was out of his mind with boredom, but when they did catch a group of migrants it was like playing a game of tag because they'd just come back again." Her elongated shrug and sad little smile spoke volumes. "He used to say that it was like a revolving door."

I nodded, thinking that his complaints echoed exactly the grievances quoted by the disgruntled agent in the article I'd read last night.

She chewed her lip for moment before tacking on, "Mom was always giving him grief about the low pay too. She said it wasn't worth him working such crappy hours and certainly not for risking his life in some cases."

I knew the next question was going to hurt, but I had to ask it anyway. "Tell me, Jennifer, do you know anything about the allegations that he...."

Fury erupted in her eyes. "Don't even say it! I don't care what you've heard or what you've read, my dad was *not*, and I repeat *not*, involved with drug smugglers. He was honest and decent and kind and he would never, ever in a million years have done anything like...like they're saying." Her voice trembled over the last few words and she pressed her lips shut.

I smiled in sympathy. "I'm sorry. I know this is a painful subject, but Walter doesn't buy the official ruling that your dad committed suicide. What do you think?"

She appeared to be straining for composure. "Like I said, he wasn't exactly himself those last few weeks, but who would be with that kind of shit coming down?" She pushed to her feet, marched to the edge of the porch and stood with her back to me for a minute before she swung around to face me, her eyes luminous with tears. "Does it sound logical to you that a man with a wife and four kids and a grandbaby on the way would kill himself the night before his fiftieth birthday party?"

Frowning, I shook my head. "No." The mournful wail of the wind seemed to accentuate the unspoken realization that passed between us. "Jennifer, did your father have any enemies?"

"Not that I know of."

We both flinched when a voice commanded, "Jennifer! Get inside right now!" I swung around. A haggard-looking woman with eyes as morose as the hound dog stood behind the screen door. Wrapped in an oversized terrycloth bathrobe, her graying sandy hair was squashed flat against the side of her head as if she'd been lying on it a long time.

Jennifer's brow crinkled. "Mom, what's wrong?"

She edged the door open, beckoning frantically. "Get in here. You shouldn't be talking to this woman. She works at a newspaper! You could be endangering the whole family."

Her choice of the word 'endanger,' coupled with the expression of fearful agitation tarnishing her dull blue eyes, set my pulse rate skyrocketing.

Jennifer fired a bewildered glance at me as she brushed by and disappeared inside the house. "Mrs. Shirley," I began, "I'm sure your mother told you that I'm a friend of Walter and Lavelle...."

She cut me off with a curt, "Did anybody see you come here?"

"What?"

"Does anyone else know you're here?" Her eyes darted all around and then widened with fright when her gaze locked onto something behind me. "Hell's fire, they're still watching me. Get out," she snarled. "Get out of here now and don't ever come back!" The door slammed in my face.

I swiveled around in time to see a white Chevy Blazer slowly cruising past the house. A lightning bolt of alarm shot through me when I recognized the beefy skinhead I'd seen earlier at the café. The menace smoldering in his close-set eyes was every bit as frightening as if he'd reached out and wrapped his hands around my throat.

11

Twenty miles later, my apprehension persisted. Keeping one hand on the wheel, I adjusted the rearview mirror again. The road was clear behind me, but the knowledge that I had been followed to the Shirley residence, coupled with Loydeen's claim that she was being watched, unnerved me. There was zero doubt in my mind that the malevolence directed towards me both yesterday and today was a direct result of my association with a person of Mexican origin, plain and simple.

The skinhead's timely appearance, combined with the Shirley woman's violent reaction, gave merit to Walter's assertion that Bob may have had some association with the Knights of Right, and his warning that the situation could get dicey had me wondering how best to proceed. I couldn't realistically take my fears to the authorities, as there'd been no direct threat against me.

I headed to the mission, determined to pick up Lupe's bag before going to the ranch. With Sunday services long over, the place looked deserted again. I parked near the pink house and entered the kitchen. Celia and the second Hispanic woman were there washing dishes, but when I asked for Sister Goldenrod, Celia shook her head and pointed to the door. I gathered she wasn't around and headed towards Javier's room.

Judging by the clean soapy smell and the shine in his dark hair, it was apparent that Sister G had given the little guy a bath. An empty plate and new stuffed toy sat next to him on the floor of the closet. The touching scene thawed the cold dread icing down my insides. Even if it was eventually revealed that Sister G's ministry was bogus, her concern for the illegals and her affection for this little waif appeared genuine. I wondered how she would react to Mazzie La Casse's request.

I grabbed Lupe's bag from the floor and Javier returned my smile with his timid one as I waved goodbye before closing the door to his sanctuary. Disappointed that I was having no luck connecting the dots in this weird puzzle, and grappling with an overpowering sense of defeat, I headed down the hall, anxious to get to the ranch, fearful that the little orange kitten might be dead. I'd definitely have a few words to say about Jason Beaumont's deplorable behavior.

I hadn't gone two steps past Sister G's bedroom door when I heard rustling followed by a soft thump. I halted, listening intently. Perhaps I'd misunderstood Celia. I tapped lightly on the door, calling softly, "Sister Goldenrod?" before easing it open to stare in surprise. The noisemaker proved to be Froggy McQueen. Balanced atop a small stepladder, he was so absorbed in rummaging around inside some cardboard boxes on the top shelf of her closet I knew he hadn't heard me. Well now, what was this? Instinctively, I knew he shouldn't be there. And wouldn't it be a crying shame to let an opportunity like this slip by? Warily, I eyed the far corner of the room and suppressed a shiver of terror before tiptoeing into the room. Why did I always torture myself with the irrational belief that a spider could vault from its web and travel by air to pounce on me?

Preoccupied in his explorations, Froggy did not notice my stealthy approach. "Where the hell did you hide it, you miserable bitch?" he muttered, stopping to wipe beads of perspiration from his forehead before reaching for a bottle of beer perched on the lower shelf. He tipped it skyward, drained it and then let out several croaking belches that actually sounded like the call of a bullfrog. The origin of his nickname perhaps?

The word obnoxious couldn't begin to describe this guy. It also occurred to me that Froggy must indeed have an alcohol problem if his drinking had begun already. It wasn't yet one o'clock. When I cleared my throat, he started so violently he almost lost his footing. "Jeezuuuus!" he cried, gawking open-mouthed at me while grabbing the shelf for support. "You scared the everlivin' shit out of me!"

"Sorry. I was looking for Sister Goldenrod."

He swallowed convulsively and clambered down, missing the last rung on the ladder and almost falling. "Ah...she's not here, but I expect her back any minute." He punctuated his statement with a hiccup.

It took all my willpower not to laugh out loud. I said nothing, just stared at him coolly until he offered up a sheepish smile. "She...um...asked me to do some cleaning for her."

"Really? You should get rid of the spider over there in the corner while you're at it." I retraced my steps, calling nonchalantly over my shoulder, "I'll check back with her later...and I'll be sure to mention that I saw you. Bye-bye now."

I hadn't gotten more than ten steps outside the door before he caught up with me. Breathless, he gasped, "Hold on a minute!"

Smiling inwardly, I stopped and wheeled around to face him. "Yes?"

"Listen," he said, nervously rubbing his hands on his faded jeans. "Do you s'pose you could maybe not mention anything about me being in her room." His words slurred just a little bit.

I folded my arms and let him stew for a few seconds. "Well, I think we can work something out."

His bloodshot eyes narrowed with suspicion. "How?"

"I have some questions I need answered."

He knew I had him and he looked like he wanted to cry. Furtively, he glanced around before making tentative eye contact with me again. "What kinds of questions?"

"For starters, how long have you known Sister Goldenrod?"

Puzzled frown lines formed a cleft Y above his mottled nose. "Why do you want to know that?"

"Do we have a deal or not?" I had the upper hand and intended to keep it.

He hesitated, running his tongue along his lower lip. "Hey, listen, I'm kinda thirsty. You wanna go out to my truck and have a beer?"

I started to refuse and then changed my mind. Alcohol is wonderful for lubricating the jaw muscles. "Sure."

Outside, he plucked two bottles from a Styrofoam cooler in his camper shell, popped the tops and handed me one. "She won't let me keep this in her refrigerators," he groused, taking a long pull from his beer and then wiping his mouth on his sleeve. "Say, I heard through the grapevine that you was a reporter," he announced in an obvious ploy to change the subject. "Bet you got some real interesting stories to tell."

"Froggy, I don't have a lot of time. Answer the question."

His face crumpled like a petulant child. "I dunno. I met her three, maybe four years ago."

"Under what circumstances?"

"She lived in the same...um...place as my sister."

Pretty vague answer. "Which was?"

"Tennessee."

Still vague, guarded. I took a tiny swallow of beer and switched gears. "Tell me something, is Goldenrod her given name?"

His lips twitched with mirth. "No, it ain't." Unable to contain his glee, he sniggered, "She don't like anyone to know because she says people don't take her seriously, but you know what her real name is?"

I shrugged. "I'm listening."

"It's Hoggwhistle. Shalberta Hoggwhistle." He let out a hoot of laughter and pounded his knee.

I shook my head in wonder. With a name like that, I could understand why she didn't want to use it. "Charming. And is she really a minister?"

"So she says. Hey, why do you want to know all this stuff?"

"I'm just curious to know why you're blackmailing her."

He made a little choking noise and his eyeballs practically bulged from their sockets. "What? Where did

172

you...I mean, I don't know what you're talking about," he stammered, his face paling visibly. He looked so uncomfortable, I almost felt sorry for him. Almost. Matter-of-factly, I said, "I think you do."

I could see all kinds of activity going on behind his eyes in an apparent struggle to decide what he would or would not tell me. "Look," he said, his tone now syrupy, "I ain't doing nothing wrong. The good Sister, well, she got into a little trouble a few years ago and says she's happy to help me out a little bit financially, if I keep that piece of information to myself."

"What kind of trouble?"

He looked everywhere but at me. "Oh...nothing much. She just spent a little time in the joint."

Nothing much? So, Sister Goldenrod was an ex-con? That certainly went a long way in explaining her coarse behavior. "What was she in for?"

"She swears she was framed," he said, holding up his right hand as if he were being sworn in. "I think it had something to do with cashing bad checks or something." His expression of contrived innocence told me he was lying but, if he'd been telling the truth to this point, at least now I had enough information to check out the story further. The rattle of a car engine made his eyes widen with alarm. "Oh, shit, she's back." He grabbed the unfinished beer from my hand and stowed it along with his empty bottle back inside the cooler before slamming the door to the camper.

I decided not to let him off the hook too easily. "I think we should talk again. Soon."

His gaze turned flinty. I'm sure if he'd been a dog, he'd have grabbed my ankle with his teeth and hung on, but since I appeared to be holding the cards, he acquiesced. "Sure, sure," he said, sliding an uneasy glance towards

Sister Goldenrod's Bronco pulling into the garage. "Maybe I could buy you a drink at La Gitana. I go there in the evenings sometimes."

I'll bet he did. "Perhaps," I said. "I'll be in touch." Damn, it felt good to see the self-satisfied smirk wiped off his face, but I was frustrated that I hadn't had the opportunity to ask him what he'd been searching for.

I watched him climb behind the wheel and rev the engine, but he didn't get very far down the driveway before Sister Goldenrod motioned for him to stop. "Why haven't you left yet?" she barked, ambling up to the passenger window, her face one big scowl. "I told you we need those groceries here by four o'clock."

"I'm goin', I'm goin'," he said, glowering as he gunned the truck towards the road. Sister G shook her head in disgust before turning a look of suspicion on me. "What were you two talking about?"

My heart faltered for a second. Minus her white robe, her disagreeable personality had reemerged. "Nothing in particular," I answered, hoping I sounded calmer than I felt. "I just stopped by to pick up Lupe's bag. She wasn't feeling well and went home right after breakfast."

My explanation didn't diminish the worried glaze in her eyes. "You didn't talk to him about Javier, did you?"

"No."

"Good. He doesn't really know anything other than he's just a little kid that I'm babysitting for a couple of weeks and that's the way I want to keep it. That man can't be trusted to keep his mouth shut when he drinks."

She was sure right about that. "Speaking of Javier, what's going to happen to him? What happens to other children in similar circumstances?"

A look of melancholy softened her crusty demeanor. "Tragic. It's just tragic. In most cases, if the powers that be can't locate a relative, these poor tykes are deported to orphanages in Mexico where conditions can be unspeakable. I can't bear the thought of that happening to him."

"What are you going to do?"

"I don't know."

Her expression of genuine distress made it harder to accept the fact that she was an ex-con in minister's clothing. Was she really here trying to rectify her past, or merely using her position to enrich herself by breaking United States immigration laws? I weighed my next move. Should I share what I'd learned from the meeting with Mazzie La Casse? For Javier's sake, for Lupe's sake, I decided to go for it.

"What?" she squawked when I'd finished. "You promised you wouldn't tell anyone about him!"

"She doesn't know who he is or where he is. Just hear me out."

She froze in disbelief as I relayed the similarities between Javier's nightmares and some of the incidents attributed to other witnesses. "My Lord," she gasped, pressing a hand to her bosom, "so, the poor baby's telling the truth?"

The whole idea was unnerving. "Well, I think it's the truth as he perceives it. Would you consider allowing her to place Javier under hypnosis? It may help him to remember more details."

"But that might scare him even more," she murmured, picking at the hairs growing from her chin. "I'm going to have to think about that."

"Fair enough."

She looked towards the house and back at me again, her forehead rumpling in a frown. "If…if I do decide to let her talk to him, where would I reach you?"

I hesitated. There was no guarantee I'd ever pick up a strong signal for my cell phone. "I'm on my way to the Sundog ranch right now, but after that, I'm not sure. I can call you later."

Still appearing undecided, she grunted, "Okay."

I started towards my car then swung back. "By the way, Lupe wanted me to ask if you'd been able to track down the smug…I mean the person who guided Javier's family across the border."

"I…haven't had time to look into that yet."

I could tell by her wary expression that she wasn't about to tell me even if she did know. "Okay, well, I have to go now. Here's my card, or you can call Lupe if anything new develops. And thanks for your hospitality." Such as it was, I added to myself, tossing Lupe's bag onto the back seat of my car. As I made a wide circle to turn, I noticed her staring at a slip of paper in her hand. Frowning, she looked up and flagged me down. "Miss O'Dell, wait a minute!" I stopped and waited while she lumbered towards me, waving the paper.

"I…I didn't mean to be so short with you," she said, breathing heavily from the exertion, "and thanks a lot for this generous donation. Every cent counts."

"You're welcome." I shoved the car into gear again, but she didn't move. I looked up at her questioningly. "Is there something else?"

"Listen, tell Lupe I did hear some news. My sources tell me that no one has seen or heard from the guy for over two weeks now."

Interesting. By the time I reached the main road and turned south, my brain felt like a wet sponge, unable to absorb one more drop of liquid. So many details whirled in my head, I couldn't think straight. What a pathetic reporter I was! Armed with all the information I had, I still didn't really know anything. This story was far different from the other two blockbusters I'd tackled in the last six months. This one seemed to have no clear focus, no apparent motive, and yet I knew that nothing this weird happens without a reason. I thought about what Mazzie La Casse had said about the unsuspecting illegals dying by the hundreds from heat and exposure in the remote regions of the southwest deserts, especially during the burning months of summer. Years could pass and still hikers, campers and Border Patrol agents would stumble upon the sad remains—a pile of sun-bleached bones, a watch, a coin, something, some sign that the person had once resided on earth. So then, how could people just vanish into thin air without any trace? Wasn't it entirely possible that during the past two weeks the *coyote* in question had returned to Mexico, been picked up by the Border Patrol or just melded into the Hispanic population? But on the other hand, if he had disappeared along with the other passengers in the van carrying Javier's mother and possibly Lupe's relatives, where was his body? Where were the bodies of all the others? More importantly, *why* were these people missing?

All at once a feeling of intense weariness washed over me. I felt utterly alone. Utterly overwhelmed. "Face it, O'Dell," I grumbled, "you're in over your head on this one." I was supposed to be on vacation, damn it! I should be at home preparing for my romantic getaway with Tally, and instead, because of my own bullheadedness, I'd chosen to make Lupe's seemingly unsolvable problem my own.

Again, I wondered what had possessed me to think I could unscramble a situation this complicated in one weekend?

Totally immersed in thought, I almost drove past the turnoff to the Sundog Ranch. I hit the brakes and turned right, passing under a graceful wooden arch flanked by several sun-faded wagon wheels. After traveling for more than twenty minutes along a well-worn dirt lane that meandered through miles of hilly mesquite and yucca-covered rangeland dotted with grazing cattle, stock tanks and spinning windmills, I began to appreciate just how big the place was. Signs along side the road warned in both English and Spanish that this was PRIVATE PROPERTY and NO TRESPASSING was permitted. Considering the ranch's close proximity to the border, the signs seemed ineffectual at best.

The topography changed subtly as I drove toward the gentle foothills of the Baboquivari Mountains. Spectacular upthrusts of smooth rounded sandstone boulders in all shapes and sizes dramatically transformed the grassy landscape. Lush green vegetation hugged the banks of a dry creek bed charting a serpentine course among the outcroppings.

I was beginning to think the road would go on forever when it suddenly widened into a sandy drive bordered by a white wooden fence and shaded by tall cottonwood trees. When I rounded a corner, an impressive two-story ranch house with a giant American flag billowing in the steady breeze jumped into view. It was a large, rambling place sporting three large dormer windows set against a red roof flanked by stone chimneys at each end. Beneath the generous overhang a wide porch wrapped around both sides. Within easy walking distance sat four white cottages nestled against the rocky hillside. Bordering the north side of the main house lay a series of outbuildings and a large red barn enclosed in pipe fencing. A string of horses stood at a long hitching post. As I drew closer, a ripple of surprise snaked through me at the sight of so many people packed into the clearing. I parked at the end of a row of cars and walked towards the house while watching two tough-looking, sun-weathered wranglers tighten saddle cinches and adjust stirrups for a group of men, women and children sitting astride the waiting horses. The air was filled with shrieks of laughter, bird song and lively chatter—a carnival-like atmosphere totally different from Tally's place, where raising cattle and breeding Appaloosa horses was considered serious business. I searched my memory. Why was it again that he'd had to come down here so many times these past few months?

"Hello," said a cheery female voice. "Can I help you with something?"

I turned to see a smiling, pleasant-faced woman standing on the porch. Smartly clad in a crisp white blouse, plaid vest and a chocolate-colored broomstick skirt, she hooked a strand of wispy strawberry blonde hair behind one ear while descending the stairs towards me.

I smiled back and extended a hand. "Hi, my name is Kendall O'Dell. You're probably expecting me."

Still smiling, she stared at me, looking slightly perplexed. "I'm sorry, do we have a reservation for you?"

After a slight hesitation, I repeated, "Reservation?"

"Well, don't worry," she assured me, appearing slightly chagrined, "we're still new at this and someone just probably forgot to write your name down. I'm sure we can find space for one more."

I stared at her uncomprehending for several seconds before turning to look again at the boisterous group of people on horseback and then back to the row of cars, many of which bore out of state license plates. And then it hit me. The Sundog was a guest ranch. It also finally sank in that some of the horses pawing the ground impatiently were handsome Appaloosas just like the ones Tally raised. Had they come from the Starfire? And if so, why hadn't Tally ever mentioned this to me? Or, I thought uncomfortably, perhaps he had and I hadn't been listening.

"If you don't mind sharing," the woman went on, "I can put you in one of the guest cottages with that nice lady from New Jersey over there on the chestnut mare."

"We've got a little misunderstanding," I said, turning back to her. "I'm here about the injured cat."

One hand flew to her mouth. "Oh, I'm sorry. You're the one Payton told us about. If you can wait a few minutes, I'll be glad to...oh, wait, here he comes now." She pointed towards the pickup rolling into the parking area. The decibel level of the noisy crowd of trail riders rose as they urged a latecomer to mount up. A heavyset man wearing spanking new blue jeans and a brightly printed shirt that clearly indicated his 'greenhorn' status, waddled towards the last horse for a leg up from the waiting wrangler. It took a couple of tries before he made it into the saddle.

I couldn't suppress a grin. It hadn't been that long ago, I'd worn a similar outfit on my first horseback ride with Tally. Had that only been six months ago? I no longer felt like a newcomer, but it dawned on me watching this group fumble around for stirrups and reins, that I wasn't that far removed from my 'city girl' ways.

"Grandma, Grandma, look what Daddy found for me!" shouted a small red-haired boy breaking from Payton's side and running towards us holding something high above his head. I returned Payton's wave of greeting as the woman knelt and spread her arms wide. "What have you got for me, sweetie?"

"A rattlesnake skin," the excited child announced, extending his hand to show her the gauzy brown and gold pattern. "Isn't that cool?"

"Yes, very," she said, recoiling slightly. She stood and brushed her skirt as Payton walked up. "I hope you're careful when you take him on these snake hunting jaunts with you." There was an undertone of reproach in her voice.

"Please don't concern yourself, Twyla," he answered evenly, ruffling the boy's hair. "Rest assured that he's never in any danger."

"If you say so." Her head cocked at the sound of a phone ringing inside the open front door of the big ranch house. "Excuse me, I have to get that." She trotted up the steps and Payton said, "Kendall—may I call you Kendall?"

"By all means."

"I'd like you to meet my son, Brett. Brett, this is Kendall."

"She has the same color hair as us," the little boy observed, staring up at me with surprised eyes.

Payton laughed. "Very true. This is the very nice lady who rescued the little kitty earlier today."

"It's actually your dad who rescued him," I told him, wishing I could add, *'And it was your malicious uncle who tried to run over her,'* but I contained myself. I would address that issue soon.

"You'll be happy to know that Dean has looked her over pretty thoroughly and seems to feel that she'll recover in time. Would you like to go see her?"

"Absolutely, and if I could use a phone...."

The steady beat of horse hooves on the sandy earth interrupted my words. When I turned to look, it seemed as if the tourists, ranch hands, and even the birds had all fallen silent. Every eye was riveted on the young, blonde woman in the hot pink shirt cantering into the clearing astride a stunning white Appaloosa with a perfect dappled-gray blanket adorning its hindquarters. Aware that she had a captive audience, she beamed us a winning smile and then demonstrated her excellent horsemanship by maneuvering the animal to rear up on its hind legs several times, each time waving her black hat to the appreciative crowd like a rodeo queen. Amid the ooh's and aahh's from the trail riders, she trotted over to us and dismounted with fluid grace. She tossed back long golden hair and fixed a pair of reflective periwinkle blue eyes on me. "Hi, I'm Bethany Beaumont. Welcome to the Sundog."

For some reason I could not begin to define, my reaction to her was unexpected, yet instantaneous. I disliked her.

12

I think she only half heard my name over Brett's excited squeal. "Mommy! Look what Daddy found for me. Can I keep it in my room?"

Her facial muscles twitched in a valiant effort to repress her disgust at the sight of the crinkly snakeskin. As he rushed towards her, she put a restraining hand against one shoulder to hold him at arm's length. "That's really…exciting, honey, but I'll look at it closer another time, okay?" she said, ignoring the boy's crestfallen expression and locking her frosty blue gaze on Payton. "I didn't expect you to be here." Her voice sounded flat, cold, impersonal.

"Sorry to disappoint you," he said, maintaining a light tone while shooting a worried glance at Brett.

"It wouldn't be the first time."

He inhaled a deep controlling breath before saying quietly, "Save the sarcasm. Now that you've seen fit to return from California, I'm afraid you're going to have to accept the fact that I intend to exercise my parental rights. You'll have to get used to me coming here."

I squirmed. Witnessing their very personal exchange made me ill at ease, but as I considered Bethany Beaumont's petite figure, stunningly beautiful features — upturned nose, flawless sun-kissed skin, rosebud lips and dimpled chin—an indefinable pang of apprehension chilled my heart.

An older ranch hand with a sun-browned face called out, "Come on, Miss B, we got a bunch of anxious cowpokes and gals champing at the bit to get a move on." As if to reinforce his statement, several of the horses whinnied and shook their heads, jangling the reins.

She glanced around and issued the man a dazzling smile that now seemed artificial to me. So far I was less than enchanted with both of the Beaumont offspring. "Be right there, Hal," she answered in a singsong voice.

Returning her attention to Brett, she bent down to eye level with him. "These nice people over here are waiting for Mommy to show them some more of the ranch, so I'll see you in a little while, okay? Now run inside and get Mommy's black jacket, it might get chilly." She cast an upward glance at the swiftly moving clouds.

"Okay!" He flashed her an endearing smile, raced up the steps and disappeared through the front door. Envying his escape, I cleared my throat and pointed to my car. "Payton, I'll wait for you over there."

Bethany stared at me blankly as if she'd forgotten I was there and then her questioning gaze flickered between the two of us. "Oh? I didn't realize you were here together. How nice." The insinuation in her voice was clear, but before I could set the record straight Payton put up a warning hand. "Kendall, stay. And, Bethany, if you still feel the need to belittle me, could you please do it in private and not in front of Brett?"

"Did I ask for your opinion?" Their eyes clashed as the little boy burst out the door and handed the fringed leather jacket to his mother. Like quicksilver, she was all goodness and light. "Thank you, honeybun." She slipped it on, grabbed the horse's reins, but then swung around to face Payton. "Oh, by the way, I thought you said you were taking him to a movie in Green Valley?"

"Our plans changed."

"We hiked near Wolf's Head," Brett volunteered. "My legs are really tired."

Irritation flared in Bethany's eyes. "Not another dreadful snake hunting escapade?" Pouting prettily for Brett's sake and possibly mine, she added, "The poor baby looks depressed. Don't tell me you forced him to accompany you again to that maudlin...*shrine* you've created for Laura?" She shook her head sadly. "I wish you wouldn't include him in your personal obsession without my permission."

Jaw muscles working in a struggle to maintain composure, he laid a protective hand on his son's shoulder. "You always have to have the last word, don't you? Just as a reminder, I don't need your permission in regards to what Brett and I do with our private time together. And you needn't worry, I know exactly what I'm doing."

Bravo, Payton. Good thing he appeared to be a low-octane kind of guy. I'd have decked her.

"Oh, yes, I forgot, you're an expert at just about everything."

A wave of embarrassment rolled through me. I could understand the petty motivation for putting her ex-husband down in front of Brett, but why did the perfect-looking creature feel compelled to air their private differences in front of a complete stranger?

Refusing to respond to her scorn, Payton's lips stretched into a tight smile. "You mustn't keep your adoring fans waiting, my dear."

"Have him home by six sharp," she said, carefully placing the western hat over her curls. "You know how disappointed Grampy Boo is if he's not in his usual place for dinner." She turned away, but not before I heard her mutter under her breath, "What a loser." Having won the confrontation, at least in her mind, Bethany grabbed the reins, nodded to me, then blew a kiss to Brett before swinging into the saddle. "Goodbye, Jack," she said, training a malicious glance in Payton's direction before cantering to the head of the waiting line of riders where she was joined by a rugged-looking young cowhand who all but devoured her with his eyes. Damn, she did sit a horse well.

When I turned back, a little zing of surprise shot through me. While Brett's eyes were aglow with admiration for his beautiful mother, the rapt expression in Payton's gaze reflected a poignant combination of pain, resentment and a trace of reluctant awe. Oh, no. Was he still carrying a torch for her?

"Why does Mommy call you Jack sometimes?" Brett asked with a puzzled frown, watching his mother ride off down the driveway chatting gaily with the dudes perched awkwardly on their mounts, holding tight to the saddle pommels.

His sheepish expression made me wonder too, but he dismissed her remark with, "It's just one of her little jokes. Now, how about we take Kendall over to Uncle Dean's place to see how the kitten is doing?"

"Can I take Rascal with us to play with her?"

"Mmmm, maybe we should wait awhile before we do that. The kitty might not be quite well enough to appreciate a sixty pound Lab just yet," he added for my benefit. "And to keep everybody happy, run in and tell your grandma we'll be back by dinnertime."

The boy dutifully skipped up the stairs again and Payton motioned for me to come with him. "Sorry about that," he said as I fell into step beside him. "I hope you didn't get the wrong impression of Bethany. Sometimes she tries to overcompensate for her innate feelings of insecurity."

I shot him an incredulous glance. She appeared far from insecure to me, and the phrase, 'Well, she's not exactly Miss Congeniality' jumped to mind, but I bit it back. "Not at all. Actually, I think she's one of the more charming people I've ever met."

His appreciative laugh filled the air. "She can be…as long as you treat her as though she's the center of the universe."

Not having the slightest idea what he was talking about and since I barely knew him, I opted not to comment. When he opened the passenger door of his truck, I halted in surprise. "I thought we were going to see the kitten."

"We are. Dean's place is about three miles from here."

"Oh. Listen, I'm really sorry to put you out for a second time in one day."

He waved away my apology. "No problem. Lucky for me, he was still here at the house when I came to pick up Brett this morning, so this will actually be my first visit there in quite some time."

I climbed into the truck. "Well, whatever. I definitely owe you one. How about I buy you dinner to make up for ruining your breakfast this morning?" The mention of food made me realize I'd never had lunch.

He smiled. "I'm tied up tonight, but thanks anyway."

"Breakfast tomorrow?"

"You don't owe me anything."

"The heck I don't. Listen, if you hadn't been available at that exact moment...well, you saved the day."

"In some cases, timing is everything. I'm glad I was there to help," he replied, shutting my door. "I happen to believe that animals are the true innocents of the world. In exchange for being cared for they offer us loyalty and unconditional love." He followed that with a wry, "And they certainly don't screw you over the way people do."

I sensed he was referring to his current 'out-of-favor' situation with his ex-wife and probably the entire Beaumont clan. Having recently been down the rocky road of divorce, I could sympathize with his situation. I knew what it was like to be drawn into the bosom of a large family, loved, pampered, and then thrown out in the cold when the marriage fizzled. It was a rude awakening to realize that, in all but a few exceptional cases, acceptance bequeathed to the new spouse didn't extend much beyond the divorce decree. Payton Kleinwort appeared to be a compassionate soul and it made me wonder again how he'd ever gotten matched up with a vixen like Bethany Beaumont. "I'm not letting you off the hook so easily," I put in. "How about lunch tomorrow? Right now, my plans are to head home in the afternoon, so I could meet you at the café there in Arivaca on my way out of town. What do you say?"

His eyes glittered with amusement. "You're very persistent."

"Yes, I am."

He threw up his hands in mock surrender. "Okay. Lunch it is, but it's going to have to be early. Will eleven-thirty work?"

"Sounds perfect."

He nodded, I nodded, and sudden silence fell between us. To fill the conversation void until Brett's return, I asked, "So tell me, how big is this place anyway?"

"In the neighborhood of fifty sections, which translates to about thirty thousand acres."

My mouth dropped. "Wow." I'd thought Tally's ranch was big, but the Sundog dwarfed the Starfire. Reaching for the seatbelt, I remarked, "The cost of running an outfit this size must be phenomenal."

He dipped his head in the direction of the riders trailing over a rise. "That's the operative word. It's been touch-and-go the last few years for a lot of the ranchers in this area and not many have survived. It was Twyla's idea to convert it into a place where tourists and other folks could come to enjoy the...ranch experience," he said, crooking his fingers like quotation marks around the last two words. "What with the high cost of feed, the drought, cattle prices being stagnant, then figuring in the taxes, well, it's not been good. Not good at all."

"You sound very knowledgeable. Do you have a ranch around here too?"

An imperceptible shadow crossed behind his eyes before he blinked it away. "A long time ago in another life," he replied, abruptly moving away from my window towards the driver's side. I longed to know the reason for his curious reaction, but his taciturn expression discouraged any further discussion of a subject that was apparently off limits.

At that moment Brett returned. Chattering happily, he scrambled onto the seat, squeezed between us, and busied himself with a hand-held video game as Payton maneuvered the truck out the driveway and turned south. The sandy ribbon of road wound its way through treeless hills blanketed with tall grass undulating like golden waves in the erratic wind. Each time we'd dip down into a wash, Brett would whoop with laughter. "That tickles! Go faster, Daddy!"

Payton arched a brow for permission and when I smiled he accelerated until my stomach soared and dipped as if we were on a roller coaster ride. All at once, he hit the brakes to avoid a jackrabbit and a loud thump from behind made me turn and peer through the back window into the camper shell. A red and white plastic cooler had launched forward striking the plastic window. There were several more stacked behind it. "You guys must have had *some* picnic," I remarked with a laugh, thumbing over my shoulder.

Payton glanced at me. "What?"

"Picnic. It looks like you have at least a half a dozen coolers back there."

Squealing with laughter, Brett pulled his attention from the beeping game in his lap. "Those aren't for food. That's how Daddy keeps his snakes cold."

"Oh, boy. I'm almost afraid to ask why anyone would want to keep snakes cold, but I must."

Payton chuckled. "It's nothing too mysterious. I collect rattlesnakes and sell them to a couple of labs in the Midwest that process snake venom for hospitals."

"No kidding? And you can make a living?"

"Not really. It's just a part-time thing to help make some extra money when I'm down here to see my favorite little guy," he said, casting Brett a look of affection as he smoothed a lock of rust-colored hair back from the boy's forehead.

I glanced down at the contented little boy snuggled against his father's side, taking note of his well-polished boots and clean, crisp clothing that smelled of fabric softener. I couldn't help but think of the contrast to poor little Javier cringing in his dark hideaway, homeless, motherless, and clutching a toy bunny for comfort.

"So you don't live here full time?" I asked Payton.

"No. I teach and work in the herpetology lab at the university in Tucson."

Brett chimed in, "Sometimes Daddy catches turtles and Gila Monsters and tarantulas too!"

A tremor of revulsion ricocheted through me. "Ugh. I can do without the tarantulas, but I thought it was against the law to capture Gila Monsters. Aren't they considered a protected species?"

"Yes. But, my job allows me to obtain a Wildlife Holding Permit."

Only half listening, my attention was fixed on an irregular jumble of wind-carved pinnacles that looked like giant volcanic chimneys. They dominated the southwestern horizon and I was pretty sure they were the same ones I'd noticed yesterday while traveling along the road to Sasabe. Pointing, I asked, "What's that odd-looking mountain range called? Is it in Mexico?"

"That's Wolf's Head. It actually straddles the border," Payton replied, slowing for a cattle guard. "And to anticipate your next question, its name is derived from a prominent rock formation on the southern tip." He hitched his shoulders, grinning wryly. "Personally, I think it looks more like the head of a mule."

I tossed him a quick glance, recalling Bethany's sarcastic remark concerning a shrine for someone named Laura, and I couldn't help but wonder why anyone would want to be buried in such a remote spot. "I'm confused. I thought we were only a mile or so from the border, but the mountain looks to be further away than that."

"Remember, the border doesn't run in a straight line. A couple of sections of the Sundog span it, as well as a huge section of Tohono O'odham reservation land which actually runs along it for, oh, I don't know, maybe seventy-five miles and then stretches south into Mexico."

As he continued talking, I noticed the saffron-tinged rangeland giving way to patches of blackened ground strewn with the withered remains of mesquite bushes, scorched yucca plants and yellowed prickly pear. The devastation expanded until it extended on both sides of the road as far as I could see. "Looks like they've had one heck of a grassfire."

"That," he said with a broad sweep of one hand, "is a perfect example of the problems caused by this God-awful border mess." The sharp undertone of resentment in his voice softened slightly when he added, "Sorry. I forgot you'd probably find a statement like that offensive."

"Why would you think that?"

He slid a sidelong glance at Brett who appeared totally focused on his game. "Well, you did say you were here to report on the rally and since I noticed that your companion is Hispanic, well, I assumed your sympathies probably lean towards the illegals."

Oops! I'd almost forgotten that was supposed to be my cover story. "Don't be too quick to make assumptions. Lupe is here on an unrelated matter, but it's my intention to do what I always do and that will be to write an objective piece containing the facts of the situation." It suddenly dawned on me that in the twenty-four hours since giving my hastily fabricated reason for being here to Hank Breslow, a genuine interest in the border problems had blossomed. The boiling cauldron of opposing forces in this region was great fodder for a feature article. Maybe several.

He flicked me a considering look before refocusing on the road. "That will be refreshing. The media's been having a field day lately pandering to these border rights groups and the Mexican politicians we're trying so hard not to offend. Their articles are completely biased and they make the ranchers in this area out to be the villains when all they're trying to do is protect their own property. Talk to Champ Beaumont. Talk to Dean. Talk to any other rancher dealing with this nightmare day in and day out." The tremor of emotion in his voice and the little splotches of color in his cheeks left little doubt where his sympathies lay. But in a quick turnabout, he concluded with a blasé, "Glad I don't have to deal with it."

A sudden ringing made me jump and I stared in astonishment as Payton fished a tiny cell phone from his shirt pocket and said, "Yeah?" He listened intently. "Really? Listen, I've got company. Catch you later," he said, abruptly ending the conversation as I pulled my own phone from my purse and powered it on. Sure enough, the 'roam' message pulsed back at me. "Well, what do you know?" I murmured, shaking my head.

"What?" asked Payton.

"Who would think there would be cell service out here in the middle of nowhere when I haven't been able to use this damn thing since I left Tucson."

He chuckled. "I know what you mean. The signal is erratic at best. There's a very narrow corridor where we can get service. The mountains probably block it." As if to demonstrate his statement, the 'no service' message blinked at me again as we dipped into a ravine. "I see what you mean."

He arched a concerned brow. "You need to call someone? I can turn around and go back until you pick up a signal again."

"Thank you, but it's nothing that can't wait until later." I tucked the phone back in my purse, content with the fact that I'd have all evening to make calls back home and probably spend some time on the Internet doing more research.

We rode in silence for another minute or two until a wooden ranch house bordered by a hodgepodge of outbuildings, corrals and tin-roofed sheds along with another building in the early stages of construction, came into view. "Is that going to be a new house?" I asked, referring to the framed-in structure.

Payton turned left into a long driveway spanned by barbed wire. "No, that's the new barn. The old one went up like a tinderbox in the middle of the night about two weeks ago." His words came out crisp and bitter.

I stared. "You're saying illegals set the fire?"

"I'm saying exactly that."

"On purpose?"

A quick shrug. "Who knows? You saw the end results as we came in. The fire spread so fast, it scorched over thirty acres of prime grazing land." He cast a sidelong glance at me. "Are you in the market for an ironic footnote to your article?" There was presumption of mocking challenge in his question.

"Always."

"Needless to say, Dean about had a stroke. He rounded up a couple of his hands and they finally tracked the group down hiding in a clump of greasewood. Now, here's the kicker. One of the them was a young woman in labor and because he was the only one around who knew what to do, Dean ended up delivering the baby." He brought the truck to a halt and shoved it into park. "Can you believe that? Instead of these interlopers suffering the consequences for being the lawbreakers that they are and causing untold damage to the ranch, the punishment for their deed was to have our own government grant the newborn American citizenship. And, of course *we* all end up paying for the mother's medical and living expenses until they're deported. Think about how fair that is when you write your story."

I definitely would. As I stepped from the truck, it struck me that nothing he'd told me so far was more indicative of the fearful atmosphere in the region than the sight of heavy iron bars crisscrossing every window of the weathered ranch house, which was encircled in a barrier of chain link fencing at least eight feet high. Two German Shepherds, barking ferociously, paced the interior, eying me with suspicion. In stark contrast to the idyllic western setting of cattle and horses grazing peacefully under an endless sweep of majestic blue sky, the house presented a disturbing picture. It more resembled a prison compound. For the first time since my arrival, I felt a flash of anger towards the undocumented immigrants, anger that American citizens should be forced to live this way in their own country. I could only imagine how the residents who had to deal daily with these problems must feel. It was little wonder the ranchers were forming coalitions and White power movements were flourishing.

"There's Uncle Dean," Brett shouted, running towards a tall, rangy-looking man of perhaps sixty whose deeply wrinkled complexion bore testimony to years spent baking in the Arizona sun.

"How you doin', Squirt?" the older man inquired, swinging him effortlessly onto his shoulders. Payton introduced me and after a hearty handshake he ushered us through the sturdy gate and into a spacious flag-stoned entryway that opened into a large room saturated with the sugary aroma of fresh baked goods. Self-consciously, I clutched my growling midsection as my gaze swept over the gleaming copper pots in the modern kitchen that occupied the left hand corner of the room. The center contained a dining area that led down two steps into an airy family room filled with bulky pine furniture, accented with tangerine and turquoise pillows. A magnificent floor to ceiling beehive fireplace dominated the right side of the room.

"What's cooking?" Dean called to a silver-haired Hispanic woman, kneading dough on a butcher-block counter.

"Oatmeal raisin cookies," she replied, flashing a gold-toothed grin. "You will also have fresh pecan rolls with honey for breakfast."

"Ah, you spoil me, Inez," he said, with a lopsided smile, lowering Brett to the floor before turning to me. "So, you've come to check on my little patient, huh?"

"Yes, thank you very much for looking after her. Is she going to be all right?"

"She suffered a nasty concussion. I stitched the gash behind her left ear and she's going to be favoring her left hind leg for awhile, but other than that, I expect she'll recover."

My mood lightened as we followed him along a narrow hallway with an uneven stone floor. As we passed several bedrooms and a bathroom in various stages of remodeling, Payton said, "You're doing wonders with the old place, Dean." The wistful quality of his words, coupled with the nostalgic glaze in his eyes, brought to mind his earlier remark about having lived on a ranch in another life and I wondered again about his poignant response.

"Thanks. I can only pray that those goddamn wetbacks don't burn the rest of the place to the ground after I've spent the bulk of my retirement renovating it," he griped, his forehead bunching in a scowl. "I should have thought twice about letting Twyla talk me and Henrietta into moving down here into this damned hornet's nest."

"I wish I could wave a magic wand and just make the problem disappear," Payton remarked with a sigh, "but I'm sure everyone over at the big house appreciates you being here to protect the southern flank."

Dean grunted his response and ushered me into a small, irregularly shaped room at the far end of the hall. It was crammed full of boxes, an X-Ray machine, a row of cages, a metal examining table and various other pieces of medical equipment that had obviously once resided in a veterinary hospital. In another corner stood sections of shelving packed full of more cardboard boxes, piles of books, and several more of the same types of coolers Payton used for his snake collections.

Brett rushed to one of the cages and wiggled a finger through the wire. The kitten lay at the farthest corner rolled into a tight ball. Disturbed by the noise, she stirred and cracked open brilliant green eyes. "She's so cute! I'll ask Mommy if we can keep her." His expectant gaze locked onto Payton, who shook his head sadly.

"Sorry, little buddy, your mom is allergic to cats, remember? That's why you have Rascal instead."

His face fell. "Oh. Where will the poor kitty live?"

"I guess she'll be going home with me." The sound of my own voice amazed me. I hadn't really made up my mind until that exact moment. I directed a questioning glance at Dean. "That is, if she's ready to travel."

He looked uncertain. "I wouldn't mind having another day or so to observe her. Any chance you could pick her up on Tuesday?"

"Not really. I was planning to leave tomorrow afternoon."

He rubbed his chin, considering my answer, then said, "Tell you what, I have to pick up my wife at the airport in Tucson tomorrow at one-thirty, but we should be back here by three at the latest."

I did a quick calculation. If I kept my lunch date with Payton in Arivaca, that meant I'd have to double back here afterwards to pick her up. But, then, that might work to my advantage, giving me a couple of hours to check out Sasabe and Morita. After that, I could just zip up route 286 instead of returning to the Interstate. "That should work out for me."

The two men beamed their approval, but tears of disappointment brimmed in Brett's eyes. In an obvious effort to distract him, Payton swept the boy into his arms. "Hey, partner, what do you say we go lasso a couple of those nice, hot cookies from Inez?"

Brightening perceptively, he clamped his hands around his father's neck and sniffed, "Okay."

I wouldn't have minded joining them for a few cookies myself but Payton said, "We'll run along and give you some time to bond with your new companion."

I thanked him and turned to Dean as he opened the cage door. "Come on over and introduce yourself."

Bending to eye-level, I reached inside to stroke the cat's soft fur. "Hi, there, sweetheart." At first there was no response and then a great rattling purr filled the cage. Slowly, she rose, arched her back, yawned, and then stared up at me with questioning eyes. Her deep orange color made me think of marmalade. Yes. Marmalade would be a great name. Suddenly, I couldn't wait to show her to Tally, but I'd have to ask Ginger if she could keep her while we were on our trip. Dean encouraged me to hold the cat so I carefully reached in and pulled her out, cradling her to my chest like a baby. As I stroked her, the vibration of her contented purrs ignited a warm glow inside me and I knew I was a goner.

"Where do you call home?" Dean asked, leaning his weight against the cluttered countertop, stuffing his hands in the front pockets of his jeans.

"Castle Valley."

He puckered his mouth. "Nice place. Ted Parkins is the doc up your way. Good man. I went to college with him a couple of centuries ago." He inclined his head towards the cat. "This little lady's been on her own for quite awhile. If I were you, I'd get her in to see him right away. She's going to need inoculations and you're going to want to get her spayed pretty soon. I gave her a shot of antibiotics, but she should have oral medication for at least another week."

Oh, dear. Now I'd have to inconvenience Ginger even further. "I'm leaving for California early in the morning. You don't have any antibiotics here, do you? I'd be more than happy to pay you for them."

He shook his head slowly, but I could see the wheels turning behind his unfocused gaze. "Tell you what I can do. I'll stop by a colleague's office on the way back here tomorrow and pick you up a bottle of the liquid. Will that help out?"

What a nice guy. I flashed him an appreciative grin. "More than you know."

"Well, all right then."

"I can't thank you and Payton enough. Did he happen to tell you how this whole thing happened?" The kitten buried her face against my chest and I held her tighter.

His face darkened. "Yeah. Said Jason was showing off again in his new truck. Man, that kid's got a wild streak that needs taming. But every time Champ comes down hard on him Twyla comes running to rescue his skinny hide. I've told my sister time and again that she's too easy on him. That boy needs to be reined in before he gets involved in something really serious."

I longed to tell him about the incident with Lupe and that his nephew's cruel behavior went beyond someone having a good time, but I knew that most people weren't too keen about receiving criticism from a stranger. "On the flip side, Payton seems like a real standup guy."

"That's for sure. And considering the string of bad luck the poor guy's had in his life, not to mention the raft of crap my spoiled ass rotten niece has dished out, well, it's amazing he even comes around anymore."

His statement tweaked my curiosity, but the thud of footsteps outside in the hallway put my growing list of questions about this affable young man on hold.

"So, does she own you yet?" Payton asked with a merry twinkle in his eye as he ducked under the low doorway with Brett still in his arms. I cocked my head in question and he grinned. "When you get to know cats better you'll soon find out which one of you is really calling the shots."

Chuckling, Dean concurred as I gently placed Marmalade back in her cage. I still couldn't believe it. I was now a pet owner and the new responsibility weighed on me. My mind spun ahead to all the things I would need to acquire for my new roommate—a litter box, food, and cat toys. Lots of cat toys.

A hazy gold and orchid twilight accented by smudges of dark, thin clouds was settling into the valley, throwing dark pockets of shadows into the deep clefts and canyons of the surrounding mountain ranges when we finally climbed into the truck. The chill wind made me wish I'd thought to bring my jacket along. Dean had declined my offer to pay for his veterinary services and as we headed back, it dawned on me that even though I'd worked out details for tomorrow, I still didn't know where I'd be spending the night. Dog-tired didn't even begin to describe how weary I felt. The hour-long drive to Green Valley was growing less appealing by the minute, so perhaps I'd best consider Twyla's offer to bunk with the lady from New Jersey. On top of that, even though the cookies kindly offered to me by Inez had taken the edge off, hunger pangs bounced around my belly, making the quest for dinner uppermost on my mind.

Brett fell asleep almost immediately and, except for exchanging a few phrases of small talk, Payton seemed preoccupied in his own thoughts, making for a quiet trip back to the main house. In the fading light, set snugly against the dark backdrop of the hills, warm light spilling from every window, the Beaumont house emitted a message of cheerful welcome. When I stole a look at Payton's rigid jaw line, I could guess what he was thinking. Total strangers were now welcome here, but that invitation no longer extended to him. The twinge of sympathy had me thanking my lucky stars that I'd stood firm against having a child early in my marriage or I'd be facing the same heartache of being a part-time parent.

Gently, he shook Brett awake and I walked beside him as he carried the still-sleepy child up the steps and rang the doorbell as any other outsider would. "This is the hardest part," he murmured to me, tightening his hold on the boy.

The door flew open to reveal a diminutive Chinese woman wearing a sour expression on her sallow, wrinkled face. "You bring boy late for dinner," she admonished Payton, reaching high to pull Brett from his arms. "Everybody eat already. Watch out. Missy Bethany not happy."

Facial muscles quivering, he relinquished his hold and then glanced at his watch. "Nice to see you too, Lin Su," he replied mildly, ignoring her criticism. "She said to have him back by..."

"Five," said Bethany stepping into the glow of the yellow porch light. "I distinctly told you dinner was at five." Eyes aglitter, obviously spoiling for a fight, she looked like a fierce lion with her golden tresses tumbling around her face. As always, injustice of any kind heightened my blood pressure and I was close to jumping to his defense when Payton insisted, "You said six." He was breathing hard through his nostrils.

"Oh, I think not," she said with playful spite, "but I guess we'll forgive you. Please try to be more considerate of other people next time."

Payton opened his mouth, shut it, opened it again and then, apparently thinking better of it, turned to me. "Kendall, I'll see you for lunch tomorrow." With that, he wheeled around and hurried away into the darkness. What a thoroughly obnoxious family. I couldn't begin to imagine what it was about these people Tally found so appealing that he'd go out of his way to come here and spend any amount of time. I made an instant decision not to stay the night. If I had time perhaps I'd stop by tomorrow, in hopes of speaking with Champ Beaumont about the location of the butchered animals found on his property. "Would it be possible for me to use a telephone?"

Her inquisitive gaze darted toward Payton's retreating taillights and then back to me. I knew she was still under the impression that we were together, but I didn't feel compelled to confirm or deny her suspicions. Let her wonder.

"In the kitchen," she said, waving carelessly towards an open archway to my left. I felt like one of the hired help as she dismissed me with an imperious nod and vanished through another doorway before I could even thank her. Annoyed, tired and hungry, I stepped into an enormous, high-ceilinged room bustling with activity and smelling deliciously of garlic, onions and other spices. Twyla stood in front of a side-by-side refrigerator barking orders in Spanish as she pulled out pie wedges and handed them to two young Hispanic girls. Another bronze-skinned woman whose blunt features identified her as Native American scoured pots at the sink. I fished my phone card from my purse and glanced longingly at the kitchen table strewn with empty plates, the remains of a salad, half-eaten dinner rolls and the well-picked bones of a barbecued-pork roast. Yum. Bet that had been scrumptious. At the far end, a burly man with a sun-crinkled face capped by a thick shock of gray hair sat reading a newspaper, his boots propped up on another chair, seemingly oblivious to all the commotion.

Her hands filled with four pie plates, Twyla's long skirt billowed behind her as she rushed by heading towards an open doorway where I caught a glimpse of gaily-chattering people seated at tables covered with red-checkered cloths adorned with kerosene lamps. "I'm sorry, Miss...ah...Miss ah...."

"O'Dell."

"Right after you left with Payton this afternoon I filled that vacant bed with another guest." She smiled a fleeting apology and hurried to feed the waiting diners, now being serenaded by someone playing a guitar and crooning a popular western tune.

Fine. I hadn't planned to stay under any circumstances. "Excuse me," I called to the man at the end of the long table, "is there a phone book I can use?"

The newspaper lowered enough for me to make out two eyes the same periwinkle blue as Bethany's. "Bottom shelf on that cart right behind you." The paper rose again, dismissing me. I shrugged. He probably assumed that I was one of the guests.

I tried several places before I found a vacancy, which I secured with my credit card. Then I called Lupe to see if she'd arrived home safely. She sounded miserable, so I didn't try to share the news of the missing *coyote* with her, just told her to rest and I'd talk to her tomorrow. I was dialing Tally's number just as Twyla returned and collapsed in a chair beside the man I assumed was her husband, Champ Beaumont. She leaned over and began speaking to him in low undertones. While I waited for someone to answer, I caught bits and pieces of her conversation that included Payton's name and my own. He lowered the newspaper long enough to gaze at me reflectively for a few seconds before returning his attention to his reading material.

When I heard Ruth's lackluster 'hullo' immediate irritation flooded my chest. What, I wondered, were the odds that Tally would get this message either? As expected, Ronda wasn't around, so I had no choice but to deal with her again. Perhaps I'd try diplomacy. "Ruth, do you have something handy to jot down a note?"

"I don't need to write anything down," she snapped. "Just say what you have to say and I'll tell him when he gets in."

I burned to say, 'Oh, yeah? Like the silly little game you played yesterday?' but I bit it back. "I'm calling from the Sundog Ranch. Tell Tally I'll be out and about all day tomorrow, but I'll be home in the evening around seven as planned."

"Anything else?"

"He can try my cell phone if he wants to."

"Okay." Click.

Nonplussed by her insolent behavior as always, I cradled the receiver and exhaled a long, calming breath before turning to thank my hosts. A little thrill of surprise rippled through me at Champ's questioning stare. He tossed the newspaper aside, jumped to his feet and advanced on me. "Excuse me, but I couldn't help but overhear part of your conversation," he said, still wearing a bemused expression. "Did I hear correctly that your name is O'Dell?"

"Yes."

"You're not by any chance from up Castle Valley way, are you?"

"Yes, I am."

His eyes blazed with anticipation. "And you wouldn't happen to be acquainted with a fine young fellow by the name of Bradley Talverson?"

I grinned. "As a matter of fact, I am."

He slapped his thigh and bellowed with laughter. "Well, why the hell didn't you say so in the first place?" He slid a beefy arm around my shoulders and turned to his wife. "Do you know who this pretty little gal is?"

Her delicate features gathered in a frown. "Well, I assumed she was with Payton...."

He tightened his hold on me, announcing in an elated tone, "Don't you recognize her name? This is Kendall *O'Dell*. You know, Tally's girl!"

Twyla's face flushed with confusion. "Well, my goodness, why didn't you say something earlier?"

"The opportunity didn't present itself until now."

"We wouldn't hear of you driving all the way over to Green Valley, would we?" Champ insisted, continuing eye contact with his wife. "I'm sure we can make room someplace for her to stay the night."

Twyla's gaze turned inward for a few seconds before she said vaguely, "Well...all the guest rooms are filled...but I guess I could have some of the girls clean out the sewing room...."

"Please don't go to any trouble on my account," I interjected, sensing that he'd put her on the spot. "I'll be fine with...."

"Problem's solved then. You can cancel those motel reservations," Champ said with a tone of firm conviction, squeezing my shoulder once more. "You had supper yet?"

"Well, no, but...."

"Say no more. I'm sure we can rustle you up some grub too."

"Of course we can," Twyla agreed, beaming me a gracious smile.

After two days of meeting people who hadn't exactly rolled out the welcome wagon, it felt really good to bask in the glow of their concern and genuine acceptance. But the pleasant fuzzy feeling diminished when my glance strayed to Bethany standing still as a stone in the kitchen doorway. There was not the slightest hint of warmth on her face. None. In fact, her eyes, frosty as two blue glaciers, were locked on me with an expression of unadulterated resentment.

13

Hours later, after being peppered with a multitude of questions about my purpose for being in the area, and plied with liquor and more food than one person could possibly eat, I was comfortably ensconced on the second floor in the family wing of the spacious ranch house. Under Twyla's direction, the two young Hispanic women had swiftly cleared out the ironing board, baskets of freshly laundered clothing, assorted boxes and the sewing machine to make room for my arrival. After such an excruciatingly long day, I could hardly wait to snuggle under the covers in the sofa bed for a well-earned night's sleep. But a hot bath sounded awfully good, so I grabbed up my cosmetic bag and headed back down the long L-shaped hallway where Twyla had conducted a brief tour just minutes earlier, proudly showing off the recently remodeled master bedroom suite with its enormous bath and walk-in closets. Bethany's ultra-cute pink and white room was located further along the hall adjacent to Brett's bedroom that boasted one bright red wall and was decorated with cheerful blue and yellow furniture.

I heard water running behind the closed bathroom door, so I killed time by wandering along the wood-paneled corridor admiring original oil paintings depicting Native American culture and western scenes filled with cowboys herding cattle and chasing down wild horses. There were several extraordinary, and I'm certain very expensive, pieces of bronze cowboy sculpture near the wide staircase. At the far end of the hall, I glanced into a partially open doorway and stopped in my tracks when the message emblazoned on a large poster hanging near the door caught my eye. DIE SCUM-SUCKING WETBACKS! Below it was a photograph of Congressman Lyle Stanley and his attractive but gaunt-looking Mexican wife. I leaned in, squinting at the small print that indicated they were entering a hospital in Tucson. The rest of the caption had been torn off and someone had stuck a hunting knife through the paper in the exact region of her heart. The protruding handle cast a menacing shadow on the wall. Whoa, mama. What, I wondered, did the Hispanic staff members think of such a blatant portrait of hatred? I cast a quick look around to see if anyone was near before edging the door open a little further. The entire room, dimly lit by the wavering greenish-blue glow of a 70's style lava lamp and a creepy skull-faced screen saver on a computer monitor, was papered with an array of disturbing posters. ARYAN BROTHERS AWAKE! SUPPORT THE AMERICAN NAZI PARTY! RACIAL PURITY IS AMERICAN SECURITY! WHITE IS RIGHT!

My initial suspicion that this was Jason's room was confirmed when I spotted a framed photo of him posing with several other skinheads in camouflage gear, smiling wickedly while proudly brandishing AK-47 rifles. I knew I shouldn't, but I couldn't resist a closer look. After a cursory glance at the empty hallway, I hurried to the junk-littered dresser and angled the photo towards the light. One of the brawny skinheads standing next to Jason was the evil-looking guy I'd seen in the restaurant and then afterwards in the white truck outside the Shirleys' house. Interesting. I put the photo back, taking note of the 45 caliber handgun and hunting knife resting alongside a pair of binoculars.

I looked around the room. To say it was unkempt would be charitable. The bed was unmade, piles of dirty laundry lay everywhere, but it was the mountain of books and pamphlets that lured me to the computer desk. Using the yellowish light pulsing from the skull, I sifted through some of the mounds of files containing newspaper clippings. Most were examples of border catastrophes befalling the Arizona ranch community, while some focused on the thousands of illegals apprehended by Border Patrol agents just in the past several weeks. Other clippings contained stories of a major drug bust, and the disturbing fact that the leaders of Mexico's most notoriously brutal drug cartel were considering moving their operations from Tijuana to the border with Arizona. I was shocked to read of recent incidents involving Mexican troops firing on American citizens inside our own borders. Whoa. No wonder Walter and his wife had called it quits.

There was also a troubling article regarding the *reconquista* movement. This well-funded Mexican activist group advocated overturning the Guadalupe-Hidalgo Treaty with Mexico and reclaiming the southwestern United States. "Unreal," I whispered, shuffling through additional articles that told horror stories of American women being raped and several local families being robbed and terrorized by Mexican gangs. There were reams of hate literature filled with crude drawings depicting the systematic execution of Jews, Blacks, Arabs and Mexicans, inflammatory anti-government material and scores of gun brochures. But when I came to information he'd downloaded from the Internet that gave detailed instructions for producing various types of explosives, and accompanying articles on how to carry out assassinations in foreign countries, my insides shrank in horror. This kid was one sick puppy.

Deep in thought, I absent-mindedly set the file back on the uneven pile, only to have the whole thing shift and begin to slide off the desk. I made a hasty grab to keep it from hitting the floor and, in the process, bumped the mouse, which removed the screen saver. Suddenly, I was staring at one of Jason Beaumont's e-mail messages. *"Merrily the feast I'll make. Today I'll brew, tomorrow bake; merrily I'll dance and sing, in four days will some strangers bring."*

How weird. Frowning, I glanced at the top of the screen for the sender's address but froze when the thump of footsteps on the stairs closed off the breath in my throat. Cautiously, I tiptoed to the door and peeked around the corner. Oh, my God. It was Jason Beaumont. Yeah, I was just the person he'd want to find snooping around in his room. I searched frantically for a hiding place. With no more than seconds to spare, I chose the age-old standby, and dove under the bed as he tromped into the room and snapped on the light. To my utter dismay, he flopped onto the bed, which caused the springs above my head to sag down until they pressed my chin into the floor. With a loud grunt, he pulled off his rough leather boots and threw them down only inches from my face. Phew! The rank smell practically made me gag, but I dared not move a muscle. I shut my eyes, breathing shallowly through my mouth until the wave of nausea subsided.

Holy crap. How was I going to get out of this one? Would I have to stay here all night? Visions of the luxurious bath, and then crawling into a cozy bed, evaporated. I could have happily kicked my own ass.

Thankfully, only seconds later, he rose and moved to the desk. I tensed. Would he notice that the screensaver was gone? I heard tap, tap, tapping at the computer keyboard and then the familiar melodic hiss as he connected to the Internet. Oh, Lord. This could be a very long night. The realization that there was nothing I could do brought tears of frustration to my eyes. I'd just decided things could not possibly get any worse when I heard claws clicking on the hardwood floor and the distinct sound of panting. The dog! Four black paws appeared in the doorway, stopped and then headed right for me. I stiffened with dread when the dog dropped to its belly and stuck its nose under the bed. Loud snuffling of the makeup bag clutched in my right hand and then silence as the dog flattened his chin on the floor and surveyed me with puzzled brown eyes. I cringed, fully expecting furious barks to reveal my hiding place, but instead his tail thumped and he let out a joyous whimper, followed by an expectant yelp. Good gravy. He wanted to play!

"Shut up, Rascal!" Jason roared.

The dog's tail swished back and forth so hard his entire rear end swayed. He scooted a little closer until his snout was against my face and then he began to enthusiastically lick my cheeks and nose. When he moved around to my left ear, it tickled so much I could hardly keep from giggling. In fact, the whole ridiculous situation made me want to scream with laughter. But the idea of being discovered by Jason was sobering enough to squelch the sensation.

"What the hell are you up to?" came Jason's gruff inquiry.

If I didn't do something fast, it would all be over. Craning my neck, I looked to my right. There were more piles of paper, shoeboxes and several huge batteries nestled among dust bunnies the size of golf balls. I reached my left hand down beside me and felt around, finally grabbing hold of something made of cloth. I pulled it forward, rolling it into a ball before shoving it towards the dog's mouth. Gross. It was underwear. Jason's grubby underwear.

But Rascal seemed thrilled to get it. He grabbed it up. Shook it. Threw it into the air, pounced, then brought it back to me. Obligingly, I rolled it up again and he whined with anticipation before scampering around the room shaking it violently in his teeth.

As expected, his noisy antics finally captured Jason's attention. I heard the squeak of the chair rolling away from the desk and the pad of stocking feet. He lunged at the dog growling, "What's this? Hey, you like my shitty boxers, boy? Well, there are lots more where these came from. Have at 'em." Laughing, he threw the shorts back to the dog and left the room.

I listened to his muffled footsteps and when a door slammed, no doubt to the bathroom where the empty tub still awaited me, I scrambled out from under the bed and made a beeline for the other end of the house. Rascal was right beside me. Once we got past the bathroom door, I slowed my pace to avoid suspicion. Before entering the little room once more, my quick backward glance confirmed that no one else was around. With a groan of relief, I collapsed onto the bed and stayed there until my hammering heartbeat subsided. Oh, boy. That had been way too close.

The end result of my foolhardy predicament left me so lightheaded that I could hardly force myself to a sitting position. Rascal sat at the foot of the bed, tongue lolling to one side of his mouth, patiently waiting for me to resume our playtime. "I don't think we've been formally introduced," I said, reaching out to pet his silky black fur. "O'Dell's the name, trouble's my game."

He scooted a little closer and laid his chin on my knee. I smiled, deciding that so far Rascal was my favorite member of the Beaumont household. I waited another fifteen minutes before venturing to the bathroom again and this time I was successful. Even as I was submerged in the glorious rose-scented bubbles, I could not stop thinking about what I had seen in Jason's room and no amount of soap seemed sufficient to wash away the appalling sensation of hostility that had permeated his room. I wished I'd had time to stay and see what site he'd visited on the Internet.

A half hour later, I returned to my room. Rascal was gone. It was barely nine o'clock but the house was quiet. Just like Tally and his family, it appeared that most ranchers retired early and rose at first light. If I'd been at the motel in Green Valley as planned, I'd be using this down time to make phone calls and go online to research the White power movement in this area. On my hands and knees, I searched the room for a phone jack but came up empty. Nothing on this trip seemed to be going as planned. When I stood up, the sensation of total weariness rolling over me was so strong it felt like my bones were melting. I could hardly get into bed fast enough.

In the pitch-black room, I lay there staring out the window at the legion of stars, a veritable celestial banquet interrupted only now and then by an occasional gauzy cloud. The ceaseless wind rattled the windows, and tree branches scratched out a soothing lullaby on the glass as I waited for sleep. But even though I tried to banish all thoughts of the past forty-eight hours, my mind continued to churn like a washer on permanent spin cycle. I thought about Lupe and Javier, Sister Goldenrod and Froggy. Mazzie La Casse's descriptions of the extraterrestrials whirled in my mind along with the disquieting conversations with Jennifer and Loydeen Shirley. I could picture the smirking face of Border Agent Hank Breslow and the malevolent warning glare from the muscular skinhead. Warning about what? And what about the perplexing e-mail on Jason's computer? The words struck a familiar chord, but I could not for the life of me remember where I'd heard them before. Its riddle-like quality seemed strangely reminiscent of Froggy's distorted nursery rhyme from last night and made me suspect that it was some sort of code. Had Jason been the recipient of his call? And if so, did that mean that he was involved somehow in smuggling illegals into the country? But what reason would he have to do that? Considering his standpoint, it seemed more logical that it would serve his interests better to make sure they stayed out.

The more I chewed on all the possibilities, the more they became a muddled mass of unconnected clues, none of which made any sense, separately or together. Payton, Brett and the rescued kitten were small bright spots, but overlaid across the top of all that was the one subject I didn't want to approach. I had deliberately avoided it all day, but at that moment I relaxed just enough for the back door of my mind to crack open and it slithered in, dragging with it a sliver of doubt that seemed to seep from the deepest, darkest regions of my heart.

If pushed to interpret the contemptuous stare Bethany Beaumont had bestowed upon me from the doorway of the kitchen a few hours ago, and combining it with the eerie premonition that had enveloped me when I first laid eyes on her, I would have to admit in my heart of hearts that I was suffering from an acute case of jealousy. Oh, I knew myself well enough to know that I sometimes tended to react impulsively, but no matter how I tried to deny it, there remained the very good possibility that her reaction to my true identity stemmed not from her father's obvious affinity for me, but instead from the fact that she may well have her sights set on Tally. And, of course, that led to the second part of my supposition. What were his feelings towards her? Was it possible that *she* was the overriding reason he'd been making so many trips down here and not, as Champ Beaumont had told me earlier, that Tally was helping them out of a financial bind by purchasing, at top dollar, several hundred head of cattle that he could no longer afford to feed? But, what proof, other than relying solely on my instincts, did I have for entertaining such a discomfiting hypothesis? Suddenly, his brooding demeanor and testy behavior with me these past few weeks took on new and disturbing significance. And what of Ginger's secretive reference to another woman, and her somber warning that I was in danger of somehow spoiling our relationship?

Growing more heartsick by the minute, my mind skated off in several different directions as I conjured up one distressing scenario after another starring Bethany the blonde cowgirl Barbie doll and Tally. "Cut it out!" I whispered aloud. What kind of an idiot was I? Tally had said nothing, done nothing to warrant these unfounded, petty suspicions. Convinced that I was just fatigued, I banished all thoughts from my mind and fell into a deep sleep that probably would have continued until noon if the rapping at my door hadn't jarred me awake. "Yes?" I croaked, propping myself up on one elbow, noting with a twinge of irritation that it was still dark outside.

"It's five o'clock," called Twyla. "If you want to go with Champ for that ranch tour you requested, you'll have to get up now."

Oh, yes. The tour. When pressed about my unexpected arrival, I'd stuck to my cover story after giving them an abbreviated version of Walter's move to Castle Valley and my desire to complete the series he'd begun on the border-jumping issues affecting ranchers. Champ had graciously offered to escort me around the ranch property and give me a real education.

Dressed in jeans and a long-sleeved turtleneck, I joined Twyla and Champ for a hearty bacon and eggs breakfast while the kitchen help worked feverishly preparing food for the guests who'd not yet ventured from their warm beds. I felt relieved that neither Jason nor Bethany was present. Maybe I'd be lucky and get away without ever seeing them again. I pushed my plate away while stifling a yawn. Even though I'd slept like a rock, I still didn't feel rested and had surprisingly little appetite. Strange for me.

Dawn was busy painting the rugged horizon a stunning turquoise blue, and streaking it with vivid magenta clouds by the time Champ finished his third cup of coffee. We had just pushed away from the table when

Twyla shot a startled look over my shoulder. "Cecil, what on earth…?"

The two Hispanic girls peeling potatoes blushed and turned away giggling, as I followed the astonished stare of the Indian cook towards the kitchen doorway. I could hardly believe my eyes. An elderly man of perhaps eighty stood there with a towel in one hand, and a bar of soap in the other, wearing an expression of total confusion and nothing more. Not a stitch. Nada.

"Christ Almighty," Champ choked, jumping to his feet and running to the man's side. "Dad? Dad, what's going on?" He grabbed the towel and wrapped it around the man's slender waist. "Twyla, where the hell is Felix? Isn't he supposed to be watching him?"

"I'll go find him," she said, hurrying from the room.

As if coming out of a trance, the old guy focused bleary eyes on his son.

"What are you doing here?" Champ repeated, gentler this time.

"I thought…well, I was…trying to find the bathroom. Guess I took a wrong turn," he mumbled. When his gaze landed on me, an odd light of recognition flickered behind his eyes. "Penelope? My God, Penelope is that you?" Grinning foolishly, he took a step towards me and Champ grasped his arm tighter. "Dad, that's not Penelope. This is Kendall O'Dell. She's a friend of Tally's."

"Oh? Tally," he repeated vaguely. "Sure, sure." His wrinkly jowls drooped with disappointment and my insides ached for this man who appeared lost in his own house, in his own head. He was obviously suffering from some sort of dementia and I wondered if it was Alzheimer's. If so, my heart went out to all concerned. I'd done several pieces on this devastating disease and knew that the victim's painstakingly slow downward spiral was traumatic for friends and family alike.

"Meester Bo," cried an equally ancient-looking Hispanic man, rushing to Cecil's side. "Why do you run away from me like that, *amigo*?" He edged a guilt-laden look at Champ and shrugged his apology. "I am filling the bathtub and I don't see...."

"That's okay, Felix," Champ responded, patting him on the back. "Don't be too hard on yourself. No harm done."

"Remember when we didn't even have indoor plumbing?" Cecil remarked with a faraway look glazing his eyes. "We heated the water in a big copper tub and took a bath once a week whether we needed it or not."

"*Si*, Meester Bo, I remember," Felix agreed, leading him down the hallway.

Champ followed their progress with a sad shake of his head. "Sorry about that."

"No need to apologize," I said softly.

His anguished sigh filled the entryway. "This is so goddamned tough to watch I can hardly stand it." His eyes looked a little moist. "You should have known him before. Big, strapping, happy-go-lucky fellow. Good husband, good father, good provider. I'll tell you what, he and my uncles and my grandpa worked their hands to the bone, working sunup to sundown, year in and year out, putting up with all manner of hardships to make this place what it is today. What it used to be anyhow."

"I wish I'd known him then too," I said.

He brightened marginally. "And could he ever spin a yarn! Man alive. He could give you a complete history about the origins of this ranch and tell you everything there was to know about this whole area going back a hundred years. Still can some days," he said, tamping his hat down over his thick hair. "Funny, sometimes he remembers stuff from fifty years ago clear as a bell, but he can't remember what he did yesterday."

"Who's Penelope?"

The reflective smile softened his craggy features. "My mother. She had real pretty red hair too when she was young. He always called her Babydoll. She died...let's see, it's been about ten years ago now. He's gone downhill a lot since then."

"I'm sorry."

He cleared his throat. "Yeah, we all are. But, those are the cards we've been dealt and with God's help we'll get through it. So now, little lady, if you're ready I'll be happy to take you to the front lines of our little war zone," he said, his voice assuming a more business- like quality.

"Give me two minutes to get my things and I'll be right with you," I said, placing one hand on the banister. I'd barely taken two steps when I heard the scrape of footsteps from above. To my dismay, Jason Beaumont clomped down the stairs towards us with a saucy swaggering gait, fastening the holster of a 9mm handgun to his waist. When his distracted gaze zeroed in on me, it was interesting to watch his cocky, self-assured expression alter with each progressive downward step. On closer inspection his initial indifference evaporated into disbelief, recognition, and finally a blaze of animosity.

"Jason," his father called out, "meet Kendall O'Dell."

"We've met," I said dryly.

He clattered to the bottom of the steps. "What... what the hell is this bitch doing in our house?" he snarled, his finger pointed only inches from my nose.

Champ's thick brows plunged into his beet-red face. "What's the matter with you, boy?"

"I hope you haven't been talking to her about any of our private family stuff. Don't you know she's one of those dumb-ass media sluts?"

Champ roared, "You'd best watch your mouth! Kendall happens to be a friend of Bradley Talverson. She's come down here to do a story on our border problems, plain and simple. Now I believe you owe her an apology."

Unmoved by Champ's appeal, the wispy strawberry-blonde beard on his chin quivered as he snarled, "I don't owe her shit. You're being set up, Dad. I know for a fact she's working for the enemy. A couple of us saw her at the rally yesterday and we spotted her twice afterwards chauffeuring that Lopez woman around town."

The affable light faded from Champ's eyes. "Is this true?"

"I don't have clue one as to what he's talking about. I was with an employee of mine by the name of Lupe Alvarez. She went home sick yesterday morning." Flushed with anger, I turned back to Jason. "No doubt made sicker by you and your moronic bunch of skinhead thugs. And by the way, I didn't appreciate your childish game of road rage either."

"What's she talking about?" There was a dangerous edge to Champ's voice.

Uncertainty ruled Jason's face for a fleeting second before he reasserted himself with a sarcastic, "It was no big deal. Me and a couple of the guys was just having a little fun. Okay, so maybe we had a few too many beers and made a mistake. Is it my fault that wetbacks all look the same to me?" Smirking, he brushed past me and disappeared into the kitchen.

Champ surveyed my heated face with chagrin. "I apologize for any trouble caused by my son. He can be kind of a hothead at times."

I gave him a quick overview of what happened, including the cat incident. "There is no excuse for terrorizing people or animals."

His skyward glance seemed to be searching for inspiration. "Look, these kids are just responding to a situation we have no control over. Folks who aren't from around here don't have any idea what we're up against. Our livelihood is at stake, our families, our sovereignty for chrissake! Most of the news reporters soft peddle what's really happening. The awful truth is, we're under siege! It's like living in a pressure cooker every single day and I guess Jason, like all of us, sometimes tends to overreact."

Overreact? I longed to ask him what he thought of Jason's open declarations of hatred and bigotry on full display in his room, but didn't want to reveal how I knew. "Who's this Lopez woman he mentioned?"

His clenched jaw made the chords in his neck stand out. "An activist lawyer who heads up one of those immigration advocacy groups in Tucson. That woman has made it her mission in life to make *our* lives a living hell. For the record, just so you get the whole picture, this Mexican bitch is suing my ass for a half a millions bucks for so-called human rights violations against a bunch of trespassing illegals who trashed *my* property!" He gulped in a couple of calming breaths, started to speak again and then apparently thought better of it, clamping his mouth shut for a few seconds before saying in a carefully controlled tone, "I'll be waiting for you in my truck."

He stomped away without another word, grabbing a set of keys off a hook beside the door. Walter was right on the money. This place was a tinderbox of volatile emotions on all sides, poised to explode at the slightest provocation. A war zone. Not a happy thought. Needless to say, the discord had my belly in a nervous stew as I raced back down the stairs after retrieving my tape recorder, camera and jacket. But, I had to admit that I was intrigued by what I'd learned so far. The yearning to solve Lupe's dilemma was still dominant, but it was a real stretch to think that I was going to come up with anything viable by this afternoon. On the other hand, the opportunity for a feature article on the ongoing border tensions was tangible. Why go home empty-handed?

In the kitchen once more, I noticed Jason and Bethany with their heads together at the far end of the table as I made my way towards the side door. The glitter of malicious humor reflected in her swift sideways glance pretty much confirmed that I was most likely the subject of their cozy chitchat. To hell with both of them. Shrugging into my jacket, I stepped outside and hurried towards Champ's green Chevy pickup, breathing in the frosty, hay-scented air and reaffirming that Rascal still retained his number one spot as my favorite member of this motley household.

14

The brilliant rays of the rising sun breaking over the distant peaks illuminated the almost full moon, poised above the western horizon like a pearly-gray medicine ball. The wind hadn't abated much since last night and, in fact, seemed to have gained strength.

Cloaked in a Levi jacket trimmed with a sheepskin collar and sipping fresh coffee from a large mug, Champ's frame of mind appeared to have improved somewhat as I climbed in beside him. He agreed to my request to use the tape recorder for our interview and then, after a couple of minutes of initial awkwardness, seemed to forget it was there.

With a look of pride shining in his eyes, he explained how the neat row of guest cottages behind the main house had once belonged to various family members. Less than a year ago, they had been completely remodeled. There were also two bunkhouses for visitors wishing to 'rough it.' I noticed that much like the Starfire, there was a hum of activity about the place even at such an early hour. Ranch hands on foot, horseback and driving dusty weather-faded pickups, exchanged friendly salutes with Champ as we cruised by whitewashed stables and pipe corrals filled with horses, sheep, goats and even a few llamas. He informed me that the smaller animals had recently been added as an attraction for guests with children. Their list of services also included trail rides, hayrides, cookouts, participation in branding and cattle roundups and even western dances. Within minutes, we left the trappings of civilization behind and headed out into the open range where straggling herds of white-faced cattle munched on smoothly sculpted hills of dry grass. Beyond the vast cactus-strewn grasslands, tier after tier of rugged mountain ranges thrust upward to collide with the bold blue sky. It was hard to believe that a single family held stewardship over such a gigantic empire when most of us are lucky to own a tiny plot of acreage at some point in our lives.

"Man, this place would be perfect to film a western movie," I remarked with a note of admiration.

He chuckled. "Did you ever see The Last Arizona Cowboy?"

"No, I don't think so."

"Well, it was made right here five years ago."

"No kidding?"

"And that wasn't the only one. We registered with the Arizona Film Commission after that and there've been four other movies shot here. A cable station was down here just a couple of months ago doing a TV movie."

"Is it lucrative?"

He edged me a meaningful glance. "Oh, yeah, definitely. They even used Brett as an extra in the last one and, before that, Jason and a couple of his buddies picked up quite a chunk of change helping to tear down some of the sets and haul stuff away."

"How exciting for everyone."

"Sometimes. Those Hollywood types can be a real pain in the ass, pardon my French. Real bossy. Demanding. And temperamental. Their crews tear up the roads something awful hauling equipment in those big trucks. They're noisy and messy, but I've got to say the meals put together by the catering companies they hire is just about the best damn food I ever ate." He laughed and rubbed a hand over his generous middle.

We rode in silence for a few minutes until he pointed to the cracked shingles of mud stretched across empty stock ponds, explaining that they were usually eight to ten feet deep with runoff from the summer rains. "That little spit of moisture we got yesterday was useless." He shook his head, scanning the distant vista with a thoughtful look. "You know, I thought my dear wife had lost her marbles when she first came up with the idea of starting a dude ranch. But, after nearly seven years of drought conditions, grazing allotments being cut, and skyrocketing fees, well, our backs were against the wall. In the salad days, we were running ten thousand cows and about one thousand bulls. Our calves were going for a buck a pound. Now we're lucky to get sixty-five cents." A little smile quivered at the corner of his mouth. "We owe your guy big time for saving our butts. Tally worked out an arrangement for taking some of the cattle in trade for some of those fine-looking Appaloosas. They make the best dang saddle horses in the world but, frankly, I'm afraid he's losing money on the deal even though he'd never admit it."

"How long have you known Tally?" I asked, moving the small microphone a little closer to him, noticing that the wrinkles crisscrossing his cheeks and creasing the corners of his eyes were so pronounced it looked as though he'd had his face pressed up against a wire screen for twenty years.

"His pa, Joe, and me knew each other since we were knee high to a bullfrog. Used to compete at the county fairs and rodeos all the time." He turned to me, grinning impishly. "Guess you can figure out which one of us came in first most of the time."

I smiled back. So that meant Champ had known Tally all his life. And it also confirmed my suspicion that Tally must be well acquainted with both of the enchanting Beaumont offspring. The uncomfortable knot of suspicion inside me intensified, but I admonished myself once again for being silly. Tally was an intelligent guy. He wouldn't have the slightest interest in a spoiled brat like Bethany.

"I'm gonna show you just a small example of our problems," he said, turning onto a narrow side road. We bounced along until it tapered into little more than a sandy path. Then, he stopped and invited me to join him outside. Strong wind gusts grabbed my hair and smacked it repeatedly across my face. "Does the wind ever stop blowing out here?" I asked, capturing my unruly locks in one hand.

"Nope. That's one thing around here that's pretty constant." We walked towards a thick grove of mesquite. I wasn't sure why until I noticed the piles of trash littering what should have been the pristine landscape. Beneath the low overhang of shrubbery was a small clearing where the range grass had been flattened or obliterated by the heavy foot traffic. A flash of irritation shot through me when I saw the piles of discarded plastic gallon water jugs. There must have been fifty or sixty of them. Scattered everywhere were empty food tins, diapers, toilet paper, beer bottles and discarded cans of a Mexican beverage called Jumex.

Empty potato and tortilla chip bags, along with dark green plastic garbage bags snagged in the foliage, snapped and crackled in the stiff wind. The mess was appalling.

I looked up and saw the aggravation in Champ's eyes. He pointed to the ground, grimacing. "My Border Patrol buddies call this a lay-up area. That's where the guides or two-legged *coyotes*, or whatever you wanna call these scumbags, drop off their loads of jumpers. They camp out here and wait for their ride. And this," he continued, moving his index finger to a well-worn footpath snaking away through the brush, "is just one of dozens of paths they've worn clean through my property all the way from the blasted border. Can you believe we just cleaned this area up a few days ago?" he huffed. "Now, along with everything else, we get to be trash pickers, and that's not all. These people kill off wildlife and set fires to cook and keep warm in the winter. I tell you, it's a goddamn losing battle."

"I saw the results of one fire when Payton drove me over to Dean's place yesterday," I said.

A heavy sigh. "Yeah, that's just the latest in a string of 'em. Considering how dry everything is we're lucky they haven't burned down the whole southern half of the state. On top of that is the five head of prime beef we've lost over the past year because my cattle eat these plastic water jugs they leave behind. Two other head escaped through cut fences and were killed on the highway. A friend of mine over at the Dunbar spread is being sued by a woman who ran into one of his bulls and is now paralyzed. Every rancher in this area is suffering because of this unstoppable invasion of our country. And make no mistake about it," he said with a curt nod, "it's just that, an *invasion*."

I had an instant vision of the big black bull I'd encountered on Arivaca Road and thanked my lucky stars I'd been able to stop in time. As we drove back towards the main road, I noticed that the glow of pride in his eyes had dimmed.

Champ tapped the horn and waved towards a horse and rider silhouetted on a windswept bluff. The rider responded by brandishing a rifle. "That," Champ said, pointing his chin at the man, "is a primary example of wasted manpower. In order to protect my own property right here in the so-called sovereign US of A, I am forced to hire extra hands to stand lookout and chase these people down when I should be paying them to put in a good day's work."

"I hope this question doesn't offend you, but I have to ask it. I couldn't help but notice that you, along with Tally and every other ranch I've visited lately, employ Mexican laborers. Isn't it just a little bit hypocritical of you guys to complain about the influx of these people when you're helping to create the problem?"

He flicked me a look of irritation. "Look, we're not talking about migrants coming here with a legal temporary work permit. It's too bad the government did away with the old *bracero* program. In most cases, it worked pretty well for both sides. No, ma'am. We're talking about having to deal with a new and more dangerous breed of criminal ilk invading our borders, and that includes these terrorist cells."

"Isn't it the Border Patrol's job to apprehend these people?"

. A shrug accompanied his tired sigh. "I'll tell you something. I know a lot of these guys personally and they work their asses off doing the best they can, but let's face it, even though things have really tightened up a lot at the legal border crossings with the National Guard helping out, there's no way on God's sweet earth they can hire enough agents to patrol the whole two thousand miles. If you ask me, I'd say the only solution left is to bring in the military."

"You mean the Army?"

"Yes ma'am. Them or the Marines! It's the federal government's job to secure our borders and they're doing a piss poor job of it. Last month me and the boys rounded up over 400 illegals," he said with a sharp laugh. "Maybe we ought to be on the payroll."

"That's a lot of people."

He snickered. "Oh, that's a drop in the bucket. You know how many were apprehended last year?"

"No."

"Over 700,000, and we're not seeing just Mexicans. If you check with the Border Patrol you'll find that Orientals are coming in, Eastern Europeans and even people from the Middle East." He shot me a grave look, tacking on, "And after what happened in New York, we can't afford to fool around. We need to be extra vigilant protecting our country's borders, because that number only reflects the people that were actually caught. You see why we're calling it an invasion?"

He had a point, a very good point.

"Do the math," he went on. "Multiply that number along the entire Mexican border and you get some idea of just exactly what we're up against. Oh, I'm sure you think I'm a hard-hearted so and so, but I have one simple question. Why don't we *force* the Mexican government and all these other corrupt countries to take care of their own people? Then they wouldn't be pouring across, using up our resources as a nation, draining social services meant for our own people, clogging hospitals, overrunning our schools, illegally voting to influence our elections and who knows what other God-awful mayhem they may have planned for us." His hands clasped and unclasped the steering wheel. "Have you heard the latest thing the damn Mexican government is up to?"

"Um... I'm not sure."

"Now they're providing survival kits to make it easier for these people to cross the desert."

"You're kidding?"

"No, I'm not," he grumbled. "I just read it in the paper. The kits contain food and water, medicine for scorpion and snakebites, salt, even birth-control pills for the women, for chrissakes! I know it's politically incorrect to be suspicious of people from different cultures, but I think Americans are finally waking up and realizing what's happening to our sovereignty. People who enter this country illegally are lawbreakers. Some of them are dangerous criminals and I'm tired of the fuzzy-headed thinkers in Washington making us feel like the bad guys for defending ourselves. You can feel free to quote me on that." His mottled complexion and heavy breathing revealed passionate opinion, but he didn't strike me as unreasonable, just a patriotic man with strong convictions. Did he approve of his son's involvement in the White power movement? I was beginning to suspect that he just might. By his tone, I wouldn't be all that surprised if his sympathies lay in that direction also. And, considering the ongoing problems, would anyone blame him?

Ahead, the road seemed to go on forever. "How are you able to monitor a place this size? It seems like you'd have to employ a hundred hands just to check out the property every day."

He chuckled. "I would if I didn't own an airplane."

"No kidding? Well, I guess that makes sense."

"Look over there," Champ said, wagging a finger towards a tower perhaps thirty feet high with a small shack snuggled at the base. At first I thought it might be a cellular transmission tower but, as we drew closer, I could see a man at the top sitting on a platform, binoculars trained on the southern horizon. "That's the newest addition in our private war against Mexico. At night we use infrared binoculars and I want to tell you, we hit the jackpot a couple of weeks back when we snagged eight packers loaded up with cocaine and heroine sneaking across about two in the morning. It was pretty nerve-wracking, because one of those suckers was armed and meant business. But, we overpowered him and held the bunch of them until our Border Patrol guys got here."

We'd stepped out of the truck and had walked no more than a few yards when a stocky young guy with a big handlebar mustache wearing a BEAUMONT RANCH PATROL sweatshirt came running up to meet us. "Hey, Champ. Glad you're here. I was just getting ready to drive over to get you."

"Rob, what's going on?"

"Trouble. Big trouble."

"Oh, Christ, what now?"

"We've had company again. I don't know how we missed 'em, but we did." He paused, flinging me an uneasy glance. "You'll probably want to come out and see this by yourself." It was obvious by his grave tone that something was seriously wrong.

Champ turned to me. "You'd better stay here."

I stuck out my chin. "What about the education you promised me?"

He hesitated a few seconds then, "Come on."

At speeds approaching the reckless level, we followed the curtain of dust billowing behind Rob's truck, bouncing along a washboard road hugged by a thick jungle of mesquite, cat's claw, palo verde trees and giant yucca plants. Lots of places for people to hide. At the foot of a rocky slope, the road opened into a small clearing where a windmill spun madly in the lonesome wind beside a series of weathered wooden stock pens. Adjacent to them stood an enormous corrugated steel stock tank spray-painted with the words *La proxima vez, los vaqueros, no las vacas.* In front of it lay half a dozen brown mounds. As we drew closer, my insides clenched when I realized the inert lumps were not rocks, but cows. Dead cows. Disemboweled cows. I fired a look at Champ as he jammed on the brakes. "Gaawd daaamn!" he bellowed, his rosy complexion fading to the color of ash. He threw the door open and leaped out to join Rob, so I grabbed my camera and hurried to catch up with them.

"How many?" he asked in a hoarse voice, surveying the grisly scene.

So far, I've counted ten heifers. But that's not the worst." He gestured for Champ to follow him and threw me a look of warning which I chose to ignore. My heart was bucking and kicking with anxious expectation as the younger man wordlessly pointed to the tank. Intense dread pressed down on me as I stood beside Champ and peeked over the side. It took a few seconds for my reluctant brain to accept what my eyes were seeing. "Good God." Recoiling, I stared down at the bodies of several bludgeoned calves. Or rather, pieces of calves. Several tiny heads with wide lifeless eyes stared back; some hooves and large chunks of flesh lay at the dark bottom of the tank

233

while other unidentifiable parts floated in the choppy blood-reddened water. The sickening spectacle sent tremors of revulsion throughout my entire being and it was all I could do to keep from gagging. I turned away quickly, inhaling deep breaths to quell the nausea while blinking back enraged tears. Considering that I'd been warned not to come, it wouldn't do for me to lose my breakfast.

"Son-of-a-bitch!" Champ thundered, pounding the side of the tank with his fist over and over. He let fly a string of profanities that would have made an Irish pub owner blush and worked himself into such a scarlet-faced rage, I thought he might have a heart attack. And then, in a poignant move that ripped at my heartstrings, he suddenly fell silent, collapsed to one knee and rested his forehead on one hand.

I finally gathered my wits enough to get the camera focused. The picture of this fiercely proud man, weeping alongside the butchered carcasses of once peacefully grazing cows, was worth far more than a thousand words.

I stole a look at Rob, hands rammed in his jean pockets, his mouth a grim line of determination. At that moment the enormity of the situation began to fully sink in. Whoever had committed this heinous act was no doubt long gone and would suffer no consequences. The two of us exchanged an unspoken glance and walked towards the truck to give Champ some time to compose himself. "Do you read Spanish?" I asked in a shaky voice, setting my camera on the passenger seat.

"A little."

"Do you know what that says?"

He hitched his shoulders, squinting at the macabre message. "Something like, next time the cowboys, not the cows."

"I see. So this is revenge for apprehending the drug smugglers last week."

"Most likely." He glared southward for long seconds before turning back to me with an odd glitter of triumph in his brown eyes. "As far as I'm concerned, these Mexican bastards are just taking up space on the planet. They've gone too far this time and they'll pay a heavy price for this. Believe me, they'll pay."

15

Immobilized by shock, I stood by the truck on jellied knees waiting for Champ to return. The brisk morning breeze had increased to wind gusts of perhaps thirty miles per hour, turning the air a dusty saffron color as it swooshed through the tawny grass and whistled around the cactus spines. Again, it played havoc with my hair and pelted my face with stinging granules of sand. The dull roar made conversation with Rob nearly impossible, so I retreated to the cab of the truck just as Champ came trudging up, his massive shoulders hunched against the wind. He seemed to have aged twenty years. The bright gleam of pride in his blue eyes had vanished and the lacework of wrinkles on his ashen face crumpled into deep canyons of bitterness.

He stopped to talk to Rob, but the mournful keening made it difficult for me to interpret what he was saying. From his hand gestures and the few fragments of words that reached my ears, I gathered he was instructing him to round up a crew to dispose of the hideous mess. I shivered again and rubbed my arms. Would I ever be able to banish that horrific scene from my mind? Probably not, but it had accomplished what no amount of rhetoric could. This really was a war. It was frightening to realize that the perpetrators of this savagery were capable of inflicting harm on anyone who stood in their way. No doubt the threat to 'get the cowboys next' would be taken very seriously and it resurrected thoughts of Agent Bob Shirley's questionable death. If indeed he had been involved in a smuggling operation, as the authorities suspected, had he also become a victim, paying with his life for refusing to cooperate any longer? Even in light of his family's vehement denials, had he decided to take his own life rather than endure a tortuous death at the hands of such ruthless people?

When Champ finally finished, Rob tore off in his truck while we headed back towards the ranch house, riding in morose silence for long minutes before he noisily cleared his throat. "I'm sorry you had to witness such an awful sight. You gonna be okay?"

"I think so. What about you?"

He darted a quick look at me. "Young lady, I need to ask you a big favor."

"Sure. Anything."

Apparently searching for the right words, he rubbed his chin a few times before continuing. "It would help me out a whole lot if you'd agree to not say anything about what you saw this morning."

My mouth dropped. "Why?"

"I've been thinking about it. Can you imagine what kind of an effect something like this will have on our paying guests and any future guests? If they get wind of this, they'll panic and stampede out of here like frightened cattle." At the mention of cattle, he stopped and swallowed hard. "Word of mouth will be bad enough, but if you print this in your newspaper, it's gonna deep six the only viable business we've got going right now." When I didn't say anything, he threw me another anxious glance. "We've also got a big chunk of this place up for sale and something like this would definitely scare away potential buyers."

I frowned. "Do you think it's wise to keep it a secret? Aren't you even going to alert the sheriff's office or the Border Patrol? Somebody?"

"Yes, yes, in due time, but I need a few days to decide how we're going handle this...latest crisis."

"What *can* you do other than turn a blind eye to all illegals from this point forward? I mean, how can you differentiate between innocent immigrants crossing to get work and hard core drug traffickers?"

"We can't. Except for the one guy in the group who was armed, the rest of the people we detained last week were just average guys, doing it for money or because they or their family members were being threatened. That's how these smuggling operations work. The top dogs rarely get caught whether they're trafficking in drugs or people."

We made solemn eye contact for a fleeting second before he returned his attention to the road. I sighed inwardly thinking about what great copy it would have made, but the dull sheen of hopelessness reflected in his gaze made my decision easy. "Okay, I'll keep it under my hat." This weekend had to have set a record for the number of promises I'd sworn to keep.

His long-drawn-out sigh broadcast profound relief. "Thanks. I really appreciate that."

Just beyond the rise ahead, the roof of the stable was visible so I knew we were only a few minutes from the house. "No problem. But, there were a few more questions I wanted to ask you before I head home."

"What's that?"

I switched my recorder on again. "Do you think there is any connection between this incident and the other mutilated cattle that were found on your property during the past two years?"

His quick glance held incredulity. "How'd you know about that?"

I reminded him again of my association with Walter. "I don't think there's any connection at all," he said, pulling up near the kitchen door and shutting off the engine.

"What makes you so sure?"

"This thing today makes me madder than hell because I know damn well it was carried out by a bunch of no good cowardly dogs, but that other stuff...well, that was just about the scariest thing I've ever seen in my life. There was no blood, no footprints around, nothing for the authorities to go on. It's still a mystery."

"Any theories?"

He arched a salt and pepper brow. "You mean do I believe that creatures from outer space landed on my ranch and surgically removed organs from my cattle?"

"That's what some people are suggesting."

He fell silent for a few seconds. "I like to think I'm a pretty normal down to earth fellow but, to tell you the God's honest truth, I don't have any explanation for what happened out there." He reached for the door handle and then turned back to me with a troubled scowl. "I can tell you this much. Whoever did it knew exactly what they were doing, but *why* anyone would do such a thing, I don't know."

It suddenly occurred to me that there was someone nearby who might have the expertise—his own brother-in-law, Dean Pierce. But, when I pictured his gentle treatment of Marmalade, a tremor of guilt tiptoed through me. How could I even entertain such a thought?

He stuck out a callused hand and I took it. "Kendall, it's been a pleasure meeting you. Next time Tally comes down this way, I hope you'll see fit to come with him and visit us again, hopefully under more pleasant circumstances."

"That would be good." I thanked him again for his time and promised I'd send him a copy of the article when it was published. There was a buzz of activity about the grounds as we emerged from the truck. Champ explained that ranch hands were preparing one group for the cattle roundup and another for a trail ride and picnic. He excused himself, saying he had to go talk to his ranch foreman and hurried away towards the barn. No doubt he'd be instructing him to keep the vacationers away from the scene of carnage.

I busied myself snapping a few photos of the main house, gardens and smiling couples on horseback. Four children, including Brett, were squealing with delight as Bethany led one of the llamas around on a halter. It was an idyllic setting and reinforced my pledge to keep silent about the shocking episode. If any of these visitors had the slightest inkling of what had happened just a few miles from here, they'd be rightly horrified and probably on the next plane out. I wondered when Champ planned to tell the rest of the family about the incident. I could only imagine Jason's reaction.

I checked my watch, surprised to see that it was only nine o'clock. Good. I still had plenty of time to get a few more shots of the ranch and make my calls before meeting Payton for lunch.

I strolled around the back of the house, snapping pictures of the cozy guest cottages and some of the kids petting sheep in the small enclosure adjacent to the barn. The children cooperated beautifully, mugging for the camera, and I got a great shot of Brett getting his face washed by an enthusiastic pygmy goat. Then showing off as kids will do, he began rolling around in the straw and dung until Bethany suddenly reappeared from the barn, shouting, "Brett, stop that!"

She hurried in the gate and began slapping at his smeared clothes, grumbling, "Now you're going to have to change before the hayride. The rest of you kids can go on into the barn. Tell Mr. Simms I'll be along in a few minutes."

Giggling, the children dutifully trooped to the barn and Bethany turned to face me. "My folks told me you're going to write an article on the Sundog. I hope you got some great pictures," she said, issuing me a sunny smile that showed no trace of her earlier sarcasm or animosity. "We could sure use a little good publicity."

"Glad to help out," I murmured warily, taken aback at her sudden turnabout.

"Did you get some pictures of our llamas?" she asked, unnecessarily fluffing her perfectly coifed curls.

"Just from a distance."

"Do you know much about them?"

"Not a lot."

She clapped her hands together. "I absolutely *love* llamas. They are the most *fascinating* animals. Why don't you go on over and get some closer shots," she suggested. "See that big black and white one? That's Maxie, my favorite. He loves to pose for the camera. Have fun!" She grabbed Brett's hand and pulled him to the gate saying, "Come on now, let's get you some clean clothes."

The little boy shot an anxious look over his shoulder. "But, Mama, you know that…"

"Shhhh! Hurry up!" she cut him off, pushing him ahead of her. "Everybody's waiting." She scooped him up in her arms, practically running with him to the kitchen door.

Still harboring vague suspicion at her unexpected friendliness, I turned back towards the llama corral. There were four of the fluffy-looking creatures and they all had their camel-like faces craned eagerly in my direction, ears straight up, their inquisitive eyes locked into mine. The big black and white one Bethany had mentioned was at the far end of the corral, grazing. With caution, I approached the smallest one and gingerly extended my hand, which it sniffed before stretching its neck upward to explore my entire face with gentle little snuffling sounds. "Well, aren't you the most darling thing," I cried, petting the woolly coat while watching the others prance back and forth. I focused the camera and got some great close-ups of their large eyes and seemingly smiling mouths.

All at once, Maxie looked up and trotted across the enclosure. Poor fellow. He probably didn't like being left out of the limelight. The others backed up as he approached. "Hey there, big guy, you want to be included, don't you?" I crooned, as he rushed up to me. Just as I reached my hand up to pet him, his ears laid back and he emitted a strange gurgling grunt before proceeding to spray my face with dank, sour-smelling saliva that reeked of wild onions.

"Oh, man!" I shouted, jumping back and wiping my face with the sleeve of my shirt. At that exact second, I knew I'd been had. Set up. And Brett had tried to warn me. Angrily, I swung around expecting to see Bethany at one of the windows doubled over in mirth, but saw nothing but the usual ranch activity. I should never have let my guard down. "What a total dufus you are," I ranted to myself, still trying to clear the nauseating smell from my nostrils as I stomped towards the house and pushed open the side door. I was heading towards the stairs to retrieve my overnight bag when Twyla hailed me from her seat in front of a computer monitor in the farthest corner of the kitchen. "Oh, hello, Kendall, did you enjoy your tour?"

What to say? I mustered a wan smile. "Well, it was certainly memorable."

"Good. Listen, Tally phoned while you were out with Champ. He said he'd be at the ranch until noon if you want to call him back."

If I wanted to? A rush of elation warming me, I backtracked to the wall phone. But just as I lifted the receiver, a giggling Bethany rushed in followed closely by the strapping wrangler she'd been flirting with when I'd arrived yesterday. Seeing me, she slapped his hand away from the seat of her ultra-tight jeans and chirped, "Did you get some good pictures of Maxie?"

I had to reach way down deep inside to control the blaze of fury searing my chest. Coolly, I answered, "They couldn't have been better." Would the wretched smell permeating my nose ever go away?

"I'm so glad." Assuming an expression of innocent righteousness, she breezed across the room. Who did she think she was fooling? Bitch.

"Mornin', ma'am," the ranch hand said to me while flicking Twyla a deferential nod as she rose and moved across the room towards me.

"Hello, Sloan," she said, her tolerant smile thin, her eyes narrowing with mild disapproval. When he was out of earshot she whispered to me, "If you'd like a little more privacy, there's a cordless phone around the corner in the living room. You can try taking it upstairs, but sometimes the reception isn't very good."

"Thank you." I shot her a grateful smile, hurried along the hall and paused in the doorway of a long, rectangular room embellished with reddish-brown leather furniture, wagon wheel lamps and colorful Navajo rugs. On a side table, adjacent to a large picture window offering a stunning view of the blue-hued Santa Rita Mountains, I spotted the phone. Calling card in hand, I was across the room in a flash and could hardly dial the numbers fast enough.

"Hullo?"

"Hi, Ronda," I said, feeling relief that it wasn't her mother, "is Tally there?"

"Yeah, he's here, but he can't talk to you right now."

My spirits sagged. How long was this silly game of phone tag going to continue? Unable to suppress my irritation, I snapped, "Why not?"

"Because," she exhaled, "he's out front arguing with a couple of pointy-headed INS officials. Try him in half an hour or so."

More than a little disappointed, I hung up thinking that the odds that we'd all be experiencing the impact of illegal immigration at the same time must be enormous.

What the heck. Might as well use the time to get the office calls out of the way.

"*Castle Valley Sun*," chirped an unfamiliar voice after two rings.

Slightly nonplussed, I asked, "Umm...is Morton Tuggs in?"

"Hold on." Click. A few seconds later, came a gruff, "Tuggs here."

"Hey, Tugg, Kendall. What's going on?"

"Oh, just the usual chaos. Well, maybe a bit more than normal, but we're coping. But, what the hell's up with you? I thought you and Tally were heading to California this week? Instead, Walter tells me you're down in Arivaca because of Lupe?"

"We're leaving in the morning." Still bound by my promise, I gave him a vague overview, citing major personal problems.

"Personal, huh?" he grunted. "And that's all?"

"Mostly."

The skepticism in his tone conveyed loud and clear that I wasn't fooling the old newshound. Oh, well. What could I do? When I returned, I'd have no choice but to level with him about Lupe's illegal status and he was going to shit a brick. Changing gears quickly, I asked, "Say, who was that answering the phone?"

"Louise."

"Your daughter Louise? Why is she there? Where's Ginger?"

He chuckled. "Manning the phones in classifieds and she's not too happy about it."

"What?" My heart spiraled downward. "Lupe promised me she'd be in today."

"She was here alright, but sick as a dog, so I sent her home."

"Oh, frap. Just what I was afraid of."

"She said you'd have a royal fit, but, hey, you're not doing me any favors by sending Typhoid Mary in here to infect the rest of us."

I weighed my options for several seconds, before saying, "Well, that settles it then. I'll be back at my desk tomorrow morning."

"You'll do no such thing."

"Tugg, a deal's a deal. In good conscience, I can't go skating off to California for a week and leave you there shorthanded."

"Bullshit. You've earned every second of this vacation. You both have."

"But, Tugg...."

"No buts. Lupe will probably be back in a day or two and Al will be back Thursday. In the meantime, we'll make do. So forget everything, relax and have a good time."

I didn't feel good about it, but he refused to take no for an answer, saying that after thirty years in the business he felt confident he could handle things. I just hoped the added stress wouldn't jeopardize his health, although he'd improved leaps and bounds since his ulcer surgery. He excused himself to take another call and I asked him to connect me to Ginger who immediately scolded me for not calling her sooner. "Sorry, there's lousy cell coverage down here."

"Whew! And here I been worried to death that you was still mad at me about the other night."

"I'm not going to tell you that it hasn't been bugging me, but what I really need now is to ask you a huge favor." I gave her an abbreviated version of the cat escapade and she crowed, "Well, ain't you a sweetie pie rescuing a poor little stray. I'm sure we can handle it."

"You don't think Churchill will hurt her, do you? She's pretty small and with her leg injured, I don't think she'll be able to outrun him."

"Don't you worry your little head. We'll shut her in Brian's room, that way Churchill can't pester her and neither can Suzie."

"You're a doll. I'll bring her by this evening. Then I've got to scoot and finish packing."

"I'm sure Tally will be as happy as a rooster in a hen house to have you back."

"I hope so. We've haven't spoken since Friday night. For all I know he's still pissed off at me about this trip."

Her sly little giggle re-ignited my curiosity. "Honey, I don't think I'd worry too much if I was you."

"Are you sure there isn't something you'd like to tell me?"

"You'll find out soon enough," she said in a sing-song tone, "and be real careful driving home, we're supposed to get another storm tonight."

"Another storm? You had rain? I think we had about twenty drops here yesterday, but that's all."

"We had us a real frog strangler and...oh Lordy, I got to catch these other lines."

I thanked her for bailing us out of a jam on such short notice and then asked her to transfer me to Walter. "Kendall!" his voice boomed in my ear. "I was wondering why you never called me back."

"Lots of reasons," I said, "but now that I've got you on the line, I have a few more questions and a favor to ask."

"Fire away."

I recapped my visit to the Shirley residence, my conversation with Jennifer and about Loydeen's evasive behavior, her accusation that my presence was somehow endangering them, how she flipped out when she spotted the skinhead in the truck and her fear that people were watching her. "Walter, do you have any idea what she was talking about?"

"No, I don't. That sounds mighty odd but you gotta take into consideration that she's been under a lot of strain and if she's taking a bunch of prescription meds...well, maybe that's why she's been acting paranoid."

I hoped that's all it was. "Walter, do you know anyone else I could talk to pertaining to this case?"

"Jennifer pointed out one of the guys at Bob's funeral to me. Said he was her dad's partner. Guy by the name of Alberto Morales or something like that, but good luck finding him."

"Why do you say that?"

"According to Loydeen, two weeks after the funeral, he resigned and moved away."

The dark sense of uneasiness nudged me again. "Hmmm. Interesting coincidence."

"I thought so too. So level with me, Kendall, what do Bob's case and your interest in my extraterrestrial piece have to do with Lupe?"

Ginger hadn't wasted any time telling everyone. "I wish I could tell you, but I can't, not yet."

Big sigh. "Gotcha. Did you get a chance to talk with Mazzie La Casse?"

"Yes, thanks for the tip. She's a great resource."

"I figured she would be. So, was I right about that rally on Saturday? Did you end up in the middle of it?"

Etched forever in my memory were Lupe's screams of terror as the skinheads closed in around my car. And I certainly would never forget the hateful aura that saturated Jason's room, nor the pitiless smolder in the wolf-like eyes of the skinhead outside the Shirley house. "In more ways than one. Speaking of that, what else do you know about this Knights of Right group other than what you mentioned on the phone the other day about the head guy being sentenced to prison? Who's running the show now?"

"I'll be damned if I know. And it's not so easy to find out anymore."

"Why not?"

"The leaders aren't as visible. Ever since the Oklahoma City bombing, most of these White supremacist groups and even some of the law abiding militia groups have decided it's better to keep a low profile rather than make themselves an easy target for government officials. In fact, most of them have gone underground. I'm not even sure that the majority of people involved in these groups even know who the actual head honcho is because most of the communication is carried out over the Internet now."

His insightful remark made the mysterious e-mail on Jason's computer even more intriguing and helped to cement my growing suspicions about him. "Hey, listen, Walter, I know you're snowed under, but I need a huge favor. I'd do it myself, but I'm going to be on the move for the rest of the day."

"Name it."

"Can you call Julie over at the sheriff's office and see if she can get me some information on a woman by the name of Shalberta Hoggwhistle? She did time in Tennessee, supposedly for cashing bad checks."

"Hoggwhistle? Are you pulling my leg?"

"Nope. And here's another name. I doubt it's genuine, but see if you can find anything on a Froggy McQueen."

"There'll be a million McQueen's. Am I checking in Tennessee too?"

"For starters."

"Anything else?"

"That should do it for now. I'll be in California the rest of the week, so you can reach me on my cell phone if you find out anything. Hopefully, there'll be better cell coverage on the coast than down here."

"Yeah, it's spotty at best. Anything else?"

"One more thing. I'm planning to make a side trip to Morita before heading out. Last Friday night you mentioned the caretaker and said it concerned another piece you'd worked on. What's that about?"

"It concerned a hiker who was killed there about a year ago."

Conjuring up the ghoulish details of Russell Greene's past made my stomach dip in anticipation. "Killed? How?"

"Apparently, he was exploring the area looking for caves and fell into one of the abandoned mine shafts. Right afterwards, the owners put up a fence, plastered the area with no trespassing signs, and hired some guy to keep people out because of the liability factor, I imagine. Too bad. It's real pretty back there, natural springs, a waterfall and it used to be neat to poke around some of the old buildings."

"Who owns the property?"

"You know, I'm not sure. Up until a few years ago, one of the big ranchers in that area owned it, but I think I remember reading that they'd sold the property to an out-of-state mining venture interested in reopening the old Yellow Jacket Mine, but you'll have to verify that."

"I plan to. Turns out you left a lot of pretty intriguing stuff on the table that I'd really like to follow up on."

He chuckled. "Well, you'd better get cracking if you plan to get all the answers by this afternoon."

I smiled. "That's good, Walter. Actually, I'm probably going to have to make another trip down here next week." I heard his other line ringing. "Hey, I know you guys are swamped so we'll talk more later. Call me when you get that info." I punched the off button and redialed Tally's number. Ronda answered again and told me to hang on a minute. I roamed around the room while waiting and decided that the privacy of my room would really be preferable while talking with him but, when I got to the hallway, the phone hummed and hissed so loudly I had to retrace my steps.

At long last, I heard footsteps on the other end of the line and the scrape of the receiver being lifted. "You are one tough lady to get hold of," Tally said with no preliminaries.

"Me? I've been trying to reach you since Saturday morning."

"Really?"

"Really. I left three messages." I bit my tongue, deciding I would not mention his mother's underhanded tactics right now.

"Did you forget to take your handy-dandy little cell phone with you?"

"No, I have it."

"Well, it's not working. I've tried calling you at least fifty times."

Hearing that made my heart soar with delight. "Sorry about that. I haven't been able to get a signal most of the time. It's a pretty isolated area, but, of course, you know that." What an inane conversation. I didn't want to talk about cell phones anymore, I wanted terribly to find out if things were okay between us, to ask if he was still angry with me, tell him that I missed him, I loved him and that I could hardly wait to see him.

"I see," he said lightly. "Has your trip been everything you hoped it would be?"

Interesting wording. Translation: *I hope you've gotten all this nonsense out of your system now, and are ready to come back home.* The standoffish quality in his voice clearly conveyed that he was still annoyed.

"By the way," he added, "what the hell are you doing at the Sundog? I thought the whole purpose of your spur-of-the-moment trip hinged on Lupe's problems?"

"It...it's a long story, most of which I'll be glad to share with you when I get back."

"What do you think of it?"

"What do I think of what?"

"The ranch."

"It's fantastic."

"The Beaumonts are a really special family, don't you agree?"

I hesitated before saying through gritted teeth, "Salt of the earth."

"I think so too," he said warmly. "So...what time are you getting in?"

I studied my watch. "I'm thinking no later than seven and Tally...."

"Uh-huh?"

It was on the tip of my tongue to babble how sorry I was that I'd come on this infuriating trip, but stubbornly all I said was, "I miss you."

His silence reined in my wildly beating heart. Apparently, I had a lot of fences to mend as a result of my rash decision. Sounding petulant he said, "Does that mean I have a shot at being number one on your list of important things for a change?"

"Tally, you've always occupied that slot and you know it." I half expected him to sarcastically contradict me, but instead, he drawled, "Well, then, I'm giving you a whole week to prove it."

I dropped my voice to a low, sexy tone. "You're on, cowboy. I plan to stick to you like a piece of teddy bear cholla."

"Hmmm. Now *that* presents a host of interesting possibilities. Do I have your solemn promise?" I could tell by the husky quality in his voice that he was finally thawing.

"I told you, I never break a promise."

"Ah...Kendall...?" The note of hesitancy told me something else was on his mind.

"Yes?"

"Having you along on this trip is...well, real important to me. I guess I've been a little worried that you might cancel at the last minute."

He had no idea how close he was to being right. "Well, stop worrying. Nothing, and I mean nothing, is going to stop me from coming with you."

"I'm counting on that...can you hang on a second?"

"Sure." Mumbled conversation in the background and then he came back on the line. "Listen, I've got to go finish up with these damned bureaucrats."

"Okay. I was going to share my little surprise with you now, but I can tell you tonight," I said lightly, wondering what he'd think of Marmalade.

"It just so happens I have a surprise for you too."

"You do?"

"I do."

Tingling all over with happiness at the expectation of seeing him in just a few short hours, I reluctantly said goodbye. And, if I hadn't gotten the little phone antenna caught in my hair and had to fiddle with it for a few seconds, I wouldn't have heard the telltale click of an extension phone being cradled somewhere else in the house.

16

By the time I reached the main highway a half hour later, the flames of anger had diminished to simmering coals of agitation. What reason would anyone in the Beaumont household have for eavesdropping on my telephone conversations? It could have been any one of them but I had a gut feeling it was Jason. I'd run into him again in the upstairs hallway when I'd gone to get my bag and he'd pinned me with such a withering look, my insides shriveled with alarm. Even though he now knew that I had no connection with the Lopez woman, why did he act as if I still represented some sort of threat? And why did Bethany get off on treating me in such a malicious manner?

Even though I liked Champ and Twyla, I'd had my fill of the brother and sister duo and had a difficult time restraining the urge to blurt out my accusation when I'd returned to the kitchen to announce my departure. Unfortunately, I had no way of proving my suspicions and as a result I wasn't feeling any too friendly. My frosty thanks for their hospitality, followed by my speedy exit, had left the elder Beaumonts standing on the porch wearing bemused expressions.

Now, as I headed towards Arivaca once more, fighting the ever-rising wind, my temples throbbed and my stomach remained in turmoil. For the next ten miles, I tried to convince myself that the memory of the bludgeoned cattle and the musty residue of llama spit in my nose, piled on top of all the other weirdness that had happened this weekend, were responsible for my feeling out of sorts. But the intermittent chills sweeping over my body and my scratchy throat told a different story. No matter how I tried to deny it the evidence was there. I was coming down with something.

Great timing, O'Dell. No, make that perfect timing—to spoil the vacation with Tally. And it was all my own doing. My dad had opined, following one of my legendary tantrums at age five, that I had been born with an extra bone in my body. A stubborn bone. Wasn't it because of my pigheaded decision to flaunt my independence that I'd exposed myself to Lupe's illness and placed my promise to Tally in jeopardy?

But, maybe I was mistaken. Maybe I was just tired. I set my jaw, determined to fight it off. "Mind over matter," I muttered to myself. Perhaps some soup and a couple of aspirin would do the trick, I thought, parking near the front door of the café.

The place was only about half full, but I'm pretty sure I recognized some of the same fossils that had breakfasted here yesterday. Raked over by their inquisitive stares, I snagged a table in the furthest corner and settled down with a cup of hot tea to wait for Payton. I actually looked forward to talking with him, but had to admit that my intentions were threefold. I certainly owed him big time for his act of kindness, but, because of his longstanding ties with this community, I felt sure he'd be a valuable resource, especially when it came to filling in more background on Jason Beaumont. No doubt he'd know plenty about the young man's past, but I had to admit that the main focus of my curiosity was Bethany. Being the obvious target of her ill will was a continued source of puzzlement to me. It made sense to think the eavesdropper was Jason, but it could just as easily have been her. But, why would either of them care about my telephone conversations?

Everyone stopped in mid-chew and looked up as the door swung open and Payton stepped inside, tamping down his windblown hair. I waved and when he returned it and weaved among the mismatched tables and chairs towards me, a series of quizzical gray eyebrows hiked up. Oh, boy. Something new to gossip about.

"Hi, sorry I'm a little late." He slid into the chair across from me. "I was on the trail of a wily rattler and time got away from me."

"Did you catch it?"

"Oh, yeah," he said, a ring of assurance in his voice. "It takes a lot of patience this time of year, because their hibernation period has begun, but it's worth the effort. An ounce of venom can save a life somewhere."

Admiration swelled inside me. What a guy. I pushed the menu to him. "I really wanted to buy you a big, thick steak, but I'm afraid the patty melt is the closest thing to a gourmet dish offered here."

Payton laughed. "That's fine. You don't owe me anything, Kendall. I was happy to help out."

"Hi, Payton," said the buxom waitress, showing him a generous portion of cleavage as she set down silverware, napkins and water. "You gonna stay around and finish your food today or will you be running off to rescue more stray pussy cats?"

Chuckling, he winked at me. "No secrets in this town, huh?" I think to please me he decided on the patty melt with fries and coffee. I ordered soup, even though I wasn't the least bit hungry. In fact, I felt a little lightheaded and figured I'd best eat something since I had a long drive ahead of me. After she left he folded his arms together in front of him and leaned in, assuming a serious look. "Listen, I wanted to apologize to you about last evening."

I drew back, surprised. "Apologize for what?"

"Leaving you so abruptly. It's just that...well, Bethany can be so...so...."

"Exasperating? Believe me, I hear you." I lowered my voice. "I hope you don't mind my asking, but since you brought it up...."

He put up a hand. "I know. I know. How on earth did I ever get hooked up with someone like her?"

"Bingo."

His attention turned inward for a few seconds before he relinquished a soft sigh. "I think I fell in love with her the first time I saw her riding her Palomino at the rodeo. We were both five years old at the time."

His dreamy-eyed expression prompted me to follow my earlier hunch. "Dean's place. That wasn't by any chance your ranch at one time?"

One reddish brow inched above his glasses. "So you've been asking about me?"

"No. I just added together a couple of the things you said yesterday and sprinkled in a little reporter's intuition."

"I see. Guess I'm pretty transparent."

He paused while the waitress delivered my pea soup and his coffee before saying, "Yes, that was our place until it was...acquired by the Sundog a few years ago. But, that's a long, sad story I'm sure you have no interest in." The undertone of careless resentment in his tone piqued my curiosity even further.

"Quite the contrary, if you don't mind answering a couple of questions."

He studied my face intensely for a few seconds. "If I answer yours, you have to answer mine."

"If I can."

He leaned even closer, saying in a soft voice, "So is it you or your friend who's having an abduction problem?"

Caught off guard, my pulse rocketed skyward and soup sloshed off the spoon. "Whaa...what are you talking about?" I asked, trying to appear cool while my mind spun off in a hundred directions. How could he possibly know anything about Lupe's missing relatives?

A sly grin. "Mazzie La Casse. I've been dying to know why you and your friend were having breakfast with her yesterday. I thought you said you were here doing a story on our border issues?"

I'd forgotten he'd overheard Lupe's remark at the scene of the accident. I swallowed a few spoonfuls of soup, regaining my composure. "Oh, that." I told him about the UFO stories Walter had been writing before he'd come to work for us, concluding with, "They sounded fascinating, so I thought it might be interesting to follow up on them. She was recommended as a good source of information on that subject."

"Was she helpful to you?"

I eyed him with interest. "Yes. Why do I get the impression that you know her?"

"Everyone in town knows about Mazzie. When she found out that I spend a lot of time tramping around in the desert in the wee dark hours of the morning, she cornered me here one day to ask if I'd ever witnessed strange lights in the sky. Apparently some other people had reported seeing what they believed were UFOs around that time."

"And?"

A guarded look crept into his eyes. "Promise you won't laugh?"

My heart beat a little faster. Oh, Lordy! Another promise. "Cross my heart."

His voice dropped to a whisper. "I have to admit I've seen a few things out there I can't explain."

"Really? Like what?"

Lips pressed in a sly smile, he said, "I don't think I want you quoting me in your newspaper. Agreed?"

"Agreed."

Appearing edgy, his gaze roamed the room before returning to me. "On several occasions, I've seen odd, pulsating lights in the sky and then poof, they were gone in an instant."

Taken aback, I tried not to stare. Of all the people I'd met, he seemed the most levelheaded. "Was this near a place called Morita?"

Puzzlement shimmered in his eyes. "Why do you say that?"

"Remember the story I told you Walter was working on? You know, the one about the Mexican immigrant the Border Patrol found hiding there."

"Oh, right, of course. No, these were further east, closer to Ruby. Don't get me wrong. I'm not claiming to have seen the mother ship landing or anything like that. More likely, the military is testing a new type of plane. We're not that far from the Barry Goldwater Air Force Range."

"Well, a UFO sighting would make for more interesting copy, but frankly it's a real stretch for me to believe that extraterrestrials are cruising around snatching people away." I grinned. "However, I'm willing to keep an open mind."

His features relaxed into a smile. "Whew. It's a relief to know you don't think I'm two bricks shy of a full load."

His story was downright tame compared to Javier's. "Not at all." Could the immigrant and Javier have mistaken the lights for an airplane? But, what about the description of the alien beings with the big eyes? Where did that fit in?

He took several sips of coffee and settled back into the chair. "So, what did you want to ask me?"

Heads craned in our direction, and a couple of senior citizens shuffled by our table at a snail's pace. I waited until they were out of earshot. "On Saturday, your friend, Joe, said Jason's folks had gotten him off the hook before. What kind of trouble has he been in?"

Payton contemplated the lint on his trousers a few seconds before answering. "Vandalism, drunk driving, disorderly conduct, to name a few. Fortunately, Champ has always been able to get him off with jail time served, or by paying off the injured party to drop the charges."

"Do you know if he's involved with any of these White power groups?"

He looked at me sharply. "What makes you ask?"

"I happened to pass the door to his room last evening and he's got some pretty inflammatory stuff plastered on his walls."

The frown lines on his forehead became more pronounced. "He was implicated in a pretty serious incident that happened here a couple of years ago."

I stared at him. "You mean the church burning?"

His initial look of surprise turned to one of perception. "Ah," he said, tapping his temple for emphasis, "Your friend Walter again?"

"Actually he filled me in on that before I got here."

"The charges against Jason were dismissed for lack of evidence, but the head honcho of the group and several others weren't so fortunate."

"Do you think he was involved?"

He hesitated, waiting until after the waitress served his sandwich. "Everybody knows Jason's got a short fuse. He's young and cocky and I don't care for some of the people he associates with, but...I don't want to rock the boat. It's...kind of important for me to stay on his good side."

"Why? He's a loose cannon, at best."

He shook his head impatiently. "He's my eyes and ears at the ranch when I'm away. I like to keep tabs on what Bethany is up to regarding Brett's welfare." He chewed pensively a moment before adding, "In fact, Brett said something the other day that really blew me away."

"What was that?"

"He asked me if it was possible to have two daddies."

Apparently Jason had not mentioned Bethany's involvement with Sloan, the hunky cowstud. It was on the tip of my tongue to reveal it, but I kept silent. It was none of my business. I'd be gone in a few hours and most likely I'd never see these people again in my life. I glanced at the wall clock and pushed away the remainder of my soup. "Payton, why did you sell your ranch?"

He pounded ketchup onto his plate. "Couldn't afford to pay the taxes. It really sucked at the time, but I guess everything happens for a reason. At least I don't have to put up with all the bullshit the other ranching families are wrestling with nowadays. I'm on neutral ground. I live in Tucson, but I still get to enjoy my old stomping grounds when I come down to visit Brett, and of course I pick up a few extra bucks doing my snake thing."

"Where do you stay when you're here? I didn't see a motel around anywhere."

"I rent a bedroom from an old friend of mine or I sleep overnight in the camper if I don't feel like driving back into town." He popped a French fry into his mouth. "Any more questions?"

Smiling, I rested my elbows on the table. "Just one, and I'll understand if you don't want to answer, but I'm dying to know why Bethany calls you Jack."

His eyes twinkled with humor. "You don't miss much, do you?"

"I try not to."

He took a big bite of the patty melt, chewed and then wiped his mouth with the napkin before saying, "You know the old saying, Jack of all trades, master of none?"

"Sure."

"That's her not-very-subtle way of reminding me of the number of jobs I've held over the years." He paused while the waitress refilled his coffee then hurried off. "My parents took over running the very successful Kleinwort ranching properties when my grandpa died, and even though he worked hard, Dad could never seem to make a go of it. Of course I didn't know that then. I just knew that it was an awesome place for a kid to live. Once I finished my chores, me and a couple of buddies from neighboring ranches would ride off on our horses and be gone all day exploring." He exhaled a nostalgic sigh. "We traveled every square inch of the surrounding desert and mountains, and I know it like the back of my hand."

"Were you an only child?"

His eyes shifted away, then back as a look of supreme melancholy clouded his features. "No," he said at length, "I had a beautiful little sister named Laura. She died three years ago."

I frowned, remembering Bethany's shrine comment. "I'm sorry. What happened to her?"

"Laura was born with an enlarged heart. She never really got a chance to run and play like normal kids, but she was a real trooper. Of course the medical bills were staggering. Little by little, my dad had to sell off pieces to the Beaumonts and a couple of other ranchers until we were down to fifteen thousand acres out of the original twenty-five." He sugared his coffee and took a sip before continuing with, "But, even so, I think we'd have been okay if...if it hadn't been for my father's sudden death. My mom...well, she went to pieces afterwards. I remember the night she packed up my sister and me and drove us over to my uncle's place near Benson. She told us she needed to get away by herself for a little while and that she'd be back to get us in a few days...but that was the last time we ever saw her."

A surge of sympathy rocked my heart. "Payton, I'm sorry. I shouldn't have pried...."

He waved away my concern. "Hey, it's old news. Everyone in this county knows about the Kleinwort tragedies so don't feel bad. Anyway," he added with a wry smile, "it gets worse."

And it did. In between bites of his sandwich and fries he relayed how he and Laura had lived with his Uncle Alvin, his new wife, Myra, and older cousin, Gordon, for the next seven years until his uncle had been laid off by the railroad. When Payton's mother had been declared legally dead, his uncle sold his house and they'd all moved back to the Kleinwort ranch. "He thought he was going to resurrect the place to its former glory, but he was no better at operating it than my dad was. So, in order to get enough money to send Gordon to medical school, he systematically sold off more acreage."

"Wait a minute, he was selling off your inheritance so your *cousin* could go to medical school? What about you and your sister's rights?"

"What rights? He was our legal guardian and I was only fifteen. Actually, I didn't even know what they were up to until a couple of years later when it came time for me to go to college. They never let us forget for a minute what a burden we'd been to them and claimed the money had mostly been spent on Laura, but I know that wasn't true." He drew little circles in the sugar that had spilled on the table as he explained how he'd become reacquainted with the Beaumonts again. "Even though I only saw Bethany at school, I daydreamed about her all the time. I didn't think she ever noticed me, but about a year later she suddenly started coming around a lot. At first I thought she was befriending Laura, and then I fooled myself into thinking she was as nuts about me as I was about her...but it was really Gordon she was interested in. He was the good-looking one. He was the smart one, but she couldn't seem to get him to notice her."

My chin sagged. "How is that possible? Is he blind?"

Chuckling, he reached into his back pocket and pulled out a wallet. "She didn't look quite the same then as she does now." He proffered a photo and I stared in amazement at a plumpish teenager with limp blonde hair and rather unspectacular features before raising questioning eyes to meet his. "That's quite a transformation."

His smile soured. "With a little help from cosmetic surgery."

"I'd wager a lot of surgery, paid for by daddy, no doubt."

"No," he said dryly, "mostly paid for by me."

"You?"

"Her therapist convinced her that she needed it to create a more positive self-image. I worked seven days a week at three jobs to support her and Brett. Plus, I had to care for Laura while she waited for her heart transplant." His voice grew somber. "The fact that my sister and I were so close was always a sore spot with my beloved ex."

"Why?"

"She was always whining that I loved Laura more than her, even though I know now that Bethany never really gave a crap about me."

"Okay, I'm totally confused now."

"Sorry, I'm getting ahead of myself. I guess, being a writer, you might want to title the rest of this sordid tale *love is blind*," he said stringing imaginary letters in the air between us. "Or maybe, men are the biggest saps on the planet, or something to that effect. Anyway, when I was eighteen, Gordon suddenly eloped with one of his professors, ten years his senior. Bethany was devastated, a total basket case, and who do you think was there to comfort her?"

"You."

"Yeah, stupid me. I figured with Gordon out of the picture maybe I finally had a chance, but she was just using me to stay close to him. We were out partying one night a couple of months later. She had a lot to drink and when she threw herself at me, well, I didn't turn her down and well...."

"She got pregnant?" I filled in wryly.

Flushing, he admitted, "You guessed it. We discussed abortion, but she said her folks would have a fit if they found out, so we drove to Las Vegas and got married. About that time my uncle died, Myra left, and I hired a foreman to run what was left of the ranch so I could keep working the other jobs."

"Did you work for your Uncle Dean?"

His pale brows bunched together. "No, why?"

"That guy, Joe, said you were a vet's assistant or something."

His face softened. "Yeah. I love working with animals. My dream was to study medicine like Gordon, but I had to drop out after a year. No money," he said with a tight smile. "So, being a veterinary technician was as close as I ever got. Bethany's happiness always came first. I worked part-time as a shoe clerk," he said, pulling down fingers, "a vacuum cleaner salesman, bartender, night-manager at a convenience store...I've lost track now, but none paid enough to provide her with the lifestyle to which she felt entitled."

"When did you have time to sleep?" I asked, my contempt for this self-centered woman rising by the second.

"I didn't. I was like a zombie. And nothing I did ever seemed enough to satisfy her. Oh, I tried to convince myself that she'd learn to love me someday, but she was still obsessed with Gordon and set about making herself into a living Barbie doll until she finally got his attention. She had her nose done, cheek implants, laser skin resurfacing, liposuction, dyed her hair light blonde, hired a personal trainer, the works."

I shook my head as he went on to explain how she'd finally ensnared Gordon in an affair that resulted in his wife leaving him. Payton, mired in debt because of her lavish spending and the astronomical medical bills piling up while his dying sister awaited her transplant, could do nothing to stop Bethany when she'd taken Brett and moved to San Francisco with his cousin. "She finally got what she'd always wanted, a big house by the bay, fancy car, all the things she said I couldn't give her because of my devotion to my sister."

"And that was a bad thing to her?"

His smile was rueful. "She likes to tell anyone who will listen that my concern for Laura bordered on obsession, but I'll tell you what," he said, pushing his empty plate to the side, "my sister taught me a lot about love and courage, and I don't regret a moment of the time I spent with her."

I couldn't help but admire his upbeat attitude considering all the crappy things that had happened to him. Instead of feeling sorry for himself, instead of suffering from some major neurosis, he appeared to have reached a comfortable level of acceptance that granted him inner peace. But, it made my blood boil to hear how shabbily Bethany had treated this very compassionate, very sensitive man. I said, "Personally, I think you should be nominated for sainthood."

Reddening, he grinned. "Well, thank you."

"So, I gather since she's back, things didn't work out with your cousin?"

Scorn danced in his eyes. "He finally saw through her shallowness, called me up, begged my forgiveness and kicked her butt out. She got a real rude awakening when she came slithering back to the Sundog thinking she was going to continue her cushy lifestyle courtesy of mom and dad. Wrong! Things had changed for them financially, so in order to stay she had to agree to pull her own weight helping out with the guests."

"What happened with your cousin?"

"He's still trying to reconcile with his wife and I'm trying to make up for lost time with Brett." He exhaled a protracted sigh. "And Bethany's new goal in life is making it as difficult as possible for me to see him. In case you hadn't noticed, she's a master at laying down roadblocks and manipulating circumstances to her own benefit."

"I noticed." I hunched forward, resting my chin on my hands. "Tell me something, what did she mean about you erecting a shrine for Laura in the desert? Is your sister...buried out there?"

He shook his head, clearly irritated. "Bethany has a habit of over-dramatizing the situation. It's really not a big deal at all. Laura's dying wish was to have her ashes spread in the spot where we used to go for picnics when we were kids. I go out there sometimes, say a little prayer and just, you know, listen to the wind. I'll tell you, it was the saddest thing on earth watching her waste away waiting...waiting for the healthy heart she never got." His voice faltering with emotion prompted me to place my hand over his. "Payton, I'm so sorry." He turned his palm upward and clasped my hand, his misty eyes brimming with gratitude. "Thank you. Thank you for caring. It was a terrible ordeal, but at least one good thing came out of it."

I noticed the four elderly diners at the next table eyeing us with eager speculation, so I gently disengaged my hand from his. "What's that?"

"It made me aware of the appalling shortage of organ donors in this country. Get this, even if one does become available, it doesn't mean the most deserving person will receive it." His lips twisted. "Money, power and celebrity go a long way in pushing certain people to the top of the list."

I eyed him closely. "Is that what happened to your sister? Did she get bumped for someone else?"

"The hospital denied it, but yes, I think so. Did you know that over sixty-five thousand people are on waiting lists for transplants at this very moment? And like Laura, over five thousand a year die before receiving either a heart, or liver, lungs or a kidney?"

"I had no idea."

"It's definitely been an eye-opening education." He fixed me with a solemn look. "Tell me something, have you ever donated blood?"

"Sure."

"And have you filled out an organ donor card?

"No."

"Did you know they're available at every blood bank?"

Guilt gnawed at me and I squirmed under his intense gaze. "No, I didn't."

"Bet you never gave it much thought, did you?"

"I'm ashamed to admit it, but no."

"Don't feel bad. Most people aren't aware of it, or choose to ignore it. That's what's so sad. Think about the thousands of fully intact cadavers buried each year in ridiculously elaborate funerals when it would be so easy to have given the gift of life to another human being." His rough breathing and passionate tone of voice had curious heads turning in our direction again. Apparently we were the lunchtime entertainment.

Blushing under the scrutiny, he steepled his hands against the flat line of his lips for a couple of seconds. "Making people aware of this problem has become my personal crusade since Laura died."

"That's all right," I answered, admiring his sensitivity. "You've convinced me. I'll fill out a donor card the very next time I donate blood."

His smile matched the sparkle in his green eyes. "Bravo." A silence fell between us and he glanced at his watch. "Well, thanks again for lunch. I'd like to stay and chat longer but I've got to make a couple of phone calls..."

"Hey, it's nothing considering how helpful you've been to me."

He rose and then hesitated beside my chair. "Do you think you'll ever be back down this way again?"

I shrugged. "It's possible."

"Well, if you do, be sure to look me up."

"You can bet on it."

"Enjoy your new kitty." Smiling, he accepted my outstretched hand and then with a final wave, strode towards the outside door leading to the saloon. When I looked around, everyone in the place was staring at me with a knowing smile. Good grief. No doubt they'd interpreted our meeting as a lover's rendezvous. Good thing I was leaving town today. I hailed the waitress for the bill. The aspirin I'd taken earlier had helped dull the beginnings of a headache but my throat was growing increasingly raw. If things worked out as I hoped, I'd snag an interview with the caretaker at Morita, collect my new kitten and then get home as quickly as possible.

I stepped outside into the wind, smarting with the knowledge that so far I'd failed to come up with anything viable to help Lupe. It weighed heavily on me as I pulled my car keys from my purse and I nearly walked by the dented orange truck before I realized it was Froggy's. I hesitated. This might be a perfect opportunity to corner the little weasel in the saloon and try to extract more information, but one glance at my watch told the story. I didn't have enough time.

I'd just stuck my key in the door when the sudden squeal of tires from behind startled me. Turning, my heart jerked uncomfortably as Jason's red pickup skidded into the nearby parking space. The nasty-faced skinhead with the pit bull eyes sat next to him. Oh, brother.

Never taking their eyes off me, they slammed out the doors and strode in my direction. I drew myself up to my full height and returned their hostile glares. "Something I can help you boys with?"

Jason's nostrils flared. "You headin' out of town now?"

Even though my heart was throwing itself painfully against my ribs, I answered coolly, "I can't see how that's any of your business."

"Cutter an' me think it is."

"Cutter, huh?" I glanced at his companion, aptly named I thought as he scraped the tip of a knife blade beneath one fingernail. His menacing stare wilted my insides, but I stood my ground. "It's surprising to know you two actually *can* think."

They exchanged a viperous look and moved closer. Backed against the car, I hastily looked around for a witness. Of course, not a soul was in sight.

Jason's lip curled up on one side. "My folks might think you're hot shit, but the rest of us don't want a wetback-loving reporter snooping around sticking her pointed nose in places it don't belong." I took offense at the pointed nose remark. "So, you better be careful," he continued, baring his teeth, "or it might get cut clean off." Cutter's guttural laugh was chilling as he swiped the knife in front of his nose.

These guys had seen way too many cop movies. I narrowed my eyes at Jason. "Don't threaten me, you little punk."

Still smirking, he slapped his buddy on the back and they sauntered towards the saloon entrance. When he reached the archway he swung back, very deliberately aimed his index finger at me and then depressed his thumb as if he were firing a gun.

17

The pea soup I'd hoped would make me feel better congealed in my belly like a cold lake as I cruised towards Sasabe, still shaking with anxiety-charged fury. My face burned and my arms felt boneless as yet another megadose of adrenaline drained from my system. Should I turn around and drive to the nearest sheriff's office and report the incident? But what had they really implied? Would the authorities accept the word of a stranger against one of their own or dismiss their actions as youthful fun? But these weren't just overgrown boys playing schoolyard bullies. Like the first time Jason and his cohorts surrounded my car, I'd sensed tangible danger behind their eyes.

The consternation swirling inside me rivaled the wind buffeting my car. Walter's instincts concerning his wife's late cousin might just prove to be true. It wasn't lost on me that this latest altercation had something to do with my visit to the Shirley household. Cutter had scurried to rat on me to Jason. Did his involvement mean that the rumor linking Bob Shirley to a White power group was true? And if so, what were Jason and Cutter afraid that I might have discovered? The chilly sensation lodged in my gut gave credence to the intuitive feeling that I'd accidentally backed into something far bigger than Lupe's story. Even though I'd apparently struck out on her behalf, my scheduled trip to Morita had suddenly taken on significance beyond that which affected Lupe. Would the elusive caretaker be able to shed any new light on the Mexican immigrant's tale of alien abductions? Would Morita hold the key connecting Javier's story to Lupe's missing relatives? And if it did, what had frightened Bob Shirley so much that he refused to discuss the incident ever again? Frustration piled onto my feelings of defeat. This was a story I ached to follow up on, but my time to bring home any significant information was running out. And I had to be honest with myself. As much as the whole situation intrigued me, did I really want to return here and embroil myself in what could prove to be another dangerous assignment? And in light of Lupe's deception concerning her illegal status, did I really want to take that risk for her? No, I convinced myself, the trip to Morita was now more for my own curiosity.

The tiny community of Sasabe was just that. Tiny. And it was for sale. A prominent sign offered it for three million dollars. Cruising along the peaceful street devoid of traffic, I noticed that a renovation effort was underway in an attempt to spruce up some of the old adobe houses and buildings. Some sported fresh pink and turquoise paint. A few parked cars and two elderly Mexican women sitting on a bench in front of the Post Office adjacent to a general store were the only signs of life. I couldn't imagine why anyone would want to live here unless it was to enjoy total silence. The road curved sharply right, dipping down past a small house surrounded by a sturdy fence topped with concertina wire, guarded by two wildly barking dogs and a scowling gray-haired woman who never took her eyes off me. When I reached the top of the incline, a large red brick facility with a white gabled roof came into view. A large sign announced that I'd reached the U.S. Port of Entry and another in English and Spanish, welcomed me to Mexico, where the pavement abruptly ended. A wide dusty road continued southward towards the twin village of Sasabe, Sonora. I drove back and waved at the bored-looking U.S. Customs official in the guard station as I passed by. There wasn't another car or truck in sight. The formidable white barrier separating the two countries snaked along the rough terrain until it dissolved into nothing more than a puny range fence. Easy entry into the country just a few hundred yards away from the official crossing. What a joke. I shook my head. Unless enough agents could be hired to stand shoulder to shoulder, forming a human shield extending along the entire two thousand mile border, there was no way on earth there could be enough manpower to stop the tide of illegal aliens.

I backtracked through town and moments later turned onto a dirt lane and bounced along, heading west. Noting the herds of cattle munching on the grassy hillsides, I presumed that I had re-entered the Beaumont property. After traveling only half a mile, I drove past a square, windowless building topped with a windsock, blowing straight out in the strong southwesterly wind. At the tip of a tiny airstrip that had been carved out of the desert floor, sat a faded red and white plane that I assumed belonged to Champ. I had a quick flashback to life in my cramped apartment in Philadelphia this time last year and found myself in awe of someone owning so much property that he had to use an airplane just to visit the boundaries.

When I glanced again at the open map on the passenger seat, a little jolt of surprise nudged me as I realized that the ghost town of Morita lay nestled in the shadows of the crooked stack of wind-sculpted rocks known as Wolf's Head. I wondered why Payton had never mentioned that fact. But, of course, I'd never asked him.

After another mile or so, I buzzed over a cattle guard and passed an overgrown track to my right. Holding the steering wheel in one hand, I studied the map again. That should take me back to Dean's place. Even though it seemed much further away, Morita was actually less than three miles from his ranch house.

A hazy rooster tail of dust ahead signaled another vehicle coming my way. Since the road was narrow, I pulled over to the right to allow what I could now identify as a Border Patrol SUV to pass. A little ripple of uneasiness skimmed along my spine when I recognized the driver. Hank Breslow. He stopped and signaled for me to roll down my window. "Are you lost?"

"No."

A prolonged hesitation then, "Where are you headed?"

I couldn't put my finger on it. Maybe it was because of the way he'd treated Lupe or perhaps it was the glint of circumspection in his eyes. Whatever, I didn't really want to tell him. But, he could easily follow me and find out. "Morita."

"Why are you going out there?"

"I need to get a few shots of the area for my article."

Appearing skeptical, he advised, "I'd be real careful if I were you. There are a lot of open mine shafts around and I don't think I need to mention that a woman as attractive as you in such a desolate area along the border could be inviting trouble in more ways than one."

I don't know why, but I sensed that he didn't want me going to Morita. "I appreciate your concern. I'll be extra careful."

He didn't look thrilled with my answer. When he didn't move I waved farewell, put my car in gear and drove on half expecting him to follow. Several glances in the rearview mirror confirmed that he hadn't. Very strange guy. Or was I just overly suspicious?

If I hadn't been traveling so slowly, searching for the cutoff to Morita, I wouldn't have seen the brilliant flash of red out of the corner of my eye. I braked and backed up, staring at the vibrant clusters of scarlet tucked away beneath the grove of cottonwood trees to my left. It was too late in the season for desert flowers. Curious, I pulled the car to the side of the road and got out.

A sense of wonderment engulfed me as I encountered an unexpected carpet of green grass encircled by manicured shrubs and clay pots brimming with flowers. Above my head, the soft whisper of leaves added to the feeling of total serenity. What was this place hidden away in the middle of nowhere? My question was soon answered when I spotted a stone marker decorated with elaborately carved angels. Two large plastic vases filled with fresh roses stood to either side. Intrigued, I sat down on the little wooden bench opposite it and read the inscription. *Sleep at last in blissful peace, darling Laura. In death lies the promise of new life.*

How touching that Payton had gone to all this trouble to commemorate the place where his sister's ashes had been scattered. Nevertheless, I couldn't deny feeling a slight sense of uneasiness when I recalled Bethany's cryptic assertion that Payton suffered from an obsession regarding his sister. I shrugged it off. Obsession might be too strong of a word. Deep devotion might be a better description. But as I again viewed the flowered oasis, the word shrine seemed more and more appropriate. Okay, I admitted to myself, maybe he was just a little obsessed. I left with a cold knot in my belly, not knowing quite what to think.

Behind the wheel again, the winding road became rougher, narrower, and suddenly dipped into a deep rocky arroyo. By the time I climbed back up to the other side, the crumbling remains of several structures crouching on the grassy slopes beneath the massive overhang of rocks caught my attention. The road curved ahead, vanishing into the distant hills, so I took the next cutoff and traveled south perhaps a quarter of a mile until the road finally dead-ended. All right! I'd finally made it to Morita.

One house, perched at the top of a small rise looked livable, so I surmised that it was probably the caretaker's residence. I pulled up to the gate and stared at the sign posted prominently in large letters. KEEP OUT!! A second one warned NO TRESPASSING UNLESS YOU CAN CROSS THIS PROPERTY IN TEN SECONDS. MY DOBERMAN CAN DO IT IN NINE. Well, that wasn't much of a welcome. Yet another less intimidating sign invited me to honk my horn and wait. Good plan. However when I honked, no one appeared. I leaned on my horn again. Still no response. Was the brisk wind carrying the sound away?

The heavy padlock on the gate latch guaranteed no entry. I sat for a moment debating. I didn't want to trespass, but I wasn't about to turn around and go home empty-handed after coming all the way out here. My gaze followed the fence line. It would be an easy enough task to climb through the barbed wire and walk to the house, which looked to be no more than a quarter of a mile away. On a whim, I powered on my cell phone, and then gawked in disbelief. Out here, literally in the middle of nowhere, the roam signal pulsed back at me. That knowledge made me feel a lot more secure as I parked the car beside a Mexican blue oak not far from the gate. I clipped the phone to my waistband and grabbed my jacket and a bottle of water from the back seat.

Opening my car door against the force of the wind roaring down the slope through the gaps in the canyon walls presented somewhat of a challenge. Man. It had to be blowing thirty or forty miles per hour and the mournful keening increased the sense of utter desolation. Russell Greene must be a real recluse to live voluntarily in such an isolated spot. But, conjuring up the story of his gruesome survival experience, along with having witnessed his cruel treatment by the boys in Arivaca, made such a decision understandable.

There were no signs of life. Just to be safe though, I locked my purse, camera and laptop computer in the trunk with my overnight bag before setting out. I searched along the fence until I found a section where the wire strands were a little further apart. Even so, I still managed to tear a hole in my jacket and the thigh of my jeans when I squeezed between them. "Crap," I muttered, pushing uselessly at the frayed material.

As I trudged towards the white clapboard house, I couldn't stop staring at the dramatic backdrop of sheer rock looming tall over the last vestiges of this once flourishing mining town. Like a lot of the old ghost towns in Arizona I'd visited with Tally, this place had a palpable haunted feel to it. Was it because the decaying ruins created a somber atmosphere, reflecting the disappointments and shattered dreams of the people who'd once lived here? The wind was making my nose run and I sneezed violently a few times as I scaled the hill and marched up disintegrating stone steps to knock on the front door. No answer. I knocked again. Nothing. My spirits plummeted, acknowledging this was my last opportunity to bring home at least a shred of hope for Lupe. I walked around the side of the house and stopped in my tracks at the sight of the gun-metal gray pickup parked in a garage with only half the roof remaining. If he was home, why wasn't he answering? I pounded on the back door, calling, "Mr. Greene? Are you there? I'd need to speak with you for a few minutes. It's important."

The silence was deafening. I backed away. There were no power or phone wires connected to the house, but a propane tank stood nearby and, on closer inspection, a small electric generator sat inside a small covered enclosure that was probably used to run a well pump located just yards from the house.

To my right, higher on the slope, I could see the dark cavity of the old Yellow Jacket Mine flanked by a tangle of rusting equipment. Eight or ten dilapidated houses snuggled below in the small valley, but on the opposite knoll stood several intriguing-looking adobe buildings, some with graceful arches associated with early Spanish architecture. I glanced at my watch, noting that I still had a half an hour to kill. Might as well look around a little bit. I wished I had brought my camera because the lighting was spectacular. Amber shafts of sunlight streaming through cracks in the ruptured rock face, contrasted with the violet shadows cast by the amazing jumble of volcanic formations. I craned my head trying to make out the particular configuration Payton had mentioned that gave the place its name, but guessed that I wasn't standing at the correct angle to see it.

Returning to the bottom of the hill, I poked around a couple of the shacks, amazed that the remains of frayed curtains fluttered at some of their windows. Inside them, I found bits and pieces of splintered furniture and rusting appliances. The corrugated tin roofs, rattling and banging in the wind, provided an off-key symphony. Like most of the other played-out mining towns in this state, Morita's remaining structures would one day be only a memory, swallowed up by erosion. But maybe not. If Walter was correct, and mining interests were investing the capital needed to reopen the mine, Morita might have a second chance at life. Starting up the other hill, my goal was a sturdy-looking sandstone building a few hundred yards away. At the top of the embankment, a savage gust of wind almost knocked me off my feet. I arched a look at the darkening band of clouds rising up over the western horizon. Some pretty serious weather must be blowing in. "Way to go, Grandma," I muttered, thinking that her 'red in the morning' proverb might prove to be correct after all. I'd check the forecast when I returned to the car.

Crunching through heavy underbrush, I reached the building and was surprised to note that it was remarkably well preserved. It still had doors and the few windows that weren't boarded up held wavy panes of glass that looked to be original. Amazing. All but a handful of the other ghost towns in the state had been vandalized beyond recognition. Trying the knob, I was surprised to find the front door locked. Disappointed, I peered inside one of the windows, astounded to see rows of ancient-looking school desks and a blackboard running the entire length of one side. Erasers and chalk sat on the metal ledge. Several brass bound trunks stood along the opposite wall next to a desk with a wooden chair pulled up close. Piles of newspapers, magazines and books were strewn about as well as other items. Squinting, I was able to make out the date on the calendar above the desk. April 1936. Cool. I would have given my eyeteeth to get inside and explore.

I turned and looked back towards the caretaker's house. Still no signs of life. Well, he wasn't doing a very good job of keeping people out, I thought smugly, moving on to the next structure that looked like it may have been a stable. Edging a look over the chest-high wall, spray-painted with odd five-cornered symbols and filthy graffiti, I drew in a sharp breath and stared at the carcass of what seemed to be the remains of a golden retriever. Closer inspection was even more disturbing. It appeared to be only the skin and fur stretched out flat like a bear rug. The skeleton of the dog wasn't there. Sick. Goosebumps danced on my arms. What happened to the rest of it? My mind flashed to the mutilated cattle stories and the disturbing rumor that it might be Russell Greene satisfying his carnivorous lust for flesh. No way. Who could eat a dog? More likely, this atrocity could be attributed to the teenagers who'd been accused of practicing witchcraft. All at once, the moan of the wind contained an eerie quality.

Definitely time to go. I started back down the hill towards the gate. At first, when I heard the muffled sound, I was unsure of what it was and assumed it was the sharp whistling of the wind. But then the distinct timbre of a voice calling from somewhere in the distance stopped me in my tracks and sent tingles of horror skating down my back. "Help! Ken....daaalll! Help me!"

What? Heart racing, my mind rebelled against the possibility that anyone could know that I was here. I spun around, searching, trying to identify where the voice was coming from. All my instincts urged me to run, run back to the car as fast as I could, but the thought that someone was in trouble made me hesitate.   What if it was Russell Greene? That would explain why he wasn't around. Had he gotten trapped inside one of the old buildings? I cupped my hands, shouting, "Hello! Is anybody there?"

No sound but the sibilant wind.   I called again. Nothing. Had I imagined it?

Suddenly, the landscape wavered before my eyes. I put a hand to my forehead. My fever must be rising. That would explain it.

I started down the hill only to freeze again. "Heeelllllppppp!"

Swinging around, I stared at a squat adobe structure partially obscured in a snarl of mesquite trees, the only other building nearby. A flash of bright yellow appeared, vanished, and then appeared again.   A distress signal? Baffled, I hurried down the hill, only to slow my steps at the sight of a section of yellow plastic caution tape flapping madly in the branches of a stunted tree. Now that was odd. I located the door around the far side of the structure. "Mr. Greene!" I shouted. "Are you in trouble?"

The wind, pushing hard at my back now, made it difficult to pull the door open. I pounded on it. "Hello? Anybody in there?" I tugged harder and it moved a few inches. Man, it was thick, possibly four inches or more. Panting with exertion, I yanked until there was enough space for me to look inside. There was only one narrow window high on the opposite wall and it was barred. The low light made it difficult to see much, but the floor to ceiling iron bars caught my eye. Was this an old jail? Fascinating. I kicked away some of the dirt and stones and was able to shoulder the door open fully. Just to be safe, I searched around until I found a boulder, which I wedged against the base to keep it from blowing shut. I stepped just inside the doorway. It was cool. Dank. And really depressing. "Hello? Is anybody in here?" As I stood there in the gloom, trying to imagine what it must have been like to be locked away on this lonely hillside, I felt a violent shove against my back. Thrown forward by the force of the blow, I barely had time to get my hands out in front of me before I slammed into the opposite wall, hitting my head hard against the rough stone. Little pinpoints of iridescent light danced behind my eyelids as I lay face down on the debris-filled floor, my muddled brain struggling to make sense of what had happened. Vaguely, I was aware of first a solid clang followed instantaneously by a heavy thud. Oh, crap.

I lifted my head up, trying to focus, and when everything stopped spinning, what I saw confounded me. Not only had the wind blown the outer door shut, the iron door to the cell was also closed.

Fighting a wave of nausea, I stood up and held onto the wall for support. Something was in my right eye. I reached up to wipe it away and my hand came away wet. Uncomprehending, I gawked at the blood for a few seconds before gingerly feeling underneath my hair. "Ouch!" There was a pretty substantial gash.

"What a jackass you are," I scolded myself mildly. Why hadn't I used a bigger rock to secure the door? Better yet, I should never have come inside in the first place. Best get out of here pronto. I pushed against the bars, expecting the door to swing open. It didn't budge. Huh? Using my right shoulder, I shoved hard several times and then shook the bars before reaching around them to feel for the lock. When my fingers encountered an empty keyhole, my blood iced up. Where was the key? I scrabbled around on the floor searching. Nothing. Springing to my feet, I shook the bars again, hoping against hope to loosen the door. "No, no, no!" I screamed. "Don't do this to me!" This could *not* be happening. Suddenly, I couldn't seem to get enough air. Oh, dear God, no. I hadn't had an asthma attack for such a long time I'd neglected to bring my inhaler with me. "Get a grip, girl," I panted. Think. Pressing my face between the bars, I stared into the semi-darkness, my eyes searching the corners near the door. What I saw made my heart shrink. My cell phone, my handy-dandy little cell phone, lay totally out of reach in the far corner, blinking its little green light at me.

18

Panic is a destructive emotion. It demolishes cognitive reasoning, rendering perfectly working brain cells useless. For several minutes I raced in circles, scratching and pounding at the solid walls of my cell screaming like a trapped animal before collapsing into a corner. Bawling like a baby, feeling worse than I could ever remember, I huddled there holding my throbbing head. My throat burned like I'd swallowed a jar of jalapeno peppers, my nose dripped and I ached all over, as if I'd been pummeled in a fight. What a time to get sick. Frantic to escape, I scrambled to my feet again and rattled the bars, yelling, "Help! Heellpppp! Someone let me out of here!"

Icy horror shimmied through me when I realized that I sounded just like the voice I'd heard only moments ago. Had it been real, or an uncanny premonition of things to come? Shit! Why did I keep getting myself into these situations? Was I terminally stupid? It hadn't been that long since my last brush with catastrophe in Morgan's Folly. I was still paying the price for that one. Oh, no! Tally! The thought of him standing impatiently in the dawn light waiting for ·me, believing I'd broken my promise to him, re-ignited my panic. Ginger's words of warning from Friday night echoed in my head. 'You're going to fool around and spoil things with Tally if you ain't careful!' No kidding. This could be the proverbial straw that soured our relationship for good. And, as usual, I had no one to blame but myself.

I slumped against the bars, wallowing in self-pity. I had no food, but at least I had some water, I thought, clutching the plastic bottle protectively to my chest. But, how long would it last me? I was locked away in the sturdiest building still standing in Morita, there didn't appear to be any way out, my goddamned cell phone was lying out of reach and nobody knew I was here. Heart thudding dully against my ribcage, I closed my eyes and concentrated on my breathing for a few minutes. Inhale deeply. Exhale. Try to think. Relax. Get your shit together and calm down.

At some point the caretaker had to show up, or at the very least he would see my car parked near the gate and investigate. Even better, Dean was expecting me to come and claim Marmalade. When I didn't, would he call the sheriff and report me missing, or just assume I'd changed my mind and gone home? No, no. Think rescue. Taking comfort in that thought, my mind cleared enough for me to take a careful look around my prison. As illogical as it might sound, my number one fear in the short term was spiders. Positioning myself in the very center of the cell, I did a slow turn, examining the corners of the room for webs. There were a number of deserted ones undulating in the breeze filtering through the window, but none appeared to have a current occupant. That allowed me a small measure of relief.

I stuck my face between the bars in the door, trying to calculate how far away the phone was. Kneeling, I reached my arm through as far as it would go, but it was no use. It lay at least a yard beyond my fingertips. I needed to find something long enough to pull the phone within reach. In the dim light, with only the mournful whistle of the wind as my companion, I sifted through piles of discarded junk looking for a useful tool. There were stacks of disintegrating newspapers, bent aluminum cans and broken beer bottles, scraps of clothing...ugh, used toilet paper, and a brittle, rusted mattress spring that looked like it might be a hundred years old. Nothing there. Now what? I moped around the cell for long minutes and then rushed towards the narrow window. Standing on my toes, I was just barely able to touch the bottom ledge. Returning to the other end of the cell, I pulled out some of the newspapers and wrapped them around my hands like oven mitts before grabbing onto the sharp metal mattress spring. It screeched and groaned as I dragged it across the concrete floor and shoved it beneath the window. I heaped newspapers on top and then, cautiously balancing myself on the wavering pile, I reached up to grab hold of the bars. I tugged with all my might, but those puppies weren't going anywhere. Damn! I screamed for help until my voice was ragged. Nothing. Nothing but the wind. Despondent beyond measure, I slid off the papers, zipped my jacket up to my chin and flopped down in the corner nearest the barred door, dismally watching the second hand on my watch tick off the minutes. Two fifteen, two seventeen, two twenty-five. Perhaps I'd just close my eyes for a little while.

I woke with a start, unable to fathom where I was for a couple of seconds before the reality of my situation pierced me like a cold knife blade. My God! It was four-thirty. If help didn't come soon, I'd be spending the night in this forbidding place. I could tell by the soreness of my skin that my fever had climbed higher while I'd slept. A few sips of water helped cool the raging inferno in my throat. Could things be any worse? The easiest thing would have been to curl up in a ball and give in to despair, but I pushed to my feet and reached around the bars to feel the lock once again. Why wasn't I able to just push the door open? How could it have locked by simply slamming shut? As I reconstructed the exact sequence of events in my mind, the tiny seed of doubt inside me blossomed into suspicion. If the wind had blown the outer door shut, where was the rock I'd placed there to secure it? I didn't know a whole lot about physics, but wouldn't it have been pushed inside also? Was my incarceration in this little hellhole really an accident of nature? What if someone actually had called my name to lure me in here? But who would do such a thing? My mind splayed out, taking several paths at once. Who else besides Hank Breslow knew I was coming here? And, why would he do such a thing? I hadn't mentioned this side-trip to anyone except Walter on the phone…oh…my…God! That meant whoever had been listening on the extension certainly knew. Jason seemed the logical culprit but for the life of me I could not figure out what purpose a stunt like this would serve. That it had been designed to frighten me was a given and might be the result of my recent confrontation with him and Cutter. But it could also have been Bethany. What was the motivation behind her apparent animosity, including her nasty little trick this morning? My mind did a couple of back flips and suddenly Payton's worry that Brett might be gaining a new daddy took on disturbing significance. Oh, man. What if she'd planned this? Clever bitch. With me out of the way, she'd be free to pursue Tally... Cut! Cut! Don't do this! Don't drive yourself crazy conjuring up imaginary scenarios that have no basis in reality. Focus. Focus on the problem at hand.

Blink. Blink. Blink. I glared at the cell phone. There had to be some way to get hold of that little sucker. And I had to do it before nightfall. Returning to the junk pile beneath the window, I began to sort through it again. Nothing sturdy enough. Nothing long enough. I wracked my brain. What if I rolled newspapers into tight cylinders? That would give me the length I needed, but what would I use as a hook? I searched every square inch of the cell, but could find nothing useful. Fighting despair, I set about rolling the pages of paper into tubes and then inserting the ends into each other until I had a paper wand about four feet long. Then, with cautious expectancy, I fished it through the bars. It reached the phone, but its weight buckled the paper time and again until my arm ached with exertion. This wasn't working. "Crap!" I yanked the tube back into the cell and in a fit of fury, grabbed it in both hands and swatted it against the bars until it was torn to shreds. As I watched the pieces waft slowly downward, I slid into a crumpled heap and sobbed into my hands. My little tantrum had solved nothing except to make me feel even more miserable. Relying on the miniscule part of my feverish brain that was still able to function rationally, I gathered some of the newspapers and, in the fading light of dusk, spread them on the cold, hard floor forming a makeshift bed. The remaining ones I tucked over and around me like a blanket. I also used several pieces to blow my nose. "See," I blabbered to the empty room, "newspapers *can* be useful for some things."

Huddled beneath the paper, burning up one minute and quaking with chills the next, I took tiny sips of my precious water, keenly aware that dehydration was a real possibility. Oh, what I wouldn't do to get hold of those apples still inside the cooler in my car and the extra water. Feeling supremely sorry for myself, I drifted in and out of restive sleep packed with nonsensical, irritating dreams until I was awakened by a brilliant ray of blue light shining in my eyes. Groggy, I propped myself up on one elbow and peered out the window, thinking it must be the moon, but when the beam disappeared I blinked in confusion and rubbed my eyes, not really sure I was awake. I stared between the bars for a long time before slipping back into a deep sleep.

A strange humming intruded into my nightmarish dreams. But when I opened my eyes, I couldn't see because of the damned blue light again. Almost blinded by its intensity, I sat up, jumping at the crackle of the newspapers falling away from me. What the hell *was* that? It couldn't be the moon unless it had changed orbit while I slept and was now setting in the south. Weak and disoriented, I stumbled to the window, stretching as high as I could. My heart rate shot through the roof at the sight of something, I don't know what, hovering just to the left of the sandstone pillars of rock. Pulsing eerily, the incandescent light brightened, turning green, orange and yellow before it zoomed upward and vanished. I should have been scared out of my wits, but instead, and perhaps it was due to my foggy-headedness, I just stared mesmerized at the indigo sky until my trembling legs refused to support me any longer. I fell away from the ledge and the sudden head rush sent me lurching back to my newspaper bed where I hunched on the chilly floor, shivering. What I had just witnessed defied logic. Either I was hallucinating or I'd just seen an honest to God unidentified flying object. Could a manmade aircraft move that fast? I acknowledged for the first time that Javier and the migrant's bizarre stories just might be true. But what was I going to tell Lupe if I ever got out of here? *Sorry, looks like your brother and uncle really were abducted by extraterrestrials.* Just thinking it made me cringe. Did I dare even tell a soul what I'd seen? Everyone I knew would think I'd slipped off the deep end. Or not. Mazzie La Casse didn't seem like a crackpot and neither did Payton Kleinwort. What about the thousands of other people all over the world who'd witnessed UFO sightings?

I tried to stop the next thought from even entering my conscious mind, but it was there front and center. Would the space creatures be coming for me now? They obviously knew I was here. Resting my forehead in my hand, I croaked, "Come and get me, you ugly bug-eyed bastards! At least that's one way I can get the hell out of this dungeon."

Okay, obviously I was losing it. I felt around for my water bottle and it was a real test of strength to keep from downing the entire thing. The rest of the night plodded along as slowly as a desert tortoise. The predicted rain I'd been anticipating finally arrived about three o'clock, accompanied by thunder, lightning and gale-force winds. It poured non-stop for about two hours. Ordinarily I would have relished the fresh-scented spray blowing through the narrow opening, but it only served to make matters worse by dampening my newspaper blanket. Great. I'd be lucky not to come down with pneumonia. Huddled beneath the soggy mass, rehashing what I'd just seen, I couldn't decide whether the strange lights had been real or a product of my fever-induced imagination.

Extreme relief poured through me when the first silvery rays of dawn seeped through the bars, ending one of the longest nights of my life. But my relief didn't last long. The pain of a thousand harpoons punctured my heart when I pictured Tally loading the horses into the trailers, checking his watch again and again and wondering where in the hell I was. Would he worry about me or harden his heart and continue the trip as planned, interpreting my absence as a sign that I no longer cared about him? Hot tears flooded my eyes. I wept until I wasn't sure I had enough strength to sit up. Eventually, however, I did. Somehow, I had to figure a way out of here so I could explain what happened. And pray he would forgive me.

At least the maddening whine of the wind had stopped, so maybe Russell Greene would hear my calls for help. One of the worst moments of my life occurred next. When I tried to shout, nothing came out but a faint crackling honk. I bowed my head in surrender. Oh, mercy. How was I going to get myself out of this one?

The morning hours crawled by and at noon I tried yelling again, but my swollen throat would not cooperate. My water bottle was almost empty. Damn, I'd been locked away for almost twenty-four hours. Why hadn't anyone come looking for me? Of course, everyone at the office thought I was happily on my way to California with Tally. But, what about Ginger? Wasn't she wondering why I hadn't come by and dropped off my new pet? Had my prior conduct convinced her that I'd become so obsessed with Lupe's problem that I'd decided to forgo my trip so I could stay and pursue the story? No wonder I wasn't missed. My reputation preceded me.

Mentally sucking my thumb, I languidly gazed at my phone. It was still blinking, but I knew the battery wouldn't last much longer. My hands were so weak I could hardly roll the newspaper cylinders a second time and as I looked around the cell searching for any useful object I may have overlooked, my gaze locked onto the old mattress springs. Hey! Some of the coils in the middle were rusted and so brittle I was able to break off an entire section. By hooking the coils into one another I created a crude circle. Padding my hands with newspaper again, I wound sharp pieces of metal around my paper pole and then attached my homemade 'net' to the end of it after bolstering it with metal bands fashioned from the springs.

Flat on my belly, I carefully fished the paper rod through the bars in the door along the floor until I reached my target. Tensing, I lifted one corner of the coils and netted the phone. Well done, O'Dell! Basking in jubilation, I pulled the phone towards me only to hear a sound that made my insides shrink. The low battery signal was bleating. Oh, no! Not now! Pulse thundering, I reeled in my prize. Half-laughing, half-crying, I hurriedly dialed 911. Beep! Beep!

"What is your emergency?" a monotone voice answered.

I opened my mouth, but nothing came out but a tiny hissing squeak.

"Yes? What is your emergency?" the female voice repeated.

"Help," I whispered, just as the battery went dead. Staring at the phone in disbelief, my last hope shattered, I was all set to give in to total panic again when I heard a dog barking. Stilled by indecision, it occurred to me that I'd finally found a use for my worthless cell phone. With fiendish delight, I whacked it against the bars as loud as I could. Bang! Clang! Bang! The barking grew closer, rising to a wild crescendo and at last I heard a voice calling, "Attila! Good boy! Did you find that son-of-a bitchin' skunk?"

I continued my frantic clanging and was praising God in a hundred ways when I heard the door being wrestled open. Light poured in as a big black Doberman charged inside and headed straight for me, white teeth snapping, its unholy howl filling the cramped interior. The silhouette of a tall, gangly man filled the doorway, blotting out the daylight. "Take 'er easy, boy…I'm going shoot that bas…" Seeing me, his voice trailed off and as he moved out of the shadows, I was actually thankful at that moment that I had no voice, or I'd have surely screamed. Instead, I gaped in wide-eyed astonishment as he stared back at me from an unspeakably ravaged face that was more alien in appearance than human. The skin on the man's face was puckered and discolored, his nose a small protrusion with two cavernous holes, and what remained of his lips barely covered his teeth. A broad-brimmed hat topping shaggy gray hair completed the disquieting picture. This had to be Russell Greene. Mazzie's account of his ordeal in the snow rushed to mind and I could only assume that his facial disfigurement was the result of frostbite.

"Attila!" he roared. "Leave it." The dog immediately withdrew. "Well, who the hell are you," he growled, "and how the hell did you get in here?"

Reverting to sign language, I shook the bars and motioned for him to come closer. "Door locked," I whispered. "Can't get out."

His brows plunged in disbelief, but when he reached for the door and yanked, a look of uncertainty glazed his dark eyes. "Well, I'll be damned. How long have you been here?"

I tried to speak, but nothing came out, so I held up a finger.

"One day?" Appearing puzzled, he asked, "Where's the key?"

All I could do was shrug.

"I didn't think this thing would lock without the key," he continued as if his statement somehow nullified my predicament. Turning, he reached high on the wall and came away with something in his hand, which he inserted in the lock and magically the door swung open.

My God. The key had been on the wall hook the entire time. I stumbled past him as quickly as my spongy legs would permit, unable to get outside fast enough. When the sunlight struck my face, all I wanted to do was keep running, but suddenly the dog was right in front of me, blocking my escape.

"Hold your horses a minute," he demanded, waving his rifle. "You've got some explaining to do. I could have you arrested for trespassing you know. Didn't you see the signs on the gate?" His penetrating, yet quizzical stare made me feel as if I was the one who looked out of the ordinary. "Hey, wait a minute. I've seen you before. You were out in front of the saloon the other day talking with the lady space cadet."

I nodded, thinking how miffed Mazzie would be by his description.

His eyes narrowed shrewdly. "So, that means you probably heard all the juicy stories about me."

Averting my eyes, I shrugged. What rotten luck. Having no voice was definitely going to put a crimp in my plans to interview him. Pointing to my throat, I felt like a kid in a school play pantomiming my need to eat, drink, and have something to write on, until his puzzlement turned to understanding. "I don't know what the hell you're up to but come on," he said abruptly, inclining his head towards the white house that looked to be at least ten miles away. Overcome by dizziness, I had to stop once or twice to rest. Finally, he swung around, asking, "What's the matter, are you hurt?"

I held my throat and head, whispering that I was sick. When he slowed his pace, gratitude swept through me. It occurred to me at that moment that no matter how awful my overnight ordeal was, it certainly couldn't compare to the torment this man had suffered. Weak as a kitten doesn't come close to describing how I felt when we finally reached the cottage. After ordering the dog to stay outside, he unlocked the door and stood aside. "You're welcome to come in...that is, if you're not afraid." The suggestion of bitterness in his soft tone, coupled with the defiant gleam in his dark eyes, made me hesitate. Being alone with any strange man in such an isolated setting would be cause for alarm, let alone one with such a disturbing background. But for some unexplainable reason, I felt no fear of him and could only hope my feminine instincts were correct as I boldly stepped inside the small kitchen. Though sparsely furnished with only a scarred card table, two chairs, an ancient-looking stove and refrigerator, the kerosene lamps adorning both the table and countertops gave the room a cozy effect.

"Do you have a phone I could use?" I whispered, indicating that mine didn't work."

"Nope."

Of course not. "Water?" I croaked, waving my empty bottle.

He plucked a paper cup from a nearby stack and nodded towards a rusty sink. While I stood there drinking, refilling it four times, he popped open a can of soup and emptied it into a saucepan. He caught me sneaking glances at his horribly disfigured face and wordlessly pointed to another door before turning his back to me. Apparently conversation was not his strong suit, but then at that moment it wasn't mine either.

The cramped bathroom, surprisingly clean considering a single guy lived here, was certainly one of the more welcome places I could remember visiting in a long time. One glance at my reflection in the mirror made it apparent why Russell Greene had been gawking at me as though I were a freak. My hair looked like a crimson explosion and my face was smeared with dried blood and black newsprint. The effect was so startling, so clownish, that I could not control the whispery yelps of laughter that resembled someone squeezing a squeaky toy. I clamped my hands over my mouth and giggled until tears forged white trails down my sooty cheeks. Thank God no one I knew was here to see me.

Using paper towels and soap, I washed up as best I could, smoothing the tangles in my hair and blotting at the stains on my jacket before I felt reasonably presentable again. On my return trip to the kitchen, I noticed that the bedroom, equally Spartan but neat, contained a narrow bed, throw rug and chest of drawers. On a battered desk in the corner sat a short wave radio, apparently his only contact with the outside world. Devoid of the usual amenities, like curtains, flowers and wall decorations, the house seemed kind of drab, but he'd obviously made a conscious choice to live hidden away from the prying eyes and cruelly wagging tongues of civilization.

Still standing with his back to me at the stove, he said, "Have a seat."

I knew my resistance was at a low point when the sight of the little table already set with a spoon, bowl, water, a bottle of aspirin, pen and paper, spawned such a rush of emotion I had to hold my breath to keep from bursting into tears. When he turned with the soup pan in hand, I experienced almost as great a shock as when I'd first seen him. A piece of burlap sacking now covered the lower portion of his damaged face. As he poured out the hot soup, our eyes met briefly and I was mesmerized by the expression of profound anguish that seemed to emanate from the depths of his soul.

I wrote on the paper. *You don't have to wear that for my sake.*

He eyed my message with wary disbelief. "Then you would be unlike most other people." He pulled the second chair around backwards and straddled it. "Eat. I don't want to have to carry you out of here."

He sounded gruff but I felt it was a cover. Men are so terrible at expressing deep emotion. His reticence reminded me a little of Tally. I'm sure the vegetable soup was good, I just couldn't taste it, but the warmth soothed my throat and restored a modicum of energy. He waited until I'd taken the aspirin and finished half the soup before asking, "So, who are you and what are you doing here?"

All I really wanted to do was get in my car and go, but there was no urgency to leave now. Tally had left hours ago so I decided to take the opportunity at hand. "Kendall O'Dell. I'm a reporter," I whispered. "I came here to talk to you about the Mexican national you found here last summer."

One brow edged higher. "Which one?"

I pulled the paper towards me and, without divulging any names, wrote a short account of Lupe's dilemma, Javier's nightmarish experience and the possible link to the man he'd turned over to Bob Shirley last June. Could he tell me exactly what the illegal immigrant said, and if he, himself, had ever witnessed anything that would shed light on the story of supposed UFO abductions in the area? Since he didn't have a phone, how had he contacted the Border Patrol that day?

After reading the questions, he raised now guarded eyes to me. "I don't know what he said because I don't speak Spanish. I found him, or I should say Attila found him, just like he found you today, hiding in one of the hoist shacks. When he saw me...saw my face that is, he started yelling and kicking like a maniac, so I locked his ass inside and flagged Bob Shirley down about two miles east of here. Luckily, his partner was Hispanic and he was able to translate what the guy was saying." His eyes flashed with self-deprecating humor. "Guess he thought I was one of the bogey men coming to get him." He glanced at the sheet again, adding, "I don't know anything about the alien abduction story. Trust me, I see lots of aliens around here but they're not from outer space and they usually leave a very human trail of garbage behind for me to clean up."

"Did you know Agent Shirley personally?" I murmured.

"Not really. Just enough to say hello. He patrolled this area all the time."

I scribbled quickly on the sheet asking him if he'd talked to Bob Shirley again afterwards. Had he acted any differently? Did he know that the agent had died only three weeks after the incident?

His bushy brows collided. "Yeah, I heard. I think maybe I saw him once or twice, but it was just a 'hi, how are you' kind of thing." The repetitious drumming of his fingers on the back of the chair was the only indication that he might be growing agitated and the careful design of his answers revealed nothing relevant. Intuitively, I knew he was hiding something. I pulled the sheet back and scrawled, *who is your employer?*

Hesitating, his shoulders tensed ever so slightly. "Why do you need to know that?"

I watched his eyes carefully and wrote, *I heard the mine was privately owned and it might be reopened soon.*

The fact that he appeared to be debating as to whether to answer sharpened my suspicions. "I've never met the owner in person."

"How is that possible?" I croaked.

He shrugged. "Simple. I answered an ad in the paper, talked to him by phone a couple of times and that's about it. He pays me real well to keep greenhorns like you from wandering around his property getting hurt or falling down mineshafts. So, if you're here hoping for a sensational story, you're barking up the wrong tree."

Undeterred, I wrote: *then what's with the yellow caution tape near the jail?*

"That's easy. My dog got bitten by a rabid skunk and had to be quarantined for six weeks." He jerked to his feet and picked up the dishes. "Look, I don't feel like answering any more questions. What I do or don't do is nobody's business. I don't bother anybody and I don't like people pestering me." He clanged the dishes into the sink and then turned around and set my refilled water bottle in front of me. "It's time for you to go."

His sudden change of tone took me by surprise. I stood on wobbly legs and waited for the woozy spell to pass before heading to the door. Grabbing his rifle from the corner, he escorted me out, whistled for the dog and carefully locked the door behind him. In silence, he accompanied me to the gate and after he'd closed and re-attached the padlock, I smiled at him, whispering, "Thank you so much for your help. You're very kind."

He stared at me a few seconds with an unreadable expression in his eyes. "Be smart. Don't come back here again."

19

Not sure whether his final statement had been a threat or a warning, I watched him and the sleek Doberman tramp up the hill in the direction of the old mine. In seconds they were lost from sight in the dense underbrush. All my instincts as a reporter were on full alert. There was definitely something odd going on here, but whatever it was would have to wait until another time. I needed to lie down. Fast. Turning, I headed for my car, only to stop in gut-chilling, mind-bending disbelief. It was gone. Impossible! Searching frantically in all directions, an air of unreality settled around me as I circled the empty spot. Was I hallucinating? No matter how I tried to will it into being, my little blue Volvo was simply not there. Panic clutched me as I sifted through the inventory of my personal belongings stashed in the trunk—purse, including wallet, credit cards and driver's license, camera, tape recorder, spanking new laptop computer, my overnight bag, and Lupe's. It was an effort to not dissolve into tears. What else could possibly happen to top off this most wretched weekend of my life? With dismal certainty, the knowledge that my car had most likely been stolen and driven across the border by now slowly seeped in. Who would believe it? I, too, had become an unwilling victim of the illegal immigration quagmire. A hard knot of rage burned in my belly along with renewed empathy for Champ and all the other innocent people embroiled in the ongoing, unsolvable mess.

Now what? I toyed with the idea of returning to Russell Greene's place, but remembered that he'd locked the door. He might be gone for hours. So, what would I do? Lie at his doorstep waiting until he came back? How ironic. I was free to go and yet still a prisoner. The distant roar of a car engine grabbed my attention and I willed my unsteady legs to carry me towards the main road. Come on, come on. Where was that adrenaline kick when I needed it? Waving my arms above my head, I arrived at the mouth of the drive in time to catch a glimpse of Froggy in his pickup as it sped past. He was singing at the top of his lungs in accompaniment to the loud music blaring from the open driver's side window. *Come back!* I shouted in a whisper, watching in dismay as he vanished around the bend. How strange. From what I could remember from the map, there was nothing west of Wolf's Head but miles of desolate desert encompassing the Tohono O'odham Indian Reservation bordering Mexico. What the hell was he going to do out there in the middle of nowhere anyway? Something clicked in my head. Was this the same road Walter had mentioned, the same lonesome road where Bob Shirley's body had been found? And if that was so, what business could Froggy have out there? To barter with the Indians for fruit and vegetables? Not likely. I stared at the dissipating cloud of dust, straining to make any kind of a connection, but I couldn't come up with a single thing that made sense. Frustrated, I turned and set out along the road in the opposite direction, with no alternative before me other than to suck it up and hike the three miles to the Pierce Ranch. Avoiding a puddle, it struck me that only in Arizona could there be mud and dust on a road at the same instant. Trudging along at a snail's pace, I heatedly berated myself for my string of piss-poor decisions. Single handedly, I'd managed to lose my car and belongings, wreck my vacation, expose myself to the flu, fail miserably as a reporter, tank my relationship with Tally, not to mention that Dean Pierce probably thought I was the biggest flake on earth for not showing up to claim the poor injured kitten. I couldn't help but ponder the similarities. Last night Marmalade had huddled injured and alone in her cage, while I'd lain ill and solitary in mine. "O'Dell, you're hopeless," I whispered, taking a swig of lukewarm water.

On the bright side, the weather was just what I'd been waiting for. In contrast to the white-hot skies of summer, it was sheer joy to walk beneath the infinite dome of rich azure blue and feel warm fingers of sunlight massage my aching back while at the same instant a cool breeze caressed my feverish cheeks. To take my mind off my dilemma and the miles I had to cover, I concentrated on the mesquite-covered hills, savoring the striking beauty of the distant mountain ranges all decked out in afternoon shades of lavender and coral accented with purple shadows taking up temporary residence in the deep ravines. A half hour later, my knees the consistency of overcooked vegetables, I panted up the far side of the rocky arroyo feeling like I'd trekked halfway across the state. In reality, I'd probably covered no more than two miles when I heard the roar of a car engine coming from behind. I swung around expecting to see Froggy's truck but instead, felt a thrill of relief at the sight of Payton Kleinwort's familiar bronze pickup. Waving frantically, I watched his blank expression turn to eye-popping disbelief as he pulled up beside me. "Kendall!" he shouted out the window. "What...what in the world are you doing out here?"

I rushed up to the mud-splattered truck, whispering, "Car stolen."

He leaned out further. "What?"

Oh, man. What a bummer trying to communicate. I held my throat and motioned for him to switch off the engine, which he promptly did before jumping out to join me. Not unlike my own, his clothes looked soiled and rumpled as if he'd slept in them all night. Ruefully, I imagined he probably had. "What happened to you?" he exclaimed, looking me up and down. "I thought you said you were going home yesterday?"

Whispering and using sign language, I was able to convey my plight. He rolled his eyes in disgust. "Oh, my God. No doubt a bunch of dirt bag Mexicans took it." He paused, seeming to search for self control before saying, "What a shitty thing to happen. Listen, I'd call the sheriff for you right now, but my cell phone is back in my room sitting on the charger. Sorry."

Thick-headed and feeling worse by the moment, I squeaked, "Could you please take me to Dean's place?"

Appearing uncertain, he hesitated several seconds, his eyes straying to his watch. "Um...sure, but first I've got to drop this last shipment off at the airstrip. My pilot is waiting to take these slippery little guys to Tucson. It's not far, just a couple of miles down the road. Do you mind?"

Couldn't the stupid snakes wait? I sighed deeply. Beggars certainly couldn't be choosers and a few more minutes really didn't make much difference at this point. Mustering an acquiescent smile, I allowed him to assist me into the cab. "I'll make this as quick as I can," he assured, his tone solicitous. He rushed around to the driver's side and we were on our way within seconds. I could tell by his curious glances that he was dying to know where I'd been and what I'd been doing since yesterday. But being the considerate man that he was, he respected my obvious inability to talk and said nothing.

Keenly aware that the coolers behind me in the camper, thumping against the plastic window, were packed with live rattlesnakes, I was just a tad uneasy. But by the same token, that seemed a trivial worry compared to what I'd just been through. I closed my eyes and laid my head back against the seat, thinking about the three vital phone calls I needed to make. First, I'd contact the hotel in California and leave a message for Tally, who was no doubt at the horse show by now. I could only pray that he would accept my explanation. Next, I'd report my stolen car to the sheriff. Now that would prove to be a challenge. I could just imagine someone at the other end trying to interpret my squeaky whispers. I'd have to impose on Payton to handle that for me, but he'd need the particulars. Lastly, I'd need to contact Ginger, ask her to go to my house, find the records of my credit cards and cancel them pronto. Whoever had my car was probably out on a major shopping spree right now. And with my driver's license gone, maybe my identity would be stolen as well. Thinking about the hassle of phone calls, and paperwork awaiting me to sort out the mess, sent my spirits tumbling to even lower levels.

As we approached the little airstrip I'd passed yesterday afternoon, I spotted a spiffy-looking white two-engine plane waiting on the runway. It was larger and newer-looking than Champ's faded one tethered near the shack. A fresh-faced guy who didn't look like he was even old enough to pilot a plane was leaning against the side of it smoking. He threw his cigarette down and opened the plane's rear door as we pulled up. "I won't be long," Payton said, reaching for the door handle. "Will you be okay for a couple of minutes?"

I nodded, whispering, "Do you have something I can write on?"

"Sure." He slid out and rummaged around behind his seat, finally pulling out a white tablet. "I always keep paper around for Brett. He loves to draw."

I mouthed 'thank you' and watched him run over to speak to the pilot. After a short conversation, they began unloading the coolers from the back of the camper and shoving them inside the plane. A glow of admiration warmed me, knowing that Payton's altruistic pursuits would provide the critical antidote needed to help snakebite victims all over the country. At that moment, the tender memorial to his sister seemed quite in keeping with his personality.

While they worked, I jotted down a short version of yesterday's events, omitting the UFO sighting, but including all the statistics on my car and Ginger's home number. Following another brief conversation and a quick handshake, the young man climbed into the cockpit and Payton trotted back to the truck. I handed the pad to him and watched his eyes widen as he read. "You were shut in the old jail at Morita all night? What an awful thing for you to have to experience," he commiserated with a sympathetic shake of his head, reading on. "Oh, man. If I'd known you were planning to go there I'd have warned you about Russell. It's a bit shocking if you're not prepared for...well, I'm sure you know what I mean."

I gave him a tired nod and whispered, "Do you know much about him?"

He hesitated. "His family owned the ranch adjacent to ours. We palled around as kids, but he was always a loner and ever since his accident he keeps pretty much to himself for obvious reasons."

Recalling his final words of warning to stay away from Morita, I reminded myself that I still needed to find out who his employer was. A sudden attack of sneezing overtook me and Payton cast me a sympathetic look as he handed me his handkerchief. "I'm so sorry you've had such a rotten time during your stay here. You'll probably never want to come back this way again, huh?"

"Not likely," I croaked.

"Well, I can't blame you," he said, shifting into gear. He eyed me curiously several times before saying, "Boy, that was some storm last night. I thought I was going to get washed away a couple of times. It was actually lucky for you that you were inside the jail. That's one of the few places left with an intact roof."

I nodded agreement and my mind slipped back to Froggy flying past me in his truck. "What's beyond the road after the turnoff to Morita?" I murmured.

Payton frowned. "What do you mean?"

The pain of swallowing made my eyes water, so I held my throat for a moment before answering. "Is there a town?"

"Not for a long way. San Miguel is the closest, I think." He glanced at me again. "Why?"

I grabbed the notepad again and then handed it to him. He balanced it on the steering wheel and read as he drove. "How on earth did you meet Froggy McQueen?" he asked, question marks shimmering in his sea-green eyes.

"It's a long story," I whispered back.

He shot me a fleeting look, but didn't press me to continue.

By the time we reached the main dirt road, the plane was in the air. Sunlight flashed off the fuselage as it banked to the right and headed in a southerly direction. Odd. Tucson was north. But then, didn't planes always take off into the wind?

Moments later, Payton swung onto the narrow lane leading to Dean's ranch. "I'm assuming your insurance will provide for a rental car until...or, and I hate to say this, *if* yours is ever located," he remarked, catching my eye. "I was planning to pick up Brett at the Sundog and spend the afternoon with him, but I can change my plans and drive you to Tucson so you'll have a car to get home today."

I wasn't sure I could even rent a car without a driver's license or proof of insurance. The grim reality was that without all those little pieces of paper and plastic, I was essentially a non-person. I beamed him an appreciative smile anyway, whispering, "I couldn't ask you to do that."

He grinned. "I won't take no for an answer."

His selfless offer cheered me, and when Dean's ranch house came into view, my morale improved even more. Soon this dreadful chapter of my life would be a distant memory. Eager to get to a phone, get my cat and go, I pushed my steps faster to keep up with Payton's as he strolled to the front door and knocked. Almost immediately, Inez swung it open, then put out a hand when he stepped forward. "Meester Dean is not here. His sister calls from the big house and he goes in a hurry, saying there is much trouble."

"Trouble?" Payton parroted. "What kind of trouble?"

She hitched her wide shoulders. "Somebody is shot."

"Shot?" He turned to me, paling with alarm. "Oh, my God! Brett! Come on." He grabbed my hand and yanked me back to the truck so fast I almost lost my footing several times. Spewing gravel behind us, he rocketed down the road, taking the curves so rapidly I feared we'd roll over. When we reached the cutoff, he jammed on the brakes and we both watched in astonishment as an ambulance, lights pulsing, barreled past towards the main road.

"Jesus, Mary and Joseph," he whispered, gunning the truck towards the Sundog. Rounding the corner that led into the wide parking area, we both gasped aloud. I could hardly believe my eyes. Replacing the tranquility I'd left only yesterday morning was the unexpected sight of four Pima County sheriff's patrol cars with lights ablaze. A white television van was parked at the mouth of the drive along with two Border Patrol vehicles, Dean's pickup and a shiny black Lincoln. "What the hell..." Payton's voice trailed off as he skidded to a stop. We both jumped from the truck and ran towards the group of people gathered at one corner of the clearing.

Following on his heels, I can only describe the scene as surreal. Tinny squawking emitted by the radios in the patrol cars rose over the emotion-charged clamor of anxious tourists gathered near the white fence where the horses had been tethered during my first visit. In the center of the clearing, two uniformed Border Patrol agents, clipboards in hand, were questioning a ragtag group of eight somber-faced Mexicans sitting in a circle on the ground. A few of them drank from gallon water jugs while others smoked and talked amongst themselves.

Rob, the young cowboy I'd met on Sunday, and still wearing a BEAUMONT RANCH PATROL sweatshirt, stood nearby conversing with several other scowling ranch hands. He turned and glared at the group, his eyes burning with a look of such fierce retribution it took my breath away. His words, 'believe me they'll pay a price for this' resounded in my ears. Briefly, his eyes met mine before he turned and stomped away, swatting his hat against his thigh. I couldn't wait to find out what had happened.

On the front steps of the house, Dean Pierce, his face flushed with anger, and a petite gray-haired woman I assumed was his wife, Henrietta, physically restrained a distraught Twyla, as two burly sheriff's deputies pushed a defiant Jason Beaumont into the rear of a patrol car. "No!" she screamed, "you can't do this! How about a little compassion for us! How about a little consideration for *our* rights as American citizens?" Little shock waves rattled around inside me when I spied Champ hunched in the back of a second vehicle. Within earshot, a camera technician was focusing on a flustered-looking television reporter interviewing a slender Hispanic woman of perhaps thirty-five who bore a striking resemblance to Lupe. Well-dressed in a smartly tailored navy suit, she smoothed her slightly disheveled hair and clothing as she spoke passionately into the camera. "That's right, Tom, Mr. Beaumont's brutal response to my inquiries is typical of the White ranchers in this region and illustrates the violence directed towards Hispanic people, especially unarmed migrants who are simply crossing to find honest work. This racist hatred is also fueled by the government's on-going lethal border policy. Operation Gatekeeper is a major factor. The unfair buildup of agents at the legal entry points is responsible for funneling innocent men, women and children into these deadly regions where as many as one thousand have died of dehydration and exposure in the past four years alone. Frankly, we're sick and tired of the Border Patrol and local law enforcement agencies looking the other way when ranchers employ these vigilante tactics and commit all manner of heinous crimes against humanity...."

Scarlet blotches stained Payton's cheeks and he swore under his breath before swiveling around to make a beeline for one of the patrol cars. "Dan, what the hell is going on here?" he demanded, addressing one husky deputy perched on the front seat of his vehicle filling out a wad of forms attached to a clipboard.

Appearing slightly annoyed, the officer scowled up at him. "I'm kinda busy now, Payton."

"I can see that but...someone said there's been a shooting. Is Brett all right? Was he involved in any way? And what's the deal with Jason and Champ? Are they being arrested? For what?" His voice had climbed to a screech.

"Why don't you take a couple of deep breaths and calm down," the deputy advised. "Now, unless Brett has been magically transformed into an immigrant male in his late teens, then he wasn't the one who took a bullet in his gut."

Payton looked slightly taken aback and swallowed hard. "Oh. Well, what happened?"

"We're not really sure yet." He nodded towards the group of illegals seated on the ground. "Apparently some of these fellows jumped out from behind some bushes and scared the living crap out of some of the guests during a trail ride earlier. There was a lot of panic when one of the horses spooked and a woman fell off. While she was lying on the ground, she claims one of the illegals roughed her up and tried to steal her horse. Champ tackled him, there was a scuffle, and he insists that his gun went off accidentally. But, the Mexican swears Champ deliberately fired at him. It remains to be seen if he'll be charged."

"With what?" Payton asked sharply.

"Whatever the Pima County Attorney's Office decides. Could be attempted murder, aggravated assault or possibly endangerment."

Pointing to the tight cluster of immigrants, Payton's eyes turned flinty. "Is there no justice? Did they tell you what these barbarians did to their cattle over the weekend? How can you guys side with these...these...depraved criminals...?"

Vaguely, I wondered how Payton knew about the butchered cattle. Dan scowled back at him. "We're not siding with anybody. Just trying to do our job. Period."

"You're right. I'm sorry." He closed his eyes and held the bridge of his nose momentarily before asking, "What does...how is Jason involved in this?"

The deputy shook his head in disgust. "Stupid kid." He went on to explain that the younger Beaumont had made a complete spectacle of himself when Hispanic activist and immigration attorney Linda Lopez had arrived on the scene with a television crew demanding to know what had happened. Apparently they'd been at the port of entry in Sasabe doing a story on the rigorous new border policies when all the excitement erupted and they'd followed Border Patrol agents to the ranch. When Champ ordered her off his property, she'd threatened him with a second lawsuit. "That's when Jason lost it," Dan stated.

"First he shoved the cameraman and then he went for the Lopez woman's throat. It took me and two other deputies to pull him off of her. He's just begging to have her file assault charges against him."

"What happens now?" Payton asked, running a knuckle back and forth across his upper lip.

A shrug. "The usual. They'll be arraigned before a judge in the morning and he'll probably set bail. In Champ's case, it'll probably be pretty high since he's already in hot water with the previous charge. Hey, look, that's about all I can tell you without compromising this case. If you've got any more questions you'll have to talk to Sheriff Musgrove," he said, thumbing towards a mustachioed man leaning in the back window of the patrol car talking with Champ.

Payton thanked him and moved away mumbling bitterly, "That meddling bitch better watch her back." Apparently forgetting that I was there, he turned and loped towards the house, most likely on a mission to find Brett. Because I needed his vocal chords to report my stolen car to one of the many law enforcement officers milling around, I scurried after him. The sudden exertion made me woozy and just a tad sick to my stomach. No doubt dehydration from the fever was taking its toll.

He rushed around the side of the house and pushed the kitchen door open. A cacophony of noise poured out, along with two harried-looking middle-aged couples with suitcases and plastic bags clutched in their hands. They jostled past us, one woman shouting behind her, "Come on, kids, we're getting out of here now. This is too much wild west for me!"

Payton and I stood aside as three kids wearing long faces trailed behind them. As they hurried towards a car bearing Ohio license plates, I couldn't help thinking that this was just the type of scenario Champ had feared most. Filled with sympathy for him, I followed Payton inside. In between the parade of other guests and members of the Hispanic staff scurrying back and forth, I spotted a tall man in a checkered shirt with his back to me, the wall phone pressed to his left ear. Bethany, clad in snug tan jeans that emphasized her perfect buttocks, stood close to him, leaning her blonde head against his bicep while she cuddled Brett next to her.

I edged a glance at Payton's features flattening with displeasure. I'm sure the sight of Bethany schmoozing with the hunky wrangler probably frosted him big time, but when I looked back at them again, icy butterflies danced a nervous jig in my stomach. Wait a minute. There was something terribly familiar about the cowboy's muscular frame.

"Well now, isn't this a cozy family picture?" Payton sneered.

Brett's head whipped around. "Daddy!" he shrieked, breaking away from Bethany's grasp to throw his arms around Payton's thighs. "The sheriff is taking Grandpa and Uncle Jason to jail!" he cried, staring up at his father for consolation. "Can't you stop them?"

Bethany peeked over her shoulder, saw me, saw Payton, and then, blue eyes aglitter, she slid her arm possessively around the man's slim waist. The culmination of all the doubts festering at the epicenter of my subconscious mind erupted to the surface. No. It couldn't be. But even as my eyes continued to reject the obvious, my tortured heart grasped the awful truth. As if in a dream, the man slowly turned and fastened startled brown eyes on me. Oh, my God! It was Tally.

20

Even if I'd had my voice, the shock of seeing him with Bethany's arm coiled around his waist like a venomous snake would have rendered me incapable of speech. In the span of mere seconds, my emotions seesawed between wild elation and wounded bewilderment. More than anything else on earth, I wanted to run into his arms, but the sight of Miss Totally Perfect, clinging to him, and him not seeming to mind, brought bitter bile to the back of my throat. In contrast, I'm certain I looked as if I'd just arrived at death's door. It was heartening to see a glimmer of relief behind his eyes, but it was gone in an instant, replaced by resentment as his questioning gaze tracked back and forth between Payton and me. "Never mind, Ginger," he barked into the phone, "she's just shown up. Yeah, I'll call you back. What? Yeah, she appears to be fine. Looks like I cancelled my trip for nothing." He slammed the receiver onto the switch hook and just stood there, breathing hard and glowering at me with a mixture of exasperation and disappointment.

"I...I can't believe you're here," I managed to squeak out, really wishing that I'd said 'what a sweetheart you are to have come looking for me!'

"Apparently," came his dry reply.

"Bradley," Payton remarked, nodding coolly, "I certainly didn't expect to see you here."

In an equally chilly tone, Tally replied, "Hello, Payton. Guess I could say the same."

What? They knew each other? Mush. My brain cells were pure mush. And then it struck me. Payton had known the Beaumont family most of his life. Of course he would have run into the Talversons during that space of time.

"Brett, why don't you run upstairs and get your things," Payton said, giving his son a little push towards the doorway.

As the little boy streaked from the room, Bethany crooned, "Now see, Tally, you were all worried for nothing. Didn't I tell you she was probably with Payton? I mean, she's practically spent the whole weekend with him."

The intimate gesture of Tally's hand coming to rest on her shoulder had my insides shriveling. "Well, Bethy, guess you were right."

Smug. She looked so damned smug. Bethy? Had he called her Bethy? Even in my weakened state, a surge of heat fueled my dormant temper.

"Where in the hell have you been?" Tally growled at me. "I've been all over this town, all over this whole goddamned county looking for you!"

Holding my throat, I grunted, "I can explain...."

"I'm not sure I want to hear it. I've already heard several versions of your warm and cuddly lunch with

319

Payton yesterday. So...is this the surprise you had for me?"

My screech of protest came out a crackling honk and I threw Payton a 'hey, how about helping me out here' look, but his hostile stare was drilling a hole through Bethany, who appeared delighted with his discomfort. Eyes sparkling with malicious pleasure she clicked her tongue. "My goodness, Payton, what a bad boy you are." Her eyes raked over his mud-spattered clothes and then zeroed in on my torn jeans. "Looks like you two have been rolling in the mud."

I glared at her, anger forming a hard block in my chest. What the hell was she up to? Skewered by Tally's look of outraged betrayal, I stood mute, benumbed by the entire situation, physically unable to say anything to defend myself. Surely he wasn't going to buy into this carload of crap? When my pathetic attempt to dispute her allegations came out sounding like a strangled hiss, I locked in to his intractable gaze, shaking my head in denial, hoping he'd decipher the SOS in my eyes. But as he surveyed our incriminatingly disheveled appearance and continued to wait stone-faced for my explanation, I could sense a gulf forming between us. The palpable disconnection of our hearts seemed almost audible and left an aching void in my chest.

"I'm positive there's a special corner in hell reserved especially for you," Payton responded in a deadly tone, meeting Bethany's wicked expression.

Consumed with white-hot rage, I took several steps forward, poised to go for her jugular, just as Twyla staggered into the room and collapsed into a chair. "Oh, dear God!" she wailed. "What am I going to do?" She stared at us as if we somehow held the answer to her dilemma. "I've got six more couples arriving this afternoon from a Chicago brokerage firm. They've pre-paid for a cattle drive plus a barbeque cookout with dancing tomorrow evening! What about the other guests? How am I going to run this place when I've got to meet with our lawyers in Tucson first thing in the morning? I might be there all day." Voice cracking, she buried her face in her hands and sobbed, "This is going to ruin us!"

Payton said crisply, "Don't worry, Twyla, I'll contact the rancher's coalition right away. We'll take up a collection to get them out."

As if not to be upstaged by Payton, Bethany sprang to her side. "Don't worry, Mummy," she crooned, slipping a comforting arm around the older woman's shoulders, "everything's going to be okay." For once, she appeared genuinely concerned. "Look, Tally's here now. I'm sure if we ask, he'll be glad to stay and help us out for a few days." She turned to him, her vivid blue eyes beseeching, beguiling. "You can stay, can't you? Please say yes. Please?"

Twyla looked up, her tear-stained face brightening with hope. "Oh, Tally, would you? We would be ever so grateful!"

Taken off guard, Tally paused before leveling me with a look that made me question whether my heart was still functioning properly. "Well, since it appears that Kendall has decided to stay on to pursue her own agenda…I guess there's no reason I can't stick around and give you folks a hand."

Twyla jumped up and threw her arms around him. "God bless you, dear boy." Then she turned to me. "Oh, Kendall, I'm so sorry about your California plans, but I so much appreciate you loaning him to us for a little while.

I'll tell you what, since Champ may not be arraigned until Thursday, you two can have our room and I'll take the lower bunk in Brett's room. Will that be okay? Blah...blah...blah...."

Strange. Her mouth was moving but suddenly her words made no sense. Maybe it was because of the loud ringing in my ears. Blackness closed around me as the floor came up to meet me.

The next thing I remember was the sensation of someone placing something cold on my forehead. I strained to open my eyes, but my lids felt like they were stapled shut. I drifted again peacefully for a while before the murmur of nearby voices intruded. "That's what I've been trying to tell you people all along!" Payton spat. "Come on, Brett, if we leave now, we'll just have time to make the movie."

Bethany called, "Have him back by...."

"I'll bring him back when I damn well please." Seconds later the slam of the front door reverberated throughout the room.

"Well, my goodness, he's in a snit today," Twyla fretted. "As if we don't have enough problems." A short silence was followed by, "So, what are we going to do with her? We can't take a chance on her infecting the other guests."

Fully awake now, I stayed still, deciding I'd glean more information if they assumed I was unconscious. A saccharine voice easily identifiable as Bethany's whined, "Tally, I'm sure you don't want to take any chances on being around her either. She's probably really contagious. Why don't we put her back in the spare room like before and you can sleep in my bedroom?"

Her insinuating offer, followed by Tally's hesitation, turned my insides to ice.

"I'm going to make this easy for everyone," came his weary reply, "and stay in the bunk house with Art."

Twyla protested, "I won't hear of it. I insist you stay in my room. Brett won't mind a little company, I'm sure."

"I've got a better idea," Bethany cut in. "Why don't we have someone drive her back to Castle Valley?"

I tensed during the extended pause and then relaxed when Tally stated, "No, I think she's too sick to travel."

I despised being talked about in the third person and forced my eyes open to stare at the dark wooden beams running the length of the living room ceiling. Flat on my back on the couch, still fuzzy-headed, I turned my head and looked up into Lin Su's expressionless eyes. "Drink," the Chinese woman said, proffering a cup to my lips. "You feel better." She placed one hand behind my neck and propped my head up. It was some kind of tea with a sweet licorice flavor. The warmth soothed my fiery throat, so I gulped it greedily. She pulled it away, cautioning, "Sip. Sip slowly."

"You're awake." The two simple words made me turn to stare into Tally's fathomless brown eyes, hoping to see the light of forgiveness there. I didn't.

"Payton explained where you were last night." His words sounded crisp. "Sorry to hear about your car."

Not sorry to hear about my ordeal or that I was so sick, just sorry about the car. The brittle tone of his voice matched his gaze, assaulting my senses, and making my heart feel like it was being pulled through a cheese grater. What was the matter with him? Still unable to talk, I shot him a perplexed look as he continued with, "I passed along all the information you gave Payton to one of the deputies and I'll call Ginger about your cards and things." He offered no apology for doubting my faithfulness, just continued to look offended and totally pissed off. A heavy mantle of guilt settled around my shoulders. It wasn't difficult to read his mind. As far as he was concerned, sick or not, my zeal to pursue Lupe's story had produced the same results. Our California trip was history. I came off looking like a total shit-heel, having broken my promise and he appeared in no mood to forgive and forget. Obviously reveling in my misfortune, Bethany's expression of haughty triumph irked me to no end.

I mouthed, "I'm so sorry," then indicated that I needed something to write on. Lin Su scooped up the little notepad sitting beside the phone and handed it to me. I wrote, '*I need to talk to you alone soon. I have some really important things to share with you*' and held it out to him. His fingers brushing mine sent a pleasurable thrill through me. Surely, he wasn't going to stay angry with me forever?

Maintaining an impassive expression, he read the note and folded it up. "Maybe later, when you get your voice back and you're feeling better." He turned to Twyla. "I think she may need medical attention."

"Oh, there's no need for that," was her breezy response. "Lin Su is our unofficial medical practitioner. She'll whip up a bowl of her famous herbal soup and Kendall will be on her feet in no time." She fastened an affectionate smile on the Chinese woman, who nodded in return. "Her medicine is better than anything you can get from a regular doctor, trust me."

Tally looked as skeptical as I felt, but said nothing. In no condition to complain, I was banished to the little ironing room again on the second floor, where I lay alternately sweating and shivering. Lin Su insisted I hand over my grungy clothes to be laundered, and since replacements were in the trunk of my missing car, I had no choice but to accept a nightgown that I assumed belonged to Bethany. She helped me into it, left and then returned to rub an acrid-smelling salve on my throat. After piling blankets over me, she plied me with spoonfuls of herbal soup and left me with a bowl of ice chips with lemon sprinkled on top for my raging thirst. Time dragged as I fretted about Tally. Where was he? Why hadn't he come to see me? How was I ever going to make this up to him? I could imagine Bethany taking full advantage of the situation and I seethed with fury. Outside the open window, the muted sounds of ranch life wafted up from below before being drowned out by the rumble of arriving vehicles. Probably the large party of guests Twyla had mentioned. From my sickbed I could hear the sounds of car doors slamming, lots of good-natured chattering, raucous male laughter, and finally someone shouting, "Yee Haw! Let's brand some doggies!"

It quieted down after a few minutes, but my ears perked up at the sound of Tally's familiar baritone, so I struggled out from under the mound of blankets and stumbled to the window in time to see him and Bethany walking towards two horses tethered to the pipe fence near the barn. I fought off a wave of dizziness, and as if to underscore my condition, Bethany's words floated up to me. "Honestly, I don't know what you see in her. She's seems like kind of a wimp."

Wimp? Wimp! My fingers tightened around the windowsill when Tally shot her a look. But, to my extreme disappointment, he said nothing in my defense, just untied the reins and swung into the saddle while Bethany smoothly mounted her Appaloosa. Watching him ride away with the self-ordained ranch queen at his side was ego-crushing to say the least. She rode like she'd been born on a horse, seemed so completely at ease with ranch life, so...perfect for him. No doubt she and his mother got along famously. An overpowering wave of desire rolled over me. I don't think I'd ever wanted him more than at that particular moment.

Feeling isolated, wretched, and supremely sorry for myself, I turned and crawled under the nest of covers, my mind playing and replaying the memory of them together until I thought I was going to throw up. Rather than continue the mental torture, I cleared my head and refocused on my story instead. Okay, O'Dell, back to basics. Rule number one: follow the clues until a link is found. Problem: both Lupe's relatives and Javier's mother vanished during the crossing process. Why and how? Possible solution, alien abduction. End of story. Time to go home. I sighed and settled into the pillow. That was easy. Too easy. I gave myself a mental kick. Come on.

Following a more logical track, who was likely to hang out at the border besides the smugglers? The uncomfortable answer had to be the Border Patrol, and that link led to the late Bob Shirley. If he had committed suicide as the authorities believed, what had his final words meant? *'I can't do this anymore.'* What? What couldn't he do anymore? Did Loydeen Shirley know? Most likely. And her look of abject terror when she'd spotted Cutter, the nasty-faced skinhead, led directly to none other than Jason Beaumont. And then, and then...what? I ended up staring at the usual blank slate until I fell into a fretful sleep.

After several restless hours, sunset finally arrived, filling the tiny room with a soft, rosy glow. I was cheered by the unexpected arrival of Rascal, who nosed the door open, trotted in and sympathetically licked my face. He stayed on the floor beside the bed until Lin Su chased him out. This time she'd brought a different-tasting tea, still sweet, but this time with a bitter aftertaste. She insisted I drink every drop before she left again, shutting the door behind her. Whatever was in it affected me almost immediately. A delicious drowsiness settled over me and the fire in my throat subsided. All my cares and concerns slipped away as I succumbed to the lethargy stealing over my body, holding me immobile. I felt mellow, definitely mellow. Yeah. And then I was soaring over lush meadows dotted with trees and carpeted with vibrantly colored flowers I hadn't seen since leaving Pennsylvania seven months earlier. Luxuriating in the sensation of tranquility, I weaved my way through a series of fantastic dreams presented in wide screen and full Technicolor, yet it seemed that I could make out the interior of my little room at the same instant. Was I dreaming that I was awake? My conscious mind reminded me that I was most likely experiencing hallucinations brought on by the high fever. One dream in particular seemed very real. In the dim light of the waning moon, I could have sworn I saw Bethany leaning over my bed, her calculating eyes carefully searching my face. I slept again, dreaming of strange hovering crafts inhabited by small beings with wide, black eyes. Imprisoned by Lin Su's powerful herbs, I kept trying to wake up, but I could not seem to lift my lids. Vaguely, I wondered if the dour-faced little woman had poisoned me.

Sometime during the night, my fever broke and I fell into a comatose-like sleep until a slight movement in the bed roused me briefly. Someone crawled in behind me and as gentle fingers smoothed my hair and then wound around my waist, a warm glow of happiness surged through me. "Oh, baby doll, my love, my sweet darling, thank God you're back. I've missed you so much. You'll never know how much," whispered the husky voice close to my ear. Smiling to myself, delighting in the feel of soft kisses on the back of my neck, I snuggled close, rejoicing in sweet contentment. Was I lucky or what? Even with my string of major screw-ups, Tally had seen fit to forgive me. And I'd never known him to be so effusive. With extreme effort I was able to lift my hand and lay it over his. Murmuring, "I missed you too," I glided back into peaceful sleep.

Dawn light was seeping through the small window when I opened my eyes, amazed at how much better I felt. Lin Su's magic potions really worked. I didn't feel sick any longer, but my thought process still seemed fuzzy. The even snoring from behind, resurrected the memory of Tally joining me sometime in the middle of the night. Sighing, I recalled his gentle words of love. How romantic. He called me his baby doll. I blinked a few times as my groggy brain slowly engaged. Baby doll? He'd never, ever called me that before. I rubbed a pattern along the back of his hand and my stomach plunged in dismay. Uh-oh. Something didn't feel right about the fingers clasped tightly around my middle. They were long and bony.

A sharp gasp from behind, followed by Bethany's outraged, "Grampy Boo! What on earth is going on in here?" had me struggling to a sitting position. In stunned silence, I turned and gaped at the doorway, unable to believe my own eyes. Standing hat in hand with Bethany's fingers curled like octopus tentacles around his elbow was Tally, staring back at me in white-faced bewilderment.

21

My gaze ricocheted from Tally to that of my befuddled bed partner, Cecil Beaumont. "You're not Penelope," he quavered, his rheumy eyes dulling in confusion. Equally mystified, I disengaged his hand from my waist. "No," I mumbled, "I'm Kendall. You've made a mistake." My voice was back! It sounded low and throaty, but, hey, it was there.

The old man's face turned beet red. "I...I...I'm sorry. Someone told me that...my wife was in here."

I fired a suspicious glance at Bethany. "Really? I wonder who would tell you that?"

He massaged his temples. "I can't exactly remember now."

"What is the *matter* with you?" Bethany snarled at me, sprinting to the bed. "Do you have to sleep with every man in the county? Come on, Grampy, let me help you out of here." She pulled him to his feet and led him out the door, hollering, "Felix! Felix, I need you right away! Tally, I'll be waiting for you downstairs."

As their footsteps faded away down the hall, I pulled the covers up around my chin, gazing sheepishly into Tally's quizzical eyes. "You have to believe me when I say this isn't what it looks like. I...I thought it was you," I murmured, running a hand through my tangled hair, terribly cognizant of how awful I must look in contrast to Bethany's blonde perfection. Damn, he looked good standing there all trim and tanned in those snug blue jeans. "Whew, I don't know what was in that last cup of tea Lin Su gave me, but I had some really spacey dreams last night. I still feel all muddle-brained."

He said nothing, just glared at me in stony silence.

Hoping to thaw his arctic expression, I added brightly, "But I do feel quite a bit better this morning."

"Well, we can all be thankful for that." The obstinate set of his jaw and undertone of sarcasm wasn't lost on me.

I groaned, scooping clumps of frizzy hair away from my face. "Jesus, Tally, nobody feels worse than I do about this whole fiasco and I don't blame you one bit for being ticked off at me. My plan was to follow one last lead for Lupe before coming home and...."

He cut me off with, "But your obsessive curiosity took precedence over me."

I slapped the mattress. "Quit saying that! You know it's not true."

"And how would I know that?"

My temper flamed, overriding the twinge of guilt. "Hey, I didn't set out to deliberately get myself trapped all night in that wretched little jail. You think it was fun sleeping on a cold, hard floor wrapped in damp newspaper?"

His shrug was unsympathetic.

"I know you're going to think I'm paranoid, but I have a bad feeling someone shut me in there on purpose."

He shifted his weight and shot me a dubious look. "And why would anyone do that?"

I shrugged. "I don't know, but I can tell you this. Someone in this house was eavesdropping on my phone conversation and knew damn well I was going there." I repeated the threats aimed at me by Jason and Cutter outside La Gitana on Monday, but his already hypercritical expression dissuaded me from voicing my suspicion that it may have been more to Bethany Beaumont's advantage to have me out of the picture.

"Oh, give me a break. This isn't a Nancy Drew novel. That sounds like a couple of guys just shooting off their mouths."

"Tally, I'm serious! Whoever was yelling for help knew my name. The next thing I know, I'm face down in the dirt. Pretty odd coincidence, don't you think?"

He leaned into the doorframe and folded his arms, staring at me as if I were an errant child. "I'm sorry you've had such an awful experience, but regardless of the reason it happened, it was you and you alone who made the choice to take this cockeyed assignment. The outcome for me is the same. You were a no-show and as far as I'm concerned, your promises aren't worth diddly squat."

"Look, I'm sorry—a thousand times sorry, a million times sorry. What do you want me to do? Can't we just continue with our plans and head on to California this morning?"

His face registered incredulity. "You know what? I think I liked it better when you couldn't talk."

I wrinkled my nose at him. "Come on, Tally, we'll only be one day late for the show."

"So that's your solution. Just leave? Right now? What about your car and the fact that you're sick?"

"Weren't you listening? I told you I'm feeling better. I'll just have to deal with the car situation when we get back."

He shook his head. "It's too late. The fact is your misadventures have…" he hesitated, turning towards the hall, then back to me, lowering his voice, "…have ended up involving me. Now *I* have to spend the whole day and probably tomorrow entertaining a of bunch of overweight greenhorns on an imaginary cattle drive…" He paused and drew in a calming breath. "But I gave Twyla my word that I'd stay and help them out, so I intend to do just that." For emphasis, he stabbed his thumb against his chest. "Unlike some people, I keep my promises."

Ignoring his disdain, I blurted out, "Does your promise to entertain extend to the talented and oh-so-charming Bethany Beaumont?"

His jaw tightened. "And what exactly is that supposed to mean?"

I fussed with the bedcovers and avoided his probing stare, feeling inept, vulnerable. "Well, you do seem to be spending an awful lot of time with her." Hopefully, I didn't sound as petulant to him as I did to myself. When he didn't respond, I glanced up and caught him observing me in thoughtful silence before he drawled, "Now that you mention it, she does seem to appreciate my company."

A flash of heat rushed over me. "Meaning what? That I don't?"

"It doesn't appear that you do as of late."

"Hey, I'm sorry I have to work for a living. I'm not some swooning little cowgirl cutie batting her baby blues and clinging to your arm like a leech…"

He cut me off with, "Don't try to turn this around. This isn't about me and it isn't about her. It's about you."

Exasperation almost choked me. "Look, you of all people know how busy I've been at the office with all the construction chaos and us being understaffed all summer!"

"Yes, and I'm also well aware of where I rank in relation to your all-important career path."

"Will you quit saying that?" I shouted so loud, my newly-returned voice cracked.

"Only if you stop demonstrating that it's true. Is it too much to ask for you to stop chasing off helter-skelter all over the blasted state and maybe spend a little more time with me at the ranch?"

It wasn't too much to ask but I wasn't ready to admit it. This was not the time or place to voice my concerns about my tenuous relationship with his ever-so-annoying mother. "Can we call a temporary truce and talk about this another time?" I asked, allowing a placating note to enter my voice. "I really need your input on some things I've found out these past few days."

He couldn't have looked less interested. "I don't have much time."

"Just give me five minutes. I think you'll be intrigued." I patted the corner of the bed in invitation. "Come on, please?"

He sighed and studied his watch. "Five minutes," he announced, crossing to perch stiffly on the edge of the mattress. I ached to touch him, have him hold me, but his demeanor wasn't encouraging. Instead, I began my explanation with Lupe's tearful request for help, only to have him interrupt me. "Wait, wait, wait. I thought you said you were sworn to secrecy and weren't allowed to divulge any details about her mysterious problems."

I grimaced. "Well, the parameters regarding my promise to her have changed somewhat since last Friday night." He listened while I filled him in on all aspects of the story, appearing surprised by my decision to adopt the kitten, and then mildly intrigued, until I got to the part about Mazzie La Casse's hypothesis linking the disappearances of the undocumented migrants to alien abduction. The unmistakable skepticism seeping into his deep brown eyes made me hesitant to repeat my own experience with the strange pulsating lights, especially since, in retrospect, I'd convinced myself that they could very well have been Border Patrol helicopters or possibly surveillance balloons launched from the army base at Ft. Huachuca.

I wished I'd had my camera handy to record the look of utter astonishment on his face. "A UFOlogist? Invaders from outer space? For chrissake! Kendall, do you have any idea how nuts that sounds?"

"Of course I do, but logically...."

"Yeah, let's do inject some logic, please."

"Will you let me finish?"

He ignored me. "You want to know what I think?"

I cupped my chin in one hand. "What?"

"For Lupe to be out of touch with her relatives for only two weeks is way too soon to fly into a panic. For my money, you've squandered our hard-earned vacation on a classic wild goose chase. Do you know how many hundreds of illegal immigrants cross the border every day?"

"As a matter of fact I've learned quite a bit...."

"Good. Then you realize that these people could be any number of places. They might be caught in the paperwork maze of deportation, especially if one or both of them has been hospitalized or jailed. Hell, they could be stashed in a safe house in Phoenix for all you know and can't get to a phone. She could hear from them tomorrow."

"I've already thought of those scenarios but...."

As if I'd not spoken, he went on with his tirade. "Or, they might already be in another state, and simply haven't contacted her yet. You're forgetting that I've had a little experience dealing with these people. Some work out fine, others just move on when the impulse grabs them. As far as that first guy found hiding in Morita, have you considered the fact that he was probably one of the smugglers and manufactured this wild story as a clever way to divert attention from himself? It sounds to me as if he wanted to be deported. Period. End of story."

Hearing him voice the same reservations I'd had, added to my feelings of self-doubt. "But what about Javier? How can you just set aside the similarities in their stories—the weird lights, both of them being chased by these supposed bug-eyed creatures, the other people traveling with them just poof, gone? Tally, people don't just vanish into thin air. Something had to happen to them."

Tally waved away my objection. "Kids make things up. It's as simple as that."

That was the fast and easy way to dismiss the entire episode, but I wasn't convinced. "What about his mother? Why would a woman walk off and abandon her child?"

"It wouldn't be the first time some Mexican handed off her kid to a *coyote*. Some people are just plain stupid. Can you imagine giving a total stranger your entire life savings and then trusting one of these scumballs to safely transport your kid to relatives in the States? Not all of the *coyotes* are men, you know," he added grimly, "The good

Sister what's-her-face over at the mission is probably up to her eyeballs in trafficking illegals, if you ask me."

The hollow feeling in my stomach returned with a vengeance. He dismissed each situation, one by one, in a very male, very left-brained fashion that was difficult to refute. "Okay, but what about Bob Shirley?"

"What about him? You said he was going to be indicted on drug running charges. Looks to me like he took the easy way out."

I fidgeted with the blankets. "Boy, if I always followed your analytical line of thinking, I'd be out of a job tomorrow."

He eyed me critically. "Face it. There's only a story here because you want there to be one."

"Not true. You've left out a major part of the puzzle."

"Which would be?"

When I articulated my theory linking Bob Shirley to the Knights of Right and the subsequent connection to Cutter, which then led directly to Jason Beaumont, he exploded in anger and shot to his feet. "What the hell are you getting at? That the Beaumonts are somehow involved in something...something unsavory?" His brown eyes were glowing coals of fury. "I've known Champ...I've known this family my entire life and you couldn't be more wrong! How did you come up with such a cockamamie idea?"

Maybe I shouldn't have, but I told him about the butchered cattle we'd discovered on Sunday, Champ's passionate reaction and Rob's callous warning of retribution. "The townspeople and ranchers in this area are fed up to their teeth with these types of incidents. They think their own government is working against them and have effectively tied the hands of the Border Patrol. They're scared, Tally. They're scared for their families, their livelihood and their future. Is it out of the realm of possibility to think that some of them may have decided to join forces with these Knights of Right kooks and taken matters into their own hands?"

"By doing what?" he thundered, flailing his arms. "Skulking around in the dark dressed up in Halloween costumes and scaring the shit out of the jumpers when they cross the border?"

I paused. "Well, unless you're ready to accept the possibility that all of these people were snatched by extraterrestrials, then yes."

"To what end?"

"Maybe it goes beyond just scaring them."

He cocked his head sideways. "Are you saying that you think they're smuggling immigrants into the country, killing them, and then what? Feeding their remains to the *maaaad* caretaker of Morita? Give me a break!"

"Hmmmm! Now *that's* a very interesting theory."

Suddenly Russell Greene's horrifying past pushed him to the top of the suspect list and his grave warning to stay away and never return took on a new and ghastly significance. If he'd not been wearing the burlap covering on his mangled face, was it possible that the first illegal and then Javier were actually describing him as the so-called bug-eyed creature? But, hadn't they both stated there had been more than one monster? And what about the sharp claws? Still...?

He groaned and flung me a look of total frustration. "I was kidding! Jesus, Kendall, use your head. These White separatist groups and the ranchers want to keep these people *out*, not bring them in."

"Maybe, but ask yourself this question. Why are all of these people having the same hallucination? The fact is, Lupe's relatives are gone and Javier's mother is nowhere to be found. How do you explain that?"

He held up a warning hand. "You know what? This conversation is over. I think you've had a little too much of Lin Su's herbal soup. We'll talk later, when your head has cleared and you don't sound quite so...delusional."

"I am not delusional," I snapped back, more hurt than angry. "There's something very odd going on here. I don't know what it is yet, but I feel it right here," I added, poking my gut.

He rose and stomped towards the doorway. "It's probably indigestion from the soup. I've got to go now and I don't know what time I'll be back."

"I know this whole thing sounds crazy, but please...please don't give up on me."

He swung around, jamming on his hat. "You sure as hell don't make it easy."

I sighed. "I know. I feel terrible about the way this has all turned out. Please give me a chance to make it up to you."

His unyielding expression sent my spirits plummeting. "Are we gonna be okay?" He took a long time to answer and all at once, it seemed as if there was no oxygen in the room.

"I guess that depends on you."

My heart stumbled over itself. "Meaning?"

"That I don't intend to spend the rest of my life being your afterthought."

22

He may as well have slapped me. Tears stung my eyes as I listened to the harsh clatter of his boots fading down the staircase. "That's right, just walk out as usual!" I called after him, well aware that he had the upper hand. What was I going to do? Flounce out of the room and walk home? If I could get my hands on the people who'd stolen my car for one second.... I pounded the pillow with my fists, not knowing which was worse, that my career was interfering with my love life or vice versa. Perhaps it was time for some serious self-analysis. Had I really given him the impression that I considered him nothing more than an afterthought? Or was a certain blonde bombshell feeding this fallacy to gain advantage? I didn't even want to face the next thought, but it rammed its way into my consciousness. What exactly had just occurred? Had we simply had another one of our fiery disagreements or had he just broken up with me?

I reached for a tissue and was dabbing my cheeks as Lin Su breezed into the room and laid my freshly laundered clothes on the arm of the sofa. "You feel better today." It was more a statement than a question.

"I guess," I sniffled.

She frowned, shoving her wizened face close to mine, her deep-set eyes searching my face. She placed her hand under my armpit and then nodded with satisfaction. "Herbs chase away fever, salve brings voice back, but," she said, eyeing me shrewdly, "body cannot heal if heart is unwell."

Dang, the woman was intuitive. Or perhaps the simpler answer was that she'd noticed the angry thundercloud on Tally's face when she'd passed him in the hall. Unwilling to discuss my personal life with her, I said, "I appreciate you taking such good care of me. But, what in the world was in that tea you brought me last night? Physically, I feel a hundred percent better, but I still can't seem to shake the fuzziness in my head."

Her mouth pinched in surprise, she shook her head slowly. "Your mind should be clear, your body growing stronger."

"If you say so, but I've never experienced dreams like that before and yet I sort of felt like I was still awake. It was weird."

Wooden-faced, Lin Su snatched up the empty cup and sniffed it. Her shuttered expression hiked my uneasiness up another notch. "I wash your clothes," she stated, pointing to my shirt and jeans.

"Thank you."

She fluffed the pillows. "Bed rest one more day."

As much as I appreciated her nursing skills, I had no desire to remain isolated in the stuffy little room for even one more minute. "No, I can't. I need fresh air." I threw back the covers.

The obstinate set of her jaw conveyed that she was unused to being challenged. "I prepare lounge in garden behind house. You rest there."

"Really, I'm fine now." When I stood up the wave of dizziness that washed over me was so strong I had to grab the arm of the sofa for support. I eased myself back into bed. "Guess maybe I'm not quite a hundred percent," I confessed. "But, I have a lot of work to do. I need to call my office and...stuff."

Was that a spark of sympathy behind her eyes? "A woman named Ginger calls many times asking for you." She pulled a piece of paper from her pocket and handed it to me. I had a hard time reading the slanted scrawl, but was finally able to decipher that Ginger had called and cancelled all my credit cards. Thank goodness I'd left my password on the list of numbers or it wouldn't have been possible. There was also an addendum to call her right away.

I looked up. "Is there a phone I can use?"

"In hallway, but first breakfast and then hot bath." With that she marched to the doorway, carrying the empty cup in her hands.

"Yes, ma'am," I murmured, saluting her retreating figure. She was the most unbending person I'd ever met, but I was grateful for her steadfast devotion to my welfare.

I laid my head back against the pillow, still mentally flogging myself about Tally. Had I cooked my goose for good this time? Never in my life had I felt so isolated, so powerless, so foolish. Lin Su was right about my being heartsick. That area of my chest felt raw, like it had been buffed with a sheet of coarse sandpaper. Did the Chinese have herbs to cure a broken heart?

Good to her word, she returned with a light breakfast of oatmeal and fruit. Once I'd finished, she ran a steaming tub and I immersed myself in her special herbal bath powders that smelled of peppermint and cloves. My skin was pink and water logged, but I felt much improved after soaking for almost half an hour in extremely hot water. Lin Su earned a spot in my heart when I realized after I'd dried off that, not only had she washed and ironed my clothes, she'd carefully mended the rip in the thigh of my jeans. I used a few toiletries from the medicine cabinet, including perfume, and wished to heavens I had my makeup case so I could apply a little blush to my pale cheeks. I couldn't seem to stop obsessing about the differences between me and the Golden Goddess of the Sundog Ranch.

Unfortunately, there wasn't enough makeup on the planet to raise me to Bethany's level. I stuck my tongue out at my reflection in the mirror and stepped into the hallway. As if on cue, Lin Su materialized in the doorway of Bethany's room wearing a puzzled frown. When she saw me, she quickly slipped whatever she was carrying into the pocket of her trousers and picked up a cup and saucer from a small table beneath an oval mirror. Having no desire to repeat last night's psychedelic dream, followed by the foggy-brained aftereffects, I hesitated as she pressed it into my hands. "I really don't care for any more tea right now."

"Drink," she stated with simple forthrightness.

Positive that the mulish gleam in her black eyes matched mine, I sensed that she had no intention of backing down although the midnight remembrance that she might have spiked the tea with something other than healing herbs flashed through my mind. But, in truth, I felt no more of a threat from her than I had from the notorious man-eater of Morita, Russell Greene. I accepted the tea with a gracious smile and took a sip.

The house seemed extra quiet as she seated me at the little phone table in an alcove near Jason's room. Before silently descending the stairs, she volunteered that Twyla had driven to Tucson and that Tally and Bethany were busy with the guests. Good. Maybe this time I could conduct my calls in privacy.

First on the list was Dean Pierce. I wanted to let him know I was still here and hadn't forgotten about Marmalade. Inez answered, told me he'd accompanied Twyla to Tucson and said she'd give him the message. With my phone card also a casualty of the car thieves, I had to place a collect call to the office. I braced for the barrage of questions I knew awaited me the moment Ginger answered the phone. It rang four or five times and a zing of surprise shot through me when I heard Walter Zipp's hearty voice answer instead of hers. "What? Kendall O'Dell? Sure, we'll accept."

"Hey, Walter, how are you?"

"Well, good golly Miss Molly, what the hell's going on? I've been trying to reach you on your cell phone since Monday afternoon."

"It's out of order."

"No shit. From what Ginger's been saying this morning, it sounds like you're out of order too."

That was an interesting way to put it. "Yeah, let's just say I've had better days. Is Lupe back to work?"

"Yeah, she's here, but completely bummed out. She thinks it's her fault that you got sick."

Actually it was. "I'll talk to her after we finish and I need to speak to Ginger too."

A pause. "Guess she's in the can...no wait, I think Tugg sent her out on an errand. She oughta be back soon. Hey, you want to know what I found out about the Hoggwhistle woman?"

"I sure do."

"Hang on a second." I listened to papers rustling in the background and finished half of the spicy-tasting tea by the time he came back on the line. "You made my job pretty easy because there sure as hell weren't any other inmates named Hoggwhistle."

"I'm not surprised."

"Your gal served three years in Tennessee for check cashing fraud and got released about eighteen months ago."

"Hmmm. That doesn't sound like a crime worthy of blackmail."

"Hang on, there's more."

My pulse rate gathered speed.

"You ever hear of a bad-assed dude by the name of Johnny Ray Barker?"

I searched my memory bank and came up empty. "No."

"Got a record as long as both our left legs. He's still cooling his heels behind bars. Seems that he and Ms. Hoggwhistle made quite a killing, so to speak, running a nursing home in some little out of the way burg and hurrying along the demise of some of their ailing patients."

"Whoa."

"Oh, yeah. She claimed the whole thing was his idea and that it started rather innocently. When the oldsters with no close relatives died, they simply neglected to say anything to anybody and continued collecting their pension and Social Security checks. But then Johnny got greedy. At the time of their arrest, the Hoggwhistle woman admitted her part in the check cashing scheme, but swore she had nothing to do with the twenty-eight bodies they found buried under the old house."

"Holy crap." My stomach locked up tight. "Was she charged as an accessory?"

"Yep, but it didn't stick. When she testified against this Barker fellow, she said he threatened to kill her if she talked, and beat the tar out of her a few times to make his point. And this guy was no dummy. Like a lot of career criminals these days, he'd kept up on forensic advances and cleverly doused the bodies with lye. The level of decomposition made it hard for the DA to build a strong case. The medical examiner's report was able to reconstruct enough to be pretty sure ten of the old folks probably died of natural causes. The rest were most likely murdered. But, they couldn't put together enough hard evidence for the jury to convict him of killing all of them. They were, however, able to get him on one count of murder with the last old guy he'd smothered just a few days earlier since he hadn't had time to get rid of the body. But, here's the kicker. The authorities calculated that thousands of dollars worth of checks were cashed, but they've never accounted for all the money."

"Did they pinpoint an approximate amount?"

"The estimate is a couple of hundred thousand."

A feathery tingle caressed the nape of my neck. The notion that Sister Goldenrod may have been involved in some petty crime was bad enough, but murder? No wonder she feared Froggy. My mind raced back to the incident I'd witnessed last Saturday night and a horrible thought surfaced. Was it possible that under the guise of aiding the illegal immigrants she was actually the person responsible for their disappearances? Was she the mastermind behind the smuggling ring, extracting large payments from the immigrants and, in lieu of providing transport, then simply disposing of them and pocketing the money? Was there enough money involved to take such a huge risk? "What about Froggy McQueen? Anything on him?"

"Haven't had time to research him yet, but I'll give you the web addresses and you can probably look him up yourself."

"They wouldn't do me much good at the moment." He whistled with amazement when I filled him in on why my laptop was missing and why I'd had to call collect. "Man, have you ever had a run of bad luck."

"Tell me about it." He promised he'd get on it right away and then wished me and Tally well before transferring me to Lupe, who spent a full two minutes apologizing. "Enough!" I protested. "It's okay. I'll survive. How are you feeling?"

"Not the best, but better."

"You're a sport to come into work anyway and Tugg and I both appreciate it." When I filled her in on what Walter told me she was silent so long I thought we'd been disconnected. "Lupe? What do you think?"

"To think she might be the one all along makes me lose all hope. This is very terrible."

"Yeah, but it would sure explain why she was so frosted when you brought me into the picture. Remember, even though the jury didn't convict her of being an accessory to murder, we really don't know to what extent she was involved."

She paused again before adding in a quivery voice, "If she is so evil, why would she call to tell me about Javier? Why would she take a chance that I might find out that she is to blame for Gilberto and my uncle to be missing? And look at the way she cares so well for all the other people who come to her for help. It makes no sense."

She made a good point. Even though I knew it would discourage her, I felt obliged to fill her in on everything else I'd found out and promised to keep her posted if I discovered anything at all that would shed light on the mystery of her missing relatives. "You may want to check in with Sister Goldenrod to find out if you can get any more information from her. You never know. She might slip and say something that would help break this case. And feel free to tell her that I'm still here at the Sundog even though I doubt she'll be interested in talking with me again."

"Okay," came her gloomy response.

"Lupe, don't give up hope yet."

"I'm trying not to." She thanked me again for going out on a limb, but her pessimism matched mine. I was on hold for a full minute before Ginger came on the line squawking like a frightened hen. "Good gravy, girl, I been in a tizzy and a half over you! Why didn't you call me?"

"I'm sorry. My cell phone is broken and I couldn't talk for two days."

"Your voice sounds like a croaky old toad. What happened? What kind of mess have you gone and got yourself into this time?"

"It's too long to go into now but...."

"But nothin'! You scared the ever-loving pee out of me when you didn't show up Monday night. Round about ten o'clock I called Tally and he didn't know anything. The next thing I know he's calling me from some ranch down yonder telling me you're lost. Then, he phones back yesterday and says you're not and later, he calls and tells me your car got stolen with all your stuff, and that you're sick as an ol' hound dog. Y'all are supposed to be over there cuddling on the beach...."

I cut in, "Breathe, Ginger, breathe. Simmer down and I'll explain, okay?" She stayed quiet while I gave her a brief overview of what I'd been through, and then she screeched, "Me oh my oh Moses! You could have got yourself killed. Girl, can't you stay out of trouble for two minutes?"

"Apparently not."

"So, am I understanding this right? Are you saying that because y'all had another one of your tiffs, you ain't going to California at all?" Was I imagining the tinge of panic in her tone?

"It was more than a tiff, Ginger. He's really ticked off this time. I'm sure if he'd had his truck with him in my room this morning he'd have jumped into it as usual and driven it right down the stairs."

She was uncommonly quiet for several seconds. "If I was you, I wouldn't worry my little head none," she sang in my ear. "When he gets over this...well, all I can say is a little bird told me that things are going to turn out just hunky-dory."

I sighed heavily. "That's a nice thought, but unfortunately there may be another reason he doesn't want to go on the trip with me."

"I'm not following ya."

I paused, battling my fragile emotions. Was I ready to share the painful knowledge that my own impetuous behavior may have tanked my relationship with Tally for good? "Under ordinary circumstances I would never ask you to betray a confidence, but I need you to level with me.

You have *got* to tell me what you know about Tally and this other woman you mentioned last Friday night."

A sharp intake of breath. "I wish I could but I can't...this time, I just can't."

Crushed by her words, my heart purged itself. "Ginger, you don't understand," I cut in, my throat tightening with anguish, "I think he's been seeing another woman for several months now." There. I'd finally uttered aloud the dreaded words festering inside me. Oddly, I felt a measure of relief.

"Whaaaat? But...but that can't be true! No, no, it's impossible!"

"Why is it impossible?" Her extended silence renewed my suspicions. "Come on, Ginger, please tell me what you know. Please."

"Oh, good Lord," she quavered. "Sugar, I am so sorry. I just...I just assumed it was you. It has to be! No. I can't believe Tally would to do something like this. It ain't like him."

"You haven't met Bethany Beaumont. Picture the most gorgeous blue-eyed blonde you've ever seen. Tack on that she's a rancher's daughter who's known Tally since childhood and rides a horse like she was born on one. Heck, I'm sure she's probably crazy about his ditsy mother and to make matters worse, she's also hunting for a guy with big bucks who'd be a great step-dad to her four year-old son. I wouldn't doubt she plans to have at least another half dozen kids to boot. In other words, she's pretty much everything I'm not."

"Oh, my Gaaawd!" she shrieked. "I can't bring myself to believe any of this." I didn't want to either, but now that I'd voiced my concerns, the probability loomed more real than ever. "Sugar pie," she said, her voice cracking slightly, "I surely would've said something sooner, but I didn't want to spoil the big surprise."

Oh, yes, Tally's big surprise. A rush of heat swept my body as I braced for the worst. "Come on, Ginger, just give it to me straight."

Still, she hesitated before fretting, "Oh dear! Well, you know that little gal who works down at Wilkin's Jewelers? Melva Scruggs?"

I tensed. "Yes?"

"She made me swear on a stack of Bibles that I'd keep my big mouth shut, but...she confided that two weeks ago Tally was over at the store picking out an engagement ring."

23

I sat perfectly still, unable to respond while a conflagration of emotions raged inside me. An engagement ring! At the same instant a flash of exhilaration sent my spirits skyrocketing to the moon, Ginger's sobering words 'I just assumed it was you' sent my heart plunging into an uncontrolled free fall. Surely, the ring was meant for me? But, God, what if it wasn't? Was I being dumped for Bethany? My thoughts whirled with confusion. But, if that was true, why the trip to California?

"Are you okay?" Ginger's urgent tone sliced into my morose thoughts.

"I don't know. I'm not sure whether to laugh or cry."

"You know something? I think maybe you're reading way too much into this whole thing. Tally might be pissed at you right this minute, but I got a whole lot of faith that he bought the ring for you and not this other gal, I don't care how pretty she is."

She sounded so confident, I wondered if she was trying to convince herself or me. "Oh, Ginger, I'm praying that you're right."

"Of course I am," she said with cheerful conviction. "Now, I know you don't cotton to taking advice, but just for once I want you to listen up for a change. The next time you see him, you grab hold real tight and plant a kiss on him he ain't never gonna forget. Then, make a point of showin' him just exactly how much you love him. And for heaven's sake, quit squabbling and pay a little more attention to the poor guy."

Back to square one of my dilemma. "All I can do is hope for the best."

"Atta girl! Hey, listen, I've got to catch these other two lines and Tugg's jawing at me from down the hall. Promise you'll call and let me know what happens?"

I made yet another promise and cradled the phone, suddenly overwhelmed with the urgent desire to be enfolded in Tally's strong arms and convince him that he meant the world to me. But, I had no idea where he was or how to contact him. I rose on shaky legs, moved to the hall window, pushed it open and basked in the warm morning sunlight. As I listened to the tranquil twitter of birds and the musical tinkling of a wind chime from somewhere below, one thing became very clear. One of us had to make some concessions and I doubted it was going to be Tally. Was it too late for me to make amends? It would have been easy to give in to the reservoir of tears dammed up behind my eyes, but I gritted my teeth and blinked them back, deciding to hold onto Ginger's words of optimism rather than continue my dizzying slide down the depression chute.

Now that the defining moment was upon me, it was time for serious introspection, time to come to terms with my reservations concerning our future together. Was I now ready to face the uncertainties regarding his mother, my qualms about altering my career path and even starting a family? Despite the fact that I'd screwed up big time in the arena of love twice already, it was humbling to realize that despite my laundry list of faults and foibles, this man, this decent, honorable wonderful man wanted to marry me. God was now giving me the opportunity to make the right decision and I'd best not blow it. That thought had no sooner crossed my mind than I heard angry tones from below growing closer and louder until it made my skin crawl to recognize the shrill voice of my nemesis. "I don't understand why you're being such a butthead about this," Bethany complained. "It's not like I'm asking for that much. Don't you want your son to be happy?"

I stiffened. Had she been in the house this whole time? Being careful to stay out of sight, I edged closer to the banister, immediately recognizing Payton's passionate response. "Read my lips. For the last time, the answer is no. No, no and no. You do *not* have my permission to shorten Brett's name to Klein."

"But it would sound so much better than Kleinwort."

"Why don't you just admit it? It's you who always detested my family name."

"But warts aren't attractive," came her petulant reply. "People usually get them removed."

Payton's sigh of exasperation floated up the stairs and I stayed perfectly still, wishing I could see their faces without letting them know I was eavesdropping.

"You'll just have to get past your personal psychosis on this subject and live with it. Why don't you take it up with your therapist during your next session?" Payton suggested with a tone of angry finality.

"Don't talk to me about therapy," she shot back. "You're the one who needs a shrink!"

"What are you talking about?"

"Hey, I'm not the one who screams myself awake at night calling out for my long-lost mommy," she added with silky sarcasm.

"We haven't all experienced your perfect rose-colored life."

"You know I love this ranch, but Brett seemed a lot happier in San Francisco when he wasn't around you so much. I think your bad luck is contagious."

"You heartless bitch." Yeaa, Payton, I crowed silently. Give it right back to her. "And speaking of hearts," he added coldly, "next week, when I attend the fund-raising banquet for transplant recipients, I'll check into getting you a new one to take the place of that black, empty cavity behind your ten-thousand dollar boob job."

Woo-hoo. Nice comeback.

"Why don't you get yourself a spine transplant while you're at it." Now they were bickering like children. I could imagine Payton rolling his eyes in disgust. "I have something to tell you," she added, dropping the sarcastic banter. "There's a good possibility that Brett and I will be moving away again soon."

"What? Where to?" His voice carried a deadly lilt.

"Castle Valley."

My heart lurched painfully as I grabbed the railing for support.

"You're utterly shameless and totally transparent. It wasn't enough that you ruined Gordon's life, was it? Now I understand Brett's question about having two daddies," Payton seethed, " and when it comes time to change his name to *Talverson*, you think I'll give in without a fight, isn't that right?"

"Hmmm. Actually, I hadn't thought that far ahead yet, but now that you mention it, it sounds like a grand idea."

Her ominous words confirmed my darkest fears, sending icy prickles of distress skimming down my arms. Was she bluffing just to get under his skin? My hands coiled into hard fists. The idea of just giving in and handing Tally over to this vicious little bitch without a struggle was simply unthinkable and my resolve deepened. The best course of action would be to confront the problem head on as soon as Tally returned, but at the moment I couldn't do a darn thing until he came back from wherever he was out on the lone prairie.

In a lethal tone Payton retorted, "The depth of your deceit is bottomless. I pity any man you get your claws into, but mark my words, you'd best think long and hard about taking my son away from me a second time."

"Oooh, somebody's trying to act assertive."

"Bethany, shut up! I refuse to play this game with you any longer. Where's your mother? I'm here to see her, not you."

"In Tucson trying to get Daddy and Jason released. She said she'd call later and let us know what's happening. Listen, I have to go now. I'm busy."

"Damn it, wait a second! When she does call, tell her that the coalition is behind Champ and Jason one hundred percent. We'll get them out."

You'd think that his gesture of good will would have thawed her shrunken ice cube of a heart just a tad, but instead she jeered, "What are you up to anyway? Are you trying to suck up to my parents and turn them against me by playing the big hero?"

"You're hopeless," Payton muttered, and seconds later a door slammed with such force, I could feel the reverberation beneath my feet. Whew. To say that they hated each other would be the understatement of the century. As far as I was concerned, she represented the vortex of evil and there was not the slightest doubt she would prove to be a formidable foe. I could only pray that Ginger's assessment of the situation was right and that my suspicions about Tally were dead wrong.

I waited until it grew silent before I descended the staircase, my mind whirling like a pinwheel in a strong wind. Lin Su was right. At this moment I needed to concentrate on getting my strength back because the biggest battle of my life lay just ahead of me.

My frame of mind improved greatly when I stepped outside into the balmy October air and followed a flagstone walkway towards the rear of the big house. The sound of nearby voices from the parking area caught my attention and I slowed my steps, surprised to notice Payton sitting in his truck having an animated discussion with Rob, Champ's gangly young ranch hand. I wished I were close enough to make out what they were saying because Payton wore an expression of stunned amazement. Seconds later, he barked something at Rob and tore off in his truck. I stood for another moment watching Rob sprint across the clearing and peel out in another pickup. Well, what had that been all about? Contrary to its peaceful façade, there was certainly no shortage of intrigue at the Sundog.

Following Lin Su's directions, I took the walkway that led around towards the back of the house, passing several discarded stuffed toys and a small red bicycle with training wheels. I met Rascal along the way and he wagged his tail enthusiastically in greeting. "Hey, there big boy, how are you today?" He allowed me to pet him for several minutes before romping away. I continued my leisurely stroll until I reached a shoulder-high brick wall with a wrought iron gate nearly hidden in overflowing vines. I pushed it open and stepped through. Immediately, a sensation of extreme tranquility settled over me. Or was it perhaps the effects of the old Chinese woman's magic tea?

The little enclosed garden was a delight to the senses, an oasis in the midst of this turbulent household. In a secluded alcove, behind a large potted cactus, I found the chaise lounge she'd prepared for me, complete with a pillow and light blanket. Beneath a swishing canopy of trees, I lay listening to the muted chatter of birds while admiring the smiling faces of Mexican sun gods adorning the babbling stone and hand-painted tile fountain. Numerous clay pots overflowing with brightly colored petunias and pansies squatted beside clusters of sturdy outdoor furniture and along the top of the low brick wall. The atmosphere of peace was so overwhelming I fell asleep almost immediately.

The soft murmur of voices woke me. My pulse surged with the hope that it might be Tally, but it was only Felix seating Cecil Beaumont on a cushioned chair near the stone fountain. He tucked a blanket around him and said he'd return shortly. Cecil gave him a vacant smile and was nodding at his retreating figure the same instant Brett burst through the gate clutching a large book in both hands. "Grampy Boo, can you read to me? Mommy's too busy."

Neither of them appeared to notice me lying behind the cactus.

The elderly man's face lit up with pleasure. "Why sure I will."

Brett laid the book in his great-grandfather's lap and flopped down at his feet, crossing his legs. "Read me the same one as yesterday."

Cecil frowned. "Why not pick a different one this time? There are lots of other good stories and rhymes."

"No," the little boy insisted, "I like that one. It's my favorite story and Uncle Jason's too. We always laugh at his name, Rumbleysti...Rumbleskil...."

"Rumpelstiltskin," Cecil corrected him with a chuckle. "Okay, little man, here we go." He adjusted his glasses, thumbed through the book and began reading. *"By the side of a wood, in a country a long way off, ran a fine stream of water; and upon the stream there stood a mill."*

Listening to the words of the familiar old fairy tale soothed me. It conjured up happy memories of carefree days spent with my parents and two brothers in the cozy house back home in Spring Hill, Pennsylvania. Before I knew it, I'd drifted back to sleep. The second time I awoke, it was a shock to realize that I'd slept for three hours. I sat up and stretched, amazed at how good I felt and delighted to find that someone, Lin Su no doubt, had prepared a snack for me and left it on the table next to the lounge. Hungrier than I'd been for days, I pulled off the plastic wrap and devoured the egg salad sandwich, apple, and was polishing off the last of the chocolate chip cookies when I heard a thin voice call out, "Hello there." Startled, I leaned around the outstretched arms of the prickly pear cactus and stared across at Cecil Beaumont, surprised that he was still in the same spot. He introduced himself, looking straight at me with no trace of recognition whatsoever. "Have we met before?"

A tremor of melancholy rippled through me. Oh, dear. He'd already forgotten that we'd met formally on Sunday and again informally during the mortifying encounter in my bed this morning. "My name is Kendall O'Dell," I said with a smile. I rose and crossed the patio, moving aside the fairy tale book Brett had left behind on the chair adjacent to him before seating myself.

He wore a bemused half-smile. "You're sure we haven't met? You look awfully familiar."

I wondered if he was remembering me or comparing me to his deceased wife, Penelope. "I'm a reporter for the *Castle Valley Sun*. I'm doing a story on the Sundog. This is quite a spectacular place you've got here."

"That it is, that it is." His gaze turned inward. "You should have been around seventy years ago. Things were a whole lot different." He launched into a series of vignettes recounting some of his parent's ranching experiences in the late 1800's when it was still Arizona Territory. While it was all interesting information, I began to feel trapped. There were a lot of other things I needed to do, like checking back with Walter to see if he'd been able to uncover anything about Froggy McQueen's background and contacting the sheriff's office to see if there was any news on my car, but fearful that I'd hurt his feelings, for the next half hour I sat and politely listened to his reminiscences about everyday life and the incredible hardships he and his family had overcome taming this rugged landscape.

It was amazing. Just as Champ had described, his long-term memory appeared to be intact. He jumped back and forth between tales of his parents battling the elements on their first ranch in the searing desert heat near Yuma, where they'd lived with no electrical power, no running water, and a covered hole in the ground lined with watered-down burlap as their refrigerator, to his own early memories of rescuing young calves from winter floods and doctoring cattle for deadly screw-worm. With the telling of each triumph and tragedy that accompanied the long drought of the 1930's, his face grew more animated. "This state has got a fascinating history. If you want to have some fun sometime, get hold of a book called Arizona Place Names. I think Champ's still got a copy in his study. You'll be surprised to find how many names of mountains and rivers and canyons, a lot of 'em right here in this area, have been changed over the years, some of them three or four times from the days of the early settlers."

"Really? Who has the authority to change them?"

He pursed his lips in thought. "Well now, I'm not entirely sure of that. Government bureaucrats, I guess, but in one particular case I know of, the wives of some Army officers stationed near Yuma were responsible. Take a look at a modern map sometime and you'll find a mountain range called the Kofas, which originally stood for King of Arizona. Nearby is another one dubbed the S H Mountains. You know how they got to be called that?"

"No."

"The spiky peaks stand all topsy-turvy and go every whichaway," he said gesturing with his hands, "and because of that, some of the troops decided they resembled a bunch of outhouses, so they nicknamed 'em the Shithouse Mountains." He cackled with glee and slapped his knee. "Now, apparently the wives took exception to that and started a campaign to change them to the Shorthorn

Mountains. Sometime later they were shortened to just the plain, old S H Mountains."

He rambled on and on, regaling me with other examples of towns and mountain ranges that had been renamed since the time of the original settlers and I really was trying to pay attention, but soon found myself daydreaming about Tally's return to the ranch. How was I going to handle this sticky situation? Should I abandon my promise to Ginger and tell him that I knew about the ring? Distracted by my thoughts, I was only half listening as he droned on and on about a place originally known as Cave Springs. I think I'd pretty much zoned him out when something he said snagged my attention. "...must be a hundred different versions of the legend of a phantom black stallion supposedly seen there only on moonless nights." He chuckled. "Now if you want to hear more details, you need to talk to Felix about how he and his two brothers used to cross over the border in the wee hours on their mules to work in the mine. He swears they all saw the ghostly creature galloping down the canyon hell bent for leather, snorting fire from his nostrils and it scared the living daylights out of them."

Something clicked in the back of my mind, but I couldn't think of what it was or why it was important. "I'm sorry. Where did you say this place is located?"

He didn't answer, just stared at me slack-jawed as if I were suddenly speaking a foreign language. "What?"

"I think you were talking about a place called Cave Springs?" I could tell by the dull sheen of perplexity in his fixed gaze that something had happened. He looked away, his mouth still moving, but no words coming out. After an extended silence, I touched his shoulder. "Mr. Beaumont, are you all right?"

He turned and peered at my face, murmuring, "Oh, yes, hello. What can I do for you?"

Oh, dear. The old guy was having one of his forgetful spells and it made me wonder how much of what he'd told me earlier was actually factual. "It's okay, " I said. "We can talk later."

"Yes, later," he repeated vaguely, falling silent, apparently enclosed once more in his own world. My throat tightened with sympathy and I sat with him another five minutes or so before rising to my feet. "I'll be right back." I should probably alert Felix or Lin Su to the old timer's seemingly catatonic state, but was hesitant to leave him alone. I got as far as the gate when Felix appeared around the corner of the house. Relieved, I motioned to him and explained the old man's condition.

"It happens more and more," he said with a resigned sigh. I accompanied him back to Cecil's chair. "Meester Bo," he said softly, shaking the old man's arm. "Time for you to come into the house. Dinner will be ready soon."

Cecil looked up and greeted him with a welcoming smile as if seeing him for the first time that day. "Felix, it's so nice to see you. How are you today?"

"Fine, Meester Bo, just fine." The elderly Mexican man and I exchanged a poignant look before he led Cecil away. With sadness, I watched the two old men shuffle back to the house. I stayed alone in the little garden a few more minutes, soaking up the warmth of late-afternoon sunlight now casting long shadows across the patio, and contemplating how lucky I really was. Poor old Cecil's deteriorating health put my present dilemma into proper perspective. At least I had some control over my immediate future. He didn't.

I glanced at my watch again. Almost four o'clock. Tally should be getting back any time now. It had been only six days since we'd last been together, but my blood ran hot at the prospect of grabbing hold of his muscular frame and pressing my lips against his sensual mouth. And that was just for starters. Delightfully preoccupied in my fantasies, I made it out the gate and halfway towards the front door when something Brett said earlier pounded at my dormant brain cells like a ball-peen hammer. *'It's my favorite story and Uncle Jason's too.'* Holy smoke! I did an about-face and rushed back to the garden, snatching up *The Golden Treasury of Children's Literature* that he'd left behind on the chair. How dense was I? Was this book the source of Froggy's fractured rendition of *Little Boy Blue* and the puzzling ditty in Jason's e-mail? My heart thumping erratically, I ran my finger down the table of contents. Oh, yeah. I fanned to the story of *Rumpelstiltskin* and began flipping the pages, speed reading, until one particular phrase leaped out at me: *Merrily the feast I'll make, To-day I'll brew, to-morrow bake; Merrily I'll dance and sing, For, next day will a stranger bring. Little does my lady dream Rumpelstiltskin is my name!'"*

My hands trembled with excitement. Was I getting myself overly agitated or was this the link I'd been looking for—the one connecting Froggy to Jason? I reread the verse. Something was different, but I couldn't pinpoint it. I wracked my brain, cursing the fact that all my pertinent notes were in the trunk of my stolen car. Think. *Think, damn it.* My head felt like it was packed with sludge from so many days of high fever, along with the magnitude of events that had transpired since last Sunday evening. I must have sat there for ten minutes sorting through the file drawers in my memory bank before the vital detail finally emerged. Four days! Hadn't Jason's riddle said '*in four days will some strangers bring*,' not 'next day' like the original text? And if one interpreted 'strangers' to mean that someone was planning to smuggle in a group of illegals then that meant...I counted the days backwards to Sunday. Good Lord! Tonight! Something was going to happen tonight! But where? And when? And, I still had no clue as to why.

I snapped the book shut, my heart racing full throttle, the urgent need to take action overwhelming. But what exactly should I do? Report my suspicions to the sheriff or Border Patrol? My shoulders sagged. And just how did I intend to prove what would probably sound like a ludicrous hypothesis? They'd probably react to it the same way Tally had. I could hear them laughing now. 'Let's get this straight, Ms. O'Dell, you want us to act on suspicions based solely on woman's intuition, the unlikely, unsubstantiated testimony of a five-year-old illegal Mexican boy with a wild UFO abduction tale and a few lines from a nursery rhyme book.' Sure, they were going to buy that.

Somehow I had to find something incriminating to prove my theory. My thoughts circled madly like a hamster racing on a wheel until the answer exploded in my head. Jason's room! Of course! And with him safely stashed behind bars, there was no better time to search it than right now. I jumped up and dashed out the gate, storming around the corner of the house so fast I practically bowled over Lin Su. Gasping with surprise, I grabbed her arm to steady her. "I am so sorry. I should have been paying more attention. Are you all right?"

"Yes." Undaunted as always, she righted herself and remarked with confidence, "Special tea make heart, mind, body strong again, yes?"

I grinned. "I don't know what your magic potion is, but thanks to you I feel great, and thank you for preparing such a nice lunch."

She nodded, acknowledging my compliment with a slight smile. "Phone for you in living room. Lady with loud voice says come quick. Very important."

Thinking it must be Ginger, I dashed up the porch steps and hurried inside, passing the open door to the kitchen where the delightful aroma of food cooking wafted out and followed me down the hallway to the living room. I snatched up the cordless phone, but when I said, "This is Kendall," a voice I didn't recognize screeched at me, "You two-faced liar! This is all your fault, I knew I shouldn't have trusted you!"

Flinching defensively, I countered the accusation. "Who is this?"

"Don't play games with me, missy. You know damned good and well who it is. What have you done with him?" came a high-pitched snarl. "Where is he?"

My senses swam in recognition. "Sister Goldenrod? What's going on?"

"You told that woman about him, didn't you?"

"Whoa. Back up. Who are you talking about?"

"That...that UFO woman...Mazzie...something or other," she blubbered, her sobs rising to a panicked wail. "How else could this have happened?" A tremor of unease fluttered inside me. "Take it easy. Tell me what's happened."

"He's gone! Javier is gone!"

24

A pang of distress ricocheted through me as I stood listening to her terse explanation. After leaving Javier in Celia's care, she'd driven to Tucson on church business. When she'd returned about three o'clock to bring him a snack she'd discovered the room empty. Celia claimed she'd checked on him about one-thirty. I checked my watch. That meant he'd been missing for less than three hours.

"Is it possible he's just wandered off someplace?" I asked hopefully.

"Not likely. The poor tyke was terrified of his own shadow. In fact, he had another nightmare last night and screamed so loud he woke up the whole house. I couldn't get him calmed down so I finally let him sleep with me."

With an impatient snort she dismissed my suggestion that relatives may finally have come for him, or that he'd attached himself to one of the many other Mexican families passing through the mission. The optimistic approach would be to embrace the idea that his sudden disappearance was simply a coincidence, but the timing bothered me. "What makes you so sure Mazzie La Casse has anything to do with it?"

"What other explanation is there?"

Sadly, I didn't have one. "Sister Goldenrod, I swear to you that I did not tell her where Javier was."

"This is a real small community, Ms. O'Dell. By now, everyone knows that you and Lupe were here. She may have put two and two together. How do I know she didn't sneak in here while I was gone? What's she going to do, use him for one of her UFO experiments? What do you really know about this woman anyway?"

Not a whole hell of a lot, I had to admit to myself, wincing as a guilty noose tightened around my heart. Had something I'd said or done inadvertently given away Javier's hiding place? "Well, if she does have him, I can't imagine any harm will come to him, but before you panic and point fingers, are you sure you've looked everywhere on the grounds?"

"Of course I did!" she barked. "I've turned this place upside down, inside out and every which way."

"Have you notified the sheriff's department yet?"

A derisive hoot. "And tell them what—that I've been harboring an illegal alien? You know I can't do that."

"You said Javier woke everyone up last night. Did that include Froggy?"

A pause. "I suppose so."

"Is he there now?"

"No, it's his day off," she said, sounding puzzled, and then she sucked in a startled breath, catching my drift. "Oh, dear Jesus in Heaven. That drunken asshole's probably been at the bar all day. By now he's blabbed it all over town! Well, shit! That means the Border Patrol got wind of it or maybe those sneaky INS people raided the place again while I was gone," she said, her voice ripe with disgust.

"Wouldn't Celia have noticed something that obvious?"

"How? The undercover people don't wear uniforms and they drive unmarked cars. They could have marched right through my kitchen and she wouldn't have known any difference."

I desperately wanted to believe that Javier was safely in the custody of the Border Patrol, or even Mazzie La Casse, but I could not shake the insistent sense of foreboding. After advising her to continue searching and to call me if anything new developed, I hung up and forced myself to refocus on the more serious problem at hand. Bent on searching Jason's room, I got no more than a few steps from the phone when it rang again. Thinking that Sister G may have forgotten something, I scooped up the receiver and was surprised to hear a male voice ask for me. "Speaking."

He identified himself as a deputy with the Pima County Sheriff's Department. They'd found my car. "Oh, thank God," I exclaimed with relief. "Where did you find it?"

"A few miles east of Amado."

"Where's that?"

"Near Arivaca Junction," he informed me, "but when I say we found it what I mean is we found what's left of it."

My stomach tensed. "What do you mean?"

"It was completely stripped."

"What exactly are you saying?"

"The people who stole it took everything but the actual body of the vehicle." His blasé monotone indicated that this was not an unusual event.

But it sure was to me. Engulfed with fury at the loss of my precious little car, not to mention everything else that had been in the trunk, I was left speechless for long seconds. "Well, this is just friggin' wonderful," I groused, blinking back tears. "What am I supposed to do now?"

"Take it up with your insurance company." He gave me the name and address of the towing company where my car, or rather the remains of my car was being stored in Tucson. Steeped in self-pity, I slammed the phone down. Time to find Tally. A cursory glance at the kitchen revealed only the Mexican girls and the laconic-faced Indian woman preparing dinner. A quick search of the grounds outside confirmed that he had not yet returned. Drat!

The waning afternoon sun, hovering in a splendid tangerine sky, streaked with patches of silver-rimmed clouds, gradually relinquished its heat, allowing the early evening chill to set in. I rubbed the mass of goose bumps skimming along my arms and headed back inside. It was closing in on five o'clock. Where the hell was Tally? I tried not to think about him out there with Bethany working her beguiling witchcraft on him, instead wrestling my mind back to the business at hand. Evidence. I had to find some hard evidence or no one was going to take me seriously. Ever. I made it half way up the staircase when the clamor of quarrelsome voices outside stopped me. I turned around just as Twyla Beaumont marched in the front door followed by Jason. Shit! My heart dropped as the opportunity to explore his room evaporated before my eyes.

"I told you I can't, Ma," he whined as his mother, appearing tired and distraught, slammed a pile of folders onto the entry table. "I got other important things to do tonight."

"No excuses," she snapped, massaging the back of her neck. "I've had about all I can handle for one day and right now I can only hope and pray we can get your father released tomorrow as well." When she glanced up and saw me, her eyes rounded in surprise. "Oh, hello," she said, re-modulating her voice to a pleasant level. "It's nice to see you up and about. Are you feeling better?"

I mustered a polite smile. "Much."

Jason's reaction to my presence was telling. He flinched violently and stared up at me, aghast, the emotions in his eyes shifting in quick succession from shock to anxious disbelief before settling into fiery hostility. Momentarily taken aback, I glared back as the discomforting realization fully registered. If I'd had any doubts before, the ferocious gleam in his close-set eyes put them to rest. He hadn't expected me to be here. No. I was supposed to be dead, locked away forever in the tumbledown jail in Morita, just as he and his conniving sister had planned. All at once, the convenient theft of my car took on a far more sinister connotation. What a rotten pair.

"Well, that's good, dear," Twyla murmured absently, turning away. "Jason, get out of those filthy clothes and put on something nice. We're going to need your help this evening with the hayride."

"I told you, I can't, " he complained, turning the threatening stare on his mother. "I don't have time to entertain a bunch of pansy-assed tourists."

Unaffected by his little hissy fit, she smacked a bunch of keys onto the wall hook and swiveled to face him. "I am in no mood to argue with you."

The fact that I was witnessing their personal exchange earned me a look of extreme irritation. He puffed his chest assertively. "I'm goin'."

"Don't talk back. The last thing I need is for you to go out drinking and gallivanting around with your buddies. You can't take a chance on getting into trouble again," she insisted wearily. "Now, I've got enough on my mind, so we're not going to talk about this anymore." Satisfied that she'd made her point, she disappeared through the kitchen door.

Snuffling hard through his nose like an angry bull, his fists clenching and unclenching, he wheeled around and charged up the stairs, peppering the air with obscenities and making sure he deliberately bumped me against the railing as he passed. When he slammed the door to his room I couldn't suppress a twinge of impish pleasure that my presence irked him, but at the same instant apprehension gripped me as his angry words rang in my ears. He had something important to do *tonight*. Not tomorrow, *tonight*. Was it just a fluke or was I trying to make something out of nothing just to prove to myself that there really was something sinister afoot? I'd been in this predicament twice already in the past six months, and like my other two big stories, I'd had not one speck of tangible evidence to validate my macabre theories. But, I'd been right. Okay. I'd arrived at another of those momentous introspective roadblocks. Time to decide whether to just forget the whole thing or have faith in my gut instincts.

I slumped down on the steps, chin resting in my hands. As things stood now, I could do nothing to stop what I strongly suspected would be a replay of whatever evil had befallen Lupe's relatives and Javier's mother. Javier. Poor little Javier. What could have happened to him? My heart ached as I pictured him cowering in the farthest corner of the closet, lost and motherless, bedeviled by nightmares, afraid of his own shadow, afraid of bug-eyed monsters, afraid of black horses. *Afraid of black horses?* I frowned. Why did that sound so familiar?

As I sat there mulling over each lead, each incident, each conversation, and together with what I'd learned these past five days, something kept hammering at the perimeter of my subconscious. I don't know if it was the result of my recent illness or preoccupation with Tally, but I couldn't fit the pieces together into any cohesive order. "Come on," I urged myself, squeezing my eyes shut. "Concentrate!"

I went over every point carefully a second time and all at once I sat bolt upright, tingling all over as Cecil's rambling tales of long ago jumped to mind. *The legend of the phantom black horse!* Was it possible that the one thing in this mystifying puzzle that had made no sense to me from the very beginning was actually the missing ingredient? My heart began to knock against my chest. There had to be a connection. If my hunch was correct, Felix was probably about the same age as Javier's great-grandfather. Hadn't the little boy said that the location of the special crossing place had been handed down through generations of migrants using word of mouth? And hadn't his mother said it was safer to make the journey during the dark of the moon? Oh, my God! Cecil had said the legendary phantom horse was only seen on *moonless nights!* I sprang to my feet and almost took a header down the stairs. My sudden appearance in the kitchen doorway startled the Indian cook so badly she dropped a pan lid. "Where's Mrs. Beaumont?" I demanded, breathlessly.

She stooped to retrieve it and eyed me curiously. "Outside in the barn preparing for the buffet dinner and dance."

I glanced out at the thickening twilight. Okay, no time to hunt her down. "Can you tell me which room is Mr. Beaumont's study?"

Again, the inquisitive look, but she shrugged and pointed. "End of the hall, last door on the right."

"Thanks!" Trotting along the dim corridor, my pulse thudding in my throat, I prayed that my hunch was right. And if it was what would I do? I hesitated in front of the closed door. As a guest in the Beaumont home, I really had no business rifling around in Champ's private study, but if I found what I was looking for I'd be in and out in a jiffy with no one being the wiser. I glanced over my shoulder one more time before pushing the door open and then closing it quietly behind me. I crossed to a massive desk and switched on a lamp that flooded the oak-paneled room in golden light. Three walls were lined floor to ceiling with bookshelves, while the fourth was plastered with large movie posters. I scanned them quickly, recognizing THE LAST ARIZONA COWBOY as the one Champ had mentioned, so that most likely meant the others had been filmed here on the ranch as well. It would have been fun to study them, but a grinding pull of urgency had me searching frantically through the book titles. "Come on, come on, where is it?" Fifteen minutes and two bookshelves later I hit pay dirt. With sweaty palms, I pulled out the copy of Arizona Place Names and flipped through it until I found locations that began with C. I ran my fingertip down the pages. Camp Verde, Canyon

Diablo, yeah, yeah, Castle Butte, Cavecreek originally founded, blah, blah, later changed to Cave Creek in 1962...and then there it was. Named after a series of caves and natural springs, discovered in 1871, Cave Springs was *re-named* to Wolf's Head in 1949 to reflect an irregular promontory. Yes! A thrill of triumph shot through me. I guess I'd known all along that Morita held the key to the puzzling disappearances. I clapped the book shut. Now all I needed to know was the immigrants' exact crossing point. I was busy replacing the book and rewarding myself with a mental high five when I heard a slight movement behind me. I jerked around and my heart swooped with alarm. Jason Beaumont, his face contorted in anger, loomed in the doorway. "What the hell are you doing snooping around in my dad's things?"

"I'm...I'm not snooping. Your grandfather suggested...."

I knew I was in trouble when he strode in, kicked the door shut and advanced on me, chest heaving. "You're lying. I knew you were a government spy."

I gulped, "You're wrong...."

He body-slammed me against the wall and grabbed my jaw in a painful grip. Teeth bared, his sadistic face only inches from mine, he snarled, "You goddamned wetback-lover. I've been on to you from day one. You got my folks fooled, but you ain't foolin' me, not by a long shot. I want your ass out of here tonight."

Paralyzed with shock, it took me a few seconds to collect myself. Struggling mightily, I managed to pry his fingers away, wrestle out of his violent embrace, and put the desk between us. "Don't threaten me, you psychotic cretin. You've got no authority...."

"Shut the hell up!" he roared. "When my father's not here *I'm* the head of this household, you got that? And I want you out of here. *Now.*"

I returned his glare, not daring to show how shaken I was by his brutal show of aggression, and more sure than ever that I was on the right track. "Tough. I can't go anywhere without transportation."

His eyes narrowed to blazing slits of hatred. "I don't give a flying shit if you have to crawl. I want you gone tonight!" He punctuated his threat by thumbing over his shoulder in the direction of Tucson. "You better not be here when I get back." After skewering me with a final warning glare, he wrenched the door open and stomped out.

In the wake of the violent confrontation, my bubble of bravado collapsed and I slumped into the desk chair, trembling with pent-up adrenalin. I no longer had any doubt that my presence here presented a danger to him and whatever diabolical plans were in the works for tonight. The throaty roar of an engine drew my attention to the window and a sickening certainty gripped me as his red pickup roared away in a cloud of dust. It was almost too horrifying to put into words, but I had to accept the grim reality as a much scarier scenario emerged. If, as I suspected, he and Froggy were indeed allies, it now seemed unlikely that Javier's unexplained disappearance today was a mere coincidence. The little boy was the only living witness to the so-called alien abductions. Alarm bells tolling inside my head, I raced from the room in search of Felix.

25

A half hour later, armed with the information I'd sought, I hotfooted it out the back door of the kitchen into the chilly night air in search of Tally. The first surprise was seeing so many vehicles parked in the clearing. The second was the startling visual of the barn lit up like a cruise ship. I crossed the shadowy parking area and paused in the doorway, bowled over by dazzling lights, the energetic blare of country music, and the size of the noisy crowd filling the enormous room that smelled strongly of hay mixed with barbequed beef. Where had all these people come from? They couldn't all be guests. Neighboring ranch families most likely. With plates in hand, young and old stood in the buffet line. Some sat at long tables eating, while others gathered near the five-piece band clapping and whistling. I caught sight of Twyla, flitting from here to there, tending to her guests' every need, beaming an artificial smile that belied her inner woes, no doubt. I knew how she felt. As I pushed my way through the crush of people, I couldn't help thinking that the animated faces and sparkling fragments of conversation interposed with bursts of hearty laughter presented a stark contrast to my escalating premonition of dread.

When I finally caught sight of Tally among a dozen other couples on the dance floor, all decked out in his tailored western suit and matching black Stetson, my heart overflowed with relief. But it was more than that. Consumed by a myriad of tumultuous emotions I couldn't begin to put into words, I studied his handsome face with a sense of wonder, as if blinders had been removed and I was seeing him with new eyes. There could be no more hesitation on my part. Problems and disagreements be damned, if he still wanted me, warts and all, he was the man I intended to marry.

I pushed my way through the throng of chattering onlookers and tried to catch his eye as he danced by with a slim gray-haired woman of perhaps sixty, all dressed up in sequined cowgirl duds and staring up at him with unabashed adoration. Yeah, I agreed. He was one buff cowboy and a much better dancer than me. Fleetingly, I remembered Ginger remarking one time how lucky I was to have 'landed' him, and as she'd put it, 'Honey, a fellow who can dance is prime meat.'

The music ended to great applause, but before I could capture his attention, a second eager woman pressed herself into his arms as the singer began to belt out another lively tune. Tally two-stepped by me again and this time we made solid eye contact. A look of mild surprise flitted across his rugged features as I waved madly and shouted, "Stop! I need to talk to you!"

Assuming a look of haughty nonchalance, he mouthed back, 'Later,' before he circled off around the floor. At first I was stung by his deliberate show of indifference and then I got it. He was getting even with me. No, maybe punishing was a better word. I hoped he'd read the desperation on my face as he twirled by a third time. He hesitated long enough to say, "Take a number, I'll see if I can fit you in," before he circled away, a slight smirk teasing the corners of his mouth. Unable to conceal the devilish twinkle in his eyes, he appeared to be having the time of his life while I had worked myself into a state of acute anxiety. How was I going to make him understand that this was no time for games?

"Would you like to dance?"

Simmering with frustration, I turned and stared blankly at a balding man of perhaps forty-five, slightly shorter than me and resplendent in a fancy fringed leather getup that would have made Roy Rogers proud. "What?"

"I said would you like to dance? No sense having someone as beautiful as yourself standing here all by your lonesome." Lips stretched in an ingratiating smile, his eyes had a hungry look as they flicked over me. Oh, Christ. He must have misinterpreted my anxious expression as one of longing. I was tempted to say, 'Get lost, buckaroo,' but managed a semi-polite, "No, thank you."

Undeterred by my rebuff, he squared his shoulders, demanding, "Are you sure?" Apparently he thought if I took a second look, I'd change my mind. His pretentious attitude reminded me of a male peacock presenting glorious tail feathers to a disinterested peahen.

"Positive."

Appearing miffed, he turned away, but loud cheers and whistles erupting from the onlookers drew my attention back to the dance floor. The spectacle of Bethany in Tally's embrace, clad in a dangerously low-cut scarlet dress, her body pressed possessively against his, sent a shooting pain through my heart. As they whirled by, her frothy dress billowing around her perfectly formed legs, I felt like a plain Jane dressed in my rumpled shirt and mended blue jeans. Suddenly, the music faded beneath the roar of blood in my ears and it seemed as if one of the movie posters in Champ's study had come eerily to life. The pivotal scene starring the ever-so-sexy Bethany Beaumont as QUEEN OF THE STARFIRE RANCH, played out in slow motion—Tally's hand pressed against her back, the generous swell of her breasts, flowing flaxen hair, flawless features. As they floated past me, her taunting blue eyes shimmered with a look of such supreme triumph that hot coals of anger scalded my chest. On impulse, I turned to my prospective dance partner and grabbed his arm. "Let's dance." He executed one of those classic double takes, but didn't object as I pulled him onto the parquet floor. "Well, now, I knew you'd come to your senses," he purred, his self-assurance reinstated.

The vocalist switched to a slow ballad filled with tear-jerking lyrics that seemed directed solely at me. *"My heart breaks into a million little pieces every time I think of losing your love..."* Time was a precious commodity, but I needed to get my own house in order before I could tackle whatever havoc lay ahead. I balked as my dance partner started to lead me towards the other end of the floor. Shifting my weight against him, I propelled us in the opposite direction towards Tally. "Ohhh," he sighed, "I can tell you're a woman who likes to take charge. I like that." He clutched me tighter, his hand inching towards the small of my back.

Suppressing a shudder of distaste, I asked coyly, "So, you like assertive women, do you?"

He leered and winked. "I sure do."

"Good." I maneuvered him until we drew even with the dancing duo, then I stopped and tapped Bethany on the shoulder. "Excuse me, I'm cutting in." Tally's face registered bemusement, but when she turned and recognized me, her eyes flashed hateful fire. I held my ground. "Bethany, say hello to Roy, he's just dying to meet someone like you." I could tell by her look of considered hesitation that she was calculating whether to make a scene or continue her role as benevolent hostess as some of the other couples slowed to eye us with curiosity. Casting a final I'll-get-even-glance, she flounced into the arms of my befuddled ex-dance partner who protested, "My name isn't Roy."

I gave the hapless guy a farewell salute, slid into Tally's embrace and when they were safely out of earshot, I looked up to meet his quizzical gaze. "Nice to see you back among the living. You're in rare form this evening," he remarked, his dark eyes searching mine. "That was a charming little display of drama, but was it really necessary?"

I wanted to kiss and slap him in the same second. "I had to do something drastic to get your attention."

One dark brow edged higher. "Oh, you got it, along with everybody else's." His gaze darted among the crowd of onlookers and then back to me. "And in case you haven't noticed, I've been rather busy."

"Apparently. Why didn't you come and check on me when you got back?"

"I did."

I shot him an uncertain frown. "When?"

"Earlier this afternoon," he answered. "But drill sergeant Lin Su said madam was asleep in the garden and gave orders that you were not to be disturbed. Period.

When Bethany asked me to help her out on another trail ride, I did, and got back just in time to change for the festivities."

"Yeah, and on that subject, what's going on? Have you become a dance instructor since I last saw you?"

Sidestepping my obvious sarcasm, he assumed a superior expression. "Based on the rave reviews of the enthusiastic ladies here this evening, I have a promising future in that arena."

A few deep breaths kept my temper at bay. "I see. So, what's the deal? Are you and Miss Twinkle Toes planning to take this hoedown on the road?"

He cocked his head, mild irritation glinting in his eyes. "Considering it's your fault that I got roped into this situation, I would think you'd be more appreciative of my position. Actually, Bethy thinks I'm quite talented," he added lightly, releasing me for an underarm turn, and when he pulled me against him again, I retorted, "Personally, I don't think *Bethy* needs any more instruction of any kind from you."

Cocooning me in his arms, he dipped his head lower, his lips brushing lightly over my ear. "Do I detect a hint of jealousy?" he whispered gruffly.

"You mean just because she's been clinging to you like a second skin for three days? Heavens no."

His deep laugh released some of the tension imprisoning my heart. "Relax," he crooned, his soft breath tickling my neck. "You know what really excites me?"

My own breathing grew a bit ragged at that point. "What?"

"Tall, temperamental redheads."

I felt like breaking into an Irish jig, but couldn't resist saying, "Are you sure? Even though she has huge perfect boobs, a picture-perfect face, she rides a horse like the wind, dances better than I can, has a ready-made family and apparently, not a single one of my glaring faults and idiosyncrasies?"

He hesitated a couple of seconds before answering, "The trouble with perfect women is that in order to be truly happy, they demand a perfect man. Last time I looked, that wasn't me."

Enfolded safely in his arms, blissfully happy for the first time in days, my tortured soul felt nourished by his gentle admission. I nuzzled my face against his neck, murmuring, "You're perfect for me." I tightened my arm around his neck, relishing the feel of his lean body, wishing the dance would last forever, but then a surge of urgency shocked me back to reality. The time! Stiffening, I drew back. "Tally, we have to go."

His eyes probed my face. "What are you talking about?"

"Several important things happened while you were gone today and I need your help."

"With what?"

"Can you drive me out to Morita?"

"What?" His sharp response drew curious stares. "When?"

"Shhhh." I glanced at my watch. Almost seven! "Actually, we need to leave right away. According to my calculations, the moon will rise a little after ten, so we don't have much time."

His jaw dropped in amazement. "What the hell are you talking about?"

More stares. "Can we go somewhere and talk privately?"

An upward eye roll. "Oh no, please don't tell me we're back to the alien abduction story again? I was hoping you'd be over all that nonsense by now."

My temper flared to life. "Tally, please listen to me. I'm dead serious about this. And anyway, I thought this would make you happy."

"Why should it?"

"Because, I want you to know you're not an afterthought. This time I'm asking you to come with me."

His scowl of pained tolerance doused my hopes. "Fine. I'll drive you out there. Tomorrow. During the day."

"No!" I whispered fiercely. "We have to go now."

"Kendall, don't you get it? I don't have this burning desire to constantly throw myself into the middle of weird situations like you do. I'm a pretty simple guy, content to raise my horses and cattle and write my little sports column twice a week. And in case you've forgotten, the last time I got tangled up in one of your fiascos, you got the scoop and I ended up with a broken arm."

"I know, I know," I replied, keeping my voice low, "and I still feel bad about that but...but...sometimes circumstances require taking a certain amount of risk. People do risky things all the time. What about firefighters? What about skydivers?"

Both brows shot to his hairline. "Oh, Jesus, does this caper involve jumping out of a plane?"

Annoyed by his flippant attitude, I cautioned myself to remain calm or he'd dismiss my explanation out of hand. "Please, hear me out. It may be a matter of life or death," I tacked on for emphasis.

That earned a skeptical frown. "Whose death are we talking about?"

"Javier's, and possibly mine if Jason comes back and finds out I'm still here."

"You're still not making any sense."

A few of the dancers twirled within inches of us, so I tilted my head towards the doorway. "Come outside with me." He resisted for a few seconds, but then allowed me to lead him off the floor. "This had better be good," he grumbled under his breath, nodding and smiling at two elderly ladies eyeing him hopefully, obviously pining for a dance.

I caught sight of Bethany still clutched in Roy's arms, and if her eyes had been fists, I'd have been pummeled to death. Just to annoy her, I waved and smiled, making sure that she noticed Tally's hand in mine.

There was a definite nip in the air when we stepped outside. The cool breeze blew my hair around my face and sent goose bumps parading up my arms. Once we were away from noise of the crowd and music, he stopped and turned me to face him. "Fair warning, if you're going to continue with this nutty idea that the Beaumonts are involved in whatever craziness you were talking about this morning, I don't want to hear it."

"Do you think I'm a good reporter?"

"Is this a loaded question?"

"Just answer it."

"Of course I do, but I happen to think you're way off the mark on this one."

I groaned through gritted teeth. "Just try to listen with an open mind. That's all I ask."

"Okay." He folded his arms and listened with an inscrutable expression on his face as I filled him in on each new aspect of the story. When I finished he shook his head sadly. "Kendall, I can't believe you're actually serious about this. Only you would be able to make a connection between a hundred-year old legend about a phantom black horse and the mindless babble of a five-year-old."

"But don't you see, Javier must have heard the identical story from his great-grandfather that Cecil just repeated to me. That's why he was so afraid to cross the border with his mother. He has to be talking about the same place."

"Fiction," he proclaimed, sagely staring off into the distance. "You should take up writing fiction."

Stung, I retorted, "That's not funny."

"I wasn't trying to be funny."

I prayed for patience. "So, you're not the least bit disturbed about Jason threatening me in Champ's study?"

A careless shrug. "Can you blame him? You really shouldn't have been going through Champ's stuff without someone's permission. He probably just overreacted."

"Overreacted? He practically choked me to death! I'm telling you Tally, he's dangerous and he thinks I'm some sort of a government spy or working in some capacity for this Lopez woman he's always snarling about. And what about when he spotted me on the stairs? He looked at me like I was a ghost. Don't you see? I was never supposed to escape from the trap he set for me in Morita. I think he and some of his Knights of Right goons are responsible for the fact that I no longer have a car."

My speech did nothing to diminish the obstinate set of his jaw. "So, you believe Jason is the brains behind some sort of phony alien abduction scheme designed to wipe out the entire Mexican migrant population as they cross the border?"

That gave me pause. "Well, I don't know if he's smart enough to be the mastermind, but I'll tell you what, his true sentiments are reflected by his choice of reading material and his violent behavior. Do I think he's sadistic enough to snuff out people he perceives as parasites? You bet I do. I also think he's afraid I'll find out what he's up to and that's why he wants me out of here tonight."

"If you're so sure something is going to happen, why don't you alert the Border Patrol? Let them handle it."

I glared up at his shadow-streaked face. "I've already thought of that. If *you* don't believe me, how am I ever going to convince them? On top of that, I suspect that one or more agents may be involved in some capacity."

If possible, his expression grew even more incredulous. "Why would you think that?"

"Because of the Bob Shirley case. Think about it. Why was he so paranoid about discussing the migrant he arrested in Morita, remember the one whose story matched Javier's? And then, suddenly, out of the blue, he kills himself two weeks later? Again, we're back to timing. It's just too perfect." I could tell by his doubtful grimace that he wasn't even close to being persuaded. "Look, I know you think I'm being pig-headed...."

"You? Pig-headed? Never."

I scrunched my nose at him. "Okay, I know this is all a bit of a stretch, and it may turn out to be nothing at all, but what do you have to lose by driving me out there?"

Following his prolonged sigh of exasperation, he lifted his hat, finger-combed his hair and settled it back into position before asking in a weary tone, "Okay, what's the plan?"

"What do you mean?"

"What do you plan to do when we get there? Are we going to attempt another one of your daredevil schemes and try to round up this bunch of thugs by ourselves? If they are as dangerous as you suspect, I'm surprised you'd want to confront them. I only have my .45 with me and I'm not sure that's going to be enough firepower."

"Who said anything about confronting them? I'm not that crazy. I think the safest approach is to find a spot to hide, hunker down, and then wait to see what happens. If I'm right, then we contact the authorities, lead them out there and then let them handle it." His thoughtful expression conveyed that he was thinking it over and I held my breath waiting for his response.

"How are you going to know where to find these people?"

"Ah, that's the beauty of it," I said, rubbing my hands with enthusiasm. "I already talked to Felix, and he gave me exact directions to the crossing place."

Even in the dim light, it was hard to miss the sly twinkle in his eyes. "I have to admit that the part where the two of us hunker down under a bush is a pretty tempting offer, but somehow stumbling around out there in the dark doesn't sound like a good plan to me. And that brings up another point. Short of shining a spotlight on them, how are we going to see anything?"

Oh, boy. It was time to tell him. "It might not be as dark as you think." He reacted to my account of having witnessed a strange hovering craft and being blinded by a bright blue beam of light with a vociferous, "Oh, come on!" He grabbed my shoulders and gave me a little shake. "Kendall, listen to yourself! I can't believe I almost bought into this crazy theory of yours. Can't you see that you're basing this whole conspiracy on two unsubstantiated UFO stories, a couple of fairy tale rhymes and a fever-induced dream? You don't have one shred, one iota, even one teeny little speck of actual physical evidence to prove your point. Give it up."

Crestfallen by his negative response, I thrust out my chin. "Fine. Don't believe me. Give me the keys to your truck. I'll go by myself."

"You'll do no such thing," he thundered.

I clenched my fists. "Tally, I was not dreaming! Listen, I'll make you a deal. Come with me. If nothing happens, you can spend the rest of my life saying I told you so, but what if I'm right? Javier's life could be at stake while we're standing here arguing."

"Or not. Again, you're making an assumption. What makes you think the kid didn't just wander off someplace? Most likely, he's somewhere else in the house or on the property and she just hasn't found him yet."

Thinking about the mission resurrected the memory of my night in the car and I gasped, "I just remembered something! That night I saw the illegals being herded into the vans, remember I told you three of the vans went north but the fourth one went south and I couldn't figure out why?"

"Yes, so?"

"The flashes! The driver signaled with his headlights and there were answering flashes from the southwest. I didn't put it together until just this minute, but now that I think about it..." I paused and turned in a circle to get my bearings. "That's it! I'm sure they came from the direction of Morita! And a Border Patrol jeep followed the van, or maybe I should say *escorted* it to its final destination."

"Now you've lost me completely."

"Don't you see? For a while I thought maybe Sister Goldenrod might be in on the smuggling scheme, I mean, I think she is in a secondhand way because she *is* harboring these illegals, but now I think Jason and his Knights of Right bunch may be siphoning off people from the groups she's bringing in, and Froggy is the snitch. That silly little rhyme was to alert Jason that they were there for the picking. Once transportation arrived, they simply commandeered one of the vans. There! Is that enough evidence for you?"

"Jeeezus!" Tally exclaimed, raising his arms in appeal to the stars overhead. "That is the most disjointed, far-fetched story I've ever heard in my entire life. I swear you are the most exasperating woman I have ever known."

I opened my mouth to tell him he was the most exasperating man I'd ever met, but was interrupted by Twyla's frantic, "Tally! Tally, where are you?" We turned to see her silhouetted in the open doorway.

"I'm talking with Kendall," he called back, unable to conceal the agitation in his tone. "I'll be there in a minute."

Shrugging into a coat, she hurried towards us, the tension on her face visible as she moved in and out of the dappled light. "I'm sorry to interrupt," she said, placing a hand on her heaving chest, "but I need your help."

"What's the problem?"

"I really hate to ask after all you've done for us today, but, could you go to Arivaca and bring Jason home?"

"Excuse me," Tally drawled, edging me a condescending glance, "did you say Jason is in *Arivaca*?"

I felt like someone had thrown a bucket of ice water on me as my carefully constructed theory fizzled before my eyes like a defective sparkler. Impossible! How could I have miscalculated so badly?

"I begged him not to go out tonight," she sniffled. "Apparently, he's been drinking and mouthing off to some of the other patrons. My lawyer says things could go very badly for him if he gets into trouble again."

Relying solely on my reporter's instincts, I cut in, "How do you know for sure that he's at La Gitana?"

She pinned me with a look of blank confusion. "The bartender called. Why?"

Unwilling to admit defeat, I pressed, "Did you talk to him personally?"

"No, Lin Su took the message," she replied, pulling the coat tighter in the quickening breeze.

"So, how do you know it was really the bartender?"

"What are you getting at?" she asked, her tone snippy.

"Kendall, lighten up," Tally warned, lightly squeezing my arm. "Twyla, isn't there someone else you can ask? I'm sort of tied up here."

"I'd go myself, but I can't leave Bethany alone to handle everything. Most of the boys are getting the horses and wagons ready for the hayrides and I can't find either Rob or Sloan," her voice broke and she buried her face in her hands, bawling, "Oh, God, this has been such an awful day. Please, Tally, if you could just do this one more thing for me I'd be so grateful."

Tally, reacting like most men do to tearful situations, shifted his stance uncomfortably. "Simmer down. I'll do what I can."

"Oh, thank you. You're such a dear boy." She dabbed her eyes. "And, Kendall, thank you for being so understanding about all of this. I really don't know what I would have done without Tally's help today."

I nodded wordlessly. What could I say? While I sympathized with her plight, nonetheless it annoyed me to play second fiddle to the mighty Beaumonts. Ironically, I was probably getting a taste of my own medicine. After she disappeared back inside the barn, it took me a few seconds to work up the courage to make eye contact with Tally. Bracing for his inevitable lecture, I cringed inside. "Okay," I sighed, "apparently you're right and I'm totally off base on this one." But his steady gaze, brimming with warm compassion, surprised me. Stepping closer, he pushed the cloud of wind-blown hair away from my face, then let one finger slide down my cheek and trace the outline of my lips. His gentle touch quickened my pulse.

"Listen, pretty lady, one of the things I admire most about you is your eagerness for doing the right thing, for fighting injustice, even down to the simple act of rescuing an injured kitten," he added with a hint of a smile. "Come on, you did your best to try and help out a friend and who can fault you for that? But let's face facts. You've been a pretty sick little filly here for a couple of days and I think you've had a little too much time to lie around and let your imagination run wild. You also had your heart set on unearthing another mind-blowing, adrenalin-popping, front page scoop, but it's time to back away gracefully and admit that you're wrong this time."

His soft-gloved indictment was ego-shattering and heartening at the same instant. Escape from this sticky situation was at hand, and it would have been so easy to succumb, but I could not shake off the gnawing sense of unrest. "I know you're going to brand me as certifiable, but I still believe something is going to happen tonight, and if we don't get out there soon, it will be too late."

Ignoring my plea, he hooked his hand through my elbow and led me towards his truck. "Look, I have to do this. It shouldn't take more than an hour and a half round trip. Why don't you come with me?"

"I have no desire to confront Jason Beaumont in a drunken rage, thank you very much."

"All right then, I have a second proposal." He stopped, pulled me into his arms and pinned me with a penetrating look. I tensed, feeling positive that his choice of words meant the big moment had finally arrived. I wanted to shout out, 'yes, the answer is yes!', but instead of the expected marriage proposal he laid on his exaggerated western drawl. "Well now little lady, hows about when I get this business out of the way, you and me mosey on upstairs to your cozy little loft and start enjoying our vacation." Without waiting for my response, he whipped off his hat and fastened his mouth firmly against mine. After so many days of mental anguish, fearing that I'd lost him, my body blazed with pent-up desire. Remembering Ginger's words of advice, I wrapped both arms around his neck and returned his kiss with a heated fervor designed to leave no doubt in his mind as to how much I wanted him, how much he meant to me. When we finally pulled apart, my emotions were in such turmoil, I could hardly stand up or think straight. Judging by his uneven breathing and the intense glow of passion in his eyes, I'm pretty sure he felt the same way.

"Ninety minutes," he intoned huskily, jamming on his hat and fishing his keys from his jacket. "Keep that fire burning." With a rakish grin, he jerked the truck door open, jumped in, started the engine, and with a final wave roared off into the darkness.

Freed from his scorching embrace, the night air chilled my skin. I watched trancelike until his taillights vanished around the bend, then strolled towards the kitchen door. It wasn't exactly the proposal I'd expected, but it was a good start I thought, congratulating myself for keeping my mouth shut for once. Still flushed with happiness, I entered the deserted kitchen and grabbed an apple from the fruit bowl. With all the activity still centered in the barn, the house seemed eerily quiet. For several minutes I munched on the apple and wandered aimlessly from room to room, basking in my newfound tranquility while desperately trying to ignore the powerful conviction still haunting me. Why couldn't I just forget the whole thing? I tried to banish all thoughts of going to Wolf's Head, but I could not prevent the unanswered questions from circling endlessly in my mind. Nervously pacing the corridor for the second time, my steps halted when the startling answer jumped out at me like a Jack-in-the-box. *Just because Jason was missing from the equation didn't mean the entire hypothesis was wrong.* What if...? I ran to the living room, grabbed up the phone and dialed Information. Dry-mouthed, I waited impatiently through the computerized voice message then punched the appropriate numbers. Three rings later a female voice shouted over clanking glass and raucous laughter, "La Gitana."

I told her who I was, where I was calling from and asked if she could give Tally a message when he arrived. "He's a real tall good-looking guy in a black hat. He'll be looking for Jason Beaumont and..."

"I'm sorry, who'd you say?"

I raised my voice. "I said, he'll be looking for Jason Beaumont."

More noise, clanking, banging, and then, "He's not here."

My pulse jumped. "What time did he leave?"

"He hasn't been in tonight at all."

I slammed the phone down and rushed around the room like a mad woman trapped in a maze. I *was* right! I was *right!* Uncertain what to do next, I dashed back to the phone, grabbed the receiver and just stood there paralyzed. Who was I going to call? No one. And time was running out. Suddenly, it was as if my brain had been switched onto automatic pilot. I ran from the room, sprinted upstairs to retrieve my jacket and raced back down again. When I reached the hook in the hallway where Twyla had hung Champ's keys, I grabbed them and ran for the door.

26

I declared myself officially over the edge. Tearing along the rough dirt road towards Wolf's Head, my rambunctious heartbeat clattering in my ears, I was so wired my adrenalin levels must have been off the charts. Oh, boy. In addition to all my other transgressions these past five days, I was now officially a car thief. "O'Dell, you're in deep guano now," I murmured, acutely aware that I really didn't have the slightest idea what I was going to do when I finally got there. I glanced at the clock. Seven-thirty-five. The intelligent, less risky decision would have been to wait for Tally's return. But that might be too late. As it stood, the trafficking operation might already be underway. Or had I missed it?

Like most people fixated on a particular objective, no matter how skewered the thinking, I'd convinced myself that if I followed Felix's directions exactly, kept out of sight and didn't try any heroics, I just might accomplish my goal and be back to the ranch before Tally returned from his wild goose chase. I had to hand it to those guys. The phony call to Twyla was fairly brilliant, serving to distract

Tally and remove my means of transportation. But they didn't know me.

I reached the cutoff within twenty minutes. Instead of turning left into Morita, I kept going, following the road around the west end of Wolf's Head as Froggy had done. Back-dropped against brilliant starlight, the jagged pillars of stone arched ominously towards the sky like gnarled black fingers. Spooky, definitely spooky. Russell Greene's warning to stay away was a sobering reminder of what might await me. With the initial rush of euphoria subsiding, the gravity of my hasty decision sank in. This was insane. There was still time to turn around. Second-guessing myself, I eased up on the accelerator and coasted until the memory of Javier's frightened eyes popped into my head. Was there even an outside chance I could somehow save that little boy? I had no choice but to try.

I jammed my foot on the gas and raced ahead until I reached the fork in the road. Swerving left, I plunged between steep canyon walls where even starlight could not penetrate the gloomy interior. It was almost like driving inside a tunnel and it was a struggle to keep my claustrophobia at bay. Thankfully, the sky suddenly reappeared to my right as the cliff diminished in height and slowly angled away to the west, leaving a trail of weirdly shaped boulders in its wake. Vaguely, I wondered if the puny flashlight I'd pulled from the glove compartment would be enough to light my way. What if I got lost? Impatiently, I pushed the thought to the back of my mind and kept driving until the ground cover became so thick it was hard to navigate as I searched for the first landmark Felix had mentioned. And then, there it was. Ahead and to the right, I caught a glimpse of the old wooden gate he'd described. I braked, cut the lights and slipped on my jacket as I slid from the cab. It took me several seconds of feeling around in the dark until I found the section of wire looped over the post. I swung the gate open, dashed back to the truck, drove through, and then ran back to re-latch the gate behind me.

After that, the road narrowed even further, finally deteriorating into nothing more than an overgrown trail. The compass on the rearview mirror indicated that I had completed almost a full circle around Wolf's Head and was now nearing the southern tip of the rock promontory that bore its name. If I was calculating correctly, Morita lay directly east of me. Okay, time to ditch the truck. With only the parking lights to guide me, I drove off the shoulder into tall range grass, coming to a stop in a thick grove of mesquite trees. No doubt the sharp spidery branches had done a number on Champ's paint job. Something else I'd have to deal with later.

Using the flashlight, I reviewed Felix's directions once more. As he'd described it to me, for generations thousands of Mexican migrants had followed a well-worn path north, crossed a wide arroyo and then entered the United States through a narrow canyon flanking a particular rock that he'd described as looking like a giant Indian teepee crowned with a hole that resembled a crescent moon. Since I was already north of the arroyo, all I had to do was walk east until I found it. He'd said it was only a mile from the wooden gate and I'd come just about that far already.

Time to go. A fiery tide of excitement washed over me as I stepped into the brisk night air, zipped my jacket to my chin and then paused to get my bearings before I set off on foot, staying low. It was deathly quiet except for an occasional skitter of some small animal scampering through the unusually tall grass. There had to be a lot of water around someplace in order to produce such a spectacular display of flora and fauna. And I could certainly understand why immigrants would choose this secluded spot as a preferred crossing place. Tucked away behind the massive spires, attainable only on foot or by off-road vehicles, the jumbled piles of boulders and lush foliage created an ideal natural barrier which provided excellent protection against the inquisitive eyes of Border Patrol agents.

I was amazed at how quickly my sight adapted to the murky landscape and how luminescent it looked even minus a full moon. The nocturnal beauty of the rough terrain struck me as almost otherworldly and resurrected thoughts of alien creatures from another galaxy. They might actually feel right at home here in this secluded dell.

The night sky was breathtaking. Amid radiant stars that seemed close enough to reach up and touch, the Milky Way glowed like a glittering river of diamonds. It was actually easier to see without the flashlight, so I switched it off. Probably safer for me too, since a beam of light out here would be spotted a mile away.

Unlike most of my childhood girlfriends and even my younger brother, I'd never feared the dark. In fact, I relished the freedom of being part of it, darting in and out through the underbrush, resurrecting the familiar thrill of playing hide and seek in the dense forest behind our house, waiting with wild heart-thumping anticipation to be discovered. Grimly, I reminded myself that this was no game.

It took less than ten minutes to locate the ancient landmark. Awestruck, I stared up at the wind-eroded fissure near the summit. It did indeed look like a crescent moon. To my advantage, there was no shortage of hiding places. I tested several possibilities, secreting myself beneath rock ledges, inside deep crevices and I even climbed a few to get a better vantage point. Finally, I settled into a cluster of boulders offering a clear view of both the teepee and the jagged fangs of Wolf's Head to my left. With the familiar cold burn of excitement in my belly, I crouched in the shadows waiting. Time crawled by and soon I wasn't sure what I feared most—something actually happening or nothing at all happening.

Another fifteen minutes passed. Then another ten. Still nothing happened. Somewhere an owl screeched. More rustling in the brush, but no signs or sounds of any humans, or extraterrestrials for that matter. The temperature was dropping rapidly, so I pulled up the collar on my jacket and blew on my fingers. Gradually, disappointment replaced my heady expectations. Crap. How could I have been wrong? I winced aloud, thinking of the ridicule I'd have to endure. 'What's that? You froze your ass off crouching under a rock out in the middle of the Arizona desert waiting to witness an extraterrestrial abduction? Priceless!' Tally would be more than bent out of shape and probably never forgive me. The Beaumonts were going to be royally pissed off that I'd appropriated Champ's truck. How was I going to explain what would appear to be totally irrational behavior? No doubt I was going to look like the biggest dufus on the planet.

I stayed a little longer and then, with a sigh of resignation, I wriggled from my hiding place and stood up. I'd taken only two steps when I froze in my tracks. Crunch. Crunch. Craning my head, I listened closely. Crunch, whoosh, whoosh. Was I mistaken, or was that the sound of stealthy footsteps whispering through the nearby brush? I ducked back in my hiding place, folding my body into the shadows as the footsteps grew louder. Hardly daring to breathe, I cautioned myself to stay calm, stay quiet. I clapped my hand over my mouth, taking in shallow gulps of air. It seemed to take forever, but the crunching finally grew fainter as whoever or whatever it was moved on. My mind swam with possibilities. It may have been as innocent as an animal passing through, an immigrant stealing by, or maybe, just maybe I was right, and these guys were on the move.

I sat motionless, my muscles aching, until sure enough, I heard more movement in the brush, then the soft thud of more footsteps rushing past. Being careful not to make a sound, I peeked over the rock ledge and squinted into the darkness. Nothing appeared to be different and then all at once a series of strange noises reached my ears. Scuffling, then what sounded like shouts of protest, more scuffling, and then silence again. My pulse shot higher. Something was definitely happening.

Even though I'd been half expecting it, when a shaft of bright blue light flashed on, lighting the clearing, I flinched violently and turned to stare in the direction of Wolf's Head. Close to one of the giant rock pillars, perhaps thirty or forty feet from the ground, hovered what appeared to be a whirling disk of rainbow colored lights.

"Holy shit." Mesmerized, I gaped at the pulsing light, which seemed to emanate from the UFO. All at once, a babble of frightened voices filled the air. Clearly visible in the grassy clearing was a small group of men and women huddling in a tight circle, shielding their eyes from the intrusive blaze. Amazing. I'd neither seen nor heard their stealthy arrival to U.S. soil. Then, seemingly from out of nowhere, a frightening creature with an elongated head and bug-like features, just as Javier had described, materialized and jumped down from one of the nearby boulders. The terrified screams of the immigrants turned my spine into an icicle. One woman carrying a baby bolted from the group, but she didn't get far before another bug-eyed creature, brandishing some sort of weapon I couldn't identify, pushed her back. The terror-stricken people were herded like cattle up an embankment towards the flying disk, which appeared to have landed at the base of the cliff. For another minute or so, their bone-chilling screams echoed down the canyon walls, but then inexplicably, they grew fainter and fainter until I couldn't hear them at all. Then I heard something else—an odd rumbling noise that lasted for only a few seconds. The blue light blinked out, the disk rose into the air, humming, rotating faster and faster until it shot over the top of the mountain and disappeared from sight. Like someone shutting off a power grid, the valley was enveloped in silent darkness again. And the immigrants had vanished before my eyes.

27

The whole thing happened so fast all I could do was stand there, paralyzed in horrified amazement, questioning my own eyesight and my sanity. Had I really seen what I thought I'd seen? Either I'd just witnessed an honest-to-goodness UFO abduction, or the slickest piece of showmanship I'd ever seen in my life. I chose to believe the latter. It was unsettling to realize that there must be many more people involved than I'd originally thought in order to accomplish such a masterful deception. And, unless I was ready to believe that the immigrants had actually been spirited aboard the 'flying saucer,' then they had to be around here somewhere. An important fact jumped to mind. The original name of this place was *Cave Springs*. Hadn't Walter told me that numerous caves and natural springs abounded within the labyrinth of rocks?

I waited, shivering with cold and anxiety, for eternally long minutes, before concluding that it was time to get my butt in gear. I'd accomplished my goal, verified my supposedly harebrained-theory, and now all I had to do was convince someone, anyone, that I hadn't imagined the entire episode. I took off running like a startled deer, turning every now and then to peer over my shoulder. Short of breath, my heart pounding like an out of control jackhammer, I scrambled into Champ's truck and locked the doors behind me. My hands shook so badly, I had a devil of a time inserting the ignition key. Hurry! Hurry! I threw the truck in reverse and peeled out. In no time, the gate loomed before me. In the split second before I decided to just crash on through it, I saw a glint out of the corner of my eye. The peripheral glow of the headlights illuminated something off to my left in the trees. I slowed down enough to take a closer look and went numb with shock. It was Tally's truck! "Oh, my God!" I shrieked, jamming on the brakes. "No! No! *No!*" For several seconds, my brain cells ceased to function. All I could do was gape in horror, and then my mind did a quick replay. The scuffling sound—the one I'd heard right before the strange lights appeared, could that have been Tally struggling with his captors? How else to explain that he wasn't here? But how could he have possibly known where to find me? Oh, no. He must have raced right back to the ranch after discovering he'd been tricked and found me missing. Obviously, he'd cornered Felix for directions and then come looking for me. A sob caught in my throat. Because of me, my sweet, darling guy had probably walked right into the middle of their trap. So that meant...? I didn't dare finish the thought. There were only two options—race back to the ranch for help or try to find him myself. No choice there. I sprang from the cab, hoping against hope that Tally had left his truck unlocked. He hadn't. "Shit!" In a futile gesture, I frantically pounded on the windows. His loaded .45 was usually in the glove compartment, but more likely, he had it with him.

No time to waste. I leaped back into Champ's truck and retraced my course, so frazzled I almost lost control of the wheel several times. Back at my original starting point, I jumped to the ground. Interminable seconds went by before my eyes adjusted to the dark once more. On a hunch, I searched in the bed of the pickup and found a heavy piece of rebar. That and my flashlight would have to make do as weapons. Praying to God for success, I headed towards the last place I'd seen the immigrants before the whirling disk had departed.

Disjointed thoughts zigzagged through my head as I ran haphazardly through the clearing and clambered up the slope. How had they staged the UFO appearance? Now that I thought about it more carefully, the size of the disc hadn't altered significantly when it 'landed' at the foot of the cliff. Being closer, it should have looked much larger, so I surmised it was mock-up of an alien craft and the people involved must be utilizing the same sort of remote-controlled device to control the disc that model airplane enthusiasts use. And the alien costumes they'd employed were certainly frightening enough to scare the hell out of anyone. But why go to the expense of carrying out such an elaborate production?

Entering the murkiness of the canyon, I switched on the flashlight again. I looked behind me, trying to gauge where the immigrants had vanished. Right about here. I crashed through underbrush, stumbling over rocks and pebbles until I reached the bottom of the cliff. Frantic, I shined the light along the uneven surface, searching for an opening, listening to the sound of my own tortured breathing. Come on! Come on! I was certain there had to be a cave entrance somewhere nearby.

Precious moments passed. No success. I slid to the ground with my back against the wall. Unable to contain my sorrow, I wept bitter tears of self-condemnation and regret that intensified the aching void in my chest where my heart should be. I had failed everyone. If Tally were in the clutches of these maniacs, they would kill him just as surely as they probably had poor Javier by now. There was nothing for me to do but go for help and pray that I could find someone who would believe my wild story. Clever, clever bastards. Even though I'd already seen a preview of their machinations two nights ago in Morita, they had almost convinced me that I was seeing the real thing instead of this elaborate ruse.

When I placed one hand behind me to push myself to my feet, my palm encountered something smooth and sharp. Puzzled, I rolled over on one hip and felt along the base of the rock. I scratched the dirt and grass away and aimed the flashlight on something that glimmered back at me. What was this? As I slid my fingers along it, I felt a chill of comprehension. It was a metal track, like those used for a sliding patio door. Oh, baby, this was no natural phenomenon. I took a closer look at the rock above it— poked it, scratched it, ran my hand along the rutted surface until I reached a deep crevice, then dropped to my knees. The track ended. I scrambled to my feet and ran the flashlight over the rock again. It was hard to tell for certain with only the faint beam, but it appeared to be of a different color and consistency than those around it. I pushed against it. Nothing. Damn it. I pushed harder. Nothing. Positioning my back against it, I propped my feet against the adjacent rock and used my legs to shove as hard as I could. It moved slightly. Euphoric with glee, I pushed until my breath was gone and suddenly it rolled open several inches.

A whiff of musty air blew in my face. Unbelievable. The damn thing was a fake. Someone in this bunch deserved high marks for ingenuity. I continued pushing until I was able to slip through the opening. Wow. The interior of the cave was black as pitch. I pressed my hand over my racing heart and dug deep for courage. I had no idea what I was heading into. As dangerous as it might be, I had no choice but to use the flashlight. The thin beam of light did little to dispel the thick darkness, but because of the cave's enormity, and the fact that I could feel air moving, at least my usual claustrophobia didn't bother me.

I shined the light around the room, marveling at the colossal stalactites and stalagmites, before noting the sloping sandy floor riddled with footprints. Gripping the rebar tightly in my right hand, I moved forward. The ceiling of the cave dropped lower and lower, until soon I was bent over in a crouch. At one point I paused, hearing a faint noise behind me. I killed the light and held my breath. I could have sworn I heard something, but after remaining motionless for more than a minute I resumed my search. Further on, I stopped again and listened to a steady plop, plop, plop. Most likely water dripping somewhere. The odor and dampness increased as I descended into the bowels of the cave, and it was noticeably warmer than the outside air. I wandered into numerous little side caves and several dead end tunnels, wasting valuable time. It was now ten o'clock.

Working my way back from yet another blind alley, I turned a corner, tripped over something, and went sprawling. The flashlight flew from my hand and blinked out. Panic rose up inside me, but I fought it down. Unhurt, but disoriented, I struggled to my feet. I took one step and almost fell over. I'd never experienced such absolute darkness. My equilibrium was all out of whack and I couldn't tell what was right, what was left, up or down. I dropped to my knees and crawled around, frantically patting the crumbly floor. The flashlight had to be around somewhere! After what seemed like an eternity, my hand finally closed around it, and the flood of relief I felt left me limp.

With trembling hands, I switched it on and gawked in bewilderment, unsure as to what I was seeing. The medium-sized room I'd crawled into was piled to the ceiling with long metal and rectangular wooden boxes, crates, barrels and piles of square blocks wrapped in plastic. Stenciled on the sides of some boxes was: **9mm cartridges**. Another read **.308 rifle**. There were numbers and symbols on other containers I couldn't decipher but I sure recognized the word **rocket.** My skin crawled. There was enough firepower in the room to start World War III!

More perplexed than ever, I hurried out and wound my way through the maze of tunnels until I saw a pale glow ahead. I doused the flashlight and crept forward. The light grew brighter. Voices. I distinctly heard muted voices. I tried to swallow but it seemed as if my throat was filled with shards of ground glass. I hesitated, fearing what I might find, yet was spurred on by thoughts of Tally. I crawled to the edge of a rocky overhang and looked down into a sunken cavern illuminated in wavering white light. The sight unfolding before me was so gruesome, so unspeakably appalling I could not immediately absorb its significance. One of the bug-like creatures stood hunched over a young Mexican man lying on a gurney, sliced open from his neck to his pelvis. The creature was systematically removing organs, immersing them in some sort of liquid solution and carefully placing them in plastic bags, which he then put into iced-down picnic coolers. The bodies, or rather what was left of the bodies of two dark-haired women, lay on a thick piece of plastic on the floor nearby. There was blood everywhere and a putrid smell I couldn't really describe.

Spanning the far side of the ampitheater-like cavern, cages had been set into the wall. I blinked in disbelief. There were people inside. None of them moved. A shudder ran through me remembering Javier's fear that the creatures would cut him with their 'sharp claws.' Fleetingly, I wished to heaven I was actually witnessing extraterrestrials perform medical experiments rather than this cruel reality being perpetrated by fellow human beings.

Below to my left were four large dog carriers. I almost shouted aloud with relief at the sight of Javier, curled up like a small animal inside one of them. He appeared to be sleeping. There was a baby in the one right next to him. On the brink of hysteria, I scanned the cages looking for Tally, but he wasn't there. I ducked lower when two more of the monster bug-men entered through an archway to my right. Now that I could view them up close, the alien disguises didn't look so frightening, but the fact that I knew there were vicious, psychotic people underneath was terrifying.

I pulled back and looked away, sickened to the depths of my soul and feeling more powerless than I ever had in my entire life. I prayed for courage and strength while trying madly to formulate some sort of rescue plan. How was I going to take on this bunch with only a piece of rebar? The fact that my mind really wasn't functioning properly came home to me when the next thought popped into my mind. Why hadn't I taken a gun from the cache of arms in the storage room? But then, would I even know how to load and use one? Why, oh, why hadn't I taken the time to enroll in the firearms safety course Tally had been bugging me about for months? Too late for recriminations now.

I almost jumped out of my shoes when a muffled voice shouted, "He's starting to come around. You wanna do this asshole next?"

"With pleasure. Bring him in."

The fuzz on the back of my neck stood on end. Did I recognize the barely audible voice?

"Wooee!" the first creature hooted. "We ought to get enough out of this batch to get us a couple of handheld stinger missiles and maybe some nukes."

"Just take the bodies to the pool," said the first man, his tone clipped.

I edged another look over the rim of the rocks and as I checked out the room a second time, certainty jabbed me in the gut like a sharp-toed boot. There was a long table piled with boxes, pans of surgical instruments, bottles and vials. The cages looked as if they'd come from a veterinary hospital. Was it possible that the man beneath the monster suit was Twyla's brother, Dean Pierce? The more I thought about it the more obvious it became. Was there anyone else experienced or qualified enough to perform this type of surgery? But, still, my mind rebelled. The day we met, I had sensed his antipathy for the never-ending tide of aliens washing across his property, seen the rage reflected in his eyes as Champ was being carted off to jail, but somehow he hadn't struck me as a man who could do something so horrendous. This was a man who aided sick and injured animals. But then, a vague memory pushed its way to the front of my mind. Hadn't there been ice chests piled on the shelf in the room with Marmalade?

"This friggin' monkey suit is hot," one of the men complained, pulling at the face covering. Even with the mask on, I recognized Jason's whiny tone.

"They stay on until we're finished, like always."

He blew out a sigh of annoyance, turned, and re-entered the adjoining room with the other man. They reappeared almost instantly, one of them pushing, the other pulling a second gurney into the room, and carelessly parked it beside the first one. When they moved away, I almost choked when I recognized Tally's lean form. Apparently drugged like the others, he lay perfectly still. I had to summon every ounce of willpower I possessed not to scream in terror and leap down from the ledge. With extreme difficulty, I kept my cool while the two men grasped the ends of the plastic sheeting containing the mutilated torsos of the women, and carried it through another opening on the opposite end of the big room. The head honcho bug man was alone, busily slicing out the young man's heart. My stomach quaked with nausea and it was difficult not to retch. Inhaling deep calming breaths, I primed for action. I scooted along the perimeter of the ledge until I came to a well-worn footpath that led down to the floor of the cavern. With measured steps, I crept down and sneaked up behind him, my pulse racing so fast I felt dizzy. I'd have only one good shot at him. Grasping the rebar like a baseball bat, I drew back and slammed him in the side of his head. The scalpel flew from his gloved hand as he lurched sideways. But I hadn't hit him hard enough because he righted himself, turned, and staggered towards me. Staring at the creepy bug-face mask, it was hard not to cut and run, but before he could regain his footing I whacked him again. This time he dropped to the floor. I inhaled a shuddery breath and stood poised, ready to strike him again if necessary. When he didn't move, I turned around and shook Tally. "Wake up," I pleaded. "Please!"

He didn't respond. I set the rebar on the floor and tried to pull him to a sitting position but he fell back limply. I shot a worried look towards the archway where Jason and the other guy had gone. Somehow, I had to get Tally out of here before they returned.

I patted his cheeks. "Come on, Sweetie, wake up!" I whispered fiercely. His lids blinked open and he stared at me uncomprehending, his pupils still dilated from whatever drug they'd administered. Damn it.

My eyes swept the room again, stopping at the gallon jugs of water sitting on the floor beside a series of giant batteries that apparently powered the generator and the lights. I grabbed a jug, tore the top off, splashed some water on his face and patted his cheeks again. He mumbled something and I placed a finger on his lips. "Shhhh. Keep quiet." He seemed to be coming around, but I doubted he'd be up to walking anytime soon. And then it hit me. Why not just roll him out of here on the gurney? My mind raced ahead. How to accomplish that was the big question. The floor of the main cave was fairly smooth, but how would the wheels handle the sandy surface of the tunnels? I heard movement behind me and swung around just as the creature grabbed my free hand and yanked me to the floor. In silent horror, I struggled to escape from his grasp, fumbling for the rebar, but he knocked it away and pinned me to the floor. With his monstrous face only inches from my own, I yelped, "Tally, help me!"

"Let her go!" commanded a loud voice from above.

He jerked, loosened his grip on me and together we looked up. I couldn't believe my eyes. Russell Greene was standing on the ledge above, his rifle trained on us. Attila, his trusty Doberman, waited by his side, teeth bared and growling. "If I don't get you the dog will," he warned, easing his finger onto the trigger. I took advantage of my assailant's hesitation and shoved with all my strength. He fell against the gurney and the inert body of the young Mexican landed on top of him.

In that split second I scrambled to my feet. Just when it seemed rescue was at hand, all hell broke loose. Jason and the other man rushed into the room, brandishing handguns. I don't really know for sure who fired first, but the roar of gunfire was deafening. Amid the shouting and flying bullets, I thought of nothing but Tally's safety. Grabbing the gurney, I wheeled it into the adjoining room, frantically searching the new cubbyhole for an escape route, but there was no way out except to go back through the main cavern.

We were sitting ducks. Sick with dread, I wrapped my arms around Tally and laid my head on his chest. "Oh, Tally, I'm so sorry I got you into this mess." I reached up and brushed a lock of dark hair from his forehead. He looked so vulnerable, so dear. "I hope you can forgive me," I murmured. "I love you. You are the most important person on this planet and there's no one else I'd rather spend the rest of my life with." Scalding tears stinging my eyes, I squeezed onto the gurney and cuddled next to him, showering his face with wet kisses, waiting in heart-stopping agony for the worst. I probably laid there at least five minutes before I realized that, other than the pitiful whimpering of the dog, no other sounds reached my ears.

I got up, cautiously peeked around the doorway and recoiled in shock. My attacker was sprawled out face down on the floor beside the overturned gurney, blood oozing from a head wound. Russell Greene lay in a heap beneath the overhang, his dog frantically licking his face. The other two men were gone.

I rushed to Russell Greene's side and knelt beside him, appalled by all the blood. He'd been shot in the stomach and I had no idea what to do to help him. "Oh, Mr. Greene," I cried. I tore off my jacket and pressed it against him, trying to stem the flow. "Hang on, I'm going for help."

He blinked a couple of times before locking his intense gaze into mine. "Wait. Please believe that I...didn't know...about... all this."

"I believe you. How did you find us?"

He sucked in a tortured breath and moaned, "Saw your pickup. Followed you." With what must have taken extreme effort, he moved his hand and wrapped his fingers protectively around the dog's leg. "Promise me...promise you'll find a good home for Attila."

"Of course, yes! But...you're going to be all right." I forced an encouraging smile, knowing on some level that it wasn't true. There was too much blood and his coloring had faded to ash gray. "Thank you," I choked, "Thank you for saving our lives."

"It's...it's okay," he murmured, his resigned smile matching the glow of serene acceptance filling his eyes. "This must be the reason...God made me stay."

It took a couple of anguished seconds for the significance of his words to sink in. "Oh, please don't die," I pleaded, thinking that compared to the real monsters of this dreadful night, his ravaged face was truly beautiful.

"Will you hold my hand for a minute?"

Blinking back tears, I grasped it and held on tight, watching the essence of life fade from his eyes. He coughed and whispered, "Thank *you*...for...being kind to me." After a few more uneven breaths, his head rolled to the side and he was still.

"Oh, my God," I whispered, so overcome with emotion I could hardly breathe. This man, this poor tragic man, had given his life for me, while Jason, the coward, had run for the hills. I felt as if I was in an unending nightmare from which I could not awaken. As I watched Attila lick the face of his dead master, I heard a groan from behind and swung around, my heart locked in my throat. The creature wasn't dead!

Molten anger welled up inside me. I picked up the rifle and, carefully avoiding the body of the young Mexican man, pointed it at the man in the blood-spattered costume. I was ninety-nine percent sure it was Dean Pierce, but I had to make sure. I had to see the face of the man responsible for such a heinous crime against humanity.

Prodding him with the barrel, I warned with more courage than I felt, "Move so much as a hair, you sick bastard, and I'll blow you away." With a shiver of distaste, I toed him onto his back. Holding the rifle awkwardly in one hand, I reached down and pulled the monstrous face-mask away. Aghast, I stared into the deranged green eyes of Payton Kleinwort.

28

When the incredible story of Payton Kleinwort's unthinkable treachery finally caught the attention of the national news three days later, the media descended on the Sundog Ranch like hawks on road kill. Print and cable news reporters from other states donned fancy western gear and clamored for interviews from anyone even remotely connected to the case. Luckily for me, I'd scooped the whole lot of them. But then I'd had a running start and a unique vantage point. Unexpectedly, I'd gained access to Twyla's computer and was able to file my front-page story with the wire services, and in time for a special edition of the *Sun* on Saturday, a full day ahead of the pack.

Following Jason and Cutter's capture and arrest Thursday morning, Twyla Beaumont, reduced to hysterics, was confined to her room under heavy sedation. With Champ still behind bars, plus Rob and Sloan being detained as possible accessories to murder, Tally made the magnanimous decision to stay and help out the shell-shocked family. Also brought in for questioning were Border Patrol agent Hank Breslow, Froggy McQueen, and

415

several other members of the Knights of Right crew. Being right there on the front lines, having access to sheriff's deputies and savvy Border Patrol officials, had given me two days to gather additional data to support the biggest story of my career to date.

While Tally was out heading up a trail ride for the guests, I made good use of the time, sequestering myself in the corner of the kitchen at the computer. Sitting there in borrowed clothing that Lin Su had kindly appropriated from somewhere, I frantically typed from memory, still lamenting the loss of all my notes, tapes, and laptop.

The price of landing this story had been higher than I'd ever imagined. I was still reeling with shock over the entire stomach-turning episode, including the senseless death of Russell Greene. Both Tally and I had been profoundly affected by his ultimate sacrifice.

As details of the horrifying discovery spread throughout the surrounding communities, I thought how ironic it was that the Beaumonts' wish for publicity had come true. Even though it was negative, it had nevertheless put them on the map in a big way.

A distressed and chastened Bethany, forced to stand in for the ailing Twyla, was swamped with calls from people wanting to come to the site of the worst serial killing spree in the history of the United States. One local entrepreneur even started jeep tours to Morita so tourists could experience the macabre thrill of being close to the heavily guarded location where the debauchery had taken place.

Payton's demonic scheme to sell organs harvested from the perpetual tide of migrants crossing the border, and then using the proceeds to buy weapons for the Knights of Right's planned overthrow of the Mexican government, was actually quite brilliant and amazingly well orchestrated, considering the number of accomplices involved.

Even now, I can't begin to describe the mind-boggling shock of seeing Payton lying on the floor of the cavern, blood oozing from the nasty gash in the side of his head and the bullet wound in the chest. Shaken, and wondering what to do next, I'd felt a profound sense of relief when Tally suddenly appeared in the archway of the adjacent room. I don't think I'll ever forget his look of total bewilderment. Having no clue as to what had transpired since he'd been struck from behind and knocked cold during his vain search for me, his mouth sagged with disbelief during my breathless summation. After a tense discussion concerning the best course of action, we'd agreed that I would be the one to go for help. But the stark fear that one or more of Payton's accomplices might return, made me reluctant to leave him.

"Go on," he'd urged, giving me a confident thumbs up. "Attila and I will hold the fort until you get back with the posse," he said, training the rifle squarely at Payton's forehead. On my way out, I opened the doors to the cages containing the migrant prisoners, including Javier, and then headed into the dark tunnels once again. It seemed to take forever to reach the mouth of the cave, but once I got out into the moon-streaked meadow, I ran faster than I ever had in my entire life back to Champ's truck. Driving like a madwoman, I reached Dean's ranch in less than twenty minutes. Within an hour I'd returned, followed by DPS officers, Border Patrol agents and members of the Tohono O'odham Tribal Police. It was only then that I realized that the long-established crossing point was actually a small section of reservation land.

It had been my sad duty to call Lupe and give her the devastating news that it was more than likely her uncle and younger brother were among the gruesome pile of bodies that divers had discovered at the bottom of the deep spring inside the cavern. Forensic experts were hopeful that, because of the cold temperature of the water, tissue samples would be relatively well preserved, making DNA identification possible in some cases. But sheriff's deputies cautioned that it could be months before all the bodies were discovered, if ever.

Payton's hospital-bed confession to sheriff's detectives, added together with statements extracted from Jason and Cutter, had filled in a lot of the gaps. Climbing inside the mind of this mild mannered, innocent-faced serial killer to try and exhume the dark, twisted motive for his diabolical behavior was a chilling endeavor. In light of events, some of his earlier statements had taken on fresh significance—his suggestion to Dean that he wished he could wave a magic wand and make the illegal problem disappear, that 'timing is everything,' and the cryptic sentiment etched on his sister's gravestone '*In death lies the promise of new life,*' no doubt held a sinister double meaning for him.

"Man, oh, man alive," Tugg exclaimed during my conference call with him and Walter late Friday afternoon, following a brief overview of events, "you must have some kind of magnetic attraction for these sickos. What's Tally's take on this thing?"

"He's glad to be alive and frankly, so am I."

Walter put in, somberly, "It's always amazing to me how these degenerates manage to justify the most horrific crimes. I guess that's the only way they can get up every day and look at themselves in the mirror."

"That's sure true in this case," I concurred. "I hate to admit it, but he had me fooled. Talk about great acting. He certainly did an admirable job of hiding his loathing for the entire Hispanic race."

"Any idea why?"

"It started when he was a child and has apparently been festering inside him all these years. When he told me that his father had died suddenly, I assumed that he'd suffered a heart attack or something. Actually, he'd been brutally murdered by a bunch of Mexican criminals who crossed the border and broke into their ranch house one night. Afterwards, they raped his mother."

"Je-zuss!" Tugg muttered. "That's enough in itself to traumatize a kid for life."

"That was just for starters." With the usual mealtime pandemonium going on behind me in the background, I explained to them how his mother's deteriorating mental condition had ended with her abandoning both children.

According to the statement Bethany had given sheriff's detectives, Payton suffered from severe bouts of depression and recurring nightmares during the short time they were married. "It really put him over the edge when his sister, Laura, died three years ago because she didn't get the heart transplant she desperately needed. I checked the date of the surgery at the University Medical Center in Tucson where she was on the waiting list. Whether it's true or not, Payton believed that Congressman Stanley's wife, who just happens to be Hispanic, received the heart his sister should have gotten." I had a quick flash of the newspaper photo on the wall in Jason's room with the knife protruding from the woman's heart. The text beneath it confirmed that the congressman's wife had entered the hospital on the exact date of Laura Kleinwort's expected surgery. "Payton was close to a mental breakdown at that point anyway," I went on. "He was working three jobs to support Bethany's extravagant lifestyle and pay the medical bills he'd incurred for his sister."

"Oh, I'm starting to get the picture," Tugg mused with an undertone of wonderment in his gruff voice. "This whole elaborate scheme of killing the immigrants was his warped way of avenging his parents' and sister's deaths. His own twisted version of supply and demand."

"True," I replied. "But remember, in his mind he was providing a valuable service by helping to alleviate the critical shortage of organs."

Walter jumped in with, "Well, how did he get away with this? Doesn't anyone ask where the organs are coming from? There must be a paper trail."

"I had a chance to get on the Internet and do a little research on this subject," I answered with a yawn. "Needless to say, I haven't slept very much these past few nights. It's been hectic and rather traumatic, to say the least."

"Small wonder," Tugg murmured.

"Anyway, in the past few years, there has been a threefold increase in demand in the United States alone. He knew he couldn't get away with selling them here because The National Organ Transplant Act passed in 1984 classifies human organs as a national resource and prohibits their sale in this country, so he had to hire private pilots to fly them *out* of the country."

"Where to?" asked Walter.

"Mexico City. From what the authorities have discovered so far, he's got contacts on the payroll at several hospitals there, including one transplant surgeon. They falsified documents certifying the legitimacy of the donors, forged signatures on consent forms, and then falsified the death certificates."

"Un-friggin' believable," Tugg marveled, as I went on to explain how I'd also learned from my research that the 'shelf life' for organs is between two and forty-eight hours, depending on the organ. It was clear now why Payton had been in such a hurry to get the coolers to the airstrip before he could drive me to Dean's ranch last Monday, following my escape from Morita. Believing that he was hauling live rattlesnakes had been disconcerting enough, but knowing now that the coolers jostling around behind me in his camper contained the freshly harvested organs of recently murdered immigrants, gave me a double case of the shivers.

"Clever," Tugg said. "The Feds would be watching flights coming in because of drug runners, but not going out."

Walter cut in with an impatient, "Is there really that much money to be made?"

"More than you'd imagine," I answered, thumbing through my research. "Mmm, let's see, a kidney can bring twelve thousand, a liver seventeen, hearts command about eighteen grand, and that doesn't include all the other organs he harvested."

"What a sick son-of-a-bitch," Tugg boomed out. "He must have been raking in a fortune! But wait a second, how the hell did he have the expertise to pull off something like this? Wouldn't you have to be a doctor?"

"Get ready, this is the worst part." The information I'd gathered from my phone interview with the transplant surgeon in Tucson had chilled me to the bone, and my heart stopped every time I thought of how close Tally had come to being the next victim of Payton's madness.

"If the person removing the organs doesn't care whether or not the donor survives, then Payton's year of medical schooling plus his experience as a veterinary assistant provided sufficient know-how to complete the job." I explained that the animal mutilations he'd performed two years ago, which also helped perpetuate the accounts of UFO sightings, served as practice for the real thing, but the most stomach-churning detail of all was the knowledge that he'd exacted his fiendish revenge on the Mexican people by injecting the migrant donors with a rarely used drug called Tubocurarine. I said somberly, "It allowed him to remove their organs while they were still conscious."

"Mother of God," Tugg exclaimed, his voice rising sharply. "Are you saying that those poor people were *alive* when he cut them open?"

"I'm afraid so, and they didn't kill them all at once. Some people were held prisoner in the cages for several days, until he was ready for another shipment. Can you imagine the horror?"

"That is the most nightmarish, most depraved thing I've ever heard of in my entire life," Walter commented glumly.

I agreed. "I can hear Payton's defense attorney now entering a plea of insanity, and who knows, the jury just might buy it."

"How'd he get mixed up with the Knights of Right?" Walter inquired.

"Through his association with Jason. These were likeminded people who felt the same all-consuming hatred towards the illegals that he did, for different reasons of course. But, nevertheless, it provided a perfect vehicle for him to carry out his sadistic plan of revenge. The group got the funding they needed to finance their mischief against the local Hispanics, influence election results to vote out politicians they believed were Mexican sympathizers like Lyle Stanley, and also purchase arms for their cockeyed plot to overthrow the Mexican government. Cripes, you should have seen all firepower they had stored in that cave. And, Walter, you were right about the fact that these groups have gone underground, except for an occasional rally." I added. "Payton came up with the idea for the coded e-mail messages after reading Brett fairy tale stories."

"So, was he the leader of the group?"

"The authorities still aren't sure and admit they may never know the identities of everyone concerned, but they do know that he was responsible for bailing Jason out under the guise of the Ranch Coalition."

"What about the dad, was he up to his neck in this scheme also?"

"No. That's why Payton didn't go to the extra expense to bail him out too. But, he needed Jason on the job that night, along with Cutter and the two other Sundog ranch hands, both of whom are members of the Beaumont Ranch Patrol within that coalition."

"So, Champ Beaumont is still in jail?"

"From what I heard earlier, he was finally released a few hours ago, and Twyla's brother, Dean, is on his way to get him now."

"What an unbelievable mess," Tugg muttered.

"No kidding."

"I still don't understand something," he continued. "Whose idea was it to lock you up in the Morita jail? I'm assuming it was their plan that you be there to witness their UFO…show, for lack of a better term."

"I still don't have the full answer to that," I replied. "But, from what I've been able to piece together from the various confessions, Jason was listening in on my phone call last Monday and he alerted Payton, who already knew I was going there before we met for lunch. For obvious reasons, they didn't want me nosing around, so they arranged to set up a UFO sighting, hoping it would either scare me off or discredit me."

"So...you don't think they planned to just let you die there?"

"Jason claims they didn't but I'll probably never know for sure because, thank goodness, Russell Greene found me."

Tugg growled, "You are one lucky lady."

"Don't I know it," I responded solemnly.

Walter interjected, "What was the point of stealing your car?"

"So no one would know I was there, including Russell. Jason claims some other group stripped the car after they ditched it near Amado. The whole scenario was designed to get me the hell out of town and believe me, if Tally hadn't shown up, it would have worked." I couldn't help remembering Payton's benevolent offer to drive me to Tucson.

"But, you were leaving that afternoon anyway, why bother to go to all that trouble?" Tugg mused.

"Because, during that same phone conversation with Walter, I told him that I planned to return and continue the investigation after my vacation. They sure didn't want to risk that happening."

"This is making me sick," Walter complained. "Okay, I have to know. Was Bob involved in this scheme?"

"Not directly, but apparently Hank Breslow was. He offered Bob sizeable sums of cash to look the other way on his rounds near Morita, but after finding the frightened migrant and hearing his UFO story, he got suspicious and told Hank he wanted out of the deal. That's when Hank cooked up the idea to anonymously implicate Bob in a drug smuggling ring. He figured that would be enough to discredit him and get him out of the picture, but Payton was afraid he already knew too much. They lured him out to the reservation that night on some phony pretense and apparently he was just starting a letter of confession for Loydeen to read to their children, in case anything happened to him, when they jumped him. Payton administered the Tubocurarine, placed Bob's own firearm in his hand and pulled the trigger."

"Where'd he get all these drugs?"

"They don't know for sure yet, but they suspect he obtained them from one or more of his contacts at the hospitals in Mexico City."

"Wouldn't they have found the drug in Bob's system during the autopsy?"

"According to what I learned from the medical examiner, they screen for social or street drugs such as cocaine, marijuana, ecstasy, barbiturates and so on, but they would not have been looking for this particular drug because it's not commonly used. I'm sure his body will be exhumed for testing now."

Walter said, "I'm surprised Loydeen didn't press the authorities on that point. She had to suspect he'd been murdered."

"She did, but Cutter and Jason warned Loydeen to keep her mouth shut and accept the verdict of suicide without question, or she and her kids would be next. You remember that agent you mentioned a few days ago that disappeared right after Bob's funeral?"

"You mean Alberto Morales?"

"Right. The intelligence guys at the Border Patrol I talked to this morning suspect he may well have been involved too, but decided to cut and run before the same thing happened to him. Apparently, it's a pretty widespread problem."

Walter blew out a surprised whistle. "Damn. Lavelle's gonna have a stroke when I tell her that he was mixed up in something this...this awful."

"That brings up another question," Tugg interjected. "What was the point of the UFO light show and prancing around in these space getups scaring the shit out of these people?"

"So that if anyone escaped, like the first guy and then Javier, no one would believe them. They had no qualms about killing off the *coyotes* that brought the loads across either. I have to admit that if I hadn't already suspected what was going on, it might have fooled me. It really was an ingenious enterprise."

"How did they figure out this kid was at the mission and that he knew anything?"

"Unfortunately, they actually traced it back to me. Because of Froggy, Payton knew I'd been at the mission and he was aware of my meeting with Mazzie La Casse from day one. Cutter saw me at the Shirley place, and when Froggy told Payton about Javier's nightmares, he finally put everything together and the poor little tyke ended up back at Wolf's Head, where the whole thing started."

"Why'd Kleinwort choose that particular place?" Tugg continued.

"He'd known about the hidden caves since childhood, so when the Morita property became available, he purchased it through a phony mining corporation he'd set up in Nevada. He posted no trespassing signs to keep people away, but when the hiker Walter told me about earlier died after falling into one of the old mine shafts, Payton couldn't take a chance on more people stumbling into his little den of horrors. He fenced the place and hired Russell Greene to keep people away from the area. Poor Russell. Payton convinced him that he and the others were conducting secret government CIA experiments for testing new weapons or some such nonsense, and for whatever reason he chose to believe it. Jason confirmed that he hadn't known what was going on inside the cave."

Walter asked, "Where'd they get all the props and costumes?"

"Ah, that's an interesting twist. They were leftovers from a science fiction film that had been shot on the Sundog several years ago. That's where they got that fake plastic boulder they used to hide the mouth of the cave." I told them I hadn't found out yet exactly what kind of equipment they'd used to simulate the UFO, but that the investigators had found a strobe light that was powered by the same type of batteries they'd used to run the generator.

Rascal came up beside my chair and nudged me with his nose. As I petted his silky fur, it triggered the memory of the giant dust-covered battery I'd seen underneath Jason's bed the night I'd been in his room. I added, "Payton got the idea for terrorizing the immigrants after Mazzie La Casse questioned him about seeing strange lights on his nocturnal snake hunts. He pumped her for information and then followed up by doing his own research on the alien abduction phenomenon."

"You mean he really was collecting snakes?" Tugg asked with surprise.

"Oh yes. It was the perfect cover. He'd pretty much thought of everything."

Walter interjected, "What about this Hoggwhistle woman? How does she fit into the picture?"

"Initially, it looks as if she'll be indicted on smuggling charges along with the rest of them. But one of the sheriff's deputies I talked with this morning says he doubts they can make the charges stick. She's claiming that she never physically helped to bring the undocumented migrants across nor did she receive any payment. She's staying with the same story that her sole purpose is to feed, clothe and provide transportation for needy people. And she can always say she had no way of knowing they were illegals."

"So...do you think she was in cahoots with this Kleinwort fellow?" Tugg asked, sounding confused.

"On the contrary. Not long after she'd renovated the mission and opened her doors to immigrants, the Knights of Right decided to put her out of business. First, Payton sent Hank and a couple of the other agents to hassle her. When that didn't work he dispatched Cutter and his goons to burn the place down, but he changed his plans after running into Froggy one night at the saloon. Froggy was tanked as usual and blabbed that he suspected that she was working hand in hand with several *coyotes* smuggling immigrants across the border. Apparently he thought she was extracting large payments in exchange for helping the migrants."

"And was she?"

"Who knows? She continues to maintain that she's merely helping people in need, regardless of their legal status."

"Humphhh!" Tugg snorted in my ear. "You know the old saying, religion is the last refuge of a scoundrel."

I laughed and went on. "Anyway, Payton decided it would be easy pickings to simply siphon off some of the illegals from her loads. Froggy got paid handsomely to let him or Jason know exactly when to come pick them up, and of course, Hank Breslow made sure they got to their final destination in Morita. Oh, and Froggy also got paid to ferry shipments of weapons out to the cave inside his camper shell."

"Pretty industrious fellow," Walter commented dryly. "He was making money all over the place. But how did he know about this woman's prison record?"

"He's Johnny Ray Barker's step-brother. He told the deputies that Barker suspected she'd hidden the money someplace before her arrest and planned to get it when she was released from prison. Froggy followed her out here and threatened to divulge her new identity if she didn't pay up. When she wasn't around he turned the place upside down hunting for the money she'd supposedly skimmed from the nursing home scam."

Walter cut in to say his wife was waiting to pick him up, congratulated me on the story and thanked me for clearing Bob Shirley's name before hanging up. I wondered how much relief Lavelle would actually feel, knowing that her cousin had been murdered instead of committing suicide. Either way, it was a tragic ending and a lot of issues were left on the table, unresolved. In fact, there'd been a lot of unhappy endings to this sordid story and I wasn't feeling too great about the results of my ability as a reporter at that moment. When I voiced my thoughts to Tugg, he remarked, "Well, I gotta say, that was one hell of a way to spend your vacation."

"It hardly classifies as one," I groused, "and look at the trail of debris left in my wake. Because of me, an innocent man died, I was too late to help Lupe, Javier is now at a shelter in Nogales, Sonora, and Sister Goldenrod hates my guts." I lowered my voice, adding, "I'm sure not winning any prizes for popularity with the Beaumonts for fingering Jason, I lost my car and all my stuff...but I think what's bothering me the most is that on top of all that I put Tally's life at risk pretty much for nothing. There's no real resolution to this border problem, so what did I really accomplish? Yeah, it's been great fun."

"Hey, whoa, whoa, time out. You're being way too hard on yourself. Because of your efforts, you've saved those people's lives, not to mention all the future atrocities you've stopped by exposing this maniac. Christ Almighty, I still can't believe he was carving these people up while they were still alive! Give yourself a pat on the back, kiddo. You deserve some accolades for your effort."

"Well, thanks."

"Quit beating yourself up. You did your best. Granted your tactics are a little dramatic," he tacked on with a chuckle.

"You think so?"

Tugg's hearty laugh echoed in my ear. "Here's a thought. Why don't you try just *reporting* the next story for a change instead of becoming part of it?"

"You sound just like Tally," I answered wryly. "He swears I'm an adrenaline junkie. Maybe I am."

"Seriously, Kendall, you're a damn fine journalist. Most reporters work their entire careers and never come across anything even close to what you've just uncovered, including yours truly. Hells bells, inside of six months you've scooped three of the biggest, weirdest stories I've ever heard of in my life. Now listen, I know how stubborn you are and you're probably not gonna want to hear this, but take a little advice from an old newshound and slow down for awhile. Have a little fun, for chrissake, or you're gonna end up with a big fat ulcer like me."

At that moment, the door behind me opened, and Tally walked in looking wind-blown, sunburned and exhausted. I waved, smiled, and said softly to Tugg, "You know something, this time I think I'll take your advice."

29

It was late Saturday afternoon before Tally finished loading all of his belongings into the pickup. While he stood on the porch saying his final goodbyes to the Beaumonts, I sat in the cab of his truck watching dark gray storm clouds gather over the crown of Baboquivari Peak, thinking that nothing would ever be the same at the Sundog. I felt especially sorry for Brett, who would one day understand the magnitude of what his father had done.

It had been a difficult weekend with Champ coming home, pale and sunken-cheeked, to find the ranch swarming with reporters, sheriff's detectives and federal agents. He'd been cordial to me, as was Twyla, but it was hard to dismiss the fact that I'd been responsible for their son's arrest. And, it was obvious by the stricken look of realization on Bethany's face when she'd witnessed Tally and me coming down the stairs together each morning arm in arm, that any further pursuit of him would be a waste of time.

I think the only person sorry to see me leave was Lin Su. I'd actually caught a glimpse of emotion in the stoic little woman's piercing black eyes after I'd given her a spontaneous hug and expressed my gratitude for all she'd done for me. Afterwards, she'd bowed her head and, in a halting voice, confirmed my suspicions that Bethany may have slipped something into my tea the night Cecil had wound up in my bed. "I find in her room," she admitted, extending a handful of colorful pills. "Maybe Missy Bethany give them by accident?" I'm sure she didn't believe that any more than I did, but I appreciated her sense of loyalty to the Beaumont family. I thanked her again for her honesty before she quickly left the room. It disturbed me greatly to know that Bethany had been willing to take such extreme measures to insinuate herself into Tally's life.

Earlier that day, Dean Pierce had arrived in his truck with Marmalade. As I hugged the kitten close to me and thanked him for his kindness, I couldn't suppress the nagging guilt that I'd entertained for one second the idea that this compassionate man could have played any role whatsoever in Payton's diabolical scheme. At my request, he'd been caring for Attila until I could figure out how to honor Russell Greene's last request. To my great surprise, Tally had agreed to take him home to the Starfire.

As if he'd known I was thinking about him, the big dog's throaty bark alerted me to Tally's approach. "Ready to go?" he asked, climbing into the seat beside me.

I beamed him a relieved smile. "More than ready."

With Marmalade curled warmly on my lap and Attila inside a carrier in the bed of the truck, we rolled down the Sundog road. When we reached the pavement and headed north, I took a last look back towards the forbidding rock towers of Wolf's Head, once again thanking my lucky stars that we'd both come out of the ordeal in one piece. We rode in silence for a while and I shot a glance at Tally's profile. We'd been so busy during the past three days and so dog-tired each night, there hadn't yet been a good opportunity to totally clear the air between us even though I thought I'd used all the words in the English language to tell him how sorry I was for the way things had turned out. He'd rejected my suggestion that we spend the remaining days of our time off in California, deciding instead to head back to Castle Valley. The knowledge that he'd never once mentioned the engagement ring weighed heavily on my heart and left me feeling unsure about the future of our relationship. Busily chewing gum, his eyes glued to the road ahead, he said nothing as the miles whipped past. Unable to bear the silence any longer, I burst out, "Okay, I'm ready. Let's get the list of I told you so's out of the way. I'm ready to accept my punishment so we can enjoy the rest of the trip home."

Tally narrowed his eyes at me before tapping his watch. "There isn't enough time to accomplish that between here and Castle Valley." If I hadn't been looking at him I would have missed the mischievous twinkle in his eyes.

"Your point is well taken," I answered humbly. "But, in my defense, this whole thing started out as a simple missing persons situation. How could I have known it would turn out like this?"

"You couldn't, Kendall, and I know better than to think you're ever going to change your ways but…."

"Oh, but I am," I interrupted. "Tugg's already read me the riot act, Ginger too for that matter, so, believe me, I've got the message loud and clear. For the time being, I've decided to turn over these types of assignments to Walter or Jim. You can chain me to the desk in the office if that will help convince you."

He arched a skeptical brow. "Really?"

"Really."

He shook his head. "You're misunderstanding me, as usual. I'm not looking to have you alter your personality to please me. Then...you wouldn't be you. I mean..." he paused, apparently searching for the right words before adding, "I love your passionate nature, your bulldog determination to see things through, and I know your heart's always in the right place, but for Christ's sake, couldn't you maybe take just a little less risk next time? Call the sheriff *before* your life is on the line instead of after the fact? I don't want to lose you, especially now that we have a family." He edged me that lopsided grin that always lightened my heart and thumbed behind him to Attila, before reaching over to pet Marmalade.

I smiled back. "Cowboy, you've got a deal. And I promise I'll take that firearms safety course now."

He flicked me a look of amusement. "After seeing the results of the way you clobbered Payton with that piece of rebar, I'm not sure you need it."

We both laughed for the first time in days. I scooted closer to him and leaned my head on his shoulder, enjoying the peaceful warmth rushing through my veins, knowing in my heart that things were going to be all right.

We were only about a half an hour from Castle Valley and the sun had just ducked behind the bank of dark clouds when Tally suddenly announced, "What do you say we pull over here and let Attila out for a few minutes?"

"You don't think he can wait?"

"Nope."

"Okay, sure."

He pulled the truck to the side of the road and while he was attaching the dog's leash, I laid Marmalade tenderly on the seat. When she looked up at me with adoration beaming from her bright turquoise-green eyes, I couldn't help remembering Payton's assertion that animals love unconditionally. Maybe I could learn something from that.

After a short hike, we reached the top of a nearby bluff and turned back to the western horizon. The splendor of the sun's brilliant scarlet rays shooting skyward from behind the mound of gold-rimmed clouds took my breath away. It seemed like a good omen. "Wow," I marveled, "have you ever seen anything more beautiful in your whole life?"

He turned to me with the sunset's bright light reflecting in his solemn gaze. "Yep, I have, and by the way," he said, tenderly brushing a strand of hair from my face, "my ears work fine."

"What do you mean?"

"I wasn't completely out when you were talking to me inside that cave. I heard every single word you said." When his arms closed around me, I melted into his embrace, returning his fervent kiss with one of my own until I thought I'd burst with sheer joy.

When he gently disengaged his hold on me and reached inside his coat pocket, my breath caught as he pulled out a small velvet box. Electrified, I braced for his words, but all at once, he seemed ill at ease. Clearing his throat, he shifted his stance uneasily. "Kendall, um...I think you know how I feel, and I know we've still got a whole lot of things to work out but...well, what I'm trying to say...."

I don't know what came over me, but before I could stop myself, the words poured from my heart. "Bradley James Talverson, will you please marry me?"

After his initial start of surprise, his eyes softened as he slipped the diamond on my trembling finger. "Miss O'Dell, I thought you'd never ask."

Please turn page for comment card

We hope you enjoyed *DARK MOON CROSSING!!* If you did, would you take a few minutes to share your thoughts with us? _____

_____

_____

We also appreciate reader comments posted on-line at Amazon.com and barnesandnoble.com!

I purchased the book at _____

If you would like to receive information regarding future publications by this author, please return this card or e-mail us at: theniteowl@juno.com or visit our website at: www.niteowlbooks.com

Name _____

Address _____ City _____ State _____ Zip _____

Mail to: Nite Owl Books, 4040 E. Camelback Rd. #101, Phoenix, Arizona 85018-2736

Ph: 602-840-0132 or 1-888-927-9600

Books are available through all major bookstores or can be ordered directly from Nite Owl Books

Sylvia Nobel currently resides in Phoenix, Arizona with
her husband and eight cats. She is a member of
Mystery Writers of America and Arizona Center for the
Book